# TENACIOUS

A KYDD SEA ADVENTURE

THE KYDD SEA ADVENTURES, BY JULIAN STOCKWIN

*Kydd*
*Artemis*
*Seaflower*
*Mutiny*
*Quarterdeck*
*Tenacious*
*Command*
*The Admiral's Daughter*

JULIAN STOCKWIN

# TENACIOUS

A KYDD SEA ADVENTURE

McBooks Press, Inc.
Ithaca, New York

Published by McBooks Press 2006

First published in Great Britain in 2005 by Hodder and Stoughton
A division of Hodder Headline



Cover painting by Geoff Hunt.
Cover and text design: Panda Musgrove.

Library of Congress Cataloging-in-Publication Data

Stockwin, Julian.
Tenacious : a Kydd sea adventure / by Julian Stockwin.
p. cm.
ISBN: 978-1-59013-119-0 (hardcover: alk. paper)
ISBN: 978-1-59013-142-8 (trade paperback: alk. paper)
1. Kydd, Thomas (Fictitious character)—Fiction. 2. Great Britain—History, Naval—18th century—Fiction. 3. Seafaring life—Fiction.
4. Sailors—Fiction. I. Title.
PR6119.T66T46 2006
823'.92--dc22

2006004000

Additional copies of this book may be ordered from any bookstore or directly from McBooks Press, Inc., ID Booth Building, 520 North Meadow St., Ithaca, NY 14850. Please include $5.00 postage and handling with mail orders. New York State residents must add sales tax to total remittance (books & shipping). All McBooks Press publications can also be ordered by calling toll-free 1-888-BOOKS11 (1-888-266-5711).

Please call to request a free catalog.
Visit the McBooks Press website at www.mcbooks.com.
Printed in the United States of America
9 8 7 6 5 4 3 2 1

THERE IS BUT ONE NELSON—*Lord St Vincent*

# Prologue

The sound of carriage wheels echoed loudly in the blackness of Downing Street. With a jangle of harness and the snorting of horses, the vehicle stopped outside No. 10 and footmen braved the rain to lower the step and hand down the occupants.

The Prime Minister, William Pitt, did not wait for the Speaker of the House of Commons, but Henry Addington knew his friend of old and smiled at his nervous vitality. "Quite dished 'em in the debate, William," he puffed, as he caught up and they mounted the stairs to the upper landing.

"It will hold them for now," Pitt said briefly.

The sound of their voices roused the household. A butler appeared from the gloom, with a maid close behind. "In here," Pitt threw over his shoulder, as he entered a small drawing room. The maid slipped past with a taper, lit the candles, and a pool of gold illuminated the *chaise-longue*. Pitt sprawled on it full-length, while Addington took a winged chair nearby.

"Oh, a bite of cold tongue and ham would answer," Pitt said wearily, to the butler's query, then closed his eyes until the man had returned with brandy and a new-opened bottle of port. He poured, then withdrew noiselessly, pulling the doors closed.

"Hard times," Addington offered.

"You think so, Henry? Since that insufferable coxcomb Fox rusticated himself I have only the French to occupy me." He took a long pull on his port.

Addington studied the deep lines in his face. "General Buonaparte and his invasion preparations?" he asked quietly.

There had been little else in the press for the last two months. Paris had performed a master-stroke in appointing the brilliant victor of Italy to the head of the so-called Army of England, which had beaten or cowed every country in Europe. His task now was to eliminate the last obstacle to conquest of the civilised world. Spies were reporting the rapid construction of flat troop-landing barges in every northern French port, and armies were being marched to the coast. Invasion of the land that lay in plain sight of the battalions lining those shores was clearly imminent.

"What else?" Pitt stared into the shadows. "If he can get across the twenty miles of the Channel then . . . then we're finished, of course."

"We have the navy," Addington said stoutly.

"Er, yes. The navy were in bloody mutiny less'n a year ago and are now scattered all over the world. Necessary, of course." He brooded over his glass. "Grenville heard that the French will turn on Hanover and that His Majesty will oblige us to defend his ancestral home, dragging us into a land war."

"Ridiculous."

"Of course."

Addington cradled his brandy and waited.

Pitt sighed. "The worst of it all is not being possessed of decent intelligence. Having to make decisions in a fog of half-truths and guesses is a sure way to blunder into mistakes that history will judge without mercy. Take this, Henry. Spencer has confirmed that our grand General Buonaparte has left off inspecting his soldiers standing ready for the invasion and has been seen in

Toulon. What's he doing in the Mediterranean that he abandons his post? No one knows, but we have enough word that there's an armament assembling there. Not a simple fleet, you understand, but transports, store-ships, a battle fleet. Are we therefore to accept that the moment we have dreaded most—when the French revolution bursts forth on the rest of the world—is now at hand? And if it is, why from Toulon?"

He paused. There was the slightest tremor in the hand that held the glass. "If there's to be a sally, where? Dundas speaks of Constantinople, the Sublime Porte. Others argue for a rapid descent on Cairo, defeating the Mamelukes and opening a highway to the Red Sea and thence our vital routes to India. And some point to a landing in the Levant, then a strike across Arabia and Persia to the very gates of India."

"And you?"

At first, Pitt did not speak, then he said quietly, "It is all nonsense, romantic nonsense, this talk of an adventure in the land of Sinbad. It's all desert, impassable to a modern army. It's a stratagem to deflect our attention from the real object."

"Which is?"

"After leaving Toulon, Buonaparte does not sail east. Instead he sails west. He pauses off Cartagena to collect Spanish battleships, then passes Gibraltar and heads north. With the fleet in Cadíz joining him as he passes, he brushes us aside and reaches the Channel. There, the Brest fleet emerges to join him, thirty of them! With a combined fleet of more'n fifty of-the-line around him he will get his few hours to cross, and then it will be all over for us, I fear."

Addington chose his words carefully: "But would it not be prudent to send ships into the Mediterranean to stop him at the outset?"

"And leave England's defence the poorer?" He pondered

for a space and continued, in an odd tone, "But, then, the decision is taken out of my hands. What I think is of no account. The Austrians are adamant that as a condition to an alliance we must provide a naval presence to protect Naples—you will recollect that the Queen of Naples is Austrian born. And as the Austrians are the only friends we have—*pace* the Portuguese—we must accede. And then, of course, there's today's dispatch from Genoa . . ."

"Genoa?"

"Yes. Something that changes the stakes utterly."

"How so?"

"We have a reliable agent in Genoa. He's reporting that the French have been active, buying barrels—four thousand of the very biggest, with ten iron hoops *but no bung holes.*"

Addington was mystified.

For the first time, Pitt smiled. "Henry, old fellow, you'll never be mistaken for a character of the seafaring species. Such barrels are tied to ships' sides to assist them in floating over shallow waters. And that is proof positive that Dundas is right. The French armament is to force the Dardanelles by this means and take Constantinople. Sultan Selim III is friendly to us and we cannot allow this to happen. I shall therefore direct that St Vincent off Cadíz forthwith undertakes a reconnaissance in force. We will return to the Mediterranean!"

# Chapter 1

Lieutenant Thomas Kydd turned in his chair to Tysoe, his servant. "An' I'll have another soup, if y' please." He smiled at his friend Renzi, and loosened his stock in the warmth of the crowded wardroom of HMS *Tenacious*. "Thunderin' good prog, Nicholas, d'ye think?"

"Moose muffle," Pringle, captain of marines, called over the hubbub. He inspected the piece of meat he had speared. "Spring moose is better in June, you'll find, once the beast has a mort of fat on him."

The wardroom echoed to gusts of laughter in response to a sally by Captain Houghton at the head of the table—his officers had invited him to dine with them this night. The older of the seamen servants glanced at each other meaningfully. The ship had pulled together in fine style: with officers in harmony so much less was the likelihood of interference in their own community.

Kydd's soup plate was removed. "Ah, I think the baked shad," he said, and turned to Pybus, the surgeon. "Not as I mean t' say I'm wearying of cod, you know."

"That, in Nova Scotia, is a felony, Mr Kydd," Pybus said drily, reaching for the chicken. As usual, he was wearing an old green waistcoat.

Kydd nodded at the servant, and his glass was neatly refilled. He let his eyes wander beyond the colour and chatter of the occasion through the graceful sweep of the stern windows to Halifax harbour, the darkness relieved by scattered golden pinpricks of light from other ships at anchor. Just a year ago he had been under discipline before the mast, accused of treason after the Nore mutiny. He had joined the insurrection in good faith, then been carried along by events that had overwhelmed them all. But for mysterious appeals at the highest level, he should have shared his comrades' fate and been hanged with them; he had never dreamed of elevation to the sanctity of the quarterdeck. Now he had won another great prize: acceptance by the other officers as an equal. Where might it all lead?

"Pray assist me with this Rheingau, Tom," Renzi said, reaching across with a white wine. There was a contentment in him too, Kydd observed. His friend, who had come with him from the lower deck, was now settled at this much more agreeable station, which befitted his high-born background.

"Mr Kydd—your health, sir!" The captain's voice carried down the table.

Kydd lifted his glass with a civil inclination of the head. "*Votter santay,*" he responded gravely.

Houghton had risen above his objections to his fifth lieutenant's humble origins after a social coup had established Kydd's connections with the highest in the land. Unaware of her identity, Kydd had invited Prince Edward's mistress to an official banquet—to the great pleasure of the prince.

"I c'n well recommend th' ruffed grouse, sir," Kydd said. A seaman picked up the dish and carried it to the captain, who acknowledged it graciously.

Tall glasses appeared before each officer, filled with what appeared to be a fine amber fluid. The captain was the first to try.

"By George, it's calf's foot jelly!" he said. "Lemon—who's responsible for this perfection?" he demanded of his steward.

"Lady Wentworth's own recipe, sir. She desires to indicate in some measure to His Majesty's Ship *Tenacious* her sensibility of the honour Lieutenant Kydd bestowed on her by accepting her invitation to the levee."

"I see," said the captain, and flashed a glance at Kydd.

The third lieutenant, Gervase Adams, shifted in his chair. "No disrespect intended, sir, but it gripes me that we wax fat and indolent while our country lies under such grave peril."

Houghton frowned. "Any officer of honour would feel so, Mr Adams, but the safeguarding of trade and securing of naval supplies is of as much consequence to your country as the winning of battles. Pray bear your lot with patience. There may yet be a testing time ahead for us all."

Houghton motioned to his steward and the last dishes were removed, the cloth drawn. Decanters of Marsala and port were placed at the head and foot of the table and passed along, always to the left, as custom dictated. When all glasses had been filled, Houghton nodded almost imperceptibly to Bryant, first lieutenant and president of the mess, who turned to Kydd as the most junior lieutenant present. "Mr Vice—the King."

Kydd lifted his glass and paused for quiet. "Gentlemen, the King."

The words echoed strongly around the table. The simple ceremony of the loyal toast seemed to Kydd to draw together all the threads of his allegiance to king and country, and with others he followed with a sincere "God bless him."

The solemn courtesies complete, other toasts were made: "Foxhunting and Old Port"; "Our brothers at sea"; and the heartfelt "A willing foe and sea room!" Red faces testified to the warmth and the wine, and when the brandy had circulated

Houghton called, "Captain Pringle, might we press you to honour us with your flute?"

"Should I be joined by our excellent doctor, I would be glad to, sir."

The marine was a proficient and sensitive player, and a lively violin accompaniment from the normally acerbic Pybus set the mood of the evening. Adams was persuaded to render a creditable "Sweet Lass of Richmond Hill" in his light tenor, and Renzi delivered a reading from his new copy of *Lyrical Ballads:*

*It is the first mild day of March;*
*Each minute sweeter than before,*
*The red-breast sings from the tall larch*
*That stands beside our door.*

*There is a blessing in the air*
*Which seems a sense of joy to yield*
*To the bare trees, and mountains bare,*
*And grass in the green field . . .*

Houghton rose to his feet. He raised his glass and said softly, "To *Tenacious.*"

"*Tenacious,*" came the reply, with more than one murmured "Bless her!" There were no ready words to describe the affection that the old 64-gun ship-of-the-line had won in the hearts of her officers, and Kydd felt a lump in his throat. He could see the others were affected, too.

In the quiet, a sudden knock at the wardroom door sounded overly loud. With rainwater streaming from his grego, the duty master's mate awkwardly handed over an oilskin packet. "Cap'n, sir—urgent from Flag."

It was unusual to the point of disquiet that the admiral had seen fit to act immediately instead of waiting for the usual morning postal round, and all craned towards the head of the table.

Houghton scanned the covering letter, then looked up gravely. "Gentlemen, you should be advised that the situation in Europe has intensified. Therefore we are to be recalled from this station to join that of Admiral the Earl St Vincent before Cadíz—we sail with the utmost dispatch."

Taking the deck for his first sea-watch since leaving Halifax, Kydd strode to the ship's side and looked down with satisfaction at the busy wake forming and spreading in a hiss of obedience, slipping astern to join the other side in a lazy track that stretched far into the distance.

He returned to the binnacle: the ship's heading was within a whisker of east by south. His eyes rose to meet a look of reproach from the helmsman and he concealed a smile. He had no right to usurp the quartermaster's responsibility for the course and knew only too well the irritation of a meddlesome officer-of-the-watch.

But these were momentous times. Since Houghton had received his orders from the admiral, he had been unsparing in his drive to get *Tenacious* to sea. Whatever additional information he was privy to had lined his face and he had issued each officer-of-the-watch stern instructions to clap on every stitch—but woe betide all should it cost even a single spar.

As he paced the quarterdeck, Kydd's thoughts turned briefly to another matter: Gibraltar was less than a day's sail away from Cadíz. It would serve his purpose well if they touched on that fortress port. It would give him great satisfaction to conclude a particular task there. He had decided on it after parting with his uncle in a remote settlement in the Canadian Maritimes.

Kydd stopped to feel the ship's motion. Under all plain sail in the brisk, quartering south-westerly, *Tenacious* heaved and rose over the long Atlantic rollers in a strong and compelling rhythm, pleasing in its regularity. He sensed the waves meeting her bow and surging aft under the keel, the vessel's slow pitch conforming to its motion. But there was something further—a trifle, perhaps, but out of harmony with the concert of movement.

He glanced across the deck. Captain Houghton was taking the air on the weather side, walking with the first lieutenant. There was a full watch of the hands on deck and others were at work on their part-of-ship. Kydd signalled to the quartermaster that he was going forward, then made his way to the foredeck and stood feeling, sensing.

The bow-wave swashed and hissed below; above him soared the headsails, taut and trim. But there *was* something. He turned to peer up, above the mighty fore-course, past the tops to the topsail and topgallant. Something was causing a hesitation, a brief interruption in the forward urge of the ship. He moved to one side until he could see the end of the bowsprit spearing into the sky ahead.

It soared and dipped but then Kydd saw what was happening. It was not an up-and-down motion. Instead, it described a circle in the sky, certain indication that the helmsman was having to ease the wheel each time the bows met an oncoming sea. That was it—a griping caused by the ship's tendency to come closer to the wind when her forefoot bit deep into the wave. Kydd was annoyed that the quartermaster had not noticed it: he knew that with every billow *Tenacious* was losing way through the water—only a tiny amount, but there were countless thousands of waves across the Atlantic.

He turned on his heel and headed back, trying to work out how to resolve the problem. The usual remedy was to move provisions or guns aft, but the ship was fully stored and this would be awkward and dangerous. Also, with but a single frigate nearly out of sight ahead, it would be prudent to leave the guns where they were.

He reached the quarterdeck and Houghton glanced at him curiously. Kydd did not catch his eye as he ordered the mate-of-the-watch, "Hands to set sail!" Stuns'ls had been struck earlier in the day and the man looked surprised. He hesitated, then hailed the boatswain.

"Mr Pearce," Kydd told him, "as we're lasking along, wind's fr'm the quarter, I mean t' take in the fore-topmast stays'l and then we'll set the large jib." The boatswain's eyebrows rose, but after only the briefest look in the captain's direction, he drew out his silver call.

Kydd knew it was not a popular order among the men. The large jib would have to be roused out from below and heaved up on deck, the long sausage of canvas needing thirty men at least to grapple with it. And the handing of the fore-topmast staysail, a fore-and-aft sail leading down from aloft, was hard, wet and dangerous, followed by the awkward job of hanking the large jib.

Houghton had stopped pacing and was watching Kydd closely. The master emerged from the cabin spaces to stand with him and the first lieutenant, but Kydd kept his eyes forward as the boatswain set the men about their tasks.

The fo'c'slemen lowered the fore-topmast staysail, the men out on the bowsprit using both hands to fist the unruly canvas as it came down the stay. This was a job for the most experienced seamen in the ship: balancing on a thin footrope, they bellied up to the fat spar and brought in the sail, forming a skin and stuffing in the bulk before passing gaskets round it. All the while the bowsprit reared and fell in the lively seas.

Kydd stayed on the quarterdeck, looking forward and seeing

occasional bursts of spray from the bow shoot up from beneath, soaking men and canvas. He felt for them.

At last the jib was bent on and began jerking up, flapping and banging, and the men made their way back inboard. Sheets were tended and the action was complete.

"Mr Kydd, what was your purpose in setting the large jib?" Houghton called.

Kydd crossed the deck and touched his hat. "The ship gripes, sir. I—"

"Surely you would therefore attend to the trim?"

"Sir, we're fully stored, difficult t' work below," he began, recalling his experiences as a quartermaster's mate and the dangers lurking in a dark hold when the ship was working in a seaway. "This way we c'n cure the griping an' get an edge of speed."

Houghton frowned and looked at the master, who nodded. "Ah, I believe Mr Kydd means t' lift the bows—you'll know the heads'ls are lifting sails, an' at this point o' sailing the large jib will do more of a job in this than our stays'l."

"And the speed?" Houghton wanted to know.

But Kydd could already sense the effects: the hesitation was gone and it felt much like a subtle lengthening of stride. He turned to the mate-of-the-watch. "A cast o' the log, if y' please."

It was only half a knot more, but this was the same as subtracting from their voyage the best part of a hundred miles for every week at sea.

Kydd held back a grin. "And if it comes on t' blow, we let fly, sir."

Houghton gave a curt acknowledgement.

"Does seem t' me she's a sea-kindly ship, if y' know what I mean, sir," Kydd dared.

The wardroom was a quite different place from what it had been a day or so before: officers sat at table for dinner together in the usual way, but now they were in sea-faded, comfortable uniform and there was always one absent on watch. And instead of the stillness of harbour repose, there was the soaring, swooping movement of deep ocean that had everyone finding their sea-legs once more.

Fiddles had been fitted round the table—taut cords at the edge to prevent plates tumbling into laps; glasses were never poured more than half full and wetted cloths prevented bottles sliding—all familiar accompaniments to sea service.

The chaplain entered for dinner, passing along hand by hand to steady himself. "Do take a sup of wine," Kydd said solicitously.

"Thank you, perhaps later," Peake murmured, distracted. He reached for the bread-barge, which still contained portions of loaves—soon they would be replaced with hard tack—and selected a crust. "I confess I was ever a martyr to the ocean's billows," he said faintly.

Kydd remembered the times when he had been deprived of Renzi's company while Peake and he had been happily disputing logic, and could not resist saying, "Then is not y'r philosophy comfort enough? Nicholas, conjure some words as will let us see th' right of it."

Renzi winked at him. "Was it not the sainted Traherne who tells us . . . let me see . . . 'You never enjoy the world aright, till the sea itself floweth in your veins, till you are clothed with the heavens and crowned with the stars and perceive yourself to be the sole heir of the whole world'?"

Peake lifted dull eyes and said weakly, "I believe the Good Book may be more relied upon in this matter, as you will find in Proverbs, the thirtieth chapter: 'There be three things which are too wonderful for me . . . the way of an eagle in the air . . . the serpent on a rock—and the way of a ship in the midst of the sea.' "

Bampton's voice cut above the chuckles. "That you can safely leave with us, Mr Peake, but we'll have early need of your services, I fancy." Adams gave the second lieutenant a quizzical look. "You don't really think we'd be cracking on like this unless there's to be some sort of final meeting with the French? It stands to reason," Bampton continued.

The table fell silent: the frantic preparations for sea, the storing of powder and shot, and last-minute fitting and repairs had left little time for the contemplation of larger matters.

Renzi steepled his fingers. "Not necessarily. All we have is rumour and hearsay. We have abandoned the Mediterranean with reason, that we can no longer support a fleet there, and therefore every vessel of ours is undefended prey. In this case we have no means of intelligence to tell us what is happening, hence the wild speculation.

"Now, we do know of General Buonaparte and his designs on England—the landing boats in every northern French port, the daily inspections of his Army of England. Do you not feel it the more likely that he will ransack Toulon and Cartagena for ships of force to swell the Brest fleet to an unstoppable power that will overwhelm us? Rather, that is, than retain them in a landlocked sea for some sort of escapade far away."

"Just as I said." Bampton snorted. "A conclusion with Mr Buonaparte, in the chops of the Channel somewheres, I'd wager, and—"

"Except we're being sent south to Cadíz."

"Renzi, old trout, you're not being clear," Adams admonished him.

"Am I not? Then it could be that I am as much in the dark as you. Are we to be part of a grand fleet about to break into the Med again? Or might it be that we being only a sixty-four—a fine one indeed as I am obliged to remark—our purpose is merely that of releasing the more warlike seventy-fours?"

At the head of the table Bryant glowered. As first lieutenant his interest in a future bloody battle and the subsequent custom of promotion to commander for an active officer had been all too apparent on the quiet North American station. The prospect of sitting out his battle far from the action was hard to endure. "There's a reason for it, never fear," he said loudly. "Jervis ain't the one to ask for ships without he's got a plan. My money's on him takin' Buonaparte as he heads north with the Toulon squadron afore he can join up with the mongseers off Brest."

It was exhilarating sailing, a starboard tack with winds quartering, mile after deep-sea mile on the same course. As they edged south the weather brightened, the vivid white of towering clouds and hurrying white-horse seas contrasting pleasingly with the deep ultramarine of the water.

The stimulating stream of oceanic air impelling them along made it hard to stay below, and when Renzi took over his watch, Kydd felt too restless to retire to his cabin to work on his divisional list, and waited while Renzi satisfied himself as to the ship's condition.

They fell into step in an easy promenade around the quarterdeck. The messenger midshipman returned to the helm, as did the duty master's mate, leaving the two officers to their privacy. They paced in silence, until Renzi said, "Dear fellow, do I see you satisfied with your lot? Is this the visage of him who is at one with the world? Since your elevation to the ranks of the chosen are you content now with your station?"

Kydd paused. "Nicholas, I've been a-thinking. Who I am, where I'm headed in life, that sort o' thing." He shot his friend a glance. "It's not long since I was in bilboes waiting f'r the rope. Now I'm a king's officer. What does that say t' you?"

"Well, in between, there was a prodigious battle and some courage as I recall."

Kydd gestured impatiently. "Nicholas, I'll tell ye truly. While I was afore the mast I was content. I allow that then t' be a sailing master was all I could see, an' all I wanted from life. Then with just one turn o' the screw, my stars change an' here I am. Makes me think—might be anything can happen, why, anything a-tall." He spun round to face Renzi squarely. "Nicholas, m' life will never be complete until I have my own ship. Walk *my* decks, not a man aboard but tips his hat t' me, does things *my* way. An' for me, I get the chance to win my own glory because I make the decisions. Good or bad, they're mine, and I get the rewards—or the blame. So, how does it sound, Nicholas—Cap'n Thomas Kydd, Royal Navy?"

Renzi raised an eyebrow. "A junior lieutenant with such ardour? Where is the old Tom Kydd that I knew?" He gave a smile, then added, "I admire your fervour and respect your passion for the laurels, but you will have noticed, of course, that Fortune bestows her favours at random. You stand just as much a chance of having your head knocked off as winning glory."

Less than three weeks later, they passed the distant blue peak of Morro Alto to starboard, marking the island of Flores at the western extremity of the Azores. Their passage in the steady westerlies had been fast and sure and it was becoming a point of honour to win every advantage, gain the last fraction of a knot. HMS *Tenacious* was answering the call.

Noon. The hallowed time of the grog issue for the hands. A fife at the main hatchway started up with the welcome strains of "Nancy Dawson," and Kydd waited for the decks to clear. It was time, too, for the ceremony of the noon sight.

Officers readied their instruments. At local apparent noon, while the men were below, they would fix the line of longitude passing through their position and thus compute the distance remaining to their rendezvous off Cadíz.

A crisp horizon, and the ship's motion predictably even: it was a good sighting. Most officers retired to their cabins for peace in the concentrated work of applying the necessary corrections and resolving the mathematics resulting in the intersection of latitude and longitude that was the ship's location at midday.

From first one then another cabin came disbelieving shouts: "Well, damme—five degrees of longitude noon to noon!"

"Two hundred and fifty miles off the reel in twenty-four hours!"

"She's a champion!"

That night glasses were raised to *Tenacious* in the wardroom, but as the ship neared the other side of the Atlantic a more sombre mood prevailed. Exercise of gunnery took on new meaning as the ominous rumble of heavy guns was felt through the deck at all hours. Who knew what trial by battle lay ahead?

Landfall on the continent of Europe was the looming heights of Portugal's Cape St Vincent, which faded into the dusk as they held course through the night. The officers took their breakfast quietly and though the fleet was not expected to be sighted before the afternoon every one went on deck straight after the meal.

"News! For the love of God, let us have news," groaned Adams, running his hands through his fair hair. They had been cut off from the world for weeks across the width of the Atlantic and anything could have happened.

"For all we know of it," Bampton said drily, "we may be sailing into an empty anchorage, the Spanish gone to join the French and our grand battle decided five hundred miles away."

Bryant glared at him.

"Or peace declared," said Renzi.

Conversations tailed off at the mention of this possibility and all the officers turned towards him. He continued, "Pitt is sorely pressed, the coalition in ruins, and the threat to our shores could not be greater. If he treats with the French now, exchanges colonies for peace, he may secure a settlement far preferable to a long-drawn-out war of attrition." He paused. "After all, France alone has three times our population, a five times bigger army—"

"What do y' mean by this kind o' talk, sir?" Bryant snapped.

"Simply that if a French or Spanish vessel crosses our bows, do we open with broadsides? Is it peace or is it war? It would go hard for any who violate hard-won terms of peace . . ."

At a little after two, the low, anonymous coast of Spain firmed in a bright haze ahead. The mainmast lookout bawled down, "*Deck hoooo!* Sail-o'-the-line, a dozen or more—at anchor!" The long wait was over.

"Gunner's party!" came the order. There would be salutes and ceremony as they joined the fleet of Admiral of the Blue, the Earl St Vincent. Kydd, as *Tenacious*'s signal lieutenant, roused out the signal flag locker and found the largest blue ensign. He smiled wryly at the thought of the hard work he knew would be there for him later: the signal procedures this side of the Atlantic would be different and he would need to prepare his own signal book accordingly.

Ahead, the dark body of the fleet against the backdrop of enemy land slowly resolved into a long crescent of anchored warships spreading the width of the mouth of a majestic harbour. As they approached Kydd identified the flagship in the centre, the mighty 110-gun *Ville de Paris,* her admiral's pennant at the main.

To seaward of the crescent a gaggle of smaller ships was coming and going, victuallers and transports, dispatch cutters, hoys. A sudden crack of salutes rang out, startling him at his telescope. Answering thuds came from the flagship.

Now opposite *Ville de Paris, Tenacious* backed her main topsail, but an officious half-decked cutter foamed up astern and came into the wind. An officer with a speaking trumpet blared up, "The admiral desires you should moor to the suth'ard of the line." Obediently *Tenacious* paid off and got under way for her appointed berth.

Kydd marvelled at the extraordinary sight before him: the grandest port in Spain locked and secured by a fleet of ships so close that the great ramparts of the city were in plain view, with a wide sprawl of white houses glaring in the sun, turrets, cathedral domes—and a curious tower arising from the sea.

At the end of the line they rounded to and came to single anchor, the newest member of the fleet. Captain Houghton's barge was in the water even as the cable was veered. Resplendent in full dress with best sword and decorations, he was swayed into it by yardarm tackle and chair, and departed to report to the commander-in-chief.

Houghton did not return immediately; rumour washed around. "There's been a fright only," Bryant huffed. "Just as the Frogs always do, made to put t' sea an' when they see us all in a pelt put about and scuttle back. Not like Old Jarvie t' take a scare so."

Adams looked disconsolate: the thought of enervating blockade duty was trying on the spirit after the thrill of the headlong race across the Atlantic.

"Still an' all, you'll not be wanting entertainment," Bryant mused. "The old bugger's a right hard horse. Marks o' respect evewwn in a blow, captains to be on deck during the night when takin' in sail and if there's a sniff o' mutiny, court-martial on the Saturday, hangs 'em on the Sunday . . ."

The captain arrived back at dusk and disappeared into his cabin. Within the hour word was passed that all officers were desired to present themselves in the great cabin forthwith.

"I shall be brief," Houghton snapped. "The situation in respect to the present threat to England is unclear. France's Army of England is still massing for invasion and there are fears for Ireland. Now we've heard that its commander-in-chief—this General Buonaparte—has abandoned it for the time being and gone to Toulon, God knows why. Now you know as much as I, and the admiral.

"To more important matters. Those who have served before with Sir John Jervis, now the Earl St Vincent, know well what to expect in the article of discipline and order. We are now a part of his fleet and his opinions on an officer's duty are robust and unambiguous. You will each consult the *Fleet Order Book* until its contents are known intimately. Any officer who through ignorance of his duty brings disrepute upon my ship will incur my most severe displeasure."

"Sir, might we know our purpose? Are we to remain while the seventy-fours—"

"Our purpose is very clear, Mr Adams. In case it has escaped your notice, let me inform you that in this port there are twenty-six of-the-line under Almirante Mazzeredo. Should we fail in our duty and let this armada get to sea . . ." His face tightened. "We lie before Cadíz on blockade, sir, and here we shall stay until the Spanish see fit to sail. Do you understand me?"

# CHAPTER 2

THE SOUND OF FIRING transfixed the wardroom at their breakfast. After just three days on blockade, any variation to routine was welcome and there was a rush to the hatchway as saluting guns announced the approach of a smart 74 from the north.

Houghton appeared on deck, wiping his mouth with a napkin. "Sir," called Bampton, who was officer-of-the-watch. "Pennants of HMS *Vanguard,* seventy-four, flag of Rear Admiral Nelson."

"Aha! *Now* we'll see some action," growled Bryant, snatching the telescope from Bampton and training it on *Vanguard*'s quarterdeck. "Ye-e-e-s, that must be him. Always was the popinjay." He handed the glass back. "Didn't think to see him back at sea—only last year at Tenerife he lost an arm to a musket-shot, had it sawn off. Right arm it was, too."

Bampton took a brief sight, then lowered the telescope. "Yes, but a vain man, very vain," he muttered.

The ship passed close by; gold lace glinted on her quarterdeck, seamen stood rigid at their stations. In *Tenacious,* boatswain's calls piped attention to the new rear admiral joining and all hands tried to catch a glimpse of the renowned victor of the great battle of St Vincent, he of the "Patent Bridge for Boarding First-rates," where he had taken one enemy ship, then used it as a stepping-stone to lead an attack on his next victim.

*Vanguard* rounded the line to join the half-dozen or so vessels close inshore, and the officers of *Tenacious* returned to their breakfast.

"Sir, *Vanguard* is signalling," Rawson reported to Kydd.

"Well?" growled Kydd, in mock exasperation at his signals midshipman.

"Er, sir—union at the mizzen topmast-head, distinguishing pennants, er, that's 'Captains repair on board Flag.' An' they are . . . let me see . . . *Orion, Alexander, Emerald,* others—and us!"

"So?"

"Er, yes, sir—acknowledge."

"My duty t' the captain, an' acquaint him of the signal, if y' please."

Houghton wasted no time: his barge disappeared quickly into a throng of small craft, but he was back just as rapidly and summoned all officers to his cabin. He motioned them to sit at the polished table, but remained standing and leaned forward, animated. "Gentlemen, I have to tell you that intelligence of the gravest kind has been received from overland concerning the French intentions." Every eye was on him. "It seems that they are at this moment massing in Toulon and are about to make a sally."

He spread out a small-scale chart of the Mediterranean. "This is far more serious than a simple adventure. It has the attention and presence of their highest general, Napoleon Buonaparte, and could mean either a mass break-out from the Mediterranean to join up with their forces in Brest, or some descent to the east in a move towards the Ottomans or India.

"They have had the Mediterranean as their private sea for too long—it has made them ambitious, and the danger this poses to our country is incalculable. Therefore I have to tell you that Sir John has determined that at last we shall re-enter the Mediterranean. There shall be an immediate reconnaissance in force towards Toulon to discover the French intentions. It will be led by Rear Admiral Nelson—and we shall be a part!"

In this major fleet off Cadíz, in addition to a full admiral as commander-in-chief, there was a vice admiral for the van of the line-of-battle and a rear admiral for the rear. Exceptionally, there was also a separate squadron whose task was to rove close inshore, harrying the enemy at every opportunity and this was the particular command of Rear Admiral Nelson.

There was a stunned silence, then excited babble broke out. Houghton grinned and straightened. "If you please, gentlemen, Sir Horatio will brook no delay. He intends to sail for Gibraltar in two days. I will not have *Tenacious* disappoint so you will bend every effort to ready her for sea. Carry on!"

The Rock of Gibraltar resolved from the haze like a crouching lion, dominating the vessels that drew up to its flanks to join the ships-of-the-line and frigates already there. As anchors plunged into a gunmetal blue sea, the thunder of salutes acknowledged the visiting *Princess Royal* as the flag of a senior admiral.

The ships came to rest and the slight breeze brought a smell compounded of sun-baked rock, goats, donkey droppings and Moorish cooking, which irresistibly took Kydd back to his service there in *Achilles*—and the adventures that had followed.

"I do believe it will now be granted to us to glimpse the grand panjandrum himself," Renzi said, looking at *Vanguard*, anchored a few hundred yards away. Kydd held back a reproof: his friend had been at the great battle of St Vincent and witnessed Nelson's achievements at first hand.

"Oh?" said Bampton. "Is he so much the swell he must parade before us?"

Kydd's colour rose at Bampton's tone.

"Not as I would say," Renzi replied. "Rather, I have heard he keeps a splendid table and is the most affable of hosts."

"Should you have seen him here a year or so ago in *Minerve* frigate you'd clap a stopper on y'r opinions," Kydd added, and recounted the daring escape of Nelson's ship from two Spanish ships-of-the-line. From the top of the Rock, Kydd had watched the whole incident. Nelson had bluffed the enemy by heaving to and, suspecting he was leading them into a trap, the Spaniards had sheered off. But the real reason for his action was that he had lowered a boat to rescue a man overboard.

The talking died as *Vanguard*'s boat was hoisted out and several figures boarded. It stroked strongly for the shore, and was met at Ragged Staff by a file of redcoats, a military band and a reception committee.

"Making his number with the governor," murmured Adams.

"O'Hara," said Kydd, with a grin. "They call him 'Cock o' the Rock' on account of him being so . . . amiable t' the ladies."

After a short interval there was a pealing of boatswain's calls and the captain of *Tenacious* departed.

"God knows, Our Nel isn't one to waste his time lingering in port," the first lieutenant said. He turned to the boatswain. "No liberty, all hands to store ship. Turn to, part-o'-ship." The boatswain called his mates and stalked forward, the piercing blast of their pipes echoing up from the hatchways. "All the water an' provisions we can take aboard—our ships are on their own once we sail," Bryant growled.

But this was work for the warrant officers, petty officers and ship's company. Kydd seized his opportunity. "Nicholas, should you step off with me, y' could be of some service, m' friend . . ."

Renzi raised one eyebrow. "Er, regarding Town Major

Mulvany and his wife, do you not think it a trifle rash to venture abroad in Gibraltar? That you may meet them?"

Kydd's infatuation with Emily Mulvany was nearly a year previously but Renzi's gibe was enough to bring a flush. "I've heard there's a new man in post now," he said defensively.

Bryant saw no reason to deny them both a few hours ashore, and within a short time they were speaking to the chief valuer for Moses Levy, the biggest jeweller in Gibraltar. "Your opinion on this, if y' please," Kydd said, passing him his hoarded treasure.

The man took the object, scratched the surface with a hook-shaped pick and closely inspected the result. Then he took down a dusty vial with a glass dropper and deposited several drops of fluid on the tiny specks.

"A remarkable piece," he said grudgingly, hefting the hunk of raw gold. "May I know where this was found?" he said, as he set it on one pan of his scales.

"No, sir, you may not." Kydd's uncle would find his haven destroyed by prospectors if ever Kydd let it be known. It had been his uncle's gift to probably the last family member he would see, and Kydd was going to see it well used.

The valuer carefully added weights to the other pan. Kydd glanced at Renzi, who seemed unaffected by the excitement. The man peered at the weights, then said, "This is what I can offer. Four hundred silver pesos on account now and an adjustment later after it has been assayed."

"That would seem equitable," Renzi said. Outside he added, "At six pesos to the guinea, an excellent trade—more than enough to . . . ?"

They knew where they had to go: a bare twenty minutes along the familiar bustle of Main Street was Town Range, the residential quarter for army officers, and in a side-street they found the garrison sword-cutler. Kydd turned to Renzi. "Now, Nicholas, understand that it's a fightin' sword I'm getting, none o' your macaroni pig-stickers."

"As you've mentioned before, dear chap."

The steel-glittered interior was hung with every conceivable hand weapon, ceremonial armour, regimental gorgets and armorial heraldry. Kydd wandered along the racks of edged weapons: this was no quartermaster's armoury, with stout grey-steel blades and wooden hilts. Here was damascened elegance in blue, gold and ivory.

"See this," Kydd said, selecting one. He flourished it—the military style seemed heavier, the slightly curved blade urging more of a slashing stroke than a direct thrust. It did, however, have a splendid appearance, the blade blued along its length with silver chasing down from the hilt, the half-basket guard ornate and fire-gilded.

"A fighting sword?" Renzi drawled.

"Aye, well, a fine piece," Kydd said, replacing it as a man stepped out from the workshop at the rear.

"Gentlemen, an honour." He spoke softly, but his eyes took measure of Kydd's strong build and upright bearing. "Balthasar Owen. It's not so often we are visited by the navy. Not a small sword is my guess," he added, with a smile, glancing at a discreet light-bladed hanger usually worn by gentlemen in the street.

"A fightin' sword for a naval gentleman, if y' please," Kydd replied.

Owen hesitated.

"The expense is not t' be considered. Let th' blade be the best y' have."

"Should you have any fine Toledo steel blades, it would answer," Renzi added.

"A Toledo blade! This will be difficult. Since the late war began you will understand . . ."

"The best steel in the world, we agree," Renzi pressed. "And in the matter of your price . . ."

Owen closed the front door. "Toledo steel is the hardest there is because it is forged from an iron heart and the finest steel lapped and folded on itself more than three hundred times. This gives it flexibility but great hardness. It can take a razor's edge that has been known to last centuries. You see, at the forge, the swordsmith works only by night. Such is their care that when the blade is plunged into the oil the heat's colour is exactly known. The result, an impeccable temper."

He paused, and looked keenly at the two. "There have been many attempts at fraud. Can you tell the singular damascening of a Toledo blade? No? Then the only one you may trust is myself—for if I sell you an inferior, then my standing as sword-cutler to the military will be exploded. Now, if I can find such a one, it would cost dear, perhaps more than three hundred silver pesos—in English money say fifty pounds."

"Very well," said Kydd immediately.

"Which is to say, no paper money, payment upon delivery."

"Aye."

"And workshop time compensated."

Kydd began to count out the Spanish coins. "Should ye need an advance t' assist in th' looking, then—"

Owen's expression eased. "As it happens, I have knowledge of two suitable blades—these are, of course, just that, blades. I will fetch them. They will be hilted here in my workshop to your instructions, er—"

"L'tenant Kydd, Royal Navy, sir." Bows were exchanged, and Owen withdrew.

Kydd smiled at Renzi. "O' course, the whole world knows o' this Toledo steel, but I never thought t' sport such a one."

"I give you joy of your expectation, brother."

Renzi, who had been tutored from youth in the art of fencing, lifted out a straight-bladed spadroon and swung it round his wrist. Then, in a glittering whirl of motion, it came to rest, the needle point an inch from Kydd's nose. "Supple, light in hand, but of no account in a serious contest," Renzi said, and replaced it in the rack.

Owen returned carrying a long package, which he carefully unwrapped on the counter top. Kydd caught his breath. Despite the ugly, naked tang at the top, the sword blade's lethal gleam shone with an impossibly fine lustre. "Take it," urged Owen. "If you look closely you might perceive the damascene workings." Kydd lifted the blade, sighting along it and feeling its weight, admiring the almost imperceptible whorls of metal colour.

"The other Toledo I have is a thirty-two-inch," Owen said, "this being only a twenty-eight."

"No, sir. Aboard ship we set no value on length," Kydd said, stroking the blade in reverence. "Sudden an' quick's the word, the shorter swings faster."

"Is the fullering to your satisfaction, sir?"

Kydd slid his thumb down the single wide groove, feeling its sensual curvature as it diminished towards the tip. "Aye, it will do."

"Then perhaps we should discuss the furniture."

Kydd's brow creased.

"Yes. The blade is forged in Toledo, we perform the hilting here." Kydd avoided Renzi's eye and listened politely. "Naval gentlemen are taking a stirrup knuckle-bow these days," he said, familiarly lifting a sword by its blade and holding it vertical. Instead of forming a round semicircle, the guard had a pleasing sinuosity, ending in a flat bar.

"You will remark the short quillion on this piece," he added, touching the sword crosspiece. "More to your sea tastes, I believe.

And the grips—for a fighting sword we have ivory, filigree—"

"Sharkskin," Kydd said firmly, and turned to see Renzi nodding. "Aye, dark sharkskin it must be. Now, y'r pommel."

"Ah, yes. You naval gentlemen will be asking for the lionhead pommel. It remains only to specify how far down the backpiece of the grip you wish the mane to extend. Some gentlemen—"

"Half-way will be fine."

"Chased?"

"Er . . ."

"Silver, gold?"

"Ah, yes. How will gold chasin' look, d'ye think, Nicholas?"

"Dear fellow, this is a fighting sword."

"I think, then, none."

Owen returned the sword to its place. "And the detailing." He pursed his lips and crossed to another rack. "Triangular langets?" he said, showing the neat little catch for holding the sword secure in its scabbard.

"Not so plain, I'm thinkin'—have you an anchor, perhaps?"

"Certainly. Would you consider damascening in blue and gold? Some blade-etching—a mermaid, a seahorse, perhaps? And the scabbard: black oiled leather, of course, with carrying rings and frog stud for belt or shoulder carriage. Shall the sword knot be in bullion or blue tassels?"

It was well into the afternoon before all details had been settled. The sword-cutler had puzzled over Kydd's insistent demand for engravings of choughs, but he had promised a sketch of the birds for the etching. For the rest, it had cost a pretty premium to command the entire resources of the workshop to have it finished in time, but he would then possess the finest sword imaginable—and there was every reason to suppose that it would soon be drawn in anger.

Back on board, the remainder of the day passed busily. Men sweated in the heat as they struck stores down into the hold; others roused out cannonballs from their lockers and scaled rust from them; more still went over every inch of rigging.

So far signal instructions from their new admiral had not been sent over, so Kydd concentrated on what he had; a detached squadron was not a fleet, even if commanded by an admiral and there might be difficulties. Probably a fat sheaf of complex signal details would arrive the day they sailed, Kydd thought ruefully.

The following day the pace had calmed. Gibraltar dockyard was not a major fleet base and had no vast stocks of sea stores. Men's minds began to turn shoreward for the last opportunity to raise a wind for who knew how long. Liberty was granted to the trusties of the larboard watch until evening gun. Kydd knew where they would head—there were establishments enough in Irish Town alone to cater to an entire fleet.

He and Renzi found time to share a pleasant meal at the Old Porter House on Scud Hill. They sank an ale on the terrace. The entire sweeping curve of Gibraltar Bay lay before them under the setting sun; Spain, the enemy, was a bare five miles distant. The two friends talked comfortably together of remembered places far away; unspoken, however, was any mention of the fire of war, which must soon reach out and engulf them both.

Soon after breakfast, a midshipman appeared. "Mr Kydd, sir, and the cap'n desires to see you when convenient."

The coding of the summons indicated delay would not be in his interest and his pulse quickened as he remembered that the previous day Houghton had spent the whole afternoon and evening with Admiral Nelson. Kydd quickly mounted the companionway and knocked at the door.

"Sir?" There was another captain with him, and a midshipman rigid to one side.

Houghton rose. "Thank you for your time, Mr Kydd. I believe you remember Captain Essington?"

Kydd's astonishment quickly turned to pleasure as he shook the hand of his captain in *Triumph* at the bloody battle of Camperdown, who had commended him to acting lieutenant in *Tenacious*. But for Essington's intercession at his lieutenant's examination, Kydd would have been for a certainty back before the mast.

"He is flag-captain of *Princess Royal,*" Houghton added.

Essington's face creased to a smile. "Lieutenant, if you are at leisure, it would gratify me should we take the air on the quarterdeck for a small while."

"Sir."

Kydd fell into step beside the eminent officer. "Your captain speaks highly of you," Essington said at length. "A source of some satisfaction to me, that the Service has seen some benefit to my actions after Camperdown."

"You may rely on m' duty, sir," Kydd said stiffly.

"I'm sure of it," Essington returned. "But today I have come on quite a different mission"—he paused while they passed the quartermaster—"which I find delicate enough, in all conscience."

Kydd tensed. He had been puzzled that Houghton had held back to allow a senior flag-captain to talk directly with him, and now this admission of *delicacy.*

Essington stopped pacing and faced Kydd. "The essence of it all is . . ."

"Sir?"

"My nephew, Bowden, has been sent to me in the character of midshipman to place upon the quarterdeck of *Princess Royal.* However, in short, I do not believe it in his best interest to serve in the same ship as his uncle. Neither do I feel a flagship of the Cadíz blockade a good place to learn the elements of his profession. Captain Houghton has been good enough to agree to exchange him into *Tenacious* where he will join the gunroom and begin his education."

"Er, yes, sir." Kydd could see no reason why he should be informed of such an arrangement.

"I tell you this in order that you be under no apprehension that he is to be accorded any privileges whatsoever beyond those extended to his fellow young gentlemen. Notwithstanding his gentle birth—and you may understand he is my sister's child—I desire that he be treated the same."

"Sir, with respect, I can't see how this is a concern f'r me."

Essington smiled. "This is then the delicacy. It is my wish that young Bowden do learn his nauticals properly, neglecting none, to be a sure foundation for his future. I do not ask you will be the schoolmaster in this, but I would take it very kindly in you should you watch over his learning. That is, his notions of seamanship will then be of prime worth, coming as they will from one whose own such are so unquestioned."

"Sir, you flatter me," Kydd said carefully. But nursemaid to a midshipman? And, anyway, as an officer he would not have any direct relationship with a midshipman: that was the province of the master's mates and petty officers.

Essington frowned. "I do not ask you will interfere, merely that as the occasion presents you do try him in the particulars, sparing neither his feelings nor time as you deem necessary."

"Aye aye, sir," Kydd acknowledged formally.

"Very well. Captain Houghton knows of my request and will hear any suggestion you may have, conformable to the requirements of his ship."

Hesitating, Essington went on quietly, "The boy is, er, eager to please, having latterly formed a pressing desire for the sea life, which will not be denied, but his ideas of life in a midshipman's berth are somewhat whimsical."

"Sir, I—"

"I have instructed him that under no circumstances should you be approached on matters not pertaining to the sea profession," Essington said. "He'll find his place soon enough—or suffer. Either way, this is not a concern of yours."

He hauled a gold hunter from his waistcoat. "I see it is past eleven—I have to go ashore now. It only remains for me to wish you good fortune, Mr Kydd, and to thank you."

Kydd watched the gangling midshipman he had seen in the captain's cabin emerge from the cabin spaces aft. The lad, in brand new blues and a too-large cocked hat, looked bewildered. Seeing Essington, he went to him, remembering at the last moment to remove his hat. His fingers worked nervously at his dirk as they exchanged murmured words; the boy attempted a last embrace and then Essington went down the side amid the ceremonial shriek of pipes. Kydd caught the glint of tears, the rigidity of barely held control.

"Mr Rawson!" he bellowed, up to the poop-deck, where he knew his signal midshipman had been working at the flag locker.

Rawson appeared at the poop rails in his shirtsleeves, then slid down the ladder to join him. "Sir?"

"Mr Rawson, this is Mr Bowden. Be so good as to convey him t' the midshipmen's berth, and settle him in—an' none of y'r guardo tricks if y' please."

Kydd turned away, feigning disinterest, but listened to the exchange that followed.

"So what do we call ye, then?" Rawson teased. "Spit it out, younker!"

"Er, Charles, sir."

"No, all of it," Rawson said, with relish. "We'll find out from the ship's books anyway."

"Well, er, it's—it's . . . Her-Her—"

"Damn it, fellow, we haven't got all day."

"Her-Her-Hercules A-A-berdour Charles Ayscough, sir," said Bowden, in a small voice.

"*Well,* now! What infernal bad luck for you!" Rawson said fruitily. "I'd wager 'The Honourable' as well?"

The boy nodded miserably. "Couldn't be bettered!" Rawson said, with a whoop. "Welcome to th' Cockpitonians. Where's your sea-chest, then?"

By later that forenoon *Tenacious* was in tolerable seagoing order, her gear inspected and renewed or turned end for end, spars scraped back and well blacked, guns and gunlocks minutely checked. Every conceivable corner and space was stowed with sea stores: a thousand miles into a hostile Mediterranean was not the place to discover deficiencies.

Sitting with the others scratching away at last letters, Kydd sucked his quill: there would be no mail sent or received as they sailed deeper into the ancient sea. He bent again over his letter to his family but was noisily interrupted by a midshipman hurtling into the wardroom. "All officers!" he shrilled. "On deck instanter—it's the admiral!"

The admiral's barge had been seen putting off from *Vanguard,* but it did not shape a course inshore as usual: with Flag pennant a-flutter it headed straight for *Tenacious,* with an unmistakable figure, resplendent in gold lace and decorations, in the sternsheets.

An appalled watch officer sent messengers scurrying while he hastily pulled together a side party. Houghton shot up from below, roaring for the first lieutenant who, when he finally appeared, showed every evidence of hasty dressing.

Kydd took his place with the receiving party of officers on the quarterdeck, nervously tugging his hat and smoothing his waistcoat. No one was in fit state to greet an admiral; it was the usual custom to alert the ship well in advance, but this was the famed Nelson, who was known to be different from the rest.

The bowman of the barge hooked on with a quite unnecessary flourish. High at the deck edge the boatswain waited with his silver call poised, his mates and sideboys in a line inward to the group of officers.

At the instant the top of a cocked hat appeared, the calls pealed out together and Rear Admiral of the Blue Sir Horatio Nelson came aboard, his flag breaking at the mizzen. Houghton came forward and removed his hat. "Sir, welcome aboard HMS *Tenacious*. Might I have the honour of presenting my officers?" The deck was absolutely still; not a man moved except around the admiral.

At the junior end of the receiving line Kydd dared a glance at the man who even now was known throughout the navy and increasingly by the general public, one whose reputation must shortly be tested in this daring foray.

Not as tall as Kydd's, Nelson's figure was sparse and drawn, in no sense that of a hero, and seemingly dwarfed by the weight of his decorations and gold lace. Kydd tried not to look at the empty sleeve pinned across his chest and the spindly legs, and tensed as the admiral approached.

"And Lieutenant Kydd, sir, fifth and junior." Houghton's tone betrayed that he, too, was affected by the presence.

"Do you come from a seagoing family?"

"No, sir," Kydd answered. "I come fr'm Guildford, in th' country." He became uncomfortably aware of prematurely white hair and the odd, milky-blue right eye.

"Then what made you follow the sea?"

"I—I was pressed, sir."

There was no avoiding the admission, but to his relief a thin smile appeared. "And now you are a king's officer, come aft the hardest way. To your great credit, sir—that's so, Captain?"

"It is, sir," Houghton stuttered.

Kydd tried to think of a suitable reply, but Nelson had passed on.

Before they entered the cabin spaces Houghton turned to the officers. "Sir Horatio wishes to address you all. Shall we say my cabin in ten minutes?"

In the great cabin of *Tenacious* a chart of the Mediterranean was already spread out on the table. Nelson wasted no time. "You will have heard from your captain the essence of what faces us. The enemy is up to mischief—but where?" He looked from face to face. "There's been no news, no more intelligence forwarded to me than you yourselves know. We're sailing into the unknown. But of this I'm sure. The enemy must make his move soon and we shall be ready, gentlemen. We have the finest sea service of the age, and we shall do our duty!" There were murmurs of approval, Bryant's sounding above them all.

"Now, to strategy. Our course will be to Toulon. We cruise off and on until we discover for a certainty what the French are doing. If they make a move to the west we fall back. I'm prepared to let Gibraltar be taken to make certain that we can hold them at Cadíz and there with the whole fleet we shall try for a conclusion." There was a shocked silence, which he broke: "We are talking now of the very security of our islands—they will not pass."

He touched the chart to the east. "If, on the other hand, General Buonaparte is considering an adventure to Constantinople he will find he is trapped. The waters are shoal and there is but the one entrance, the Dardanelles. There he will find us waiting, and he will see that it will bring the Turks into close alliance. And if they are further east, to the Levant perhaps, the Red Sea, we shall fall on their lines of supply."

He straightened painfully, his face grim and set. "But all is vaporous posturing until we have met their fleet and disposed of it. While it exists, the Mediterranean is a French lake. All our striving must be to entice it to sea and bring it to battle. That, gentlemen, is our entire strategy. Questions?"

The heightened feeling was almost palpable. Bryant asked boldly, "What will be our force, sir?"

"*Vanguard,* yourselves, *Orion* and *Alexander,* with three frigates. Too big to discourage from looking where we please, too small to think we engage. Big enough to lure 'em out," Nelson snapped, and waited for another question.

"Signals, sir. We haven't yet the new instructions," Kydd found himself saying. The others frowned, but he was concerned that he did not yet have a signal book ready for any major fleet action in prospect.

"Neither will you," Nelson said briefly. "You are in a detached squadron of Sir John's fleet off Cadíz. His signals therefore will still apply." He then turned to Kydd and smiled grimly. "And if any ship of the enemy lie ahead, why, our duty is plain and no signal required."

There was a stirring among the officers. These were not the highly planned, intricate tactics of a fleet in line-of-battle: service under this admiral promised to be a time each would remember.

After the men had finished their grog and noon meal the officers sat down to dinner. The wardroom was alive with only one topic.

"A proud man, but conceited," Bampton said firmly. "Vanity does not a leader make, in my opinion."

"Oh, so you have personal knowledge of our famed commander?" There was an edge to Adams's voice.

"Not directly. But I have heard—"

"Let the man's actions speak for 'emselves, I say!" boomed Bryant.

Bampton came in instantly: "They have."

"Oh?"

"Orders. Do you call them orders? 'If you see an enemy ship, damn the signals and close with him.' What kind of orders are those? In a fleet action there has to be detail—every circumstance foreseen, all manoeuvres planned in such a manner that every captain will know what is expected of him. As for signals—is this an example to our junior officers? Are *you* satisfied, Mr Kydd?"

Kydd had no experience in a fleet action as an officer. As a master's mate on the lower deck during the battle of Camperdown he had never been privy to the wider tactical picture on the quarterdeck. Now, as a signal lieutenant, he was expected to act as a crucial link in the chain of command.

"He's a fighting seaman, that I like," Kydd said firmly. "A rear admiral, but goes out in th' boats himself at Cadíz, takes the fight t' the enemy."

"Seeking a reputation at the cannon's mouth."

Bryant snorted impatiently. "A plain-sailing admiral—*I*'m satisfied, an' *I* surely know what will answer with him."

Kydd finished his meal in silence, and went up on deck. A lone figure stood by the hances. It was Bowden, staring out, unseeing. Kydd approached, but before he could say anything the lad had moved away.

"Tysoe!"

Kydd's servant appeared quickly: the *Princess Royal* was giving a grand reception that evening in honour of Admiral Nelson, and all Gibraltar would be there.

"Full fig 'n' sword."

"Certainly, sir." Kydd held back a smile—Tysoe was never more contented than when he was arrayed in his finery. "The silver buckles, sir?"

"Of course." Kydd knew that this was Tysoe's way of ensuring he would not follow the modish wearing of Hessian half-boots and pantaloons in place of knee-breeches and stockings.

But Tysoe was not privy to the real purpose of the evening. The function was a ruse—seeing a grand party begin, the watching Spaniards would conclude that there would be no martial activity in the fleet that night or, indeed, the following morning. But while the affair was proceeding the darkened vessels at anchor were being prepared. Directly the officers returned in the early hours they would put to sea, and at dawn the Spanish would realise that the English fleet had sailed—but out of their sight and in the opposite direction to their expectation: back into the Mediterranean at last.

At dusk boats put off from all ships, heading for the glittering spangle of lights on *Princess Royal*'s quarterdeck. The sound of an orchestra and excited voices floated across the still water.

Kydd mounted the side and was greeted by the flag-lieutenant. The effect of so much blue and gold of the navy and the scarlet and gold of regimentals was breathtaking under the soft lanthorn light.

An officer of equal standing in the host ship took him into the throng. Seaman servants circulated with wine; ladies stooped to admire the flowers that adorned the bitts round the mast and marvelled at the vivid colours of the flags of every nation draped along the bulwarks.

Kydd felt a well of contentment: this was what it was to be a king's officer, to taste the sweets of his own achievement in a world he had entered by right, the stage upon which he would perform for the rest of his professional life.

He saw his host bringing forward a young lady, who dimpled with pleasure on seeing Kydd. "The Honourable Arabella Grantham. Believes she saw you before," he added enviously.

"Y'r servant, Miss Arabella," said Kydd, essaying a deep bow.

"Mr Kydd, you might not remember, but when you were King Neptune I was a cygnet." She giggled.

It stopped him short until he recalled the fancy-dress assembly he had attended the last time he had been in Gibraltar. "But o' course! The cygnet! Er . . ."

Impulsively she pressed forward, eyes wide. "Mr Kydd, it would make me very happy if you could . . . I have no right—"

"Y'r pleasure is my command," he said immediately, feeling smug. Renzi would be impressed with this evidence of his developing urbanity.

"Er, yes. Mr Kydd. What I'd adore more than anything in this world . . ." her eyes dropped, but the lashes fluttered as she finished breathlessly ". . . is that you do introduce me to your famous Nelson."

A lowly junior lieutenant? Sir Horatio Nelson? "Miss Arabella . . ." he began. Her blue eyes looked up at him beseechingly. He glanced aft. It was easy to spot Nelson; he was conferring at the centre of a distinguished group of senior officers and their followers.

"If y' please." He offered his arm awkwardly and navigated them through the throng, warning her of the odd ringbolt and hatch coaming, rehearsing the words he would use that would excuse the impertinence of approaching a flag officer without leave.

Nelson looked distracted as he listened to an anecdote from a jovial admiral who was clearly his senior. It did not take a great leap of imagination to grasp that he would far rather be ranging the seas than dallying in port.

Kydd waited for the account to finish and the guffaws to die, then addressed Nelson with trepidation: "S-sir, might I present Miss Arabella Grantham, who did express t' me a desire to make y'r acquaintance and will not be denied."

Nelson gave Kydd a cold stare, before which he quailed. Then the gaze turned on the young woman and was transformed. "Why, my dear, you are to be gratified this instant," he said. "Do you now meet Admiral Nelson of the Blue, at once your devoted admirer!" He bowed, then took her hand and kissed it. "Lieutenant, your discernment in the matter of beauty is to your credit, but I can only lament that it is much in evidence you have failed in your duty. This young lady is without the means of refreshment on this warm night."

"Aye aye, sir," said Kydd. He noted that the hand had not been released, bowed and went dutifully in search of some punch.

Tempers on deck were fraying in the hot night as *Tenacious* made ready for sea. "Get forrard this instant, damn your blood, sir!" an officer threw at Bowden, as the hapless midshipman was jostled by men too busy to tell him where to go.

"It'll be stuns'ls, o' course," the master said. Unable to risk the revealing bending of sail before the concealment of dark they were now faced with the task of sending up the long bolsters of canvas almost by touch. Casting under jib, as the large fore and aft sail mounted, it became plain from its limp flap that the light wind had backed even more easterly and they were once more held in the thrall of the Rock.

"This will need more than stuns'ls," Houghton snapped. "I'd hoped we'd make our offing by dawn, but now . . ."

"Sir, *Vanguard* is putting her boats in the water," Bampton said carefully. This implied a hard time for all.

"Yes, I can see that," Houghton said irritably. "But what will they do?" There was no question but that they must follow the motions of the admiral, and there were two alternatives he could take: tow the heavy warships out with every boat available, or warp out.

"Their launch and large pinnace only in the water, sir."

"Then it's to warp." He turned to the boatswain. "Mr Pearce, see to the launch and red cutter." They would lay out an anchor ahead of the ship and heave up to it using the capstan, then take it out and repeat the process, inching to sea by main force.

"Mr Kydd, if you are at leisure you'd oblige me by taking away the launch," Houghton said. Adams was to have the cutter.

Hoisting out the heavy boat would take time, so Kydd went to his cabin to change into a comfortable seagoing rig, then mustered his boat's crew. It was going to be hard, sweaty, painful work with the half-ton of the kedge anchor slung from the boat and the even bigger weight of the catenary of hawser stretching to the ship.

Kydd was glad to see Dobbie, a petty officer built like a prize-fighter, in his party. "Sir," he acknowledged, with a gap-toothed grin. "Better'n being down in th' cable tiers." The familiarity would have irked some officers but since his "duel" with Dobbie in Halifax—when the seaman had accused him of betraying the mutineers at the Nore, and Kydd, although an officer, had been prepared to defend his name in the time-honoured fashion of the lower deck—Kydd had reason to tolerate it. Besides, Dobbie was right: in a short while the job of the men coiling in the heavy, wet cable in the hot, fetid gloom of the orlop would be all but unendurable.

He turned to a boatswain's mate. "Pass the word for Mr Bowden."

"Er, 'oo was that, sir?"

"Mr Midshipman Bowden, if y' please."

The calls echoed down the ship. After some delay a breathless Bowden hurried up, managing to doff his hat and trip over at the same time. "M-mr Kydd, sir?" Even in the dimness the apprehension in his face was plain.

"Please t' accompany me in th' launch." It would be instructive for Bowden to see men at the very extremity of labour.

The launch smacked into the water and was brought round to the side steps where it hooked on. The boat's crew tumbled down the ship's side and took their places.

"A-after y-you, sir," Bowden said.

There was a stifled chuckle among the men on deck, and Kydd said, "No, lad, it's after *you*. Senior gets in last, out first."

Two capstan bars and a dark-lanthorn were handed down. The light was hot and smelly, but would be vital in the work to come. Kydd settled in the stern. There was no rudder for this work: Dobbie would handle the steering oar.

"Shove off," growled Dobbie, to the dark figure of the bowman standing right forward. Obediently the boat-hook was wielded and they moved out into the calm, black waters, but it was only to ease down to the mizzen chains, where the kedge anchor was stowed.

"If y' pleases, sir," said Dobbie. Holding a capstan bar in each hand he motioned towards the midshipman's unfortunate choice of seating in the centre of the boat.

"O' course. Shift out of it, Mr Bowden."

The bars were placed fore and aft over the stroke thwart and the transom, and the kedge anchor swayed down and was lashed into place, its long shank easily spanning the width of the boat with flukes one side and stock the other. The launch squatted down in the water with the weight.

"Out oars!" Movement was heavy and slow as they made their way along the dark mass of the ship to her bow. Within her bulk there would be hundreds of men taking their place at the capstans—with hawsers out to two boats, both the main and fore jeer capstans would be manned by every soul that could be found to keep up momentum.

Their hawser was paid out to them and Kydd himself doubled it back through the anchor ring, holding it while Dobbie passed the seizing. He knew they were under eye from Houghton on the fo'c'sle, and he would be merciless to any who delayed their departure. Then began the slow row out: a deep-sea lead line streamed out with them to tell them when to let the anchor go.

Heavy and unresponsive, the boat was a hog to pull and the night was warm and close. There was none of the usual muttering and smothered laughter that showed the men in spirits: this was going to be a trial of strength and nerve.

"Holy Jesus!" bawled Dobbie. "Are we goin' t' let *Orion* show us th' way out o' harbour? Let's see some sweat, then!" With the weight of iron and endless curve of hawser there was no way that redoubled effort would show in increased speed, a dispiriting thing for men doing their best. But if they flagged, the heavy boat would rapidly slow.

In the moonless night it was difficult to make out expressions, but Kydd could see the unmoving, dogged, downward set of their heads. He glanced to his side at Bowden, who was staring at the straining men, pale-faced.

In the silence, ragged panting and the synchronised clunk and slither of oars in thole pins was loud in the night air. Kydd looked astern; the black mass of the ship seemed just as close and he determinedly faced forward. Dobbie caught the movement and turned on his men: "God rot it, but I'll sweat the salt fr'm yer bones—lay inter it, y' scowbunkin' lubbers! Y'r worse'n a lot o' Dublin durrynackers!"

Kydd knew what they must be enduring—muscles across the shoulders and forearms burning with pain, turning hands on the looms of the oar to claws, but if they were to be out in the cool breezes to seaward before dawn . . .

A low groan came from the anonymous dimness forward. Kydd frowned: if this was an expression of discontent, he would take the steering oar himself and send Dobbie there. He knew that the hard petty officer kept a rope's end handy and he would have no compunction about letting him loose.

Suddenly there was a disturbance—a tangle of arms and cries of alarm. "Oars!" Kydd roared. "Dobbie, get forrard an' see what it is." They had lost momentum.

Dobbie ran down the centreline on the thwarts. Kydd heard grunts and felt the boat sway. "It's Boyd, sir—bin an' taken poorly. I've got 'is oar!" Dobbie shouted hoarsely.

"Give way," Kydd ordered, still at the steering oar. The thunk of oars began immediately; the men knew only too well how hard it was to begin again from a standing start. He blessed his luck at having Dobbie but noticed Bowden's hands clutching the gunwale. They twitched convulsively.

At last they reached the mark on the lead-line. "Oars!" The boat quickly slowed and stopped.

Dobbie padded back down the boat. "Now, Joe," he said to the stroke oar, who stood up, took out his knife and began sawing at the lashings of the anchor. When they had fallen away the two took the end of a capstan bar each in cupped hands.

"Go," said Kydd. The two men strained upwards, bodies shuddering with effort, then the anchor began to shift, to slide, until it toppled off the stern of the boat with a sullen splash, taking the hawser with it. The boat bobbed in relief.

"Hold water larboard—"

"Belay that!" Kydd ordered. "Lay t' y'r oars—five minutes, no longer." The anchor would take time to sink to the sea bed and there would be time then to resume their task.

The men eased their bodies gratefully as best they could.

"Mr Bowden, go forrard an' see what you c'n do."

The lad got to his feet and made his way clumsily forward, kept upright by hands from indignant seamen. He reported back: "A-a form of calenture, I think, sir. He's still unconscious. H-his friends have him out of the way in the middle of the boat, and I've put my coat under his head. A-and I—"

"Ye did right, Mr Bowden." Then Kydd turned to Dobbie. "Out oars—carry on."

They returned under the bows of *Tenacious,* passing Adams in the cutter going out; having two boats at work meant that precious momentum would be preserved. All too soon the unseen labourers on the gundeck capstans had brought the ship up to her second anchor and the weary round must begin again.

The torment continued into the early hours: the same hot, lifeless night air, fathomless dark sea, gasps, panting. The gigantic black bulk of the Rock had receded so slowly and there were still no breezes. On either hand the anonymous blocks of the rest of the squadron showed that they, too, were enduring—but at first light it could be seen that their mission of stealth had not succeeded.

They were nearly clear of Gibraltar Bay as the featureless grey of early dawn took on the colour of day. To starboard the Spanish fort of Punta Carnero woke to life, and the flat crump of guns sounded across the bay. It was in the nature of a salute—a derisory recognition that, despite all their efforts, whoever wished might see the British make sally once again into the sea from which they had been proscribed for so long.

# Chapter 3

The squadron did not pick up a breeze until the mighty Rock was well astern, its shape receding in the bright haze. Then, with the ever-constant east-going current invisibly urging them on, a chuckle of water began at the forefoot.

Topmen crowded up in the yards to extend the sail width with stuns'ls, and the master exerted every skill to trim the complex machinery of canvas and rope that was driving their ship. Ahead was Nelson's *Vanguard: Tenacious* could not disgrace herself.

Kydd was not on watch as officers were not required to keep the deck, but the whole ship's company wanted to take sight of the ancient sea, closed to them until this moment. Renzi stared into the blue expanse ahead, his expression calm but an unconscious half-smile in place. Kydd suspected his friend was contemplating the dangers ahead in this maelstrom of competing nations that was the cradle of their civilisation. But he seemed distant and preoccupied: it might well be more than that. Kydd remembered a letter Renzi had received in Gibraltar that had had a noticeable effect on his friend, but he knew of old that Renzi would disclose the distraction only when he was ready so he would not press matters.

There was no reason why he should go below, but Kydd

could wait no longer. He had taken a peek at the package earlier, but there had been no time for more. Despite his lack of sleep, the thought of what he would see now thrilled him. With guilty excitement he mumbled an excuse and hurried down the companionway.

Tysoe had taken possession of the long, oddly shaped article for him while he had been aboard *Princess Royal* and it was still in its brown-paper wrapping. Kydd opened it carefully, hefting the precious weight and feeling like a child with a long-awaited gift. The black gleam of oiled leather, then the martial gilding of the top of the scabbard—and suddenly it was in his hands, the weapon that would probably be by his side for the rest of his sea life.

He clicked open the langets securing the sword and eased up the blade far enough to see engraved just below the hilt, less than an inch in size, as neat a pair of Cornish choughs as he could have wished for.

With a lethal slither, he withdrew the sword from its scabbard; the half-length bluing of the blade was as handsome as he had remembered. He came to point, the action seeming so natural, the sword in flawless balance. Kydd drew it close in admiration. Mesmerised by the steely shimmer, he flourished it slowly, feeling its grace and accuracy, the sharkskin grips sure and true. He stood to lose his life if enemy blood caused it to slip from his hand.

Reluctantly he slid the blade back into the scabbard. It was unbelievable that he could be the owner of such a fine weapon.

He gathered up the appurtenances: the belt with its frog, a matching baldric—a broad strap for shoulder carriage of the sword complete with a bold gilded fouled anchor device—and a beautifully worked sword knot. Eyeing the tassels doubtfully, Kydd resolved to replace it in combat with a securely spliced manila lanyard. He hung the sword by its rings, left the rest on his desk for Tysoe to stow and returned on deck as nonchalantly as he could.

The favourable south-westerly firmed but backed more to the east; stuns'ls to leeward were struck as they were backwinded by their topsails. The master frowned at the sight of *Vanguard*'s lee stuns'ls still abroad. "Not as I should say, but for a raw captain Berry hangs on t' his canvas a mort long," he muttered.

An hour later, the winds were further towards the south-east and the remaining stuns'ls were taken in. "Hands to quarters!" Houghton snapped. Under plain sail there was no need to worry over delicate sail set and he would have his way with gun practice. "Mr Kydd, you will take post as second of the gundeck for now, if you please."

Kydd had been expecting this. In battle, in a hard-fought slugging match, a signal lieutenant might well find himself employed at the guns, replacing a killed or wounded gundeck officer—in fact, that very instance had provided his own elevation to the quarterdeck.

The long twenty-fours of *Tenacious* were powerful weapons but Kydd had cut his teeth as a young man on the thirty-two-pounders of *Duke William;* any others were lesser beasts.

The crews mustered on the gundeck, throwing off muzzle lashings, taking down the rammers, sheepskin staves and other implements. The bark of gun captains was loud in the close air as they goaded men to their stations. It seemed impossibly crowded but there was a pattern in the seething mass and Kydd waited on the centreline.

Adams was in charge of the forward half of the gundeck standing, like Kydd, well clear of the throng. He caught Kydd's eye, removed his hat and performed an exaggerated bow. Kydd grinned and returned the gesture, then turned back to his section.

Dobbie was gun captain but also quarter gunner, responsible for the after four guns on the larboard side. His squat, powerful build was perfectly suited to hard work in the low decked spaces. Kydd watched as Dobbie bullied crews into place: two to throw off the cross seizings and bight the fall of each side tackle, others hauling the training tackle to the rear of the gun and standing braced to take in the sudden slack when the gun "fired," the remainder ready to train the guns round by brute force with handspikes under the carriage wheels.

Sudden daylight as the gunports were opened. The sharp squeal of small blocks gave an edge to the preparations and Dobbie thrust over to his gun captains, peering at their gunlocks, checking their gunner's pouch and powder horn.

Each gun captain was responsible for his own gun, then immediately to Dobbie, who in turn would answer for their effectiveness to Kydd, a hierarchy of responsibilities upon which Kydd could not trespass.

"Gun crews mustered, sir," Dobbie reported, touching his forehead. A midshipman hovered, theoretically having charge of the guns under Kydd, but wise enough to give Dobbie room.

"Thank you, Dobbie," Kydd said, and walked across purposefully to one of the guns. He removed the cover of the conical match tub. Inside, he could see that the perforated head had its full complement of unlit slow-match hanging down—in action, should a gunlock fail, one would be used to touch off the gun. He eased it off and peered inside. "But where's our water?" he said mildly, turning to Dobbie. If a piece of the lighted match fell, water would be needed to douse it quickly. The look Dobbie gave the gun captain suggested that no further action would be required.

"Ye know the captain permits no sham motions," Kydd said,

careful to direct his remarks in general, "all t' be as in battle, stand fast the shot 'n' cartridge." He let it hang, then turned to the nearest of the gun crew. "Y'r station at quarters?"

"After tackle o' number eleven larb'd," he said instantly.

"And?"

"Second division o' boarders." He was listed to be called away to board the enemy in the second wave when the trumpet sounded.

"And where do ye find y'r weapons?"

"Ah—forrard arms chest?"

"T' see this man knows his duty afore he sees his grog," Kydd replied briskly to the midshipman, who hastily scrawled in his notebook. He turned to go back to his place on the centreline but heard the smothered chuckles of a powder monkey clutching his cartridge box.

"Now then, y' scallywag," he said. "Do ye tell me, what is y' duty should there be a fire at the gun?"

The youngster's eyes went wide. "Er, tell Mr Jones?" he squeaked.

"I'm sure the gunner will know of it b' then," Kydd said, then glared at the midshipman. "The younker t' tell you of his duty before *you* get y'r grog."

The ship's company of *Tenacious* had been together for some time now and practice was becoming more a matter of detail. Gun captains could be stood down while second gun captains took over; men could exchange stations and be equally proficient; they were hardening well.

Kydd paced slowly down the deck amid the heavy rumble of cannon, but his mind strayed to the poop-deck. That was his principal station in battle, heading the signals team, a task requiring the utmost coolness under enemy fire. An admiral had only the medium of signals to bring his fleet round to meet a sudden threat and if the signal lieutenant blundered . . .

"Carry on," he snapped to the midshipman. There was little further he could contribute to the ongoing sweat and toil—he would go up and see how Rawson, the senior signal midshipman, was spending his time in the absence of his officer.

With so many men below at the guns the decks seemed deserted, but as Kydd hurried up the poop ladder he was reassured to see his men at work. Rawson turned and touched his hat. "We're doin' some exercising with *Emerald,* sir," he said, gesturing to the lithe frigate on their beam. "An' they're not up t' snuff is my opinion," he confided.

"An' it's not *your* duty t' pass judgement on others, Mr Rawson," Kydd admonished him.

A seaman whipped down the current hoist, which Kydd saw was number 116: "your signal hoist cannot be distinguished."

Kydd glanced about: the flag locker was neatly stowed, the seamen quietly at their posts at the halliards. "Signal log?"

"Sir." The small portable table near the mizzen mast was rigged, the rough log open, ready for recording every signal received and sent. He enquired about the signal flares and swivel gun for attracting attention at night.

"Brought up an' stowed in the half-deck, sir." All seemed in order. Then he noticed a figure hanging back on the other side of the deck. Gaunt-faced and despondent, it was Bowden. He was also sporting the beginnings of a black eye.

"What about Mr Bowden?" Kydd demanded.

"Er?" Rawson said in surprise. "He's not as who might say a prime hand—"

"Do we not all have t' learn?" Kydd snapped, in rising irritation. "Why isn't he at the log or haulin' on a line or some such?"

Rawson looked dogged and Kydd rounded on him: "Get up t'

the main masthead this instant—you'll maybe have time then t' think o' something."

He realised part of his anger was directed at himself: he owed Essington a service, but there was little he could do about Bowden. Somewhat more sensitive than the others, the lad was clearly suffering.

What he needed, Kydd saw suddenly, was what sailors called a "sea-daddy," someone in whom to confide, who would place things in perspective for him. With a pang Kydd remembered Joe Bowyer, a kindly old seaman who had sailed with Cook and who had befriended him in his early days at sea and fired in him a passion for the life.

But who was best suited to this? Kydd knew that he as an officer could not fulfil the role. Then it came to him. Poulden: a fine seaman, with a gentle manner. He would be ideal. He was in the same division as Bowden, and now he would have a word with the first lieutenant to put him in the same watch and station. Pleased, he called, "Mr Bowden!"

The lad hurried across and Kydd handed Rawson's signal telescope to him. "Do ye know aught of signals? No? Then now's a good time t' learn." He continued, "This is y'r signal book. Adm'ral Nelson relies on us to get his wishes known to our captain, and if we're slack in stays . . ."

The powerful squadron sailed deeper into the Mediterranean, crossing the prime meridian in barely three days and raising the peak of Minorca's Mount Toro in a week. As they shaped course north for Toulon the tension increased. Every vessel they sighted now would be an enemy, and if the French fleet sailed they would be directly in its path. No one believed that Nelson would stand aside tamely, and all readied themselves for the ultimate challenge.

The line of rendezvous was reached, a parallel of latitude off Toulon that would be their station while two frigates ranged ahead off the port. Their intelligence would be vital in the coming struggle.

Even as the squadron took up position *Terpsichore* frigate returned with a prize. Late in the afternoon *Vanguard* hove to and signalled for all captains. In a fevered buzz of speculation Houghton took away his barge; rather less than an hour later he was back. "All officers," was his first order, and while the line of men-o'-war got under way again, the officers of *Tenacious* assembled in the great cabin.

"News, gentlemen," Houghton said, looking from one to another. "In short, I am happy to say we are *not* too late. The French have not sailed. *Terpsichore*'s prize is *La Pierre,* a corvette of the French navy. Admiral Nelson's staff have questioned the crew closely and they, being inclined to boastfulness, have been free with their information.

"I have to tell you now that the rumours we have been hearing are substantially correct. This armament is of prodigious size, reported by many at over thirty sail-of-the-line and hundreds of transports. And their chief general, Napoleon Buonaparte, arrived in Toulon some days ago and is now reviewing his troops and siege train. It seems these troops are, at this moment, embarking in their transport. Gentlemen, Admiral Nelson believes that they are to sail directly."

"Sir, does he know *where* they're headed?" Kydd asked.

"No," said Houghton flatly. "It seems that this Buonaparte is keeping his plans even from his officers. In the absence of any reliable facts we can only assume that the most credible is a lunge west to join with the Spanish, then out to the Atlantic, north for a junction with the Brest fleet and then . . . England."

"Indeed—why else the troops?" muttered Bryant. Louder, he asked, "Do we know anything of their commander, sir?"

"Yes. This is Admiral the Comte de Brueys, a gentleman of the old France. He has been at sea since the age of thirteen and has seen much service. He knows the Mediterranean well, and flies his flag in *L'Orient,* which is of one hundred and twenty guns," he added heavily.

"Sir, what are our orders from the admiral? I have seen no orders yet, sir."

Bampton sounded peevish, but Houghton responded courteously: "Sir Horatio has been good enough to open his mind to his captains. We understand sufficiently well what are his wishes. These he will communicate by signals, which will be few in number but each of which will be of the highest importance.

"Besides, we are a reconnaissance squadron, on detachment only, and our orders therefore are those of our commander-in-chief Admiral Jervis. I commend their thorough perusal by all my officers."

"Then, sir, our duty is clear," Bryant said vigorously. "We hold to the line of rendezvous—"

"The prize has been sent to Cadíz with dispatches, detailing the situation in Toulon," Houghton interrupted. "Earl St Vincent will determine what manner of action might be required."

"And in the event the French sail before then?"

"I have the strongest opinion of Admiral Nelson's leadership in this affair," Houghton said stiffly. "We all know our duty, sir."

The sky was deep blue, white clouds towering and the sea a-glitter as the squadron headed along the rendezvous line under easy sail.

The order came to "exercise small arms by divisions." Kydd knew the weapons well: the boarding pike, an eight-foot shaft with a forged pick head, was purely for defensive purposes; the tomahawk was seldom used as a weapon, its value in scaling ships' sides and cutting away netting; a pistol had but one shot and then became a club. Kydd had no doubt that the cutlass was the prince of weapons.

He waited while sailors shuffled into line on one side of the deck facing him. For the main part, these men were unblooded in battle, strangers to the hatred and violence of hand-to-hand combat. They would preserve their own lives and bring victory to their ship only if they had skill at arms greater than that of the enemy.

Kydd stood in shirt and breeches, the sea breeze ruffling across his chest. "I'll have y'r attention now, if y' please." It seemed an age since, as a pressed man, he had listened while a lieutenant gave him the lesson he was about to impart to these men.

"I'm now going t' save your skins. I'm telling you how to fight—and win!" He signalled to Poulden, who came forward. Kydd took up a cutlass and admired it theatrically, letting its lightly oiled grey steel blade and plain black hilt catch the sun. There were murmurs at the sight. "Now, see here," he said. Poulden advanced on him with his own cutlass; Kydd slowly raised his own blade and brought it down towards Poulden's unprotected head, but well before the blow fell, Poulden lunged forward with the point, directly at Kydd's chest. "You see? Should you slash at your foe he'll be inside you with a thrust—it only needs an inch or two o' steel to end the fight."

A figure to one side caught his eye. It was Bowden, an intense expression on his face. Kydd wondered what he could be thinking. There was no way to prepare anyone for the impact of finding a living person at the end of a blade who must be killed by the plunge of that same steel in his body—before he killed you.

"Laffin," Kydd called. The dark-featured boatswain's mate came forward. "Take this!" he snapped, throwing one of the two wooden practice swords at him. "On y'r guard, sir!"

Laffin waved his sword sketchily but Kydd performed a crisp

front prove distance manoeuvre and tapped his ear smartly. The man recoiled and brought up his sword to point, which Kydd had no trouble evading. Nettled, Laffin began a laborious assault. Instantly Kydd's sword slithered along the inside and in a last flick laid the way open for a fatal lunge.

"You're a dead man, Laffin. Ten seconds." Kydd's eyes took in the rest of his division. "Ye're all a lubberly crew who are going t' leave me alone on an enemy deck while you're all being pigstuck around me. Now we'll learn some real fightin'."

Using Poulden, a fair swordsman, as his opponent, he demonstrated the positions—guard, assault, half-hanger—and the importance of footwork. He knew his swordsmanship did not have the elegance of a fencing master but was workmanlike, forged in the struggle for survival in the short, brutal encounters of boarding.

"Now, shall we see what ye've learned? I'll take th' first dozen, Mr Rawson." The deck by the mainmast was soon filled with figures flailing and clacking at each other under the amused eye of the watch on deck.

Suddenly Kydd bellowed, "Prince o' the poop!" The fighting stopped. Kydd leaped up the ladder to the poop-deck, where he leaned over the rail and looked down with a devilish smile. "I'm defendin' my poop—any who dares t' take it from me?"

Rawson made the first challenge with a creditable show but was transfixed after tripping over a taffrail knee. The next two were quickly disposed of, but then a voice came from the rear: "I, sir! I do answer your challenge!" Renzi mounted the ladder and came to an elegant salute at the top.

Kydd knew his friend was a truly accomplished swordsman, who had been tutored by masters in his youth, but did not believe he would use his skill to disgrace him before his men. Kydd answered the salute gracefully and ceremoniously proved distance.

The tips of the plain wooden blades held each other at point, then began their lethal questing: flicking, clacking, from inside guard to St George and assault; left cheek, point, shift and guard again. The thrusts were thoughtfully considered, held off for that fraction of a second that allowed a perception of intent by the audience.

Renzi's expression was polite, amused. For some reason this annoyed Kydd and he dared a thrust of force. Renzi retreated to a series of guards as Kydd continued to smack at his blade with loud *cloks*.

Kydd was about to overbear Renzi when Renzi's face hardened. His sword flicked out like a barb of lightning, never the same move, probing, testing, vicious.

It chilled Kydd: this was not his friend—this was a terrifying enemy with lethal intent who would batter his way past his defences and finish the contest in death. There was no sound from the onlookers. Renzi moved forward, forcing Kydd into a tiring defence, everything he did of no avail against the faultless automaton bearing down on him.

The end must come—unless . . . He tensed, let his right leg bunch and sank as if brought to his knees. Renzi drew back his blade for the final downward thrust that would end with the point at Kydd's throat—but Kydd's blade flashed out low, and took him squarely in his unprotected upper thigh.

"Ha! You see!" Kydd cried loudly. "My man is now spit, wounded. He falls to the deck—he is now helpless, at my mercy." Kydd knew his unfair move would never be seen in a gentleman's fencing studio, but where was the referee on an enemy deck?

Renzi drew back slowly, his gaze reptilian. He let his "sword" drop to the deck with a clatter.

Through sparkling royal blue seas, the sun beating down, the squadron advanced to the end of the line, then went about and back again while energetic frigates cruised far ahead and abeam, ready to notify the slightest move of significance by the enemy.

Kydd prepared as best he could. He had to be familiar not only with the signal flags but with their tactical and strategic meaning: in the confusion of battle he had to be able to piece together the fleet commander's intentions from brief glimpses of bunting at the halliards and inform his captain accordingly.

The *Fighting Instructions* held all that he should know, but he was troubled that his one experience of a great battle of fleets was now a jostling memory of chaos, powder-smoke and noise, which made it hard to know what his own ship had been doing, let alone others.

And that was supposing they fell back to Cadíz and became part of a much larger fleet. If the French put to sea, Nelson would probably sacrifice himself and his little squadron to delay them—it would be less a fleet battle than a heroic destruction. So much depended on the next days. Distracted, he paced the deck forward.

Out of the corner of his eye he saw Bowden sitting on the fore-hatch with Poulden, a laborious long-splice under way. The lad's look of concentration was intense and Kydd was pleased to see his work had a fine seamanlike appearance; Bowden looked up shyly at him.

The afternoon wore on. In the dog-watches he would exercise with the cutlass again, and on the following forenoon there would be muskets and a target dangling at the yardarm. He passed Renzi, standing gazing at *Vanguard* ahead. He was clearly deep in thought and Kydd had not the heart to disturb him.

In the evening, cutlass drill was delayed. Houghton had been talking with the master, who made no secret of his distrust of the weather and both watches took off the royals and sent down the masts. Before the end of the dog-watch the breeze had freshened from the north-west. "Don't care what they calls it—*mistral* or *tramontana,* it's bad cess to us if'n it's coming from the nor'ard," the master said gravely.

It was peculiar in Kydd's experience: cloudless skies and exuberant seas, perfect weather, but the wind was increasing to a degree that in English waters would give rise to concern for the future.

After supper Kydd arrived to take over the watch. *Orion* and *Alexander* were ahead and under topgallants while the frigates closed up for the night. "Rather you than me, old pickle," Adams said cheerfully. "Master thinks a tartar's blowing up." He disappeared below.

Kydd eyed the canvas and sniffed at the wind. "M' duty t' the captain an' I advise taking in th' courses," he told his messenger.

Houghton came on deck. "I see *Vanguard* has still her royals abroad," he said suspiciously.

"Aye, sir," Kydd said carefully, "but *Orion* an' *Alexander* have taken 'em in and, if I'm not mistaken, there is *Alexander* going t' topsails now." As if reading Houghton's thoughts, he added, "And we're still stayin' with Flag, sir."

Admittedly, their line was now more of a gaggle in the evening gloom as they watched lanthorns jerkily mounted to the mizzen top of *Vanguard*. "Very well. You may use the watch on deck only, Mr Kydd." Houghton hesitated then went below.

It would mean a longer, harder job but the watch below would not be disturbed. However, within twenty minutes the wind had changed from an insistent stream to a buffeting, squally threat. "Mr Pearce, I mean to turn up all the hands in striking courses," Kydd told the boatswain, who went to fetch his mates. Houghton arrived quickly. The seas were higher, but in a way that was peculiar to this landlocked sea: short, steep and rapid, meeting the bow in a succession of sharp explosions of white.

Their consorts began distancing themselves: sea room was becoming necessary in the increasingly boisterous conditions, even with the half-moon's occasionally cloud-dimmed light. "Keep the men on deck, Mr Kydd," Houghton said, drawing his coat round him.

In less than an hour it had worsened. The moon was now all but obscured by lower-level racing scud and the topsails bellied and tautened to iron-like rigidity. "I'll trouble you to close-reef the tops'ls," Houghton ordered.

Men crowded into the weather shrouds and began climbing. It was murky and indistinct—Kydd knew they were going as much by feel and familiarity with their aerial world as sight. They would be deadly cautious, transferring hold from one hand, one foot to another only when it felt secure. Slamming wind gusts could shake the hold of the unwary and send them, helpless, to their death. When they reached the tops and eased out on the yard they would no longer even be free to hold on—balancing on a thin footrope with empty space beneath, they had to lean over and, with both hands, fist the maddened canvas into submission, then secure the points with a reef knot.

Still the wind increased, hammering in from the north-west with a flat ferocity. At one in the morning a particularly savage squall shook and pummelled the ship. With a report like gunfire, the topsails blew to pieces and *Tenacious* fell off the wind until fore and aft sail were set to stabilise her.

The wind's noise in the bar-taut rigging was a rising howl that tore at the reason; this was nature gone mad. Seas, driven up by the frenetic wind, caused an ugly roll, which threw serious strain on spars and rigging. Preventers and rolling tackles could help, but when squalls and rain clamped in there was nothing for it but endurance through the long night, with occasional half-glimpsed pinpricks of lanthorn light all that could seen of other ships.

Finally dawn came in a grey welter of cold spray and whipping wind. As the light extended, lookouts in the tops spotted other ships scattered around the gale-lashed seascape, calling their names down one by one as they recognised them. The vessels altered course to form up the squadron once more.

But which was the flagship? And there were no frigates. All that could be seen were two ships-of-the-line and another further off that must be Admiral Nelson. Yet there was something not right with the distant vessel. As they beat their way closer it became clear: *Vanguard* had lost her entire foremast as well as all her topmasts, and was surviving with scraps of sail on what remained.

With tumbled masts and no steadying canvas aloft, the ship rolled grievously, on every plunge showing her copper or submerging her lower gunports. Conditions on board would be indescribable, but she was still gallantly holding a course.

Houghton took a telescope, braced himself against the savage roll, and focused on the stricken vessel. The master moved up next to him. "A boat cannot live in these seas, Mr Hambly," Houghton said. "We can do nothing for them."

"No, sir," said Hambly, neutrally. "But on this board he stands into mortal peril, sir . . ."

"The land?"

"Corsica, sir. Dead to loo'ard an' not so many miles." The awesome force of the gale from the north-west had driven the squadron towards the craggy coast of Corsica to the south-east—but how close were they?

"He must wear, o' course."

With the wind blast on the larboard side any sail that *Vanguard* could hoist would only impel them further towards that coast. They must therefore bring the gale to the other side and let her drive before it. But with no possibility of setting any kind of sail forward there would not be the leverage to bring the big 74 round. She was trapped on her course.

"They'll tack, then?"

"No, sir," Hambly responded. "She wouldn't a-tall get through the wind's eye. I fear we're t' see a calamity very soon, sir."

It was inconceivable: the greatest fighting admiral of the age, in his own flagship, beaten on to the rocks, then almost certain death—or, at best, survival and humiliating capture by the French.

"We have to do something, damn it!" Houghton rasped. The other two ships were lying tentatively on her beam; in these surging conditions it was too risky to get closer.

"Could stream rafts for survivors when . . ." No one took up Kydd's thought and he resumed his sorrowful gaze at the doomed vessel. In all conscience they could stay with the ship only until that fatal last half-mile.

Then there was sudden movement on her decks. The rags of sail still up were brought in until the ship was bare. Without the steadying of high canvas she began a sickening wallow, the merciless wind nearly abeam. A flicker of paleness showed around her plunging bow.

"Ah!" All eyes turned to Hambly, who cleared his throat self-consciously. "Er, that is t' say, it's clear they have right seamen aboard *Vanguard*. That's a sprits'l they're setting an' they'll wear ship with that."

A spritsail was an ancient sail from another age, one spread below the bowsprit and long since disappeared from modern warships. The effect of the diminutive sail, set so far forward, was immediate. Painfully, *Vanguard* began to pay off under the leverage, rotating slowly until the seas previously battering her from abeam now came under her stern. She gathered steerage way and, bracing the spritsail yard hard round, showed canvas on her mizzen, completed the turn and finally wore round. At last the threat of shipwreck was averted.

The quarterdeck of *Tenacious* erupted in shouts of admiration—now their flagship had a chance! Only one frigate could be seen: the others must have been blown to—who knew where?

The storm showed no sign of calming and the last frigate fell away into the spindrift, then disappeared.

It was now a matter of enduring the jerking, bruising motion; a tedious, wearying period that stretched time and deadened the spirit. A second night drew in, but before the light faded a flutter of colour showed at the admiral's mizzen.

"Mr Kydd!" Houghton handed over his telescope. The image danced uncontrollably and Kydd adopted a foul-weather brace, right elbow jammed firmly to his side, the other against his chest with his feet splayed wide. Without needing to refer to his pocket signal book he knew the hoist. "*Alexander*'s pennant, 'pass within hail.'"

Then *Orion* closed cautiously, and finally it was the turn of *Tenacious.* Coming up slowly on the flagship's leeward side they saw the damage—topmasts missing, foremast a splintered stump, lines of rigging tangling on the decks—it could not possibly be repaired at sea.

Without doubt the cluster of figures on her quarterdeck would include Admiral Nelson. Kydd clung to the shrouds listening as Houghton brought up his speaking trumpet and hailed, "Flag ahoy!" His voice was strong and well pitched, but it was nearly lost in the uproar of the swashing seas between the madly surging vessels.

"Do ye hear?" came distantly across from the flagship quarterdeck.

"I do, sir."

"Have—you—charts—" Houghton held up a hand in acknowledgement "—of Oristano?"

Sardinia. So the admiral was seeking a dockyard in Sardinia under their lee. "Have we? Quickly, Mr Hambly."

"No, sir, nothing more'n a small-scale o' that coast."

"Regret—no—charts."

The remote figure waved once and the ships began to diverge. The admiral had three choices: to chance unknown waters and a possibly hostile port in Sardinia; make a lengthy return to Gibraltar in his crippled ship; or, when the weather abated, transfer to one of the others and scuttle *Vanguard*.

Darkness came and the long night brought no relief from the hammering northerly. Only when dawn's cold light imperceptibly displaced the blackness was there a moderation in the welter of torn seas. *Alexander, Orion* and *Tenacious* came together once more.

"She's signalling!" Kydd's eyes were sore with salt spray as he tried to read *Vanguard*'s hoist. "To *Alexander:* 'prepare to take me in tow.' "

"Now we'll see what they're made of, I think," said Bryant, wedging himself against the outside corner of the master's cabin and calmly contemplating, across the chaotic, tumbling seas, the heroic feat of seamanship now demanded.

"Boats won't swim," said Kydd, similarly exercised.

"Can float off a keg wi' a messenger line," mused the master, "if *Alexander* dare take a wind'd position." This was where the main difficulty lay: to allow the keg to float downwind, or any like manoeuvre, implied placing *Alexander* upwind. The huge windage of the 74s at slow speeds would ensure they drifted inexorably to leeward but it would be at differing rates for different ships and weather conditions. The consequences of the ship to weather drifting faster and colliding with the one to leeward, with all the inertia of one and a half thousand tons, was too horrific to think about.

*Alexander* lay off, preparing her move. Any close manoeuvring was deadly dangerous in the wild seas and it would take extreme care to pass over the line safely. She wore round in a big circle and approached *Vanguard* from astern and to windward.

Sail was shortened down to goosewinged fore-topsail and storm staysails, and she approached with the buffeting wind on her quarter. Closer, she eased the sheets of two of the three staysails and lined up for her run—she was clearly trying for a close glancing approach to *Vanguard*'s poop with one fleeting moment to get the line across.

The voluted beakhead of *Alexander* slowly approached the carved stern of *Vanguard*. As she did so, the scale of the independent plunging and rearing of the two ships was evident. *Alexander*'s bowsprit and its complex tracery of rigging speared closer. Then, in seconds, the situation changed. A chance convergence of wave crests into a larger one rose up on *Alexander*'s outer bow at the same time as its trough allowed *Vanguard*'s stern to slide towards her.

It looked as if the two ships would merge in splintering ruin but then the fo'c'slemen on the foredeck of *Alexander* boomed out the fore-topmast staysail to weather by main force and by small yards she yawed giddily and slid past.

Kydd strained to see any tiny thread of black rope against the white water indicating a line had been passed. There was none. The 74 plunged past *Tenacious* on her way round once more and Kydd could see activity on both ships. But when the light line had been finally passed across from *Alexander* it would in turn bring aboard a heavier hawser, then probably one of the anchor cables roused up from the tiers in the orlop. At more than a hundred and twenty pounds for every fathom streamed it would be a fearsome task to manhandle.

This time *Alexander* came up to leeward of the stricken flagship, necessarily head to head to bring their fo'c'sles adjacent. Kydd used his signal telescope to watch: he could make out a lone seaman in the forechains with his coiled, heaving line tensed, waiting.

The two ships closed, *Alexander* deliberately keeping well to leeward as she edged ahead. They began to overlap—the seaman started to swing his smaller coil in readiness—but even as he did so it became obvious that the windward vessel was catching more of the wind's blast and drifting down fast on the more sheltered leeward. *Alexander*'s bowsprit sheered off rapidly.

Once more the big man-o'-war went round ponderously. Once more the seaman in the chains began his swing, and once more it proved impossible. Time wore on. In *Tenacious* hands were piped to dinner, and the heaving line was cast twice more. The afternoon watch was set—and on the next pass a line at last was caught on *Vanguard*'s foredeck.

Those watching in other ships dared not breathe as the dots of men on her fo'c'sle scrambled to bring in the line, but *Alexander* was falling away fast. Kydd knew what they had to do: a dark cavity in *Alexander*'s stern windows was where her cable would be led out, but first *Vanguard* must hold fast the precious light line while a stouter rope was heaved in from *Alexander* and manhandled through the hawse-hole, where it would be led to the main capstan.

Below in the sweating gloom this hawser would be heaved in, its distant other end seized to the main cable issuing out of *Alexander*'s stern windows as it was led from the giant riding bitts further forward.

It was now only a matter of time. Little by little the great cable, nearly two feet in circumference, was drawn across the foaming sea until *Vanguard* was finally tethered.

The weight of the seven hundred feet of heavy rope between the two ships formed a catenary, a graceful curve in the cable that acted as a giant spring in the towing, absorbing the shocks and fretful jibbing of the storm-lashed ships. *Alexander* showed small sail, then more, until reefed topsails gave her enough force to pull *Vanguard* in line and then, miraculously, begin a clawing, slewing motion ahead.

As if in respect to the feat performed in the teeth of its hostility, the wind moderated from a full gale to a sulky bluster, then later to a steady north-north-westerly. And foul for Oristano.

The ships, limping at no more than walking pace, could not lie close enough to the wind to overcome the current taking them south, and the only dockyard on the west of Sardinia was left astern.

"What now, do you think, Mr Hambly?" Houghton asked. There seemed to be no avoiding a long and chancy tow back to Gibraltar.

Adams brightened. "Sir, when I was a mid in *Cruizer* we chased a corsair to Sardinia, and he disappeared. We found him in San Pietro Bay, south of here, in as snug a harbour as you'd find within forty leagues. I believe Admiral Nelson could lie there in perfect peace while he repairs enough to sail back to Gibraltar."

"Mr Hambly, lay me within hail of the flagship."

It was a notion clearly to Nelson's liking and the tow was shaped more southerly. The winds diminished rapidly to a pleasant breeze, and with the sun now strong again and in the ascendant, wisps of vapour rose from the water-logged decks.

A distant lumpy blue-grey appeared from the bright haze ahead. "San Pietro island, sir," Adams said smugly. "Our anchorage lies beyond."

After several days of danger and hardship Kydd found the prospect of surcease and peace attractive. But as the sun went down so did the breeze and those who had cursed the wind were now regretting its failing. Sail was set to stuns'ls but their forward movement slowed to a walk again and then a crawl. The night came languorously in violet and pink, but no breeze blew from the Sardinian shore. A half-moon rose, stars pricked the heavens, and the ships remained drifting.

Then Kydd saw something that awakened memories of an Atlantic night when death had risen out of the darkness to claim his frigate. "Breakers, sir! I see breakers!" Barely perceptible, but distantly picked out by moonlight, there was a white line of surf—the storm swell driving into the shore. It seemed that the other ships had spied it: there was movement of lanthorn light around their fo'c'sles. Without doubt they, too, would bend their best anchors to their cables.

*Tenacious* found out the sombre truth with the rest: there was no wind to haul off the land and the water was bottomless. It was unjust. Weary after so much strife they now faced another night of dread, feeling the sullen swell rolling under their keel, relentlessly bearing them towards the dark mass of the land while the sails hung useless in the moonlight.

They were long hours—restless, waiting, fearing the dawn and starting at every flap and shiver aloft, it was hard simply to endure. The deep sea lead was cast regularly; eventually it touched bottom at three hundred feet but this was too deep for anchoring.

When sunrise came it was soft and warm, welcoming them with the deep blue of the morning sky—but the royal blue of the open sea changed to the liquid green of inshore. Constrained by the dead weight of the tow, *Alexander* and *Vanguard* had not been able to take advantage of every little shift in the night breeze and now lay significantly closer inshore.

From the quarterdeck of *Tenacious* it looked a grave situation. The two 74s, still joined by the long cable, were now within a short distance of the shore and it was heartbreaking that after all their efforts the flagship would end in the breakers they could now clearly see.

"*Alexander* must cast off th' tow," murmured the master, shaking his head. At least one ship of the two would then escape. But there was no indication that this was planned—no boats in the water to take off the ship's company of *Vanguard,* no general signal of distress or move to abandon ship. Both men-o'-war drifted on, carried together towards the bare, nondescript coast.

Then, as if relenting in its tantrum, the wind returned; just enough to fill the sails of *Alexander* and allow her to crawl past the craggy northern cape of San Pietro island. Safely past, a signal hoist mounted in the flagship. "Sir! Our pennants and, 'assume the van,'" Kydd said.

"Means us to lead the way, I believe. Mr Adams, this snug harbour . . . ?" *Tenacious* stole round the southerly point of the island, led in by Lieutenant Kydd in the cutter with a hand lead-line sounding ahead. Kydd had put Poulden on the lead-line and Bowden on the simple signal flags relaying back the depths; there was time enough to spy out the land.

They entered a fine inlet between San Pietro island and another; the enfolding bay was sheltered from everything but a southerly. They could anchor there in perfect peace with space enough for twenty ships—and it was good holding ground: shells and soft shale came up with the lead.

The bare, scrubby land shimmered in the glare of the morning sun and Kydd scanned it cautiously for any activity. There were some vestiges of cultivation on the steep slopes and the occasional red-tiled farm dwelling but no fortifications that he could detect.

He completed his sweep of the little bay and told Bowden to indicate with his white flag over red that he considered it worth bringing in *Tenacious.* Then he prepared to carry out the second part of his orders.

As he pulled deeper into the bay he looked for any signs that the local inhabitants might be hostile. Already dots were appearing on the sandy beach and dunes. "Stretch out, if y' please,"

Kydd urged the rowers. If he was to represent the Royal Navy to a foreign power, he would make sure his men did not let him down. He turned the boat towards a knot of people, and when it beached, allowed himself to be chaired ashore by two seamen.

"L'tenant Kydd, His Majesty's Ship *Tenacious,*" he announced loudly, bowing in a general way to the people and bringing an immediate hush to the crowd. "Er, anyone speaks English?"

Dressed in the exotics of the inner Mediterranean they looked at Kydd with curiosity. He picked out the most dignified of the men, and repeated the question. The man started in consternation, threw out his hands and jabbered fearfully. "We come t' repair—in peace, that is," Kydd tried again, but could feel a rising tide of unease. More people arrived and he saw the curiosity replaced by scowls. He glanced back at his boat; he had deliberately not armed the seamen with him and had not worn his own sword.

A swirl of movement at the back of the crowd caught his eye: a donkey was coming down a track to the beach, ridden by an officer of some kind. Laughter broke out from the boat's crew at the comical sight of the man's legs flapping out to the sides of the diminutive beast.

"Silence!" roared Kydd, aghast. The officer came to a stop and slid to the ground, his face dark with anger. He wore an odd folded hat with a scarlet tassel and a faded but flamboyant uniform that ill fitted his corpulent figure. The seamen could not stifle their mirth and Kydd ground out, "I'll take the cat t' the next man who so much as grins, s' help me." He bowed as low as he could to the officer, who stiffly returned the gesture, after he had snarled something to the crowd, which subsided obediently. "L'tenant Kydd," he began again, but the officer broke into impassioned speech, gesturing at *Tenacious.*

"Sir, I can't understand . . ." Frustrated, they glared at each other, speechless.

*"Pardonnez-moi, mon commandant,"* Bowden came in awkwardly, *"mais si vous avez le français . . ."*

The officer's expression changed fractionally and he answered in gruff, choppy French. They exchanged sentences and Bowden turned to Kydd. "Sir, this officer comes from Fort Charles on the island. He's a captain of militia and therefore an officer of His Sardinian Majesty. He demands to know by what right we are coming ashore."

All Kydd knew was that Sardinia was a neutral country. "Thank ye, Bowden. Do you tell him we're only here a short time to repair storm damage an' mean no act o' hostility." Bowden relayed his words—some of the crowd understood what he said and passed it on to the others. The officer stiffened. Kydd looked at Bowden impatiently.

"Sir, he says that under the terms of their treaty with France, Sardinia may not allow an English vessel to enter any port in the kingdom, and that is his final word."

Kydd saw there was no moving him—no argument or show of force was appropriate. On the other hand no repairs could be contemplated if the ships would be at the mercy of unfriendly local forces. "Bowden, listen carefully. I want you t' say this so the others can hear, you understand?"

"Yes, sir."

"Tell him that we agree not to enter his port, just anchor offshore." That was no concession—the little cluster of buildings and small wharf he could see at the inner coast of the island could not possibly take four ships-of-the-line. Bowden did as he was told. "Now mark this," Kydd went on. "Tell him that a big ship has many sailors—they must be fed. If any has livestock or vegetables, they can turn them into English silver this very day, should they bring them here to this beach."

Excitement grew as the word spread. The man Kydd had

addressed earlier now pushed across, wanting to know if the English sailors preferred beef or mutton, and small boys raced off with the news. The officer barked at them, but the mood had changed: here was instant prosperity for this tiny settlement and it would go ill with him if he stood in its way.

He hesitated, then turned to Kydd once more. Bowden translated: "Sir, he says that, after consideration, he finds that if we keep out of the port the terms of the treaty are not in violation. And, sir, he wishes us an enjoyable visit."

The shouts of approbation that followed forced a smile from the officer, who clambered aboard his donkey, lifting his hand in farewell. Just at that moment three great ships-of-the-line came into view, filling the pretty bay with their warlike majesty and unanswerable presence.

The officer nearly fell off the donkey in fright. Kydd said quietly, "I dare t' say, our admiral would be satisfied with the usual salutes . . ."

Nelson brought his battered flagship to rest, then signalled, "captains to report condition of ships for sea." In addition to the usual readiness statement, an assessment of storm damage was required, and *Tenacious* hastened to comply.

For her junior lieutenant this meant accompanying the boatswain and carpenter on their rounds, a task congenial to Kydd's heart as it was an opportunity to make a closer acquaintance of his ship.

They began at furthest forward and, in a borrowed pair of sailor's trousers, Kydd was soon out on the eighty-foot length of the bowsprit with the two warrant officers. His experience in a Caribbean dockyard had shown him the difference between the dark, weathered fissures in timber a shipwright would call a "shake" and therefore ignore, and the long bright-sided splits that would betray the much more serious condition of a sprung spar. He inched along the jibboom horse, careful to check under as well as above.

The foremast came next. They used a girt-line with a boatswain's chair at each side of the mast to close-inspect the fat timbers of the foremast, a "made" mast constructed of several pieces keyed together instead of a single length of timber. It was unlikely to have sprung, and they moved on quickly from the foretop to the topmast.

As they worked, Kydd noticed the deference Pearce, the hard boatswain, was according the carpenter. Both were standing officers—they would remain with *Tenacious* even when put into reserve—and had been together for years. Kydd had never paid much attention to the carpenter, who figured on no watchbill and went about his business with little fuss.

They spread out over the yards, the older men moving deliberately while Kydd attended to the pole royal mast, and then it was time to move to the mainmast. As they inched out on the mainyard the double strikes of eight bells sounded, announcing grog and dinner for the hands.

The job had to be finished but Kydd could not in all conscience order the other two men to press on without something to eat. He leaned over the big spar and hailed the deck. "Mr Rawson, ahoy!" The midshipman looked upward. "Be s' good as to light along some scran for us—we've a job still t' do aloft."

The upper yards were completed and they descended to the maintop just as a hand waved through the lubbers' hole from below. Kydd went over. It was Bowden, weighed down with a seaman's mess-kid slung round his neck. He took the steaming vessel, realising that it must have taken considerable resolve for the raw lad to make the climb. "Where's Mr Rawson? I told him to bring this."

"Ah, he had other duties that pressed, sir," Bowden said neutrally. Kydd suspected that Rawson had coerced Bowden into making the climb, hoping for a spectacular disaster. Bowden disappeared, but then a younger midshipman popped into view, passing up a bag containing a loaf of bread, local oranges and mess-traps.

Kydd was quietly pleased at Bowden's climb up the mast and his initiative in co-opting another midshipman, who had not finished yet: he extracted a bottle of claret from his coat. "Your servant said t' give you this."

Kydd spread out his victuals. "Gentlemen, shall we dine?" The boatswain hesitated before he dipped his bread into the common pot. "Mr Feakes, if y' please?" Kydd encouraged the carpenter, who bent to his plate. "You've been carpenter aboard f'r some years, I believe?" he asked.

"Aye, sir. Since launch."

"That's before th' war, then."

"Sir."

"Bin wi' the old girl at the First o' June, he was," Pearce put in admiringly. "An' with *Cybele* in India."

The Glorious First of June—the first great fleet action of the war, and both Feakes and *Tenacious* had been there. Kydd looked at Feakes; there was no sign of those momentous, dangerous times on his lined face and he warmed to the old sailor.

Kydd felt the stout bulk of the mainmast at his back as he took in the stately soaring of stays and shrouds, halliards and pendants in their precise curves, the sweetness of the deck-line from high above as it passed from bowsprit to old-fashioned stern. This was a ship to love, to remember with fondness down the years. He felt a curious pang as he thought about Feakes and *Tenacious* growing old together.

Kydd's feelings for *Tenacious* turned to a catch in the throat, however, as he realised that in the near future enemy shot might smash its way into her vitals. This time she might not be as lucky as she had been at the Glorious First of June and Camperdown. He got to his feet. "We'll carry on," he said gruffly. "Our Nel's a-waiting f'r our report."

Captain Houghton and the first lieutenant left for *Vanguard* with Kydd's report as first dog-watchmen went to supper. Within the hour they were back. "Pass the word for Mr Feakes—the carpenter, ahoy!"

The captain's barge conveyed the carpenter to the flagship. It was dusk when he returned and hurried directly to Houghton's cabin. Minutes later Bryant was summoned, and before much longer the word was out: to Nelson's considerable satisfaction, Feakes had given out that *Vanguard* could not only be jury-rigged for the retreat to Gibraltar but might conceivably be put into some kind of shape to meet the French at sea.

In a race against time the flagship had to be fitted for sea with the only resources they had: spare spars, twice-laid rope and willing hands. And in recognition of Feakes's faith and intelligent direction, *Tenacious* was to perform the most difficult task. She would lash alongside *Vanguard* and, in a feat of seamanship that would stretch every talent aboard, she would be used to extract the stump of foremast and lower in the new to the flagship.

That night Feakes and his mates transferred to *Vanguard* and set about readying the ship for a complete replacement of all topmasts. *Orion* would craft the new mizzen topmast, *Alexander* would provide a fore-topmast while *Vanguard* herself would work on the main. Within two days the preparations were complete.

In brilliant sunshine and under curious eyes from ashore *Tenacious* was warped in close to *Vanguard*. As the ship working the evolution, *Tenacious* had charge of the operation—Bryant stood at the bulwark with speaking trumpet and the manner of a bull mastiff: should any hesitate or fail they could depend on an instant reaction.

When the partners of the foremast had been knocked out *Tenacious*'s main-yard was braced around and with stout tackles and guys clapped on it, the ugly, splintered stump of the foremast was plucked out like a tooth. Getting the new one in was a more serious matter: the raw length of the three-foot-thick lower mast might, if it slipped, plummet down and transfix the bottom of the flagship.

It took the entire forenoon but by midday *Vanguard* had her masts made whole once more. A fore-topmast had been fashioned from a spare main topgallant mast and hoisted into place and her bowsprit strengthened by "fishing" across the weakened part with timber lengths.

In less than four days Nelson's flagship had been transformed from a storm-shattered wreck to a ship-of-the-line ready for sea—reckoned by all hands to have been made whole again and set to take her place in the line-of-battle.

Admiral Nelson wasted no time. The squadron set sail, re-formed and shaped their course. There was no talk of retreating to Gibraltar; they would sail north. Their duty was clear and unchanged—to return off Toulon and resume their mission.

Gun practice and combat preparation intensified to a high pitch as they neared the rendezvous to collect their frigates, which were vital to the squadron: they would look into enemy ports and report in detail.

But as the lookouts searched the horizons a lone sail was spotted, boldly crossing their course. It was a Balkan merchant vessel. Stopped by *Orion,* she had intelligence of such import that the admiral called an instant conference. The storm that had driven them south had allowed the French to slip out of port and away.

It had finally happened. The feared Napoleon Buonaparte

was at sea and headed for an unknown destination with an immense fleet of overwhelming numbers: fifteen ships-of-the-line and fourteen frigates, with brigs, cutters, gunboats—seventy-two warships in all. But these were not the heart of the fleet: in four hundred transports there were tens of thousands of battle-hardened troops. This immense armada could have only one purpose.

Nelson's response was immediate. The awesome fleet had to be found, and for that he needed his precious frigates to extend the line to comb the seas. There was no choice: they must crowd on sail to reach the rendezvous as fast as they could and then, with the frigates spread out abreast, begin the search. When the enemy was found Nelson would detach one ship to report back to Cadíz for orders while continuing to shadow.

They reached the appointed place but there was not a frigate in sight. *Orion* searched to the east along the line of latitude while *Tenacious* took the west—but there were no frigates.

They waited at the rendezvous. Dusk fell and night gave time for contemplation of the situation. Dawn arrived—and no frigates. The day passed. Even the meanest imagination knew what it must be costing their helpless admiral. Night, another day, and still no English sail. In the afternoon a garrulous fisherman was stopped—and he had news: in some vague position not so far away he had chanced upon a great fleet passing, at least ten, perhaps a dozen ships-of-the-line, which he thought to be English—clearly incorrect, given that Nelson's was the only squadron in the Mediterranean.

In a friendless sea with every man's hand turned against them and utterly outnumbered, Nelson and his little band were faced with a quandary—what to do next.

# Chapter 4

"Sail hooooo!" The masthead hail stilled all talk and halted work on deck. Far to the west they could detect the merest pale flicker against the sparkling horizon. The squadron kept tight formation: this might be the first of a powerful French force sent to deal with a few impudent English ships reported to have entered *their* sea.

But there were no additional sail. The vessel tacked about to reveal the two masts of a humble brig. It was no outlying scout of the enemy fleet, just one of the countless workhorse craft of its kind in the Mediterranean going about its business. *Tenacious* returned to her routine.

However, the brig made no move to turn away. It stood on, its course of intersection one which would bring it close to the flagship. Curious eyes followed its steady approach until, at two miles distance, *Vanguard*'s challenge, accompanied by the crack of a gun, brought a flurry of bunting to its halliards.

"Correct answer f'r today—can't make out her pennants," Kydd said, flicking through his signal book. She was apparently English, in a sea where they had thought they were the only members of His Majesty's Navy.

*Vanguard*'s yards came round as she heaved to, allowing the brig to come up and deliver dispatches—with news that changed the situation. The reconnaissance squadron was to be no more: a powerful force of ten ships-of-the-line was on its way to join Nelson to transform it into a battle fleet. The fisherman had been right—he had seen English ships. There were cheers of joy. At last the tables had turned: no longer the fearful trespasser, they were now the predator.

Admiral Nelson's orders were not long in coming, and covered everything from the disposition of men-o'-war in a tactical formation to the issue of lemons and fresh water.

Kydd settled down to write up his signal book. Nelson's instructions were clear and vigorous and although there was not a flood of new signals there were a dozen general signals and fifty-six concerning tactical manoeuvres, all of which had to be carefully detailed and indexed in his pocket signal book.

The most important were those covering their preparations for the chase. The fleet was to be tightly formed, in three columns a nautical mile apart and each ship two and a half cables from the next ahead. Divisions for battle would be signified by a specific triangular flag; these were empowered to take on the enemy independently.

But it was the Fighting Memorandum that had the officers talking. It spoke in powerful terms of close combat during which "should a captain compel any of the Enemy's ships to strike their Colours, he is at liberty to judge and act . . . to cut away their masts and bowsprit . . ." and that ". . . possession of ships of the enemy should be by one officer and one boat's crew only, that the British ship may be enabled to continue the attack . . ."

The overall tenor of the orders was encapsulated in one single stirring sentence: ". . . this special observance, namely *that the destruction of the enemy's armament is the sole object* . . ." This was real fighting talk. No intricate manoeuvres, no time wasted in forming a line-of-battle, just forthright demands to fall upon the enemy in the most direct and effective manner at hand and the confident assumption that the English fleet would prevail.

The wardroom was abuzz long into the night with the implications for individual initiative, the risk for Nelson in trusting his captains with the close-in climax of a battle, and the probability of a rapid conclusion—one way or the other.

First one, then a multitude of sails lifted above the horizon. After an anxious wait the ships were finally revealed to be the longed-for reinforcements. For three days the newly formed battle fleet lay hove to. Boats plied busily between ships as captains met their admiral and officers reported to the flagship with their order books to receive the details resulting from strategy realised into tactics by the fertile mind of their chief. When all was complete, the collection of fourteen warships was as one under a single command. It was time to go in chase of the French fleet.

Signal guns on *Vanguard* cracked impatiently. In three divisions, led by Nelson and supported by Captain Troubridge to larboard of the line and Captain Saumarez to starboard, the fleet began its quest.

Kydd was anxious, but it was not the hazards of storm or enemy that made his palms moist: it was the knowledge that he and his ship were under the eye of the most famous fighting admiral of the age. They were daring to become one of an élite band of ships and men beginning to be known throughout the Royal Navy: Troubridge of *Culloden,* Hallowell of *Swiftsure,* Foley of *Goliath,* Hood of *Zealous.* To see the crusty Houghton return from colloquy with Nelson, eyes alight and pride in his voice, Kydd knew that this was a professional pinnacle in his career and, whatever happened, he must not fail.

• • •

Nelson's first move was to the eastward, rounding the north of Corsica with his fleet in tight formation, laying to in the evening off the sprawling island of Elba. It was vital to gain intelligence on the whereabouts of the French armament. To blunder into it round the next point of land would be disastrous. All that was known was that the French had sailed, and because the reinforcements had come from Gibraltar without sighting them the armada must have passed north about Corsica and then down the Italian coast—to Rome? Naples? Malta?

With not a single frigate to scout ahead there was little choice: the brig *Mutine* was pressed into service. The game little vessel would look ahead into the bays and harbours of the coast of Italy and hope she could survive any encounter with the French.

Meanwhile the fleet would stop any vessel that dared show itself. These were few: a terrified Moorish xebec swore that he had seen the French fleet at Syracuse, and a tunny fisherman solemnly declared that he had sailed through the entire armada not far to their immediate south three days previously. The land of Corsica and north Italy under their lee were French now and hostile so would not provide reliable intelligence.

Nelson could not wait: the trail was going cold. The English fleet weighed anchor and stood to the south, broadsides loaded and in fighting formation—but all they met was *Mutine* on her way back to deliver her report. No sighting, not even a rumour.

The battle fleet followed the coast south. The old port of Civitavecchia was a blue-grey smudge to the eastward as *Mutine* looked cautiously into it. Another day brought a misty grey Rome to the horizon. On they sailed until the limits of French occupation were reached. This was now the Kingdom of the Two Sicilies—independent but neutral by treaty of amity with revolutionary France. Naples was important enough, though, to serve as the seat of the senior British diplomat in the Mediterranean, so surely there they would receive reliable intelligence on this most sinister event of recent times.

Neither Kydd nor any in *Tenacious* was able to catch sight of the famous city. Only the massive cone of Vesuvius was recognisable above the lumpy coastline as the fleet hove to far out in the Bay of Naples, ready to get under way in an instant to meet the enemy. Nelson remained aboard his flagship while the trusty *Mutine* sailed inshore, bearing his flag-captain to the ambassador.

Within two hours Troubridge was hastening back to Nelson, observed by an impatient fleet. This had to be the news they so badly needed. Speculation rose to fever pitch when the flagship at last hoisted the "lieutenant repair aboard" signal that always preceded the issue of orders.

The first lieutenant of *Tenacious* was sporting enough to toss a coin for the task, and it was Renzi who occupied the sternsheets of the barge sailing out to *Vanguard*. There was some delay before the craft returned, but when Renzi came up the side steps he wore an enigmatic smile and excused himself to attend upon the captain.

When he emerged he was surrounded instantly by impatient officers. "Gentlemen!" he protested. "I have but done my duty by the order book—do you suppose I am made privy to all the strategical secrets of Sir Horatio? That he confides his fears and anxieties to me, to be—"

"Nicholas!" Kydd pleaded. "Be s' good as to tell y'r friends what you saw—and heard, o' course. Are we to—"

Renzi paused for a moment, then said firmly, "It's Malta." The island was almost at the geometrical centre of the Mediterranean and astride the main east–west sea routes. With a stone-built fortress of great antiquity and a magnificent harbour, it had been ruled for seven hundred years by warrior monks, the Knights of St John Hospitallers, who still held feudal court over the Maltese.

"How do you know?" Renzi was pressed by several at once.

"I was there when Captain Troubridge was still aboard, pacing about the quarterdeck with Nelson. It seems, gentlemen, that the armament was recently seen passing southward. It is perfectly logical that Malta is the objective."

"Surely a descent on Sicily is to be recommended?" Adams said. "With this, Buonaparte has Naples and the rest of Italy and can split the Mediterranean in two—a far greater prize, I believe."

"Therefore what better than to take Malta as a safe harbour for the seizure of Sicily? Do not neglect the attraction of the gold and treasure of seven hundred years."

"A pox on all this talk!" Bryant grated. "Let's be after 'em afore they sets ashore—wherever they're headed."

"I think we'll find our answer at the Strait of Messina," Renzi continued equably. "Our French tyrant must pass through and then we'll see what kind of course he shapes."

Kydd remembered that the strait divided Italy from Sicily but was hazy about the details. "They'll be close enough t' spy from ashore?"

Renzi raised an eyebrow. "When you recollect that these very same are the lair of the Scylla and Charybdis of the ancients . . ." He paused, but in the absence of cries of understanding he went on: ". . . which are the terrors that lie in wait for the unwary mariner each side of the strait that he must brave if he wishes to pass through.

"On the one side, there is Scylla who dwells in a cave high up. She will dart forth her snaky heads, seize sailors from the very decks of their ship and bear them away shrieking to her den. And on the other is Charybdis, who engulfs the laggardly in a frightful chasm into which the seas rush with a mighty roar that may be heard for leagues. I fear it is this passage we must ourselves soon hazard . . ."

There were no ancient monsters, but the narrow strait held another threat: only a mile wide, it was a perfect location should the French fleet, having got wind of their presence, desire to lie in wait. The English, without scouting frigates and having no room to turn and manoeuvre, would be helpless.

During the night they passed Stromboli, its lurid orange flaring up to deter them. They reached the strait but no French warships loomed. However, it was clear they were expected: the scrubby foreshore was crowded with people. The fleet hove to and boats came out immediately. One with an enormous union flag made straight for the flagship.

Bryant brought the news from *Vanguard* they had been waiting for. "Malta, right enough! An' caught in the act—the consul said the Grand Master gave up the island to this Buonaparte only a week past. Much plundering an' such but now he's to account to us."

"Aye," Kydd answered. "But we'll settle him, depend on't." He remembered the time he had spent in the last days of Venice, another antique civilisation, with centuries of continuous history, brought down by the same ruthless leader. He felt bitter that the world he had grown up in, with all its traditional ways, its colour and individuality, was now being dragged into chaos and desolation by this man.

The flagship picked up her pilot for the passage and, ignoring the hundreds of boats that now surrounded them, the fleet formed line for the transit. From the fervent cries and theatrical gestures of the populace there was no doubt that they saw Nelson's fleet as their only safeguard against the dreaded Buonaparte.

There were currents as fast as a man could run, but they met no other perils as they passed through the strait. The eastern Mediterranean: few aboard had been in this half of the ancient world. To the south were the sands of North Africa and far to the east the fabled Holy Land. On the northern side was Greece, the classical fount of civilisation, and then the Ottomans in Constantinople. Every one was now under threat of war.

Ahead, a bare two days' sail, was the victorious enemy. Would the fleet stay within the fastness of the Grand Harbour, reputedly the greatest stronghold in the Mediterranean, or, with their greater numbers, would they chance an encounter at sea? Would Napoleon Buonaparte himself take command on the flagship? With stakes so high, nothing short of a fight to the finish would serve: Nelson would ensure this. Possibly within a day these waters would witness a battle whose like they had never seen before.

It was crucial that any piece of intelligence was brought to bear. From every ship in the fleet, boarding parties were sent away to stop and question all vessels of size, but with little result: it would be a brave merchantman who ventured close to Malta during these times.

They stood to the southward, ready for whatever might come at Malta. Yet again the signal hoisted in the flagship was "investigate strange sail." And once again it was *Tenacious*'s pennants that accompanied it.

"Your bird," grunted Bryant to Kydd. The sail was now visible from the deck and it was small.

"Aye aye, sir," Kydd answered, without enthusiasm, and went to his cabin to change into a more presentable frock-coat, then buckle on his sword. Rawson could be relied on to muster the boat's crew. They had time: *Tenacious* had left the line and was thrashing out under full sail to intercept. Only when they had stopped the vessel would he take away the cutter, which was now kept towing astern.

This was not his first boarding and he had grown weary of trying to make himself understood to those who had every reason not to understand him.

It was yet another of the myriad small craft plying the inland sea, a brig of uncertain origin that had led them on a fine dance and now lay under backed mainsail, awaiting Kydd and his party.

As so often there were no colours flying. Idly, Rawson speculated on the short passage across. "An Austrian, I'd wager. Surly-lookin' crew—be trading with Sicily, sugar f'r wine or some such. What d' you think, Mr Hercules?"

Bowden sat with his face turned towards the brig and said nothing. There was only need to take one midshipman, whose task was to stay in the boat and keep the seamen from idle talk, but Kydd wanted Bowden and his French with him. Rawson's animosity towards the boy irritated him and no doubt made the lad's life hard in the crude confines of the midshipmen's berth. "Pipe down, Rawson," Kydd snapped irritably. But there was nothing more he could do for Bowden that would not be construed as favouritism; the lad must find his own salvation.

The boat bumped alongside and Kydd stood up as the bowman hooked on the shabby fore chains. He stared directly at the only man on deck wearing a coat instead of the universal blouse and sash of the Mediterranean sailor, probably the master. The brig reeked of dried fish. Eventually the man growled at one of the sullen seamen, who threw a wooden-stepped rope-ladder over the side.

"Thank 'ee," he said politely, and mounted to the deck. "L'tenant Kydd, Royal Navy," he intoned, bowing.

Significant looks were exchanged and there was a low mutter among the other men beginning to gather. "Which is the captain?" Kydd said loudly. "*Cap-tain,*" he repeated slowly. There was no response. "Bowden, ask 'em in French, an' say who we are." Still no one replied. They stared stonily at Kydd.

"Th' captain!" Kydd said sharply.

"Is mi," the man in the coat grunted, keeping his distance. Kydd understood his reluctance: he might now be making a prize of their vessel or, at the very least, pressing men and he was backed by the mighty presence a few hundred yards away of a ship-of-the-line.

"Y'r papers," Kydd said, miming the riffling of paper.

The master eased a well-thumbed wad out of his waistcoat and handed them across without expression.

"Ah—a Ragusan." Although the language of the registry certificate was none that he could decipher, the vessel's origins were plain. Ragusa was a busy port in the Balkans opposite Italy and, as far as Kydd could remember, still ruled by the Bourbons and therefore not an enemy.

He pulled out the crew list and gave it a quick search: it was unlikely that a British deserter would be careless enough to sign up under his own name, but this had happened in Kydd's experience. He recognised the layout of a bill of lading, but it was incomprehensible. The next document was a little less oblique, but as Kydd pored over the certificate of clearance from Chioggia, which he remembered was near Venice, he sensed a sudden tension. Should they be found to be carrying cargo bound for any French possession, by the rules of war it was contraband: they stood to have it and the ship seized as lawful prize.

However, his orders were plain: they were not for prize-taking but for the acquiring of intelligence by any means, after the source had been shown to be friendly and therefore reliable.

With a smile he closed the papers, and fixed the master's eye. "Fair winds, then, Cap'n, and a prosperous voyage to ye." The brig was obviously trading with the enemy—how else could they survive commercially in the eastern Mediterranean? It was their bad luck that the English had chosen to enter there now.

Bowden started to translate but the man waved him to silence. "Got luck, *tenente,*" he said stolidly, and, more strongly, "By God grace, to wictory of the *francesi,* sir."

"Thank you, Cap'n," Kydd said, with a little bow. "Have you b' chance seen 'em at sea on your voyage?" he added casually, making rocking motions with his hands.

"No, *tenente.* Not as after they sail fr'm Malta."

Kydd couldn't believe his ears. "They have left Malta?"

"*Certamente*—all ships, all men, now sail."

This was incredible. It was much too soon for the invasion fleet to sail back to France, but if not, where were they? He had to be sure. If on *his* word Nelson stopped looking around Malta for the fleet and went off in some other direction . . .

"Captain, I have t' know! Very important!" The man nodded vigorously. "What day did they sail?" asked Kydd.

"Ah, *seidici giugno.* You say . . ." He frowned in concentration, then traced sixteen in his palm and looked up apologetically.

Just four days previously! "Captain, what course did they steer when they left?"

"*Che?*"

Kydd ground his teeth in exasperation. "Bowden, tell them."

"Sir, it seems in this part of the Mediterranean they only have dog-Italian or German. I—I don't know those." He flushed.

Kydd turned back to the master. "What—course—they—steer?" He aped a man at the wheel peering at a compass.

"*Scusi,* they not seen by me," he said, turning away.

The fleet had sailed after invading Malta. Now the French

were close, very close—but this was about as much information as he was going to get. "Thank you, sir, you've been very helpful," Kydd said. He hailed the cutter alongside and tumbled in. "Stretch out, y' buggers, pull y' hearts out—the Frogs're close by!"

"You are quite certain, sir?" Admiral Nelson fixed Kydd with a stare so acute it made him falter.

"Er—sir, you'll understand I had t' win his favour, so I overlooked his contraband cargo as prize—"

"Rightly so!" Nelson snapped. "It is never the duty of a naval officer to be gathering prizes when the enemy is abroad."

"—and therefore, sir, he had no reason t' lie to me."

The stare held, then Nelson turned to his flag-lieutenant. "Fleet to heave to, and I shall have—let me see, Troubridge, Saumarez, Ball and Darby to repair aboard directly."

Kydd waited, uncertain. On the weather side of the quarterdeck Nelson paced forward, deep in thought. He saw Kydd and said absently, "Remain aboard, if you please. We may have further questions of you." The slow pacing continued. Kydd kept out of the way.

The first boat arrived. Boatswain's calls pealed out as a commanding figure with a patrician air and wearing full decorations came up the side. The young officer-of-the-watch whispered to Kydd, "That's Saumarez o' the *Orion,* a taut hand but a cold fish betimes."

Next to board was a well-built, straight-eyed captain in comfortable sea rig. "Troubridge, *Culloden,* second senior, o' course. Fine friends with Our Nel from the American war. Don't be flammed by his appearance—Jervis thinks him even better'n Nelson." Nelson greeted him warmly and began to walk companionably with him.

A voice called loudly from the poop-deck and a signal lieutenant appeared at the rail. "Sir, the strange sail we saw earlier—

*Leander* signals they're frigates." *Culloden* and *Orion* hauled their wind and prepared to close with them.

Nelson stopped: frigates were a significant force and the first French warships they had seen. He hesitated for a second, then ordered, "Call in the chasing ships." The signal lieutenant disappeared to comply. "I rather think that with the French fleet close, I shall keep my fleet whole," he added, to the remaining officers.

Another captain arrived, a man with deep-set eyes, who punctiliously raised his hat to Nelson even while the admiral welcomed him.

"Ball, *Alexander.* Much caressed by Our Nel since he passed us the tow-line in that blow off Sardinia." Kydd looked at him. There was little of the bluff sea-dog about the ascetic figure, nothing to suggest that this was a seaman of courage and skill.

The last was a slightly built officer with guarded eyes. "Darby, *Bellerophon.* Keeps t' himself, really."

"Shall we go below?" There was a compelling urgency in the tone.

Kydd followed them in trepidation into the admiral's quarters where the large table in the great cabin was spread with charts. "Do sit, gentlemen," Nelson said. His clerk busied himself with papers. Kydd took a small chair to one side.

"*Tenacious* stopped a Ragusan brig not two hours ago. Lieutenant Kydd—" he nodded at Kydd, who bobbed his head "—performed the boarding and is available for questions. I am satisfied that he has brought reliable word.

"He has found that the French armament is no longer at Malta. It has sailed. And we have no indication of course or intent. None. I do not have to tell you that our next action is of the utmost consequence, which is why I have called you together to give me your views and strategic reasoning."

Saumarez broke the silence. "Sir, are we to understand that

this is in the nature of a council-of-war?" he said carefully. It was an important point: if a later inquiry found Nelson's decision culpable, the formalities of a council would provide for him some measure of legal protection—at the cost of involving themselves.

"No, it is not. Kindly regard this as—as a conference of equals, Saumarez," he said, with a frosty smile. "Now, to business. The French have left Malta. Where are they headed?"

He looked at each captain in turn. "I desire to have you answer this question. Do we stand on for Malta or steer for Sicily? Or do you consider it altogether another destination?"

Kydd recalled that this was Nelson's first command of a fleet of ships in his own right: was he seeking support for a command decision that should be his alone?

"May we have your own conclusions first, sir?" Troubridge asked.

"Very well. They might be on their way back to France after their conquest, but I doubt it. And, besides, they'd find it a hard beat with transports against this nor'-westerly. No, in my opinion they are headed further into the eastern Mediterranean." He stopped.

"The Turks and Constantinople," murmured Troubridge.

"I think not."

"The Holy Land? There's plunder a-plenty there and a royal route to India across Mesopotamia." It was the youthful-looking Berry, present as captain of the flagship.

"Possibly." As there were no further offerings, Nelson declared incisively, "There is one objective that I think outweighs all others. Egypt."

There were mutterings, but Nelson cut through forcefully: "Yes, Egypt. Should they take the biggest Mediterranean port, Alexandria, they have then but twenty leagues overland and they are at the Red Sea, and from there *two weeks* to our great possessions in India."

Saumarez stirred restlessly. "Sir, saving your presence, I find this a baseless conjecture. We have not one piece of intelligence to support such a conclusion."

"Nevertheless, this is my present position," Nelson said. "I should be obliged for your arguments to the contrary. In the absence of news we deal in speculation and presumption, sir. We must reason ourselves to a conclusion. This is mine."

Troubridge leaned back with a broad smile. "'Pon my word, Sir Horatio, this will set them a-flutter in Whitehall. Conceive of it—the entire fleet dispatched to the most distant corner of the Mediterranean, to Egypt no less! The Pyramids, the desert—"

"Whitehall is two months away. The decision will be made today." The reflected sun-dappled sea played prettily on the deckhead, but it also threw into pitiless detail the admiral's deep lines of worry, the prematurely white hair, the glittering eye.

"Then I concur," Troubridge said. "It has to be Alexandria."

"Should Alexandria be captured, our interests in India will be at appalling risk. This cannot be allowed." Unexpectedly, it was Saumarez.

"Yes. Captain Ball?"

"It seems the most likely course, sir."

"Darby?"

"Putting to sea in a wind foul for France does appear an unlikely move unless their intentions lie eastward."

"Anything further? No? Then it shall be Alexandria. Thank you, gentlemen."

A thousand sea miles to the east—to the fabled Orient: the Egypt of Cleopatra, the Sphinx, the eternal Nile. And a French invasion fleet waiting for them there. The English fleet prepared accordingly.

The most vital task was to crowd on as much sail as possible to try to overhaul the French and force a meeting at sea before the landings. The winds were fair for the Levant and, with stuns'ls abroad, the fleet sped across the glittering deep blue seas for day after day. There was little sail-handling with the winds astern, and for watch after watch there was no need to brace and trim: the steady breeze drove them onward in an arrow-straight course for the south-east corner of the Mediterranean.

Gun practice filled the day: gun crews were interchanged, side-tackle men put on the rammer, the handspike, and gun captains were stood down while the seconds took charge. It was fearful work in the summer heat, tons of dead iron to haul in and out, twenty-four pounds in each shot to manhandle. Gun-carriages squealed and rumbled even in the light of evening.

At daybreak, as soon as there was the slightest lightening of the sky, doubled lookouts at the masthead searched the horizons until they could be sure there was no strange sail. Then, after quarters, the men would go to breakfast among the guns that shared their living space. And always the thought, the secret dread, that the enemy were just ahead, a vast armada covering the sea from horizon to horizon that would result in a cataclysmic battle to be talked about for the rest of time.

It took the English fleet less than a week to cover the distance, keeping well away from land and stopping all ships they could find for the barest clue as to the French positions. In the morning light, a hazy coastline formed ahead and the fleet went to quarters. Ships fell into two columns and prepared for battle, keyed up to the highest pitch of readiness.

The low coast firmed and drew nearer. Kydd raised his telescope to a dense scatter of white against the nondescript sandy shore, the straggling ancient town of Alexandria with its Pharos

Tower. He passed quickly over the tall minarets and the lofty sea-mark of Pompey's Pillar amid the pale stone sprawl of a medieval fort. The forest of black masts that they sought was missing.

Kydd knew from such charts as they had that the port had two harbours, each side of a mushroom-shaped peninsula of land. The fleet passed slowly by, telescopes glinting on every quarter-deck, but at the end it was all too clear that there was no French fleet at anchor anywhere in Alexandria. The disappointment was cruel.

*Mutine* hove to closer inshore. A boat pulled energetically from her to *Vanguard*. Was she returning with longed-for news? Conversations stilled about the deck as the ships lay to. Within the hour, boats were passing up and down the fleet with their message—no French fleet, no news whatsoever of it.

Kydd kept his glass trained on the flagship. He could make out people on her upper deck, some moving, some still, and once he recognised a small, lonely figure standing apart. It was not difficult to imagine the torment that must be racking their commander. It had been his final decision to come to Egypt to seek the French, but they were not here—it might be that they had been comprehensively fooled and that the enemy was on his way in the other direction to Gibraltar and the open Atlantic, to fall upon England while they were in this furthest corner of the Mediterranean.

In hours the fleet was under weigh and *Tenacious* was stretching to the north-westward, ship's company stood down from quarters. The sea watch was set and word was passed that Houghton, who had been called to the admiral before they set sail, wished all officers to present themselves in his cabin.

"I am desired by Sir Horatio to acquaint you all with the position we find ourselves in." It was unusual—unprecedented, even—that Houghton had sat them informally round a smaller table with an evening glass of sherry. This was not going to be the official passing on of orders.

"I will not attempt to conceal the dismay the absence of the enemy has caused the admiral," Kydd caught Renzi's eye but there was nothing in it except sombre reflection, "and the dilemma this causes. Our vice-consul tells us that there have been no French forces upon this coast, save some Venetian frigates and small fry. He also swears that the Ottomans have found our own presence as unwelcome as the French, and intend to resist any move of aggression. In this we can see that there are definitely no major enemy forces in the vicinity."

The officers waited patiently as Houghton continued, "Trading ships in harbour have been questioned and are adamant that there are no French at sea. It is as if they have vanished."

"Then, sir, we are obliged to conclude that Admiral Nelson is wrong in the essentials," said Bampton, heavily. "And thus we are beating to the nor'ard on speculation!"

Houghton's eyes narrowed. "Take care, Mr Bampton. This is the commander of the fleet you are questioning."

Bampton's lips thinned and he continued obstinately, "Nevertheless, sir, it seems we are at sea on a venture once again with not a scrap of intelligence to justify it. I am at a loss to account for his motions."

Houghton put down his glass sharply. "It is not your duty to account for the actions of your commander. Recollect your situation, sir!"

Kydd felt for any man who, faced with a decision, put action above faint-hearted inaction, and said strongly, "T' put it plain, he has no intelligence t' work with—so what do you expect, sir? Lies in port waitin' for word t' be passed, or figures something an active officer can do?"

"And that is . . . ?" said Bampton acidly.

Houghton came in quickly: "Sir Horatio feels that the objective still remains in the eastern Mediterranean, possibly the Turks—Constantinople, perhaps. Consider: if this great armada prevails over the Ottomans then not only Asia Minor but necessarily the Holy Land and Egypt fall to the French."

Kydd's mind reeled with the implications. "And then he'll have cut the Mediterranean in two."

"Just so. We shape course to the north, gentlemen, to Asia Minor and the Greek islands, again seizing every opportunity to gather intelligence where we may. The enemy cannot hide a fleet of such size for ever."

As they left the cabin, Renzi murmured to Kydd, "Even so, Nelson will be hard put to justify his conduct before their lordships of the Admiralty—twice he has missed them, and for a junior admiral on his first command . . ."

In the steady north-westerly it was a hard beat northward, close-hauled on the larboard tack with bowlines at each weather leech. As they struck deeper into the north it appeared not a soul had seen anything of the French and the further on they sailed the less likely a mighty descent on Constantinople seemed.

It was passing belief that the passage of such a great fleet had gone unnoticed, and when they attained the entry-point of the Aegean and therefore Constantinople without finding a soul who had heard of a French fleet, it was time to take stock.

"Ah, Mr Adams—returned from the Flag with orders, I see." Even Bampton was curious as he watched the young officer spring over the bulwarks on his return from the flagship. Houghton opened the order book and studied the last entry, then snapped it shut. He would not be drawn and, with a frown, retired to his cabin, leaving the deck to his officers.

"Well?" demanded Bryant. Others sidled up: the quarter-master hovered and the master found it necessary to check the condition of the larboard waterway.

Adams adjusted his cuffs. "I must declare," he said lightly, "Our Nel is the coolest cove you'll ever meet—French armada loose, who knows where, and he won't hear any as say it won't end in a final meeting. So, it's to be a continuation of the same, battle-ready night and day until we come up with 'em."

"Dammit, Adams, does he say *where* we're lookin'?" Bryant hissed.

"Well, I was not actually consulted by Sir Horatio but, er, I did overhear him speaking with Berry."

Kydd smiled.

"And it seems that if we've not sighted 'em by twenty-seven east, then we beat south about Candia, back to the western Med."

"Quitting the chase!" said Bampton, with relish.

"Fallin' back on Gibraltar, more like," Bryant snapped. "No choice."

Kydd growled, "All th' same, this Buonaparte has the devil's luck—how else c'n he just vanish? No one sees him an' all his ships?"

"Remembering the size of the Mediterranean, above a million square miles . . ." Renzi put in.

"But not forgetting that we haven't touched land since Sardinia. Wood 'n' water, stores—we can't go on like this for ever," Bampton observed.

"If I don't misread, Nelson is not y'r man to give away th' game. He'll hunt 'em down wherever they're hidin' and then we'll have our fight. He's had bad fortune, is all," Kydd declared.

Bampton smiled. "My guineas are on that before August we'll have a new commander—mark my words."

• • •

The signal for the fleet to come about on the starboard tack was hoisted within the hour and obediently the ships shaped course westward, close-hauled and taking the seas on their bows.

Renzi did not go below. There was a pleasing solitude to be had when the men went to breakfast: thoughts could flow unchecked to their natural conclusion, and the deck, with a minimum of watchmen about, was his for the walking.

His mind strayed to the letter he had received in Gibraltar: it was from his father who, in his usual bombastic manner, had insisted that he come home to discuss his future. There was little chance of that in the near term but there was no point in putting it off for ever. The next time he was in England he would return to face him.

Peake, the chaplain, came up from below, interrupting his thoughts. "Nicholas, I was told you always took the air at this time," he said, in his precise manner. "I do hope you will not object to my company."

The deck lifted in response to a comber under the bows and he lurched over to grip a convenient downhaul. A double crossing of the North Atlantic had not improved his sea-legs.

"You are most welcome, Padre," Renzi answered warmly. He had respect for the man, who was the most nearly learned of all aboard, one with whom he could dispute Rousseau, natural law, ethics, or any other subject valued by an Enlightened mind. The chaplain had volunteered for the sea service as his contribution to the struggle against France but, with a life perspective best termed literal, he was not preserved from the torments of midshipmen and irreverents by a saving sense of humour.

"As Milton has it, 'In solitude, what happiness? Who can enjoy alone, or, all enjoying, what contentment find?'" admonished Peake.

"Just so, Mr Peake. Yet please believe I have a desire at times to withdraw from the company of men—but merely for the contemplation of the sublime that is at the very essence of the sea." He had not the heart to discourage a man so manifestly reaching out.

Renzi saw Peake look about doubtfully at the straining sails and hurrying waves. The fleet's progress west was necessarily against the same streaming north-westerly that had brought them eastward so rapidly. Now at each watch there would be anxious glances to the flagship for the signal "prepare to tack," the warning that, yet again, there would be all hands at the sheets and braces for the hard work at putting about. Peake would see little of the sublime in such sea-enforced labour, Renzi mused, then enquired, "You are not enjoying your watery sojourn? Such lands as you've seen would cost a pretty penny to experience were you to ship as passenger."

"I do not value such adventures. Canada, I find, has an . . . excess of colour, and what I saw of Gibraltar does not spark in me any great desire for sightseeing."

"Yet you have chosen the sea life?"

"I feel a certain calling. At the same time, I will confess to you, sir, in a sense it weighs heavily."

"Oh?"

Peake turned to face him. "Nicholas—I think we might be accounted friends? Fellow believers? That is," he hastened to add, "in the essential rationality of the objective man when detached from corporeal encumbrances?"

"I warm to Leibniz and his position before that of your Spinoza and his Deductions, Mr Peake."

"Quite so—we have discussed this before, as I recollect. No, sir, what I face might be considered a . . . dilemma of conscience."

"Ah! Bayle and the Sceptic position," Renzi said, with keen anticipation.

Peake winced. "Not as who should say, sir. I will be frank—in the lively trust in your discretion and the earnest hope that you will assist me in coming to a comfortable resolution."

"My discretion is assured, sir, but I cannot be sanguine about my suitability to aid you in a matter of churchly ethics."

"Never so, Renzi. Allow me to set forth the essentials. Since childhood I have been charmed by the *rightness* of nature: such nicety in the disposition of leaves on a stem, musculature in a cat, the flight of a swallow. In fine, Renzi, it is life's vitality itself that, for me, is of all the world the greater worth."

He looked closely at Renzi, then out to the immensity of the sea. "Here is the dilemma, my friend. I had an adequate living as curate in a peaceful village in Shropshire, and you may believe that for the quiet and reflective mind there are few occupations that can better that of a country parson.

"When the revolution began in France I was puzzled. Then an *émigré* French family came to the village and I learned of the true situation while attending upon the matriarch, who had lost her mind at the experience." His voice strengthened. "This is the reason for the offer of my services to His Majesty—that in some way I was playing a part in the defending of my country against such unspeakable horrors."

"A noble part, Mr Peake," Renzi murmured.

"But in my time on *Tenacious* I have learned much indeed. The sailors are rough fellows but in their way are as tender as babes to each other. And the midshipmen, scamps and rascals indeed, but I feel that they act as they do out of a need to retreat from martial horrors to the innocence of their so recently departed childhood."

Renzi's eyebrows went up, but he said nothing. Peake drew a

deep breath and continued, "What I am saying is that I have been privileged to see a species of humanity, *nauta innocentia,* that perfectly displays the qualities of life-cherishing animation that I so value. So you may recognise the anguish I feel when the captain calls for practice with his cannon—*those mortal engines, whose rude throats could counterfeit the dread clamours of Jove!*

"Renzi, my friend, please understand, it causes me the utmost pain when my unruly imagination pictures for me their purpose—the tearing apart of the sacred flesh of life and its utter and final extinction. Be they enemy of my country, I cannot prevent the betraying thought that even so they hold within them the same vital flame.

"How can I bring myself to accede to my captain's constant pressing to hurl unrelenting maledictions on the French in sermon and prayer when I find myself in such brotherly commune with their life-force? How can I hate an enemy when I understand only too well what it is to contain life within you? Whatever should I do? Nicholas—I'm torn. Help me do my duty."

The beat west was tiring and dispiriting, long miles of vigilant ships but empty sea. A distance further than a complete Atlantic crossing, weeks turning to months—and still not even the wisp of a rumour of a vast French fleet.

South of Crete, with the ancient land of Greece left to starboard, they were traversing the width of the Ionian Sea and approaching where they had left with such hopes a long month before. There was now a pressing need for provisions and water. In these lonely and hostile seas the only possibility was the Kingdom of the Two Sicilies and of these the closer was Syracuse, on the eastern shores of Sicily.

The hard-run fleet, each ship with the blue ensign of Rear Admiral Nelson aloft, sighted the rugged pastel grey coast of Sicily at last and prepared to enter the ancient port. The sleepy town lay under the sun's glare to starboard, mysterious ruins above scrubby cliffs to larboard. It was a difficult approach with troubled waters betraying rocky shoals extending menacingly into the bare half-mile of the intricate entrance.

Once inside, the spacious reaches of an enfolding harbour welcomed the ships. One by one they dropped anchor. People gathered along the seafront, hastily filled bumboats contended to be first out to the fleet, but with decorum proper to the occasion, England's union flag arose on each man-o'-war's jackstaff forward.

But before they could proceed, the local officials had to be placated. It was difficult for the city governor: any favouritism towards the British might be construed as a violation of neutrality by the suspicious French, and at first he was obstructive and implacable. It required an exercise of ingenuity and tact to arrive at a form of words that allowed a show of resistance, after which his attentions could not be faulted.

Every vessel hoisted out her boats for the hard task of watering. The massive casks had to be manhandled from a spring or rivulet ashore and floated out to the ship where they would be finally hoisted out and struck down into the hold. The enthusiastic townsfolk endeared themselves to the thirsty mariners and Renzi's classical soul when they pointed out the continued existence of the famed Fountains of Arethusa, an aqueduct from ancient times bringing water from the interior to the town and perfectly capable of supplying the wants of a whole fleet.

Kydd was touched that Admiral Nelson with all his crushing worries had noticed that the cask wine taken aboard for the men's grog issue was being affected by the heat. His orders were that for every pipe of wine two gallons of brandy were to fortify it. He made sure as well that depleted victuals were promptly restored from local sources—lemons by the cartload, endless wicker baskets of greens, and beef on the hoof. In the sunshine spirits rose.

Idly Kydd watched Poulden in the shade of the massive

mainmast patiently work a long-splice for Bowden. The lad had lost his pale complexion to a ruddier colouring and his gawky sea gait had steadied to a careful stepping. His body was now more lean than willowy, his expression poised and composed.

Voices rose on the quarterdeck, attracting Kydd's attention. *Mutine* had just entered harbour after another reconnaissance. She went aback close to the flagship and Hardy, her commander, stepped into her boat. "She'll have something t'say, I believe," Kydd said, vaguely aware of a shadowy world of plots and spies, and the surreptitious allegiances of greed and trade that were the main source of information in this part of the world.

"Probably that the French by now are past Gibraltar," said Bampton, sourly. He had come on deck at the first excitement and was still buttoning his waistcoat.

The master came up behind them. "*Mutine* showed no signal on enterin'," he said pensively. "Does this mean she has no news t' offer?"

It would be beyond belief if this crossroads at the very centre of the Mediterranean, touched at by merchant vessels plying both sides of the sea, did not have some word of the French.

Houghton emerged on deck, sniffing the wind and trying to look indifferent to the tension. The quarterdeck fell quiet as a flagship pinnace approached them. Her youthful flag-lieutenant punctiliously doffed his hat to the quarterdeck and then the captain. There were murmured words as Houghton took delivery of a packet of orders and retired to his cabin. The flag-lieutenant waited.

"Have ye news, sir?" Kydd asked him boldly.

Others edged over to hear the reply. "News? You mean the French forces?"

"Yes."

"Oh—then no news, my friend."

"None?"

"No sighting, if that's what you mean, sir."

"Goddammit, we still don't know where the buggers are!" exploded Bryant, pushing past Kydd.

"That is not what I said, sir," the lieutenant said. Bryant went red, but before he could continue the officer confided happily, "You should have seen His Nibs when Hardy brought in his report. In as rare a taking as ever I've known, capering around his cabin like a schoolboy."

"Y'r meaning, sir?" barked Kydd.

The lieutenant was now surrounded by eager officers. "My meaning? I thought it was perfectly clear, sir, no sighting of the French fleet anywhere . . . in the western Med. And *that,* to those with the perspicacity to remark it, means they must necessarily be in the east—Sir Horatio was correct in his first assumption."

"Then—"

"Then, sir, it is quite apparent, if we discount the seas north, around to the east where we have cruised so recently, it leaves only the Levant and the south. Sir, it can only be Egypt."

"Why, then, did we not sight—"

"We were too hasty in our descent on Alexandria. We hauled past them in the night, Sir Horatio believes, and thus found an empty port. Should we clap on sail this instant we should find them there at anchor within, their army probably ashore. Then, sir, we shall have the *rencontre* we so ardently desire."

Houghton stepped out briskly from his cabin. "You have heard, then, gentlemen," he said, with satisfaction. "I can tell you that we sail for Alexandria on completion of stores and, you may depend upon it, we shall have an encounter within the week."

One by one the ships-of-the-line slipped past the lighthouse and small fort at the tip of the long neck of land upon which old Syracuse shimmered in the bright sun, their next landfall the even more ancient land of Egypt. The breeze held and strengthened and the fleet stretched out over the sparkling sea under all sail possible.

Bampton was not persuaded, however. "Still our motions are driven by conjecture—where is your evidence? They are not in the west—but who has considered that, having taken Malta, they are satisfied and have retired back to Toulon? Evidence!"

As if in answer to his words, the fleet stood on for Greece. With the Peloponnese in plain sight Nelson sent in Troubridge of *Culloden* to speak with the Turkish authorities. The big 74 sailed into the wide bay towards Koroni castle. When he returned, he finally brought news that the French had been positively sighted—steering south-eastward. They had been seen some weeks before but it was a mystery as to why they had gone so far to the north instead of making a straight run of it to Alexandria. It was the master who grasped the significance: "Cabotage, sir," he told Houghton. "They're a lubberly crew hereabouts an' navigate by following the coast along, point b' point, and never a notion of workin' a deep-sea reckoning. We sailed direct, got there before 'em."

*Culloden* was followed by a humble two-master, astern. This was a French wine-brig that the same obliging governor who had given them their vital news had also graciously allowed to be carried off as prize from under the guns of the castle. Later the wine would be transhipped to the fleet as rations.

"Please take a chair, Mr Kydd." Houghton's manner as he greeted Kydd in his cabin was odd—tense, perhaps, Kydd thought. But that could be because he had only recently returned from conclave with Nelson. During their long chase the admiral had made it his practice to see his captains in twos and threes in the great cabin of *Vanguard*. There, together, they would share his fighting vision and intentions, playing out the possible settings for combat.

"I'll not mince words. We are about to be joined in battle with an enemy of great force. It will be a hard-fought contest, which is vital to our country. But I have the utmost confidence in Admiral Nelson and his battle plans, which we have discussed thoroughly. It only requires we follow where he leads and I've no doubt whatsoever of the outcome."

He paused and looked at Kydd intently. "As I recollect, this will be your first experience of the quarterdeck in an action of significance, in the line-of-battle."

"Sir." Camperdown, his only fleet action, did not count—he had been below with the guns and at no time had really understood what was happening outside his ship. And, besides, he reminded himself, it was before he had been raised to be an officer.

"It is the custom of the Service for the duty of signal lieutenant to be devolved on the junior. You have discharged this duty to my satisfaction so far, sir, but you will forgive my concern when you reflect that at this time of supreme crisis, when it is crucial the intentions of the commander be known—and only by signal—I am obliged to place the safety and honour of my ship in one who has had no officer-like experience of a fleet action and who is the most junior aboard."

Kydd flushed. "Am I then t' be superseded, sir?"

"What is the signal 'division designated, to harass the enemy rear'?"

"Why, blue burgee signific an' number twenty-nine, both at mizzen peak, sir," Kydd said instantly.

"The night signal to haul to the wind, and sail with starb'd tacks on board?"

"One light at th' ensign staff, one in the mizzen shrouds, an' fire one gun."

"And to larb'd?"

"Two lights in the fore-shrouds—that is t' say, one above the other—and two guns."

Houghton nodded, and Kydd saw that behind the hard expression his captain needed reassurance before a great battle.

Houghton got up and stared out from the stern windows. "That is well, Mr Kydd. I can see that you have applied yourself to your profession." He paused, then continued softly, "Sir Horatio is a fine leader—a great man, I believe. There we may see a ruthless determination to achieve victory that spares neither himself nor his officers: I've seen it in no other man. I would not have *Tenacious* fail him, Mr Kydd."

"Aye, sir."

Houghton swung round. "Remember always that the best plans and dispositions are as nothing if they cannot be communicated. We have no repeating frigates, therefore a great deal depends on your vigilance and attention to duty." He hesitated. "I would wish you well, Mr Kydd."

At midnight, Kydd handed over the watch to Renzi and went below to the darkened wardroom to turn in. From the chart, he had seen that they would make landfall on Alexandria the following morning, and as he slipped into his gently swaying cot unsettling thoughts came to trouble him.

There could be no mistaking the gravity of the situation. The enemy would fight to the limits to repulse any attempt to overthrow their position as lords of the Mediterranean—at stake was their chance at a break-out into the outer world and an unstoppable path to complete domination. Two great fleets would meet in mortal combat tomorrow to determine who would be future masters of the sea and, therefore, the course of history.

He tossed restlessly, eyes open in the hot darkness. It might well be his last night on earth. Into his mind came the horrors of mortal wounding, the dark hell of the cockpit and the surgeon's saw—or would it be quick? A heavy shot tearing him in two? He shied from the possibility of personal extinction and tried to focus on half-remembered religious shibboleths, but they had small enough meaning now. Should he perhaps ask Mr Peake to spend some time with him tomorrow, to seek strength in the sturdy faith of his fathers?

He rolled over restlessly and forced his thoughts to the commander, the illustrious Nelson, he of Calvi, Tenerife, the "patent bridge" at St Vincent, the savage boat fighting at Cadíz. Now there was one who would not suffer night terrors to trouble him. His written orders were full of words like "victory," "destruction," "duty," "honour." There was even a clause directing that a single lieutenant and midshipman should take possession of defeated enemy ships, however big, the better to allow their ship to move on and engage another.

Kydd felt better: there was no doubt that Nelson's fleet would conduct itself in the best traditions of the Royal Navy. And, therefore, so would he. His anxiety ebbed. Professionally he felt confidence: seamanship and courage were what were required now. And besides, a small voice offered, it might well be that the French were not in Alexandria, having vanished again . . .

The morning dawned hazy as the sun rose on sparkling deep blue seas. The north-westerly was picking up, the fleet perfectly on course: they would raise Alexandria later in the morning. Nelson had signalled to *Alexander* and *Swiftsure* to sail on ahead to report and all eyes were on the pale horizon, impatient for news.

Land was sighted: again the unmistakable flat, dun-coloured dunes and lofty palms of Egypt. And far ahead the sprawl of a city—Alexandria. *Alexander* was standing off the port; everyone aboard *Tenacious* turned to her signal lieutenant. What was the news?

As they drew nearer, the Pharos Tower resolved distantly out of the morning haze, and there were tantalising glimpses of the masts and rigging of what could only be a vast amount of shipping. Still there was no signal. Kydd waited for the simple two-flag hoist, number eleven, "enemy in sight," followed by a compass bearing. The details that came after would be the most interesting: the number of ships-of-the-line and frigates; lesser vessels would not concern the admiral.

He kept his glass trained. All along the deck not a word was spoken. His arms began to ache—but then it came. Feverishly Kydd deciphered the signal, bellowing down to the tight group waiting on the quarterdeck: "From *Alexander,* sir, 'two ships-o'-the-line an' six frigates, French colours.'"

This could be at best only a trivial remnant of the great armada for which they were so desperately searching. A roar of dismay echoed about the ship, along with shouts of anger as word spread below.

Kydd slumped. It was too much. They had been fooled again. The French had disappeared with the devilish fortune they seemed to command and there would be no mighty battle that day. He caught sight of Houghton's expression of devastation—for him there was now no prospect of promotion or prize-money. Beside him Bryant stood disconsolate; the seamen at the upper-deck twelve-pounders were outraged and voluble.

The fleet began to string out as ships no longer under the urgency of the line-of-battle quested forlornly for the missing enemy. A hard-run chase of many weeks, spirits high, keyed up with tension and now this . . .

"Sir!" Rawson pointed to one of the two 74s that had reached furthest to the east. There was colour at her signal halliards. Kydd brought up his glass. It was number eleven. "Enemy in sight!" he bellowed.

A storm of cheering broke out. Trembling with excitement Kydd tried to steady the telescope. "Sixteen sail-o'-the-line—at anchor—bearing east b'south—four frigates." Twenty miles from Alexandria, snugly at anchor within Aboukir Bay near the mouth of the Nile, they had found their quarry—at last.

# Chapter 5

"Distant four leagues. Mr Hambly, what do you consider our speed over the ground now?" Houghton still had his glass up, looking intently at the long menace of dark lines of rigging over the sandy point far ahead.

The master pursed his lips and glanced over the side. "Five, five an' a half, my guess, sir."

Houghton lowered his telescope, and swung round to look astern at the straggle of ships, some two or three miles off. "I see," he said thoughtfully, resuming his watch ahead.

"Sir?" Kydd ventured.

"Well, I fear you may not rely on action today, Mr Kydd."

"Why so, sir?"

"There will not be time enough. Should we wait until all our ships have come up, then form our line-of-battle, at five knots it will be hours before we can close on the enemy. And sunset comes at seven or so—no, we'll not be fighting today. Tomorrow when they come out, this will be when we force a conclusion."

The bay opened up with the tiny Aboukir Island at the western side. There was breathless quiet. Inside, in an endless line of ships parallel to the shore, was the French fleet. Bryant growled, "Damme, but they're well placed." With the land to their backs the French had a wall of guns more than a mile and a half long waiting for any assailant willing to risk passing the island, which, they could see, was occupied and armed.

Kydd's attention was all on the flagship: complex dispositions would need to be communicated concerning arrangements for the night. The enemy must not be allowed to escape but the British ships could not anchor too close inshore. Nelson might risk standing off and on, sailing out to sea and back again, possibly with half of his fleet . . .

Then bunting appeared on the poop—and a single signal soared. Kydd hesitated as the image danced in his eyepiece. "Prepare for battle!" he roared.

Houghton gaped. "Good God! He means to bring 'em to action now!" With a grim smile he turned to Bryant. "We have three hours—I believe we'll clear for action now."

A ship-of-the-line could clear for action in fifteen minutes if necessary, but this day would be the hardest fought of their lives—things were better done in the cool of forethought than the heat of battle. Victory could depend on the smallest precaution having been properly attended to.

Kydd's action position was on the poop-deck at the signals; there was little to do in readiness beyond the mustering of the bunting in the flag locker and ensuring that the log was at hand, signal halliards cleared and free, the handful of seamen and Rawson in no doubt about their duties. Here, preparation was of the mind. Kydd knew by heart most of the hoists he could foresee and his signal book had been brought up to date with the very latest that had been entered in the fleet commander's order book. He reviewed the provisions for night signals: complicated specified arrangements of lights in varying configurations and "false fires"—wooden tubes of combustibles that burned with a blue light and had several meanings, depending on how and when they were deployed. And, most important, the recognition signal for British ships only now circulated to the fleet. It would be four lights in line, hoisted high to be as visible as possible above powder-smoke. The lighting rig had been checked twice by the boatswain, who also had a spare charged at hand.

Kydd tucked his signal telescope under his arm and paced slowly, conscious of a thudding heart and tight stomach but resolutely refusing to steal a look into the bay.

"Mr Kydd!" the captain called from the quarterdeck.

"Sir?"

Houghton looked energised, but wore a hard expression. "I've no doubt your men at quarters are mustered ready."

"Aye, sir."

"Then as you are at leisure, you will probably wish to take a turn about the decks," he snapped.

Kydd understood. As other officers were occupied with their quarters at the guns and elsewhere, he was being asked to keep a roving eye on the clearing for action, perhaps steady the men as they anticipated the slaughter to come.

This was no sudden, frantic sighting of the enemy: it was a cold, considered approach. *Tenacious* would face her ordeal in perfect battle order.

At this moment *Vanguard* would be similarly engaged so there would be no communication in the immediate future, and Rawson, with his handful of seamen, could be trusted to stand by at the signals. "Take the glass," Kydd told him, handing over his telescope, "and any signal from the flagship I want t' know about instantly, d'ye hear?"

The entire ship's company was at work, an ants' nest of activity. Men taking up shot for the garlands alongside each gun jostled past Kydd; streams of sailors brought up hammocks and soaked them to form barricades in the fighting tops for the marine musketeers. A party was at work on the *sauve tête,* the netting spread twelve feet high above the deck to protect against rigging shot to pieces falling from aloft.

The boatswain and his mates were methodically laying out essential damage-control gear—rigging stoppers and lengths of line that could be secured above and below a severed rope to restore its function. Jigger tackles were becketed up under the hatchway coaming, canvas and twine ready to repair important sails at hand, as were grappling irons to hold an enemy alongside while they boarded. Kydd smiled wryly: *Tenacious* would probably be the smallest man-o'-war in the line—any boarding would likely be in the other direction.

He glanced aloft at the massive lower yards, tons in weight. Chain slings were rigged to support them should the tye blocks at the mast be shot through, and the braces to heave round the yards were augmented by preventers and pendants to handle the heavy spar if cannon fire knocked it askew. From forward he heard the reassuring sound of grinding steel as the gunner's party put a final edge on the tomahawks, cutlasses, pikes and other edged weapons.

Down the main hatchway it was a different kind of bustle. Cabin bulkheads were knocked away and officers' personal effects were struck below in the hold. He saw his own cabin dismantled, the desk where each day he had faithfully written his journal taken bodily by two seamen to the hatch, preceded by his cot and chest. Renzi's cabin was treated in the same way, and when the long wardroom table had been disassembled and carried away there was nothing to spoil a continuous sweep of the gundeck right to the stern, the torpid eighteen-pounder gun with which he had familiarly shared his cabin now awakened and readied for fighting.

On the gundeck more preparations were in train. The gunner had unlocked the grand magazine and stringent fire precautions were in force: fearnought firescreens and leather fire-buckets were around each hatchway and in the magazines lanthorns were put in sealed sconces. Wearing felt slippers, those inside this area would make up cartridges and pass them out to the chain of powder monkeys, who in turn carried them up to the guns. Kydd shivered at the fearful thought of being confined here in a blazing battle, with no knowledge of the outside world, the tons of powder in plain sight their only company.

He moved forward and saw Renzi, who gave a grave nod before turning back to a quarter gunner with orders. Images of Camperdown flashed before him. This place was not named "the slaughterhouse" for nothing: within hours it would be a hell of smoke and noise, smashed timbers and screaming. And after sunset the dim gold of battle lanthorns would be the only light they had to fight the guns.

The preparations continued. Spare gun-breeching ropes and tackles were laid around the hatchways and arms chests for boarders were thrown open on the centreline. Gun captains returned from the store with a powder horn, gunlock flints, pouches of firing tubes, all the necessary equipment to bring the great guns to life. Finally, the decks were strewn with sand and galley ash, then wetted. This would not only give a better grip for the men at the gun tackles but help them retain their footing in blood.

Kydd's last stop was the orlop, where the surgeon made ready and the carpenter gathered his crew. As part of battle preparations, the men held in irons there were released, given full amnesty for their crimes in the face of events of far greater moment. He was about to go down the ladder when a breathless Rawson dashed up. "Signal, sir. 'Prepare t' anchor by the stern.'" His eyes were wide.

"Thank ye, I'll be up directly."

By the stern? Had Rawson misread the signal? He hurried back to the poop, pushing past the busy swarms and snatched up the signal log. There it was, and repeated by *Orion* and others.

"Mr Kydd," Houghton called from the quarterdeck.

"Sir?" Kydd hurried down the poop ladder.

"Do you not understand Sir Horatio's motions?"

"Er, t' anchor by the stern? Not altogether, I have t' say, sir."

"Then, sir, mark the enemy's position. They are anchored in line along the shore away from us *and directly down the wind,* I'll have you note. Without doubt the admiral wishes to advance on them from there, then lay his ships alongside an enemy and stay—in short, to anchor. But should we anchor in the ordinary way, by the bow, then as is the way of things we will rotate round to face the wind and—"

"O' course! We'd be cruelly raked until our guns bear again."

"Undoubtedly. And additionally—"

"With springs on th' cables we c'n direct our fire as we please."

"Just so, Mr Kydd."

With one signal—two flags—Nelson had levelled the odds.

"Then you will oblige me, sir, in taking a cable through a stern chase gunport."

"Aye aye, sir. Making fast t' the mizzen?"

"Yes."

Kydd saluted and left the deck, happy to have something of significance to do in this time of waiting. "Mr Pearce!" he called to the boatswain. "We have a task . . ."

It was no trivial matter, rousing out the hundred-fathom length of twelve-inch stream cable from below, then ranging it along the gundeck from where it was seized round the fat bulk of the mizzen mast, through the gunroom and out of one of the pair of chase ports. With the wake of the moving ship foaming noisily just feet below, the thick rope had to be heaved out of the stern and passed back along the ship's side beneath the line of open gunports and to an anchor on the bows. The cable was kept clear of the sea by a spun-yarn at every third port ready for instant cutting loose, and at the bows it was bent on to the anchor.

Bryant approached the captain. "Ship cleared for action, sir." There was a taut ferocity about the first lieutenant, Kydd saw, almost a blood-longing for the fight. He wondered if he, too, should adopt a more aggressive bearing.

"Very well, Mr Bryant. There will be time for supper for the men before we go to quarters, I believe—and everyone shall have a double tot, if you please."

Kydd called Rawson over: "Go below an' get yourself something t' eat, younker—*after* you've seen y' men get their grog." It would not be long before they went to quarters. The enemy was now in plain view, on the right side of a low, sandy bay fringed by date palms, and inshore of a guardian island no more than thirty feet high, their line stretching away into the distance. On the left were some higher sand hills, which Kydd knew from their rudimentary chart was the Rosetta mouth of the Nile with its distinctive tower. In the evening sun he picked up knots of people coming down to the water's edge: there would be a big audience for the evening's entertainment. He wondered if the famed General Buonaparte was watching, perhaps from the small medieval castle at the mouth of the bay.

He went below: the men were in spirits, rough-humoured as he remembered himself when he had been one of them, the old jokes about prize-money, the lottery of death, the exchange of verbal wills.

In the wardroom he stuffed his pockets with hard tack, an orange and a large clean cloth, then accepted his fighting sword and cross-belt from his servant. His uncle, who had provided the fine blade, was now unimaginably distant. He eased out the blued steel far enough to glimpse the Cornish choughs, then clicked it home again and buckled it on. Whose blood would it taste first? Or would he yield it in surrender to great odds?

As he left he felt a stab of foreboding—he was going out on deck and perhaps would never return. But he shook it off and as he reached the upper deck his eyes immediately searched out the waiting enemy.

"This is a grave and solemn moment, Mr Bryant," admonished Houghton, breaking into the first lieutenant's avid description of what he had once found in a captured French ship. "We shall mark it with due reverence. Pass the word for the chaplain." At length the man appeared. "I desire to see a short service before we open hostilities if you please, Mr Peake."

"A—a service?"

"Yes, certainly. Do you not feel it wise to seek the blessing of the Almighty on our endeavours?"

"You mean—"

"Do I have to instruct you in your duty, sir? A rousing hymn to get the men in spirit, some bracing words about the rightness of our cause, doing our Christian duty, that sort of thing. And, of course, finish with a suitable prayer calling for a blessing of our arms on this day. Steadies the men, puts heart into them. Make it brief—we'll be at the guns in an hour."

As he hurried along the upper deck Renzi saw a figure he recognised, clinging to the bulwarks, head bowed. "Why, what's this, Mr Peake? At your prayers, I see," he said. With most of the men below there were only a few curious pairs of eyes to gawp at them.

Peake lifted his face: it was a picture of misery. "I can't do it, Mr Renzi," he said thickly.

"Cannot do what, sir?"

"The captain wishes me to—to speak words of violence, to

incite men to acts of bloodshed, and this—this I find in all conscience I cannot do, sir."

Renzi knew the man was finished if he was unable to function as expected. It would be construed as common cowardice. "We must discuss this," he said, taking Peake firmly by the arm and urging him below. They passed through the main-deck with its gun crews animated by grog. One called out, "What cheer, the sin-bosun—ye'll have work enough t' do afore we sees the sun again!"

When they arrived in the orlop the cockpit table was ready laid with shining instruments; the surgeon lifted a fearful-looking long knife, and began stropping it deliberately. Peake shied away under his direct stare.

"Mr Pybus, you'd oblige us extremely by allowing us the temporary privacy of your cabin," Renzi said.

The surgeon laid down the knife. "Dear fellow, I can think of no better lair to wait out this disagreeable time. By all means."

Renzi sat Peake on the patient's stool. "Mr Peake, you came forward to serve His Majesty, is this not so?" There was no reply. "And now your country needs you—and in particular at this time, *you,* sir," he added forcefully.

Peake stared at him as Renzi pressed on. "Our ship's company—all hands—are putting their lives at peril in the service of their country and their fellow man. They look for meaning and surety, words they can carry with them in their hour of trial. Can you not feel it in your heart—"

"Mr Renzi. You are no practised hand at dissimulation, so speak direct, sir. You assume a lack of moral fibre in me, a reprehensible shyness in the face of mortal danger. Let me assure you, this is far from being the case."

"Then, sir, what prevents you in the performance of your divinities?"

"I have referred before to my abhorrence of any man seeking to wreak violence upon a fellow creature. I do not propose to explicate further."

Renzi bit his lip. His immediate duty was to the gun crews under his command, and thence to his ship, and time was pressing. "Do I understand that you take exception to the form of words used by the captain?"

"Of course I do!"

Renzi did not speak for a space. "Then if *your* words to the men, suitably chosen, are thereby made acceptable to you, you would feel able to deliver your service?"

Peake looked doubtful, but answered, "If they did no violence to my precepts, Mr Renzi."

"Then to the specifics." Renzi produced paper and a pencil. "In fine, to which phrases do you have objection . . ."

"*Aaaall the hands!* Clear lower deck, *aaall* the hands lay aft!" In the short time left to them before their ordeal, the men of *Tenacious* would bare their heads before their Maker to seek a benediction. With the officers standing on the poop-deck, an improvised lectern at the rail, the men assembled on the upper deck below.

"We shall begin with that well-loved hymn, 'Awake My Heart; Arise,'" Bryant announced.

The fiddler stepped forward, nodded to the fife and both struck up. The men sang heartily, their full-throated roar a testimony to the feelings that the simple communal act was bringing. The hymn complete, the men stood silent and expectant. The chaplain stepped up to the lectern, glancing nervously at the captain. He cleared his throat and took out his notes. "Er, at this time, you men . . ."

"Louder, if you please, Reverend," hissed the captain.

The chaplain looked uncertainly over the mass of faces before him and tried to speak up: “That is to say, as we sail towards the enemy, er, our mind is drawn to our forebears who in like manner faced the foe.”

Houghton’s stern frown lessened and he nodded approvingly. Emboldened, Peake snatched another look at the paper and continued: “Yea, our antecedents of yore indeed. We think of them then—the staunch faith of Themistocles, indeed the dismay of the Euboeans at traitorous Eurybiades.” He peered at the paper once more. “Are we to be as Achilles, sulking in his tent—”

“Get on with it!” muttered Houghton. The men were becoming restless: some threw glances over their shoulders to the dark ships of their adversary.

“—while loyal Myrmidons do the bidding of others? We must always remember that this was the same Achilles who had prayed for the destruction of the Achaeans, and from it we may understand—”

“That will do, thank you, Mr Peake,” Houghton rasped.

The chaplain looked grateful, and raised a tranquil face heavenward. “Let us pray.” A spreading rustle moved over the assembly. “We will pray for God’s divine guidance in this matter.” A barely smothered snort came from the first lieutenant. Undismayed, Peake went on calmly, “As we contemplate the dreadful hurts we are going to inflict on these Frenchmen, the despoliation of bodies and minds that are the inevitable consequence of modern war—”

“Mr Peake!” Houghton’s voice was steely with warning.

“—that we must nonetheless visit on their living bodies as they seek to do to our own—”

“Mr Bryant! Beat to quarters!” roared Houghton. There was a moment’s astonishment, then the ship dissolved into frantic movement, whipped on by the volleying of drums at the hatchway.

Already at his station on the poop-deck, Kydd could see it all unfolding: in minutes men were standing to their guns, manning the fighting tops behind barricades of hammocks, or deep in the magazines. The boatswain's party stood to on deck, ready to attend to the many special duties about the ship.

Now the die was solemnly cast. Each man would stay at his post until the battle was won, or lost, or he was taken below to suffer agony under the surgeon's knife. They stood silent and watchful as their petty officers reported to the master's mates, who then informed their officers that the men were now at their fighting stations. Then they stood easy, dealing in their individual ways with the fact that they were being borne steadily towards whatever fate was to be theirs.

"Sir, Flag is signalling," Rawson said, his voice unsteady.

Kydd realised that this was not only the midshipman's first big fleet action but probably the first time he would be under hostile fire from a man-o'-war. Kydd took up his telescope. "Number forty-five at the main, forty-six at the mizzen. Which is?" He was trying to keep the youngster occupied during the approach.

"A—a—" The lad's face contorted as he tried to get the words out.

"Quite right. M' duty to the captain, an' Flag signals 'attack enemy's van and centre.' Quickly now!" There would be little time to worry about him when battle had been joined. He swung forward and settled his glass on the enemy line.

On the face of it, the French admiral had chosen well, anchoring close in with the shore, his broadsides facing seawards. And the bay was shoal—there was tell-tale white water and troubled rippling at awkward places. However, there were no reliable British charts of the area: they would have to take their chances on the attack. But, crucially, there was an element the French could not command: the wind. It could not be more fair for their approach, the north-north-westerly blowing directly down upon the van of the enemy line and towards the rear. The English could choose the time and the precise point of their attack.

Once they reached the line, however, there would be no alternative but to stand yardarm to yardarm and smash out broadsides until there was a conclusion. Kydd could see that about a third of the French men-o'-war were larger even than the biggest of their own and in the very centre of their line a monster towered above the others mounting, from the number of her gunports, 120 or more guns. The regularity of their positions indicated that they were probably secured to each other with stout cables, effectively preventing any attempt at breaking the line.

In the swiftly setting sun the French force looked awesome, and it was now their duty to throw themselves at this wall of guns whatever the cost. Again, a presentiment tightened Kydd's bowels: this day would see a clash at arms of such an immense scale it would test every man to the limit.

A signal hoist rose rapidly up the flagship's mizzen halliards. Kydd had been waiting for it and hailed the quarterdeck: "Form line-of-battle as convenient."

It was now the last act.

"Rawson, hoist battle ensigns." It would be the white ensign; although a rear admiral of the Blue squadron, Admiral Nelson had chosen the white as being more visible in the dark: some said it was because he had a personal fondness for the purity of white in the colours.

As Rawson bent to the flag locker, Kydd added, "Captain wants t' see four of 'em, and hoisted high." He turned back to the flagship. As he watched, her own battle ensigns mounted swiftly, enormous flags that would leave no doubt whatsoever about her allegiance. And not four but six eventually streamed out proudly. Bull roars of cheering erupted from their men.

Another hoist: "alter to starboard." The English fleet now shaped their course to round the little sandy island but were in no recognisable line-of-battle. In their haste to close with the enemy they strung out eagerly, *Zealous* and *Goliath* vying with *Vanguard* for the position of honour in the lead, others crowding in behind. *Tenacious* found herself pressed by *Culloden*, which had cast off her prize under tow and was coming up fast, while *Swiftsure* and *Alexander*, astern but under a full press of sail, hastened to join them from where they had been off Alexandria.

One by one the anchored ships answered the challenge: colours soared aloft until every ship in the line flaunted the tricolour of France, and the first shots of defiance thudded out from the medieval fort at the end of the bay. The English ships did not deign to waste powder in reply.

*Goliath* now led the race: with a leadsman in the chains taking continual soundings she rounded the shoals at the point of Aboukir Island and headed directly across for the first ship of the enemy line, closely followed by *Zealous*. The anchored fleet opened fire, the evening twilight adding a viciousness to the stabbing flashes piercing the towering clouds of gunsmoke. Kydd could feel the deck shaking from the massed thunder of guns.

Battle had been joined. The action that was going to determine the future of the world was beginning. Kydd's pulse raced and he found he was clutching the hilt of his sword. How would this night end? Who would be the victor? And would he be alive to see it?

The English fleet held fire as they approached, single-mindedly heading for the van of the line. Kydd lifted his glass eagerly to witness the first British ship grapple with an enemy. It would be *Goliath:* she was flying towards the first of the enemy line as if to win a race, still with silent guns.

Kydd shifted the telescope quickly to the flagship. A final hoist flew: "engage the enemy more closely." He snatched a quick look at Rawson. The lad was pale but determined, and smiled back bravely. "You'll remember this night, Mr Rawson. We both will."

"Don't y' worry of me, Mr Kydd—I've a duty to do, an' I'll do it." He crossed over to the signal log and carefully entered the details. Kydd resumed his watch on *Goliath*.

Everything depended on staying clear of the rocky shoals that lay unseen all around. In the lurid glow of a vast sunset *Goliath* reached the first ship-of-the-line. The enemy ship's fire slackened and grew uncertain as the British 74 passed the point of intersection, for not only could her guns no longer bear but when *Goliath*'s helm went over to cross her bows she could only wait for the ruin and death that must surely follow.

From only a few yards' range a full broadside slammed into the unprotected bow of the hapless French ship; thirty-two-pound shot smashing and rampaging through the entire length of the vessel in an unrelenting path of destruction. Through the swirling powder-smoke Kydd strained to see *Goliath* wheel about, but to his astonishment she continued on, her rigging visible beyond—on the inside of the line!

"Damme! What's he about?" Kydd had not seen Adams arrive—he had made an excuse to leave his post at the guns below to see the excitement before they in turn were engaged. "He stands to take the ground and there, o' course, he'll be helpless!"

"No, I think not," Kydd said, holding the image in his eye. *Goliath* had passed further along, her guns seeking a fresh target, while *Zealous* stretched out to reach the same point. "Ye know what I think? He's seen the anchor buoy—these Frenchies are at single anchor, and he knows they've swung to th' wind. Stands t' reason, they have to leave room to swing an' that's where he's going to place his ship." It was daring and intelligent and the move was from individual initiative, not the result of a signal. It deserved to succeed.

*Zealous* reached the line—again the erupting billows of gunsmoke. In the gathering darkness gun-flash illuminated it eerily from within. The Frenchman's foremast toppled and crashed. The British ship's helm went over and she likewise ran down the inside, slowing after her stern anchor was slipped, which brought her to a stop abreast her helpless target to begin a relentless pounding.

Kydd's fist thumped the rail as he willed *Tenacious* to join the fight. A shout came from behind, from one of the signal hands. "Sir! *Culloden,* she's—" Kydd wheeled round and peered into the twilight. Next astern, *Culloden* lay unmoving, stopped dead and at an unnatural angle of heel.

"She's run aground, God save 'em," said Adams. In her hurry to clear Aboukir Island she had shaved the point too closely. "Can't be helped. Now they'll miss the sport."

A signal hoist jerked up *Culloden*'s masts, then another. Kydd deciphered them and hurried down to the quarterdeck to Houghton. "Sir, number forty-three—*Culloden* is aground an' warning us, and does recall *Mutine* f'r assistance."

Houghton stopped pacing. "The warning is more for *Swiftsure* and *Alexander,* I should think," he muttered, looking at the developing battle ahead, then back to the helpless man-o'-war. "More to the point, what possible use to Troubridge is *Mutine,* a contemptible little brig?"

"There is no other," Bryant said shortly, eyes straying to the noise and gunfire of the battle.

"Mr Bryant, *we* must assist."

"*We,* sir?"

"Of all the admiral's ships, which do you think he can most spare? We are the smallest, the most insignificant of his force, but we *are* a ship-of-the-line and have the size to be of consequence in assisting."

Bryant spluttered, "Sir! They must take their chances! We have a duty—"

"Mr Hambly, haul us out of the line and bring us to, a cable's length off *Culloden*. Mr Kydd, signal her that we are coming to assist. Mr Bryant, you will go in a boat and speak with Captain Troubridge, requesting his orders in respect of any assistance we might be able to give."

*Tenacious* would thus be denied the glory of the grandest fight in history in order to stand by a stranded ship. Kydd held his silence as he returned to his station. Lifting his telescope again he could see the thrilling sight of *Audacious* following *Zealous*. As he watched, her passing broadside at the luckless enemy sent her mainmast toppling like a felled tree. The main body of the English fleet now reached the head of the line; *Theseus* and *Orion* followed the others inside. As close as Kydd could see, the firing was one-sided: the French had not prepared for action on their inshore sides.

Near Aboukir Island *Tenacious* hove to, well clear of the unfortunate *Culloden*. Her boat pulled for the motionless 74, watched sourly from the ship by frustrated seamen while the battle raged on without them.

Kydd stared helplessly at the great spectacle: now the flagship was coming down on the French line—she, however, chose the seaward side and the vengeful French gunners smashed out their anger in broadsides. Undeterred, *Vanguard* selected her prey and, anchoring by the stern, eased to a stop and began her own cannonade. Others followed their admiral, and Kydd's last sight of the battle, before darkness and vast quantities of powder-smoke split by gun-flash hid his view, was the black shapes of the remainder of the English fleet streaming into action down the French line.

Where *Tenacious* was hove to there were only the sounds,

overloud in the dark, of backed sails slapping and fretful, the slop of water against her side and the monotone grumbling of seamen.

Out of the dark Kydd heard a hail, then confused shouting. A telescope was of little use now and he tried to make out the source. He saw a glimmer of light from a lanthorn in their boat, the rowers laying into their oars like lunatics and the first lieutenant standing, ranting, urging. The boat surged alongside. Bryant heaved himself up and bounded on to the quarterdeck. "Sir—Cap'n Troubridge thanks you for your concern, but advises we should lose no time in joining the fleet."

A roar of cheering erupted and, without orders, seamen clapped on to the braces. Houghton said calmly, "We shall pass down their line and the first Frenchman unengaged is ours."

The yards came round and *Tenacious* resumed her charge. Little could be made out at the distance but as they came closer individual fights resolved, illuminated by furious gunfire. Ships lay together in palls of smoke and it was clear that the first half of the French line was in trouble. The inspired action of *Goliath* passing down the inshore side had resulted in it being pitilessly battered from both sides.

Men ready at her guns, *Tenacious* finally reached the head of the line. The totally dismasted wreck of the first ship lay unresisting under the onslaught of *Zealous* and *Audacious*. They reached the third, and the easily recognisable form of *Vanguard*, her opponent laying to her anchor alongside and also suffering from two English ships at work on the opposite side. Then the smoke drifted clear and there, proud and free above the enemy tricolour, flew a large white ensign. It brought savage cheers from the men, redoubled when the second in line fell silent. Her colours lowered, followed shortly by the hopeless wreck of the first.

*Tenacious* sailed on but even before she reached the fourth, hoarse cheers went up when it could be seen that she, too, had given up the fight. Was it victory that night, so soon? But four ships taken out of the dozen or so left two-thirds of the French fleet ahead. Nelson's plan of concentrating his forces at the head of the line and overwhelming the stationary enemy one by one was a brilliant success so far, but with *Tenacious* the last to enter battle there was no more strength left that could be brought to bear on the rest.

Downwind of the head of the line Kydd could now smell the battle: acrid powder-smoke, heated gunmetal and ancient wood-dust blasted from old timbers. There was also the pungency of damp burned timber—fires had been recently extinguished.

In their path was an English ship lit almost continuously by her guns, smashing low into her antagonist, whose vicious return fire was in turn causing visible ruin to her timbers. But settling in place on her inshore side was another English ship, beginning her cannonade from the opposite side. The noise was hellish, scores of the biggest guns in the fleet contending furiously with even bigger French ones in a ceaseless thunderous drumming.

Ahead at the centre of the line the huge flagship *L'Orient* was now in action with two English ships and beyond her another French two-decker was smashing out her broadsides at a smaller ship. It could not be long before they themselves must join in the action, and Kydd had no illusions about their chances: they were the smallest vessel in the English fleet and a fraction of the size of the French flagship—or any of the enemy for that matter.

As they came to pass the three vessels Kydd looked down from the poop at *Tenacious*'s little quarterdeck command group. Suddenly Bryant pointed energetically to the French ship. Her foremast was already down, and as her mainmast majestically crashed to the deck in a tangled ruin, Kydd could see what had excited Bryant. The massive sides were no longer unmoving: she had either cut her cables to escape the terrible punishment or they had been simply shot away, and now she was slowly dropping out of the line.

And leaving an opening! Houghton's roared orders could be heard clear above the din. Seamen scrambled up the shrouds to take in sail, and forward, others rushed to clear away the anchor. *Tenacious* slowed, waiting as the French vessel slipped away, trailing wreckage and the stink of defeat.

It was a shrewd move: instead of lying alongside a heavier enemy to be pounded by bigger guns Houghton was taking the opportunity to slip between the stern of one and the bow of the other and, while he took position, fire with impunity into both. The stern anchor went down in a rush, the cable slipping away rapidly. But the move had been seen by the big ship next down and while her guns could bear they opened up on *Tenacious*.

Kydd stood in the darkness on the exposed poop-deck feeling the slam of unseen shot and debris. At this moment he felt more for the old ship than for himself: she had endured at Camperdown in an earlier age, and she was his first ship as an officer so he had a tender feeling for her that made any hurts the more grievous to bear.

A missile whistled past, the eerie sound fading as it passed into the blackness beyond. Kydd noticed Rawson, pacing determinedly at his side, his youth touchingly apparent: the youngster would be a different person before the night was over. It was all he could offer, but Kydd said conversationally to him, "O' course, th' musketeers aboard the Frenchy can't see us in the dark."

"Secure the flag lockers, if y' please, sir?" Rawson replied, with an effort. His face was pale but composed in the flickering light.

"Why, yes. We'll not be seeing flags again this day." Now there would be signal lanthorns in the flagship's rigging to watch for and all the detail of night signalling to worry about.

*Tenacious* sailed inside the arc of fire of the enemy, whose guns stopped one by one as they approached the bow of their target; on her foredeck dark figures were running from the light upper-deck guns. The sudden crash and blast from their own guns took Kydd by surprise. So close, their iron balls could not miss and when the smoke cleared the beautifully ornamented bow was scarred and pitted with blotches of ugly blackness.

Then their stern cable told and *Tenacious* slewed heavily round the quarter of the enemy ship-of-the-line. Yet again, Nelson's prescience was confirmed: springs on the cable, controlled from the capstan, meant that the ship as a whole, with its lines of guns, could be aimed by slackening and tightening on the appropriate spring.

Their guns resumed with a crashing broadside, but the enemy replied with venom—they would be made to pay for their boldness. The French guns were heaved round by handspike to bear aft as far as possible, then opened up on them savagely. Kydd felt the deep concussion in the pit of his stomach, and the heavy balls took *Tenacious* in her hull, sending splinters sheeting and skittering about. Twisting chain shot, langridge and other ugly, man-killing evil whirled through the night air.

Kydd's skin tightened. Being at idleness in the open was so different from action on a gundeck. Here, he could only sense countless muzzles seeking their target before they exploded into violence; below, there was furious activity, the means and duty to hit back.

The guns of *Tenacious* smashed out again in an ear-splitting crash. At such close range the strike of their shot was visible on the enemy side and pieces of wreckage tumbled into the short space of ruddy water between the vessels. The stench of powder and ruin was overpowering. A shriek from forward ended in a bubbling death-cry—three marines ran to the poop and set up a firing party aiming far up at the mizzen fighting top of the enemy from where the muzzle flash of muskets stabbed downwards.

Again the space between the ships was enveloped in powder-smoke, but Kydd detected a different pattern. Beyond the end of the length of their target glided the shadowy bulk of another ship coming into position at her stern. Before she had anchored, her guns on the far side exploded into action—the powder-smoke alive with gun-flash like summer lightning, quickly followed by her near side, a savage broadside into the French ship's stern quarters. With four lanthorns in a line at her mizzen peak she had to be an English 74—the *Swiftsure,* Kydd thought. She had slipped into place between their own adversary and the flagship, firing at both from each side of guns. He tried to make out the mighty man-o'-war just past their opponent and saw that she was now set upon by three English ships in a mind-numbing cannonade.

The battle was now reaching a peak of ferocity. The shattering slam of guns made it difficult to think; back along the line their own flagship was impossible to see in the darkness. Kydd felt the frustration of helplessness. "Stay here. I'm going t' the quarter-deck," he said suddenly, to his men. Anything was better than the aimless, nervous pacing, and he had a duty to advise the captain of his inability to sight more than the most elementary signals.

Houghton and the first lieutenant were pacing slowly together in grim conversation, followed by several midshipman messengers. Kydd touched his hat and delivered his report. "Thank you, Mr Kydd," Houghton acknowledged, barely noticing him. "Do you hold yourself in readiness here for the time being."

Kydd joined the master near the helm watching the captain's clerk attempting to scribble into a notebook by the light of a feeble lanthorn. His duty was to minute events as they happened but Kydd wondered how accurate his jottings could be, given that they were made in near darkness, their author half blinded by the flash of guns and probably petrified with fear.

A sudden iron crash and ringing tone, like a struck anvil, sounded forward as an upper-deck gun took a square hit from a round shot. There would be carnage as it dismounted and Kydd felt pity for the casualties.

Ahead, the hulking enemy man-o'-war was showing every sign of fight—but Kydd's attention was taken by a petty officer running aft and touching his forelock to the captain.

"What is it?" Houghton said.

"Sorry, sir, don't know what t' do, like."

Kydd stared at him. What would take a hardened seaman like that away from his post in battle?

"It's like this, sir. Number three larb'd nine-pounder took a hit an' it did fer its crew." He hesitated, as if to spare the details.

"Come on, man, give your report!" Houghton spat out.

The petty officer continued, in a puzzled voice, "We goes t' see what's t' do. There's nothin' we can do f'r two o' them an' we goes to heave 'em overside and then—and then the parson, he comes outa nowhere an' stops us!"

"Stops you? The chaplain? What do you mean, stops you?" Houghton's anger communicated itself to the seaman, who recoiled.

"Sir, I can't just scrag th' chaplain—not the parson, sir!"

"Dammit!" Houghton exploded. "Get that ninny off the deck—now!"

"Sir." Kydd hurried forward with the petty officer. The gun lay shattered and dismounted with a weal of bright steel across its breech. A man lay crouched, sobbing in pain while another sprawled unmoving. And the chaplain, wild-eyed and trembling with emotion, stood over a third.

"Why, Mr Peake, what is it?" Kydd said. It dawned on him

that this was probably the first time the chaplain had seen guns fired in war.

"S-s-sir, I have difficulty in finding the words. This—this blackguard," he stuttered, "I saw with my own eyes, telling his men to take the fallen and—and drop them into the sea! I cannot believe his contempt for the dead! He is blind to humanity! He—he does—"

Suddenly, severed by a shot aloft, the entire length of an eighty-foot main topgallant lift slithered down in an unstoppable cascade, throwing Peake forward into the pin-rail. Kydd picked him up and steadied him. "Mr Peake, why are you here? Your duty—"

"My duty is to be with my flock wherever they've been called, even to this barbaric struggle, and—and to do what I can."

He seemed both pathetic and noble at the same time. Kydd felt unable to respond harshly. "Mr Peake—your duty is not here on deck, or at the guns."

The chaplain looked at him resentfully. "You will speak to this man, then? Tell him—"

"He is doing *his* duty, Mr Peake. The dead have t' be cleared from th' fighting space of the living or every sacrifice is in vain." Kydd took a deep breath. "They will be remembered, sir, that y' may rely on—and by every one o' their shipmates as they'd wish it. This is the custom o' the Service, sir, and may not be put aside," he finished firmly.

"I—I cannot—that is to say . . ."

Kydd paused. There was no lack of fortitude in the man but an edge of madness was lapping at his reason. "Come, sir, there are those that need ye," he said, and drew him away.

He took Peake firmly by the arm and led him below, past the bedlam of both decks of guns, down to the after hatchway and past the sentries to the orlop.

If ever the parson needed a glimpse of hell, thought Kydd, this was it. There was no daylight in the gloomy cavern but lanthorns were sufficient to show such a scene that Peake held back at the bottom of the hatchway ladder, rigid with horror. Spreading out from the base of the ladder where they had been brought and left, wounded men lay moaning and writhing; some were ominously still. Cries of pain and mortal despair filled the air, almost drowning the rumbling of guns run out on the deck above.

Further into the orlop, in the space outside the midshipmen's berth known as the cockpit, a table had been set up on three sea-chests, a smaller spread with the dull gleam of medical instruments. A bunch of lanthorns above gave light to this operating table and Pybus, almost unrecognisable in a bloody apron, was directing the surgeon's mates and loblolly boys in preparing the next man for his attention.

Kydd's gorge rose, but he stepped resolutely round the wretches on the deck, and pulled Peake to Pybus. The doctor looked at them briefly. "You'll wait your turn with the others," he snapped, turning his back. Kydd was shocked at the change in their dry-humoured surgeon—his black-rimmed eyes were sunken but there was an iron control and ferocious purpose. "Get out of my way," he snapped crossly. A seaman was lifted on to the table, his lower leg a grisly tatter of blood and bone fragments below a kerchief tourniquet. The man was white with pain. His eyes rolled as he understood where he was being laid, but the loblolly crew took his arms and legs and spreadeagled him with ropes to four stanchions.

Kydd and Peake were mesmerised. The seaman's bloody trousers were cut away quickly, the sudden touch of the surgeon's mate making him flinch with dread. A leather pad, dark with stains, was put into his mouth, and as Pybus approached, the man's piteous eyes fixed on his, following his every move. His body was rigid with terror. "Hold still, and I'll not make a mistake," Pybus said levelly, and closed in for the job.

Unable to look away Kydd saw Pybus take his bloody knife and thrust it up between the man's thighs. It did not hesitate: in a whirl of movement the knife sliced, in a single practised stroke, clear round the entire leg. A mind-freezing howl came from the wretch on the table, who writhed hopelessly against his tethers, but without delay Pybus took his saw—much like a butcher's—and applied himself to the bone. While the man fought and shrieked into the leather in his teeth the harsh grating of the saw continued until the pitiable remnant of leg separated and fell with a meaty thud. It was retrieved and dropped into a tub.

Pybus took his needle and, standing astride the stump, swiftly sutured across a flap of skin left for the purpose, then stood aside to let his mates treat it with spirits of turpentine. The whole procedure, incredibly, was over in less than two minutes. He mopped his forehead, then said thickly to Kydd, as he wiped down his blade, "What are you here for, then?"

"Ah, Doctor, I have here Mr Peake, who desires t' be of some use." He felt faint but carried on: "Er, if ye could indicate to him any who might have need o' some, er, comfort of religion, why, please t' inform him."

For a space Pybus regarded them both, his expression unreadable. "You might see to him," he said, pointing to a quiet figure pulled to a sitting position against the ship's side. "He's ruptured his femoral—no hope, he's only minutes left. Oh, and that powder monkey, his face burned so, and calling for his mother . . ."

Kydd made quickly for the hatchway; the chaplain would find employment enough now. For a moment the cocoon of belief in his own invulnerability slipped and terror seized him at the thought of his own maiming and subsequent descent into the orlop. But that way led to nightmares and cowardice, and he crushed the images.

Deliberately he shifted his thoughts to Renzi and paused at the top of the ladder to the gundeck to catch a glimpse of his friend. There, it was a different kind of hell. Men worked their guns by only the dim light of battle lanthorns in the stinking, thunderous gloom amid thick, swirling powder-smoke. Consumed with a wild thirst from the acrid fumes, they were unable to see their antagonist in the outer darkness but for the deadly flash of their cannon muzzles.

This was brutal, killing work, serving the iron beasts like slaves—knowing that whichever was the first to falter would lose the battle. Gun captains drove on their men with hoarse cries and curses, locked for ever in the ceaseless rhythm of swabbing out hot muzzles, loading and running out, a manic imperative that pushed men on and on to heroic feats of strength and endurance.

It was impossible to see across the deck and he feared for his friend. Then Renzi, his uniform stained grey, appeared from a gusting swirl of smoke, calm and pacing slowly with a half-smile that stayed in place. Kydd's joy and relief at seeing him metamorphosed a cheery wave into a grave doffing of his hat, which was equally solemnly returned.

Kydd bounded up the ladder and out on to the familiar dark chaos of the open quarterdeck. He looked about for the pacing figures of the captain and other officers, but when he located them they were motionless, all their attention in one direction: beyond the stern of their adversary and across a short stretch of sea, the enemy's mighty flagship was afire.

# Chapter 6

Fire! Seamen could brave gales to go aloft or stand fearless against the deadliest cannonade but the elemental terror of fire aboard ship could turn the hardest man to craven panic. And Kydd had a personal dread of it. In the Caribbean, in *Seaflower,* he had seen a ship ablaze: they had tried to claw against the wind to save the sailors but, helpless, had been forced to watch their end—a choice of being burned alive or throwing themselves into the water to sharks in a feeding frenzy.

"Seems t' be aft, around the mizzen chains, the poop . . ." Kydd forced his voice steady as he trained his signal telescope on the intermittent flaring on the big ship's after-end, where her signal crew would be gathered. His imagination supplied the details. There would be frantic scrambling to extinguish the flames before they took hold; fire-buckets dashed at them by men held with feral dread as if charged by a wild bull. Sailors would be taken from the guns, from below—everyone who could be spared would be put to work for a bucket chain before the engine and hose were brought into play.

"Mr Pringle!" Houghton wheeled on the captain of marines. "Take six of your best men to the foredeck. They are to kill any man aboard the Frenchman who attempts to douse the flames. Am I understood?"

"Yes, sir—clear the deck of any enemy approaching the fire."

Kydd froze with horror—but he understood. If the huge enemy ship was destroyed by fire it was as satisfactory as if she had been reduced by hours of bombardment. It was unlikely that the French would abandon their proud flagship to the flames while it was possible to save her. Soon there would be so much death and pain, men who would find it in themselves to defy the bullets for the sake of their ship and be struck down, others who would know the bitter taste of self-loathing when they discovered they could not.

The conflagration lessened and wavered, then returned as their murderous fusillade achieved its object. Shots came, too, from *Swiftsure*. Unchecked, the flames mounted, licking dangerously along the edge of the driver boom, little wisps flickering upward and along. It would not be long before the fire took strong hold and then there would be no turning back—timbered, and with tarred rigging, the man-o'-war would become an inferno.

Kydd watched as one figure, black against the light of the blaze, raced along with a bucket, then was cut down. The figure toppled into the flames where it thrashed for a little, then was still. More figures darted and fell, and Kydd tore his eyes away. "A terrible sight, sir," he said to Houghton, who was watching with Bryant. Houghton cast him a curious look. "Even if they are Frenchies," Kydd finished lamely.

The blaze was spreading about the poop and its light now tinged the faces of the officers in *Tenacious* as they stared at the awful sight. They resumed pacing: there was no need to make the job of any vengeful French sharpshooter the easier. The master pulled out a large kerchief and wiped his forehead. "Does strike me, sir, that such a monster must have a mort o' powder aboard. The blaze reaches the grand magazine, why, it would put a volcano to shame!"

"There is that, of course, Mr Hambly. Do you wish me to allow them to extinguish the fire?" A grim smile belied Houghton's words. "Yet a reasonable course for her captain would be to strike now to save life—but I doubt he will do that."

"Then, sir, do you not feel it prudent t' shift berth? If she explodes it will put every ship to hazard." Bryant came in.

Houghton took three paces more before replying. "Consider, Mr Bryant. Our people have been fighting for long this night. They're exhausted and can't in all mercy be expected to stand at a capstan. But should we cut our cable in the darkness we cannot easily range another through the stern-port and therefore we lose our advantage. And in any event I am obliged to point out that while our immediate opponent remains at her anchor, so must we."

"Aye aye, sir."

As always in the sea service, duty would stand well before consideration of personal safety. But the fearful logic of war dictated that the enemy could not be allowed to save themselves or their ship. The end, therefore, would probably be cataclysmic.

The pitch darkness was now rolling back with the light of the burning ship; as the blaze strengthened and leaped, the entire bay was illuminated and Kydd imagined a fearfully fascinated audience of thousands watching from the lines of ships—and they themselves were at its very centre, the massive three-decker the next after their own adversary.

Houghton turned to Kydd. "I want to know the moment she shows any sign of yielding." But even with her after deck uncontrollably on fire her lower guns continued to crash out against her tormentors: there would be no easy end for this proud ship.

"Pass the word for the boatswain and gunner. Mr Bryant, I rather fear that we must remain for the final act. I would have you prepare *Tenacious*." There could be no more dangerous situation, a burning powder keg of gigantic dimensions about to explode near to them.

"Cease firing. Secure the magazines." On the upper deck men glanced fearfully across at the flaring torch that was the enemy's after deck, then cleared their own of cartridges and all combustibles.

The boatswain sent men aloft with lines; fire-buckets were hauled up and emptied over the sails furled along the tops of the yards, the decks sluiced. "I'll have a sentry on the cable, if you please, Mr Pringle." There would be some who might be tempted to cut the cable and run. If they did, it would only send them blundering downwind straight into the deadly blaze.

Flames had now run along *L'Orient*'s deck and were reaching up into the masts and rigging in a crackling flare that cast the scene in a ruddy orange. Kydd felt a creeping awe at the approaching moment of doom.

Houghton turned to them all. "Gentlemen, I do believe we should now consult our situation. We shall run in the guns and secure the gunports. So, too, the hatches must be battened, but I believe *we* must take our chances under the half-deck."

Carrying dripping swabs and leather buckets of water, men took their last look at the blazing ship as they went below. Then the gratings over the hatches were covered with the thick tarpaulin more usually to be seen in stormy weather, and secured with battens hammered into cleats. Kydd reflected on the hell below, in the stinking closeness each thinking that the very next instant could bring the titanic explosion that would crush them to oblivion, or capsize the ship and drown them all.

"God damme, but this business sticks in my throat," Bryant growled.

Kydd saw that men from the ship were now beginning to jump from her decks into the sea and worm from the gunports to drop into the water. Yet still her guns fired, her colours flew. It was madness, an insane defiance against the inevitable, but from a sense of glory, honour?

Houghton watched with grim concentration. Then he turned abruptly to Bryant. "We cannot stand by and see those brave fellows drown. Is the launch still at the boom?"

"It is, sir, but—"

"Then take it, Mr Kydd. Do what you can before . . . the end."

"Aye aye, sir." His mind raced, crowding with images of the Caribbean inferno, his dread of fire threatening to unhinge him. He took a long, deep breath, then made his way to the bulwarks. For protection the launch and cutter had been placed on the unengaged, sheltered side of the ship. The launch was their biggest boat but it seemed so frail a bark to approach such a maelstrom of fire. He pulled back and sought out Rawson. "Go below. Get a petty officer an' six. Don't tell 'em why."

Rawson returned with Poulden and six hands, who gaped in awe at the burning ship. "The cap'n wants us t' see if we can save some o' the Frenchies yonder," Kydd said, forcing a tremor from his voice.

One of the seamen spoke up, "Aye, well, they're sailors an' all, aren't they, mates?" Others rumbled a cautious agreement, held by the grim spectacle.

"Then into th' boat, lads," Kydd ordered. "You too, Mr Rawson," he added.

Alongside the dark bulk of *Tenacious* the boat seemed no refuge and Kydd fought down a rising panic.

"Heading where to, sir?" said Rawson quietly.

"The Frenchy, if y' please." Any swimmers would be fanning out in all directions and would be lost in the dark. The only real chance for saving more than one or two would be to stand off the burning flagship. They left the shelter of the side of their ship and came into full view of the blaze, which now bathed the whole bay in firelight as bright as day. When it became apparent where they were heading one of the seamen looked behind him and cried out, "Be Jasus—she's goin' ter blow!"

"Shut y' trap," Poulden growled instantly.

"She goes, we all go!" another seaman said fearfully and the boat's speed fell off.

"Be damned t' your infernal shyness!" Rawson said, in a most creditable rasp. "See *Swiftsure*? She's damn near alongside, and not a-feared." The English 74 was within half a pistol shot of the flaming ship, off her bow from where she had been slamming in her broadsides and there was no indication that she was about to pull away.

It was puzzling why she was so close yet was making no moves to save herself. Kydd shook his head: the grandeur and horror were having an effect on his senses. He roused himself. "See there, y' swabs! There's other boats out, an' they're not hanging back. Do ye want t' shame *Tenacious* in front o' them?"

A cry rang out from the bowman who was pointing to a shadowy blob in the fiery path on the water. "Go," Kydd snapped at Rawson, who obediently put the tiller over. They came up to the dark shape.

"Oars!"

The bowman leaned over and grappled. "Bear us a fist, Ralph," he called. The two tugged and suddenly there was a weak stream of words, followed by retching.

"Anyone speaks French?" Kydd demanded. He turned to Poulden. "Get him down in th' boat, search him, and if he's trouble, throw him back."

"Give way." The boat continued heading towards the appalling tower of flame, alive and magnificent but touching every primordial nerve in Kydd's body. They were close enough now to hear the fierce roar of the flames; against it the battlefield sounds were a dull background.

Another survivor shrieked as he was pulled aboard. Sounds of his agony continued then stopped suddenly. Clambering back, Poulden reported quietly. "Sorry, sir, 'e was all burned like."

"Over th' side," Kydd said, without hesitation. He watched as others were pulled in but it was becoming unreal, the martial thunder of guns and battle overlaid with closer sounds of humanity in distress, yet all in terrified thrall to a cataclysm that could happen before he drew his next breath.

They heard a tiny cry in the night and a ship's boy was heaved in over the sternsheets; he was shivering hysterically and scrabbled for the bottom of the boat, whimpering. "Leave him alone," Kydd growled.

The ship was now afire from stem to stern, a towering conflagration of horror that had to be visible as far as Alexandria itself. Cannon still fired from her lowest line of guns. It was bravery at an insane level, in conditions that could not be imagined.

Kydd's boat continued on. Two men were found, roped together, one probably could not swim. They floated away, both dead. Another, levering himself up the gunwale, heard English being spoken and, with his last gasp, cursed the uncomprehending seamen and slipped to his death. Still more cries came from the darkness.

Then—faster than thought—a searing white flash leaped over Kydd's entire vision, with a suffocating slam of superheated air. In a trance-like state, Kydd tried to make sense of the disorder—and the fact that he was still alive.

His sight cleared at the same time as a wave violently rocked the boat, sending them all into a tangled heap. Water flooded over the gunwale. The boat righted and all eyes turned to the conflagration. An immense fiery column climbed skywards, and at its base there was just foam and vapour. The flagship and a thousand men had vanished.

Slowly, other features in his landscape became perceptible. There was *Swiftsure*—so close, and yet untouched. In a flash of insight Kydd realised the reason they themselves were not destroyed: the force of the explosion had been vast but it was nearly all vented upwards in an inverted cone, and therefore the safest place in fact was close to the ship.

Rawson's bloodless face turned to Kydd, mouthing silent words at the sheer wonder of their survival. Others uncurled from foetal positions. Some made half-hearted efforts to retrieve oars, several bent to find the bailer and start sheeting out the water that half filled the boat.

Kydd turned to the task in hand but as he tried to shake off his disorientation, he saw a silent splash rear up to seaward—and an icy fear gripped him. The mighty explosion had blasted skywards perhaps thousands of feet. Now the pieces of an entire battleship were falling slowly back to Earth.

There were more splashes, near and far—and an enormous one that ended with a jagged spar spearing back up from the depths. Others trailed tangles of rigging and plunged spectacularly, with an increasing rain of smaller fragments still trailing wisps of flame.

Then came a gasp of pain and the flurry of beating hands. Kydd tore off his coat and shared it with the nearer men, Rawson threw his to the men forward. They cowered under their pitiful shelter, feeling the strike of particles and larger burning fragments, flinching at the thought of a giant missile coming down on them. Kydd's skin crawled as he imagined the four tons of a cannon a thousand feet above hurtling down on their little boat.

The pattering and splashing all around seemed to go on for an age—but no great piece came near. It was only when the lethal rain had petered out that Kydd could accept reality: the blast cone had projected most of the wreckage well beyond them.

He waited a little longer, then ventured out from under the coat, staring around wildly. Where there had been a fiery column before, a sullen towering of black smoke shot through with sparks now hung. A desolate stink of cinders and ruin lay pungent on the air.

An eerie stillness reigned over the battle scene, an awed recognition, perhaps, of the catastrophic event so much greater than any local affray, guns fallen silent in respect at the sudden removal from the Earth of the greatest object of before. Then, accentuating the unreality of the scene, the calm silver of a rising moon settled softly over the still ships.

In the launch not a word was spoken as each man came to terms with what he had experienced. Kydd drew on his coat again and pulled himself together: there may still be those in the water, God forbid.

"Out oars—come on, lads, let's be havin' ye. There's sailors out there, lookin' t' be saved . . ." It was going to be a long night.

Kydd tossed and turned. Sleep was hard—his mind reeled with stark impressions of fiery grandeur, horribly burned bodies, shattered wreckage. They had returned only a couple of hours before dawn to a ship whose company was dropping with exhaustion. Men were asleep at their guns and place of duty. After six hours' hard fighting they were now at the extremity of weariness.

He became aware of someone close by. It was Rawson. "Sir, m' apologies for waking you, but it's dawn an' Admiral Nelson is signalling."

Kydd raised himself on an elbow and tried to focus his thoughts. "Oh? Er, well, I'll be up presently." Rawson turned to go, but Kydd added quietly, "An' thank you, Mr Rawson." The youngster had known that dawn would allow signals to be seen and, although he was as exhausted as Kydd, he had made it his duty to be up on the poop-deck ready with *Tenacious*'s answering pennant.

Going wearily up the ladders Kydd was aware of his tiredness: his feet plodded forward, his mind in a daze, and he had to take several seconds to orient himself when he reached the signals post.

"Number fifty-five with our pennants, sir."

Kydd fumbled in his little signals book.

"That is t' say, 'assist ships in battle,' sir," Rawson said gently, his eyes hollow. "I've acknowledged, sir."

He had had no right to do so, but Kydd was grateful. "The captain—"

"I've sent word, sir." A brief spark of youthful high spirits showed as Rawson confided, "An' would you credit, they had t' bang a pot to wake him."

"More respect to y'r betters, younker," Kydd answered, but suppressed a grin. By long custom of the sea, a seaman could be shaken awake but never an officer—that might be construed as laying hands on a superior, a capital offence. The men must have been hard put to think of a way to rouse their captain.

Kydd went down to the quarterdeck to await Houghton, prudently using his signal telescope to spy out the morning situation. Despite his weariness he was awestruck at the scene of devastation and ruin.

The entire enemy van, ship after ship in a line, had hauled down their colours. Their opponents were still at anchor opposite them in the same position from where they had thundered out their broadsides. But there was an interval of more than half a mile from where the flagship had been; the remainder of the line had abandoned their places downwind of the inferno to edge away to the south. They were now in an untidy gaggle well into the bay. Two looked as if they had run aground during the night;

three or four others were still in a fitful exchange of gunfire with two English 74s.

"Good morning, sir." Houghton was dishevelled and lacked a shoe, but his coming on deck was sufficient to bring order to the desultory scenes of ruin and weariness.

"Thank you, Mr Kydd. What is the state of the action at this time?" His voice was hoarse and abrupt. Bryant appeared from forward and Houghton turned to him. "We shall assist as ordered. I mean to weigh and proceed this hour, sir. Every man possible at the capstan, stand fast the topmen. We shall muster at quarters as we sail for the enemy."

Kydd could not shake off his daze of tiredness. Not even the sight of the undamaged enemy they had yet to fight, outnumbering the few English ships in any condition to confront them, was sufficient to raise an emotion.

They fell before the wind and sailed south, directly towards the thunder of guns. It seemed so cruel, so unfair. The fight appeared to intensify as they approached. Ahead were but two English ships and a quick count of the enemy gave nine sail of force waiting. *Theseus* was passing abeam under a full press of sail but when Kydd searched astern there were no other English ships on their way to join them. The four of them would face the French alone.

Like a band of fighters squaring up to another gang, the four English formed up together and faced their opponents, anchoring in a line, and the firing began almost immediately. Their main opponents were the three 80-gun battleships and a 74 opposite, more than a match for them all, but in addition there were five ships inshore—three frigates and the two ships-of-the-line that had grounded.

Kydd paced at his station. His function had little meaning in a sub-battle with no designated commander but he would remain at his post until called upon. It would be Renzi and Adams on the gundecks below who would be the hardest worked—they must be calling on all they could think of to keep their exhausted men toiling at their guns but if it was not enough . . . Rawson paced beside Kydd, hands firmly crossed behind his back.

A vicious whir above ended in the twang of parted ropes. The French were firing high with chain-shot to try to bring down the rigging and disable them. Debris tumbled, and Kydd could feel solid hits thudding into the hull of *Tenacious*. Once or twice there was the wind of passing round shot but no deadly musket fire at these longer ranges.

Their guns crashed out at the two battleships around but the winds were backing westerly and the gunsmoke swirled up and around them in choking clouds. Bowden emerged from the hatchway to the gundeck, blinking in the sunlight. He was grey with fatigue but held himself with dignity as he reported to Houghton, then turned away to return with his orders. At that moment a round shot slammed across the deck and Bowden was flung down in an untidy sprawl. He did not move.

Kydd's fuddled brain struggled to take in the significance of the lifeless figure. Seamen from a nearby gun crew rushed to him but with a tearing cry Rawson ran forward, knocked them aside and lifted Bowden's body. The head lolled back, revealing a livid wound that oozed scarlet.

"He lives!" Rawson croaked.

Recovering, Kydd stepped forward. "Get him t' the doctor," he told the seamen. There was a chance that Pybus could stem the tide of death in the young man—presuming that the doctor himself had not succumbed to exhaustion. At least he could tell the lad's uncle in all sincerity of his complete devotion to duty. Kydd made no move to stop Rawson going below with Bowden as juvenile rivalries were now swept away in the horrors of war.

The firing intensified for a period then slackened. Two of the French 80-gun ships veered cable and eased round further away from the English line. This exposed the two grounded ships to heavy fire. The closest lost her fore-topmast, but before it had finally settled over her bow in a snarl of rigging her colours jerked down. The situation was changing fast: another English ship arrived and anchored next to a frigate, which loosed her broadside, then struck her colours.

Kydd's fog of weariness began to lift. The focus of gunfire now shifted to the four remaining ships of the original French line, but Kydd's attention to these was cut short when Houghton sent for him. "Mr Kydd, do you take possession of the French seventy-four."

To take possession? It was every officer's dream to board a vanquished enemy and this day Thomas Kydd would do so! It was incredible, wonderful. All trace of fatigue left him. "Aye aye, sir," he stammered. He had no doubt, however, of why he had been chosen: he could be spared in the continuing conflict—others would continue the fight.

"Carry on, Mr Kydd." Houghton gave a dry smile and turned away.

Kydd's heart rose with pride, but the formalities must be observed. His mind scrambled to recall the procedures as he told a messenger, "Pass the word for Mr Rawson."

The midshipman appeared, his features drawn.

"How does Mr Bowden do?" Kydd asked.

"He's near-missed by a ball. Mr Pybus says he is tolerably sanguine for his life but he's sore concussed an' will need care."

"Which can be arranged, I'd wager," Kydd said. "But now we go t' take possession of the Frenchy yonder," he added briskly. It had the desired effect. The resilience of youth ensured that a smile appeared on the midshipman's face. "Beg Mr Pringle for a half-dozen marines and ask the first lieutenant for a boat's crew." There were things to remember—he had heard of the embarrassment of one lieutenant who had arrived triumphantly aboard a conquered ship but had omitted to bring along a flag to hoist over that of the enemy.

And he had no French to deal with their captives, but that could be remedied: "We'll have Petty Officer Gurnard in the boat." This man, he knew, came from Jersey in the Channel Islands and would have the French like a native.

He wished he could shift from his grey-stained uniform to something more presentable, but all his possessions were struck below in the hold. His cocked hat was passed into the boat, where the crew and marines waited, then Kydd swung over the bulwarks and down the side.

They pulled steadily towards the motionless French ship-of-the-line and as they did so the men began to cheer and whoop—the second vessel aground had lowered her colours. "Silence in the boat!" growled Kydd. He would see to it that the surrender was seemly and in accordance with the strict and ancient customs of the Royal Navy.

As they rounded the stern, they saw, below the shattered windows and trailing ropes, the vessel's name: *Heureux*. "Means 'happy,' sir," the nuggety Channel Islander offered.

"Thank you, Gurnard," Kydd replied, thinking it an odd name for a ship-of-the-line. "We shall find a better when she's ours, you may depend upon it."

The bowman hooked on at the side steps, ignoring stony looks from the French seamen above. Kydd addressed himself to the task of going up the side. It would be disastrous if he lost his footing or stumbled. He jammed on his hat firmly and, keeping his sword scabbard from between his legs, he heaved himself up.

The noisy jabbering lessened as Kydd stepped aboard. A knot

of officers stood before him, their eyes hostile; around them were scores of seamen, staring and resentful. Others were coming up from below, filling the decks.

An older officer with the gold of authority removed his hat and gave a short, stiff bow. Kydd returned it, removing his own hat.

"*Je suis Jean Étienne, le capitaine de vaisseau national de France* Heureux." His voice was hoarse.

"L'tenant Thomas Kydd, of His Britannic Majesty's Ship *Tenacious.*" Bows were exchanged again as Gurnard translated, the captain's eyes never leaving Kydd's.

*"Pour l'honneur de la patrie . . ."*

Gurnard spoke quickly to keep up: it seemed that only in the face of so patently an overwhelming force and the unfortunate absence of their great commander had they been brought to this pass. "He seems t' be much concerned, sir, that you, er, recognise the heroic defence of their vessel . . . He says, sir, t' avoid further, um, effusion o' blood it were better they acknowledge their present situation . . ."

*"Par conséquent . . . à bas le pavillon . . . je rends le vaisseau."*

"An' therefore he must strike his colours and give up the vessel." A hush fell over the upper deck as the word rippled out.

Kydd returned the intense look gravely. "I sympathise with Captain Étienne's position, an' can only admire the courage he an' his ship's company have shown." He searched for more words but it was difficult to suppress the leaping exultation that filled his thoughts. He tried to think of what it must be like to yield up one's ship. "And I do hope, sir, that th' fortune of war sees you soon returned t' a fitting place of honour."

The captain inclined his head and stepped forward. His eyes released Kydd's as he unhooked his sword and scabbard from its belt fastening. There was a pause for just a heartbeat, then

Étienne held out the lengthy curved and tasselled weapon in both hands.

It was Kydd's decision: if there had been a truly heroic defence he had an option to return the sword; in this instance, he thought not. With a civil bow he accepted the sword and handed it smoothly to Rawson. Étienne made a courtly bow, then straightened. It was impossible to discern any emotion in his expression.

"Thank you, Captain. I accept th' sword of a gentleman in token of the capitulation o' this vessel." Something like a sigh went up from the watching company as Gurnard spoke the words of finality and closure.

Kydd paused and looked about: this was a memory that would stay with him all his days. He turned to a seaman. "Hoist our colours above th' French at the mizzen peak halliards, if y' please."

Facing Étienne he said directly, "If you'd be good enough to leave the magazine keys with me, sir . . ." There was no compromise in his tone: any madman with a taste for glorious suicide could put them all in mortal peril.

Étienne muttered briefly to another officer who left and returned with a bunch of keys, which he handed to Kydd, who gave them to the sergeant of marines. "Now, sir, you are free t' go about your business until I receive my further orders. Good day to you, sir."

Kydd's role was over. The marines had secured the magazines, the French sailors were dispersing below to whatever consolations remained until they were taken in charge. But while he waited to be relieved from *Tenacious*, Kydd declined, out of respect for the feelings of the officers, to enter the cabin spaces and wardroom and remained on deck.

Absently, his steps led him up to the poop-deck, to *Heureux*'s signal position under the two big flags that floated overhead. He sighed deeply. The bay of Aboukir in the glittering purity of early morning had all the desolation and grandeur of a dying battlefield. Every man-o'-war in the French line stretching away to the north lay in the stillness of surrender, ship after ship, some broken, mastless wrecks, one lying inshore with only her upper-works above water and, closer, a frigate still afire.

Resistance in the south was nearly at an end; the last two ships of the French line had cut their cables and were now fleeing with two frigates—but Nelson was signalling, urging *Swiftsure* and the others in chase. Only two enemy were left: one was drifting helplessly on the shoals and the other was no more than a defiant wreck that must shortly be silenced by the English ships coming down in reinforcement.

Kydd shook his head in silent admiration. It was a victory on such a scale as never before in history—not merely the winning but the complete annihilation. "Victory" was not strong enough a word to describe what lay before him.

# CHAPTER 7

"GLORY BE, IT'S INCREDIBLE!" breathed Rawson, gripped by the glittering expanse of the Bay of Naples covered with hundreds of boats whose joyous passengers shouted and waved wildly. They had come to see Nelson, hero of the Nile, grand conqueror of the dreaded French with their dreams of empire, terminator of the ambitions of the greatest general of the age.

"Be sure an' you'll not see the like o' this again," Kydd responded, equally awestruck. As they drew closer he saw the seafront, coast roads, quayside and the ramparts of castles all black with massed sightseers.

Sounds of music and the martial thumping of drums came towards them from three flag-bedecked barges rowed abreast in which musicians enthusiastically beat out "Rule Britannia" and "God Save the King." A ceremonial felucca forged into the lead, her foredeck packed with an angelic choir in laurel leaves. Not to be outdone, the noble barges in the colours of the Kingdom of the Two Sicilies and Great Britain pulled strongly seawards towards the battle-worn men-o'-war.

Kydd glanced astern. Rear Admiral Nelson was standing on the quarterdeck of his flagship. *Vanguard* was under tow by *Tenacious:* the foremast that had been repaired after the storm off

Toulon and seen her through the long battle had not survived the squally weather they had encountered within sight of Stromboli. Kydd snatched a quick look through his telescope. Over his gold-laced frock-coat the admiral wore a red sash with the resplendent star of the Bath over his breast; spangles of light came from his gold and silver medals. Unmistakable with his empty sleeve pinned up, he stood grave and unmoving in the centre of the quarterdeck from which he had fought his great battle.

Nelson had retained only two of his squadron, *Culloden* and *Alexander*—the rest had been dispatched to Gibraltar and tasks about the Mediterranean. He had employed *Tenacious* to assist his battered ship back to Naples, the only friendly port in a friendless sea.

More boats arrived and the bay filled with noise, colour and excitement. One vessel in particular caught Kydd's eye, a rich and stately barge with an imperious female figure in white gossamer gesticulating hysterically in its prow. He saw at the ensign staff that this was an English official craft of high status, probably the ambassador.

Before he could confirm it, Rawson exclaimed, "Flag, sir—she signals." It was "cast off the tow." *Tenacious* would round to, and wait for *Vanguard* with her reduced sail to overtake and precede her into harbour.

The press of boats advanced and one by one the upper-deck guns of *Vanguard* began to thud—twenty-one for the King. *Tenacious* followed gun for gun, her brave show of flags streaming out in the smoke. The ambassadorial barge at last reached the flagship, which backed topsails while a small party was helped up the side. A large union flag broke at the mizzen and *Vanguard* moved ahead slowly to her anchorage.

Even before she had swung to her anchor she was surrounded by clamouring watercraft. Guns banged and thudded from the towered castles ashore as salutes were exchanged and shrieks of feminine delight greeted the thunder of the flagship's guns, which had last spoken at the Nile.

The tide of boats enveloped *Tenacious* as well. Nobles and wives, courtiers and mistresses, all had come to see the famed warriors of the sea. Renzi's Italian was much in demand as the flower of Neapolitan society was escorted aboard and given a tour of one of Nelson's famed men-o'-war.

A richly ornamented royal barge put off from the shore. "Quickly, lad," Kydd told Rawson. "Rouse out y'r Naples standard an' as many ensigns as y' can find. Hoist 'em for breaking at fore, main 'n' mizzen." The navy had a way of invisibly hoisting a flag and setting it a-fly at exactly the right time, by folding the bunting tightly and passing a hitch round it. At the signal a sharp tug on the halliard would burst it open to float proudly on the wind.

The royal barge headed directly for the flagship and curious eyes made out the long figure of the King in black velvet and gold lace as he joined the ambassador on the quarterdeck of Nelson's ship, then went below. An hour later the King returned on deck, to resume his ceremonial barge for his return, Admiral Nelson prominently at his side.

"Gentlemen!" Houghton called for attention, holding a paper. "Tonight every officer of the fleet shall be a guest at a grand official banquet in our honour. I desire each of you to exert every effort in your appearance . . ."

In the evening twilight boats of the fleet made their way inshore. As each pinnace touched at the quayside it was met with surging crowds and strident huzzahs of *Bravissimo! Nelson, il vincitore di Abukir!* The officers stepped ashore in a cloud of flapping birds released by fishermen.

Open-top carriages whisked them away, through noisy, ecstatic crowds, into the maze of streets behind the massive fortress that dominated the foreshore, and after a short journey they arrived in the courtyard of a dark stone Romanesque building.

They were handed down by liveried footmen, and conducted into a reception room entirely in red and gold, with extravagantly ornate chandeliers. For Kydd, the simple blue, white and gold of the naval officers stood out clean and noble against such overpowering opulence.

A receiving line was in progress at the opposite end of the room. Officers conversed self-consciously as they waited their turn while servants bore round flutes of iced champagne. It all had a giddying impact on Kydd's senses. He glanced at Renzi, who winked.

"You have met General Acton?" a nearby equerry asked.

"L'tenant Kydd, HMS *Tenacious,* an' I have yet t' make His Excellency's acquaintance," Kydd replied, remembering what he had been told: Acton was the English-born prime minister of Naples, known afar as a master diplomatist.

The room filled with more blue and gold, the champagne came round again, and Kydd found himself being politely addressed by the general, who was arrayed in a handsome embroidered uniform, complete with a sash at the waist. Kydd had taken the precaution of having Renzi move through the line before him, so his civil inclination of the head and his polite notice of the austere woman at the general's side was a model of urbanity.

Others arrived: one Italianate officer, improbably in black leather buskins, had a large scimitar hanging from a broad belt, his moustache working with the effort of conveying his emotions at the magnificent victory.

A short peal of trumpets in the next room summoned all to dinner. Kydd knew his duty, and as a junior officer obediently entered the banquet hall among the first, and was ushered to a table far from the place of honour awaiting its hero. A small ensemble *in sordina* delicately picked its way through "Rule Britannia" while the purple and gold banquet hall filled with sea officers trying hard to appear unaffected by the magnificence.

"Boyd, third o' the *Alexander.*" The cherubic officer on Kydd's right introduced himself.

"Kydd, fifth o' *Tenacious*. An' proud t' take the hand of any out o' the ship I saw so handsomely take th' admiral under tow in that blow off Corsica."

Boyd broke into a grin, which widened when the officer opposite Kydd leaned over to offer his hand as well. "Aye, that was clean done indeed," he rumbled, his older face creased with memory. "You should really have been there to see Our Nel in a passion, shaking his fist at *Alexander* for disobedience in not casting off the tow. Oh—Hayward of *Vanguard,*" he added.

A lieutenant from the flagship attracted interest immediately, but Hayward deflected it by addressing Kydd. "*Tenacious*—was it not an impudence for a sixty-four to lay herself alongside an eighty and have at her?"

Kydd chuckled. "We saw our chance when one o' the French fell out o' the line. It gave us a berth off the stern o' *Franklin* an' we didn't waste our powder."

The conversations died as the orchestra trailed off into silence and all eyes turned to the doorway. Then it burst into a rapturous "See The Conquering Hero Comes!" as General Acton appeared with Nelson, who looked frail and tired but was clearly enjoying the occasion.

They processed up the room together, each table rising to clap and huzzah the commander as he passed. At the high table Nelson stood in his place for a moment, looking out over his officers, who had achieved so much in his name, then bowed low to left and right. A storm of cheering erupted that continued long after he had taken his seat.

Excited conversation resumed while soup appeared in gold-rimmed bowls; Kydd was now experienced enough at formal dinners not to expect it to be hot.

"Damme, but this is a night to remember," said Boyd, dipping his spoon with gusto. "Can't say, however, as I'd know any of 'em up there with His Nibs," he added, nodding at the high table, which seemed to be populated mainly with Mediterranean-looking notables.

"It's a puzzler t' me," Kydd said, "why the King's not here as well t' welcome the admiral."

"Why, it's not such a mystery," Renzi said calmly, helping himself to a sweetbread sautie.

The others, not knowing Renzi, raised their eyebrows.

"Our noble host is the prime minister, no less, of the Kingdom of the Two Sicilies, a certain John Acton—who also happens to be an Englishman employed in that post. The King dare not show his approbation of our late action in too formal a manner with the French at his borders and a treaty in place—but he cannot, of course, prevent a display of natural feelings at such a victory from an English national . . ."

"Do ye think we'll meet the King, Nicholas?" Kydd asked.

"I do—but in another place, I believe."

"And the ambassador, you would say he is diplomatically absent from a private party, will you not?" Hayward said half defensively.

"Indeed. That would serve to avoid adding moment to the occasion."

Hayward leaned back. "You seem unusually well informed for a sea officer, Renzi."

"I was at Naples on—on another occasion, sir. I had reason

then to be grateful to the ambassador for his politeness in the matter of accommodation. A charming host of another age: a learned gentleman whose shining qualities and lucid brain mark him out far above the common run."

He had the table's attention so continued, "He has served in post since 'sixty-four, and there is not overmuch he does not know about the character of your Neapolitan. A sprightly man, if I might remark it, he is accounted the best dancer in the palace and is greatly esteemed by the Royal Family, thereby being of inestimable value to the cause of Great Britain."

"But he's of an age, I gather," Boyd mumbled, through his haunch of lamb.

"Perhaps, but he has married a young wife who keeps him in spirits. Her entertainments are legendary, you may believe. Thirty-five years his younger, but they are devoted."

"What's his name?" demanded Kydd.

"His name? Sir William Hamilton—his wife, Emma."

The attention of the officers returned to the food. "Be sure to accord that dish the homage it deserves," said Renzi to Boyd, who had begun to address a creamy rice platter with tiny white shavings arranged neatly on top. "Those are the immortal white truffles of Alba, and will amply reward your delicacy in the tasting."

The courses came and went; the din of conversation increased with the flow of wine and the need to try to put aside the stark imagery of recent times.

"You know, we missed by a whisker bringing the French to battle while they were still at sea," said Hayward reflectively. "That day when we couldn't find 'em near Malta and thought they'd gone to the westward? It seems that those frigates we chased off were scouts ahead of their main fleet—while we were hove to in our council-of-war they crossed our wake."

There were wry grins but several officers stared at the tablecloth and others had furrowed brows. Boyd broke the spell. "Er, Kydd, were you not out in a boat at the Nile?"

The images rushed in. "Aye, I was . . ." But it was impossible to find the words to describe the events of that night and he ended muttering at his plate.

"I'll tell you a singular thing," said a neat-featured man to the right. "Innes, *Swiftsure.* After the Frenchy blew itself to kingdom come, Ben Hallowell, our Owner, thought to fish out of the sea a good stout length o' the Frenchy's mainmast. Then has the audacity to get Chips to make it up into a coffin, which he then presents to his admiral. And well received it was, by all accounts."

"It was indeed," Hayward agreed. "Keeps it by him in his sea-cabin."

"How singular," murmured Renzi.

"But th' hero of our age!" Kydd said vigorously, glancing up to the table where the admiral held court among his noble admirers. He turned to Hayward. "Our Nel—I've heard such catblash about his character. Is it true? How do you . . ."

Hayward stroked his chin. "A man of strong views and stronger convictions. And only two words will serve with him—'duty' and 'honour.' Woe betide any officer who forgets himself in this particular—he's as merciless as Jove.

"Yet the men love him, and he feels his captains are, as Shakespeare has it in *Henry V,* a band of brothers. When he's to hand, you believe that nothing can fail. But this is not to say he ignores the lower orders—I've seen him climb the mizzen shrouds to show a green midshipman the way, and you'll all have seen his order book filled the half over with instructions for the well-being of the lower deck."

Innes turned to Hayward and asked, "Has he married?"

"Yes, but I've never met the lady. I've heard he took her as a widow in the Caribbean. No children."

Laughter gusted and swelled around them and the mood changed. "Renzi, if you've been here before, pray tell us the essence of the place," Innes said, abstracting the largest piece of roast hare.

"Ah—Naples. The seat of the Kingdom of the Two Sicilies, ruled by Ferdinand the Fourth, lately in treaty of amity with the French. The Queen is sister to Marie Antoinette, and has her views on the character of the French nation. The court has been termed grotesque and cruel, although the people adore their king—"

"Belay all that, if y' please," Kydd interrupted pleasantly. "Should we want t' step ashore, what diversions c'n we expect?"

"Naples? That Goethe considers the third city of the world? A tolerable number of diverting entertainments—we have Vesuvius, which swallowed the Roman Pompeii, an inordinate number of churches, arts and cultures—"

Kydd smiled ruefully at the others.

"—but in all this we have to remember that there are Jacobin spies on every corner, those who would slit a throat for two piastres and ladies who must be accounted the most rapacious of their species. And shameless . . ." Renzi finished.

A sudden roar of acclamation went up from the table next to them as the officers lurched to their feet to raise their glasses to Nelson, who moved on and stood quite near Kydd. "Wine with you, gentlemen!" he said, handing over his glass for refreshing. "Our late victory owes all to my gallant band of officers, whose conduct was in the highest traditions of our Service. To the health of His Majesty!"

"Damnation to th' French, sir!" Warm with wine Kydd's elation was rising. "Success attend ye always—an' in a bumper!"

Nelson gave a short bow and looked at him quizzically. Kydd had an impression of a deeply incised face haggard with fatigue, a slight, almost delicate body, flint-like gaze and febrile energy.

"Kydd, is it not? Aft through the hawse, and now an ornament to his profession."

Speechless with pleasure, Kydd bowed awkwardly. "Th-thank you, sir," he stammered.

Officers scrambled to set their glasses a-brim. "To you, Sir Horatio! And Old England's glory!"

*Tenacious* would have to wait her turn for repair at the Castellammare dockyard, a dozen miles across the wide bay. In the meantime there seemed no reason why the delights of the city should not be sampled.

"See Naples and die!" Renzi murmured, as the two friends stepped ashore. From the time of their adventures in Venice, Kydd had known that Renzi had been on the Grand Tour expected of the gentility and had visited many cities in Europe. He knew little more other than that he had been accompanied by a dissolute companion who had extended his education into areas Renzi refused to speak of, yet at the same time had also kindled in him a deep love of learning.

"How fine t' play the hero," Kydd said, as they strode together down the broad seafront road. On every side passers-by waved and cheered, while women threw flowers over them. A Neapolitan officer stopped before them and bowed elegantly, rising with an elaborate gesture of welcome.

"Why, thank ye, sir," Kydd said happily, seeing the pleased surprise on the officer's face at Renzi's gracious reply.

Beggars hobbled towards them and small boys ran up chanting. Kydd made to find a coin but Renzi pulled him on. "These are the *lazzaroni*—if you give to one you'll have the whole city round your ears." Leaving the seafront they went up into narrow streets past meat stalls, joiners working in the street, hucksters, pedlars, performers. After the purity of the sea every port had a characteristic smell for all sailors—that in Naples was compounded from the garlic-laden pasta cooking on every street corner, a universal underlying odour of fish and the ordure of horses.

"Where are we bound, Nicholas?" Kydd asked.

"You wished to see the sights of Naples. If we are fortunate we will soon have the opportunity to take our fill of the most diverting curiosities . . ."

Not far from the royal palace Renzi pointed out, a little further up the hilly streets, a relatively modest building. Kydd saw it bore the arms of Great Britain. "The embassy?"

"Of course. I am to renew acquaintance with Sir William Hamilton and his amusing wife, I believe."

The doorman accepted Renzi's card and ushered them both into a drawing room. Presently a tall, aristocratic gentleman with striking eyes and a hooked nose entered, holding Renzi's card and looking puzzled. "Lieutenant Renzi?" He looked at them keenly, then suddenly exclaimed, "Mr Laughton! You have the advantage of me, sir, I had no knowledge of your arrival, and—"

"Sir, I am known in the sea service as Lieutenant Renzi."

Kydd had long known of his friend's past, and how, for deeply held moral conviction in respect of a family act resulting in the suicide of a youth, he had self-sentenced himself to a period of exile in the fo'c'sle of a man-o'-war. Renzi had taken the name of an obscure medieval monk, who had placed the love of learning above the distractions of the world.

"Very well." The keen eyes rested for a moment longer on him, then shifted to Kydd.

"Sir, may I present Mr Thomas Kydd, a lieutenant in the Royal Navy who is my particular friend."

"The honour is all mine, gentlemen, to be in the presence of two such who have lately met with so much success in the destruction of England's enemies."

Kydd and Renzi bowed, and Hamilton went on, "Regrettably my wife cannot receive you as she is at this moment with the Queen."

"Sir, do not stand on ceremony for our sake. My friend wishes merely to make the acquaintance of the author of the celebrated *Campi Phlegraei*, to perhaps view some small curiosities, treasures of an enquiring mind."

Hamilton's expression eased. "You were always of a persuasion to discover your classical education at source, as I remember, Mr Lau—Mr Renzi." His intelligent eyes turned on Kydd. "Do you, sir, know aught of the Pausilypon, the Serapeum of Puteoli, perhaps?"

"It would please me well t' see 'em at first hand, if that were possible," Kydd said stoutly. His answer would serve whether these were places or things.

Renzi hurried to his rescue: "Since I have been absent, sir, has progress been made at all on the discoveries of Herculaneum?"

"Indeed so! Should you be at leisure on the morrow, it is my practice, as you may recollect, to mount to the rim of Vesuvius in the interests of science. It would certainly be possible to visit Ercolano on our way. Might I suggest the hour of eight o' clock?"

Herculaneum turned out to be a dusty expanse of crumbling ruins, picked over by paid labourers and dilettantes. Kydd was glad they had taken the precaution of shifting to shore clothing and stout shoes.

Renzi was in his element, happily exchanging observations on the House of Argus, Pliny the Elder and other unpronounceable names. Kydd was glad for him, but it seemed an age before they resumed their carriage and made for the colossal, glowering presence of the volcano.

"Has it been, er, angry at all since . . ."

Hamilton smiled. "We had a brisk entertainment in 'seventy-nine, certainly, and have had some alarums since. But had you confided your unease to me before we left I could have provided you with a phial of the blood of San Gennaro, which infallibly protects those who venture on the slopes of Vesuvius."

"That won't be necessary," said Kydd, and stared out at the scrubby countryside. It grew thin and bare and, with a sudden thrill, he caught sight of the first brown-black hardened lava flows. A little further on the carriage stopped at a small gathering of waiting retainers and horses.

"We shall ride to the end of the track, gentlemen. Then we will be obliged to walk the rest of the way." Hamilton swung astride a pony and led the party in single file up a steep path that wound round the massive flanks of the volcano. They rode in silence, the uneasy quiet and garish rocks speaking to Kydd of a devilish underworld that lay beneath him ready to explode at any moment.

The soil lost the last of its vegetation, its colour now an inflamed dull red. Then the track petered out and the horses were slipping on the grey-black cinder that covered everything in sight. "Now we walk," Hamilton said, and dismounted.

They trudged up an incline, the cinders crunching underfoot. The acrid pungency of the volcano hung on the air. Renzi glanced at Kydd's set face and grinned. "You are in the best of hands, brother. Sir William's writings on the character of volcanoes are applauded throughout the civilised world."

Kydd muttered, in a low voice, "Y' know well that I can't abide fire—and now y' asks me to look on the fires o' hell itself."

Hamilton affected not to hear. "I'd give half my fortune to be in England when they receive news of your famous victory."

Renzi chuckled. "There'll be a scramble on 'Change, I'd wager," he said. "Pitt will see his chance to turn the credit to hard coin—it will quite put the opposition to the blush."

"No doubt," said Hamilton, regarding Renzi curiously. "But you must appreciate that the greater effect will be here. Conceive of it—not just a victory over the French but their annihilation! They now have no means to support their claim to the Mediterranean. In short, the careful building of colonies and garrisons since you were driven from the Mediterranean is as nothing now. All are isolated and ripe for our seizing, one by one and at our convenience.

"You will be aware that Turkey has declared against France and is opening the Dardanelles to our ships. Austria is much heartened—as you will know the Queen of Naples is the daughter of an Austrian emperor and is now in raptures. Dare we hope that a Second Coalition is possible?"

Renzi nodded quietly.

A crooked smile appeared on Hamilton's face. "But what I relish most is the sure knowledge that at this very moment the first general of France, Napoleon Buonaparte, is stranded helplessly in the deserts of Egypt with above thirty thousand of his best troops—and no hope of rescue."

Kydd swelled with pride. Their hard chase and heroic battle had brought about an abrupt change in the balance of power of far more significance than any of the endless land battles he had heard about. And all this could rightly be ascribed to the achievement of one man: Horatio Nelson.

"We're masters of the Mediterranean for now, sir," Renzi said respectfully. "What do you see as our probable future course?"

Hamilton's low chuckle was almost inaudible. "We have won

a great victory, Mr Renzi, but we have by no means won a war. We are sadly beset on all sides, with precious few friends and no recognisable strategy for turning defence to aggression."

A fragment of low cloud enveloped them in a cool embrace, its sombre light depressing. Then it dissipated and the warm sun returned. Stopping suddenly, Hamilton turned and pointed to the Bay of Naples below, a breathtaking sweep of scores of miles. "There, sir, beyond the point of Posillipo, it is there you should ask your question."

"Bacoli?" said Renzi, puzzled.

"No. I speak of the cave of the Cumaean sybil, which still exists. Perhaps you should seek your future at the feet of the prophetess, receive your oracle as did so many from distant lands in the time of the ancients."

The three stood on the flank of the volcano, held by the vast panorama with all its beauty and antiquity. "I believe we must press on—it's another hour yet," Hamilton said, glancing down the track to where a laden mule and servants followed behind them.

Eventually the ground levelled and they found themselves standing on the rim of Vesuvius. Kydd felt his palms sweat in a way they never had even at the height of the battle, for the track was only a few feet wide, meandering along next to the colossal maw of the volcano. A Stygian stink of steam and sulphur hung on the air, but to Kydd's mingled relief and disappointment there was no heaving hell of fire in the interior, merely dead scree slopes and untidy heaps of grey ash from which vapours issued.

While Renzi helped Hamilton with his stakes, chain measures and thermometers, Kydd wandered along the path, fascinated and repelled. It felt like some great sleeping beast that was harmless until a careless act woke it to terrible life. He was not sorry when Hamilton concluded his work and they set off down the track to the horses.

When they arrived it was already late afternoon and a spectacular sunset promised to the west, directly at their feet.

"Sir," Renzi said suddenly, "it would gratify my spirit beyond words were we to linger a while to partake in the close of this day . . ."

Hamilton grunted as he heaved himself up on to his pony. "I understand you, Renzi, please believe me, but tonight I am to receive someone who has travelled far, and must prepare. Should you wish, however, I shall send my carriage back for you."

"That is most kind in you, Sir William," Renzi said, with a bow.

Kydd sighed with exasperation, but as he had seen in the South Seas, Renzi was always most at peace in the midst of one of nature's displays and it would not be a kindness to fret about moving on. They settled on the cinders and watched the unfolding beauty. "And afterwards, dear friend, we shall sample the entertainments of the night at the first hand," Renzi said softly.

There was peace of a kind here, on the flanks of a volcano that had devoured all of two ancient towns, but to Kydd it was the peace of the dead. What he could not get out of his mind was the magnitude of their recent success—and all the consequence of a single mind's contriving and command.

"'Like madness is the glory of this life,'" Renzi murmured, his eyes fixed on the gathering rose and gold display.

"What was that you said, Nicholas?" Kydd asked politely.

His eyes still on the gathering sunset, Renzi declaimed, "'Let Rome in Tiber melt, and the wide arch of the rangéd empire fall. Here is my space. Kingdoms are clay.'"

Kydd frowned. "That's as may be, Nicholas, but you'll agree, we've a famous victory t' be proud of."

Renzi, rapt with the heavenly closing ceremony of the day, said nothing.

"I've been thinking about things," Kydd said seriously.

"Working through m' life, y' understand."

"Oh? What did you conclude, brother?" Renzi answered distantly.

Kydd held on to his temper. "I was considering m' position in the light o' recent events," he said.

"Ah, yes."

"Do ye want t' hear, or no?"

Renzi turned to Kydd. "Of course, dear fellow—do fill and stand on, as it were."

Kydd caught his breath. It was difficult enough to put into words the powerful feelings he had found within him, the insight into himself that he sensed was there for the perceiving. "It's—it's that steppin' ashore a hero, I—I find it agreeable, is all."

"Some would find it diverting," Renzi murmured, his attention clearly elsewhere.

"What I mean is—if y' take my meaning—I'd rather it were me, my doing, my victory." His eyes burned. "Is it so necessary to crave pardon f'r the sin of ambition? Why should it not be me?"

"Indeed, why not?" Renzi said drily, then noticing Kydd's anger he sat up. "That is to say, it would be well to reflect that to be in the character of a hero necessarily involves elements of chance as well as merit."

Kydd glowered at him. "Chance? O' course there's chance. Was it mischance or luck that had me in the Horse 'n' Groom sinking an ale just when th' press-gang went in? Or when *Seaflower* went ashore over the reef in that hurricanoe?

"I don't deal in logic overmuch—I've seen too much o' how quick the world c'n go all ahoo to worry about plotting m' course too far ahead. But what I've learned—an' it's a lesson well taken—is that when things are on the flood f'r you, take it in both hands an' clap on all sail. If it's going a-foul then snug down an' ride it out without whining."

"This is an observation I cannot disallow."

"I've been fortunate, this I'll be th' first t' admit to—a foremast hand crossed t' the quarterdeck. But who's t' say that this is an end to my portion o' luck? Where will I go to next?"

"Quite so. Be you always ready for anything that chances by."

"No!" Kydd snapped. "That is not what I'm going t' do."

"Er—"

"I've seen how a reg'lar-built hero goes about it. Nelson—is he one t' wait for what comes his way? Heaves to 'n' waits f'r the enemy to sail over to him? No! He makes his chances by rising up an' seizing 'em."

Renzi watched him but made no comment.

Kydd folded his arms. "You see, Nicholas, from this day forward, I'm t' make my own luck. Like Adm'ral Nelson I'm looking for my chances an' taking 'em the very instant I see them. An' if that means perils an' hazard t' me, then this is what I must do, an' I hope I won't prove shy in that hour."

As the heat of his words cooled he gave an awkward smile. "So y' see—I mean t' make something of m'self, is all."

Looking at him seriously, Renzi said quietly, "This I can see, brother. Let us pray it leads you not into tempestuous waters some day."

"Nicholas, be sure an' this is what I mean—"

"'Finish, good sir; the bright day is done, and we are for the dark . . .'"

Heat built quickly in the morning calm. The ships lay listlessly at anchor in the bay and Kydd and Renzi walked languidly about the decks of *Tenacious*. The gunports were triced open to allow the small zephyrs to bring some measure of relief to the humid conditions in the 'tween decks.

Boarding nettings were not rigged below them, less in respect of the unlikelihood of unfriendly visitors than in recognition of the disinclination of seamen to desert in such an unfamiliar port.

Bumboats, however, were always to be seen alongside, hoping to entice sailors through the open gunports with gew-gaws.

Wiping his forehead, Kydd tried to ignore his dull nausea and uncertain footing, and asked Renzi, "Tell me true, did you mark what th' dwarf was doing with the blackamoor and the straps?"

Renzi avoided his eye. "I rather feel that on this occasion we were unfairly gulled into a lower class of entertainment owing to our—our agreeable acquaintance with the famed Lachryma Christi wine."

Kydd peered over the side at the bumboats, but he was not an officer-of-the-watch in harbour: this was a job for a master's mate who would turn sullen if advised of his duties by an idle officer. Signals were now in abeyance: in port the admiral would distribute his orders and dispatches by midshipman and boat, and in any case it was rumoured that Nelson had accepted an offer of hospitality from Sir William Hamilton and was staying ashore in their house, resting.

Treading carefully around three seamen who were eyeing him warily, he noted that their splicing and bolt-rope sewing had not progressed far since his and Renzi's last turn round the deck, for this was the second occasion that the boatswain had been too "ill" to take charge of his men.

It was inevitable, the toll on discipline and spirit in a harbour of such allure. Rawson and Bowden had sampled the delights together, overstayed their leave and were now confined to the ship, while Adams was refusing morosely to show his face ashore after a mysterious encounter involving a lady.

Other incidents were more serious: one seaman had been brought back by his messmates stabbed in the neck, and over fifty were unfit for work. It was proving difficult to overcome the lassitude that seemed to pervade the air after their recent extremity of effort.

With Houghton and Bryant away up country inspecting fortifications, Bampton had been left acting captain and at seven bells there was the depressingly more frequent "clear lower deck—hands to witness punishment."

"Sir, Henry Soulter has been a top-rate petty officer an' fo'c'sle hand, always ready t' step forward when there's perilous duty to be done—"

"It's not his character that's at question now, Mr Kydd," Bampton said acidly, "it's his actions. Did he or did he not make threatening gestures and thereafter strike Laffin, boatswain's mate?"

Kydd stifled a weary sigh. He had the essence of the matter from Soulter's friends. Inflamed by unaccustomed *grappa*, Soulter, a gifted seaman and steady hand, had responded too readily to taunting of a personal nature from Laffin and had laid into him. Unfortunately this had been witnessed by Pringle, the captain of marines, who had thought it his business to take the matter further.

It was splitting hairs as to whether Laffin was in fact Soulter's superior, but if it were so adjudged then it was a very serious matter indeed, requiring a court-martial and the death penalty not discounted.

"Aye, sir. Soulter admits th' charge, but states that it was under much provocation that—"

"There can be no extenuating circumstances in a crime of this nature, Mr Kydd," said Bampton, importantly. "If he admits the charge . . ."

Kydd's temper rose. Soulter was in his division and he knew his value, but now Bampton was playing God with them both. "He does," Kydd snapped.

"So, striking a superior. This is a grave charge, Soulter."

"Sir," Soulter said woodenly.

Bampton let it hang, then said, "This should result in your court-martial, you villain. How do you feel about that?"

"Sir."

"However, in this instance I am prepared to be lenient. Mr Kydd?"

"Sir, I'm certain Soulter did not intend a disrespect t' his superior and now regrets his acts," he said stolidly. Kydd knew that Bampton would never hand a court-martial to Houghton on his return and felt nothing but contempt for the show he was making.

"Very well. Soulter, you are to be disrated as of this hour and shall shift your hammock forward immediately."

Soulter's eyes glowed, then went opaque.

"And you shall be entered in the master-at-arms' black book for one month."

This was shabby treatment indeed: the man would revert to common seaman and Laffin would therefore have free rein to indulge his revenge. Not only that: for a month Soulter would be cleaning heads and mess-decks before all the seamen of whom he had been in charge before.

The men were dismissed and went below for the noon meal. Kydd sat at the wardroom table without appetite. It could have been worse—at least there were no lashes awarded for an act that was so predictable for top fighting seamen kept in idleness in a port of this nature. He would see to it that Soulter was reinstated at the first opportunity. Kydd brightened: he knew Soulter was a popular petty officer, fair and hard-working. By the unwritten rules of the lower deck he would have been seen to be unjustly treated and therefore would not be demeaned before the others by his impositions.

"I'm getting t' be a mort weary of Naples, m' friend," Kydd said reluctantly. "It's not a place f'r your right true shellback."

Renzi did not hasten to offer a further run ashore. Kydd had noticed his distaste for the squalor of some streets. Renzi was no prude but Kydd had a feeling that it sat uneasily with the classical splendours that filled his head.

After a space Renzi said smoothly, "You wish to depart these shores? Before you have been introduced to culture of altogether a different sort, an evening of entertainment of a far more . . . decorous nature?"

"Oh?" said Kydd, without enthusiasm.

"An invitation from Sir William that even the admiral feels it an honour to accept . . ."

"Nelson!"

"A select few will be there, you may be sure. The ambassador honours us greatly for our interest in antiquity, and should you be absent, it will be noticed, I fear."

"But Nelson—an' probably some of his captains?"

"Almost certainly."

In the warm dusk Kydd ran his finger about the constricting circle of the stock round his neck, irritated as well by the tickling of the frilly starched jabot under his chin. He consoled himself that a naval officer's full-dress uniform was a trial at times but was far easier than the elaborate frogging and tight pantaloons of the army.

The Palazzo Sessa was ablaze with lights and rich banners flew from each corner of the building, crowds massed outside hoping to catch a glimpse of the hero of the hour. The two officers passed through the doorway to cheers from the excited people. After the dimness of a violet dusk the light of massed chandeliers was overpowering, highlighting rose-bloomed faces and sparkling jewellery over ample bosoms.

"I say, you're Kydd of *Tenacious,* are you not?" The left

epaulette and single ring at the cuff proclaimed him a commander, a captain in the quaint naval way of an unrated ship, even if he was younger than Kydd.

"Aye, sir," said Kydd.

"My father has mentioned you," he said, with just a hint of the supercilious. "But I see these knaves are neglecting you. Here," he neatly abstracted a champagne flute from a passing tray, "should we not be well primed to salute the honour of the all-conquering Nelson?"

He took a long pull at his glass before Kydd could recollect himself enough to utter an unconvincing "Sir Horatio—victor o' the seas!"

"Yes, well. Must make my number with Carraciolo, the bumbling fool." He thrust through the assembly and was lost.

Kydd looked round for Renzi and found him talking with a thick-set post-captain who stood bolt upright, the champagne flute in his fist looking diminutive. "Ah, Kydd, please make the acquaintance of Captain Troubridge."

"Sir, a pleasure t' see you again. An' dare I offer m' consolation on *Culloden* takin' the ground as she did and missing the sport?"

"Damn charts—but a glorious occasion, hey?"

Kydd caught a sight of the commander he had spoken to before. On impulse he asked, "Sir, are you acquainted with th' officer over there speakin' to the lady in blue?"

"I am," Troubridge answered, looking at Kydd oddly. "That's the captain of *Bonne Citoyenne* and, as you should know, he is also Nelson's son."

"I—I—"

"Step-son, that is to say. Josiah Nisbet."

"I see. Thank ye, sir."

The buzz of conversation increased, then fell away quickly as a hush spread over the room. A trio was coming down a staircase that led from the apartments above: the ambassador with Nelson and between them, an arm on each, a cherubic but striking lady whom Kydd had not seen before but who must be Emma, Lady Hamilton.

The hush was broken by a single cry of *"Viva il conquistatore!"* It was taken up all over the room in a bedlam of joyous shouts. Nelson, in his splendid decorations, responded by beaming and bowing to left and right.

Lady Hamilton struck an imperious pose and cried, "Avast, all ye! I present Duke Nelson, Marquis Nile, Baron Alexandria, Viscount Pyramid, Baron Crocodile and the Prince of Victory!"

Laughter and patriotic cries burst out and the three descended into the gathering. Presently the ambassador held up his hands for silence. "For those who love Naples, an evening of civilisation. Pray come with me, let the entertainments begin!"

In the drawing room a semicircle of elegant chairs in two rows faced a small ensemble of harpsichord to one side, two violins to the other. The musicians remained in a bowed position while the guests settled.

Kydd found a chair in the second row from which he could see Nelson and the Hamiltons. They were in fine form, Sir William animated and relaxed while his lady seemed to be in full flood of sociability towards her distinguished guest. Nelson appeared equally engaged, his responses to Lady Hamilton's sallies almost boyish in their artlessness.

Hamilton rose and faced his guests. "I know you will be amazed and delighted when I tell you that I have persuaded the famed tenor Romualdo Farrugia to perform for us tonight. He will begin with Pergolesi's 'Lo frate 'nnamorato,' of course in the original Neapolitan dialect . . ."

Next to Kydd Renzi stirred with interest. "Farrugia! What a coup! In *opera buffo* the finest in all Naples—which is to say the world."

A short, dark man in an extravagantly rich costume strode out and bowed low, then fixed his audience with a fierce gaze. A cascade of notes on the harpsichord concluded with entry of the violin continuo and the piece began. It was magnificent: the effortless power of his voice infused every note with its full charge of emotion and significance. Kydd had never heard anything like it.

The singer retired to a storm of applause. Hamilton rose and turned to the guests. "Equally fortunate is it that the noted soprano Bellina Cossi is delaying her return to Vienna to perform for us tonight. She sings about a shepherdess at the banks of a river who does not feel inclined to waste herself on a lukewarm lover . . . Of course this is the Scarlatti cantata 'Su'l margine d'un rio.' "

The beauty of the crystal clear notes, their passion and tenderness moved Kydd and he felt detached from his hardy sea life. The music, just as it had in Venice, lifted him into an untouchable realm of the spirit. In a warm haze he heard Hamilton announce a duet—a scene from a recent Cimarosa opera, *Le Astutzie Femminili.* He let the music wash deliciously over him, and was sincerely sorry when it was over.

"An intermission," Hamilton announced, "but do not despair. We shall shortly have our own particular entertainment for you . . ."

The scraping of chairs and murmured conversations were muted under the lingering spell of the music, but livened as the guests partook of sweetmeats and Lachryma Christi. They returned to stand informally about the front of the room.

"Are you prepared?" called Hamilton. "Then—Act the first!"

First one, then another black man in turban and baggy trousers came through the door. Naked from the waist up they carried between them a long scarlet curtain on brass rods. Intrigued, the guests watched as the men took position; they bowed and when they rose, so did the rods, suspending the curtain in a creditable imitation of a miniature stage.

"Ah! I believe I know what is to come," said Renzi. Mysterious bumps and scrapes sounded from behind the curtain. Urgent whispers could be heard, and then Hamilton emerged. *"Ecce!"* he called—and swept aside the curtain.

At first Kydd could not make out what was happening, but then he saw that it was Lady Hamilton in a theatrical pose, standing motionless before a large upright seashell in a flowing classical Greek robe, all composed within an empty picture frame. Candles were held artfully by the ambassador to throw a dramatic light upon her. Kydd was astonished at the diaphanous material of her gown, which left little to the imagination, and a *décolleté* that would be thought *risqué* even at the theatre. At the same time he saw that the chubbiness had not extinguished a very real beauty—an expressive and angelic face raised to heaven that was the quintessence of innocence.

"Aphrodite rises fr'm the waves!" Several shouts vied with each other. They were rewarded with a smile from the enchantress and then the curtain closed. It opened again to a different pose: an ardent, lovelorn entwining around the branch of a tree, beseeching an unseen figure, and still in the filmy gown.

"Glycera frolicking with Alcibiades!" A slight frown appeared while protracted but jovial disputation took place.

"Cleopatra and Antony receive the news!" called Renzi at length, to be thrown a dazzling smile. Kydd looked to see how Nelson was receiving the entertainment and was startled to see the gallant admiral wildly applauding each manifestation, always gracefully acknowledged by Lady Hamilton.

Places were resumed for the second half, Dorabella and Guglielmo from *Così Fan Tutte*. Kydd had seen Lady Hamilton sit with Nelson again, her arm laid on his and not removed. He glanced about: no one seemed to have noticed except possibly Troubridge, who stared forward stonily.

The plot of the scene was whispered brokenly by Renzi. It seemed to be nothing but unlikely disguises and trifling complications following a wager, but the music carried Kydd along once more.

At the end, Hamilton thanked the performers and added, "Our entertainment is concluded for tonight, my friends and honoured guests. The hour is late, but for those who wish to indulge there is a faro table in the next room."

The guests rose in a babble of excited talk as Hamilton and his lady escorted Nelson to the next room. "What do we do now, Nicholas?" Kydd whispered.

"At this hour we have the civilised choice: to linger or depart immediately," Renzi replied. "Nothing will be imputed from our actions."

"Would it be at all curious, should we desire t' see a faro table without we play?"

"I don't think so, brother," Renzi said. They moved into the next room where already a large card table was set out. Lady Hamilton stood behind Nelson, urging him excitedly. A footman offered iced champagne, which Kydd found most acceptable in the heat of the night.

Feeling happy and expansive, Kydd remarked to Renzi, "Y'r foreign cant is all pedlar's Greek t' me, Nicholas, but the music! I have t' say, it leaves me with th' hot shivers."

Renzi nodded. "Of the first rate. The pity is to escape it in Naples. In the nursery, your tradesman in the street, all are singing from the heart wherever they be. A truly gifted people."

It seemed there were others who wished to linger, some at the gaming table, others promenading before the inattentive hero of the Nile. Kydd accepted another glass of champagne while he looked about the room. "Have ye noticed? We're the only l'tenants," he said proudly, discounting the indeterminate Neapolitan army officers. It was an agreeable observation and he sighed with the sheer joy of the moment.

"So it seems," said Renzi, turning to see the origin of raised voices.

It was Nisbet. The young commander had approached the faro table and confronted his step-father, red-faced, his cravat hanging askew. From their distance it was impossible for Kydd and Renzi to make out the words, but the reaction of bystanders was eloquent enough.

There was a scuffle and more shouting, and in a room suddenly quiet Troubridge and another officer frogmarched Nisbet past them and into the night. The room burst into horrified talk; Lady Hamilton stared after them, her face chalk-like.

A colonel lurched towards Kydd, telling everyone he could find of what he had heard. "Damme, but his own son near calls him out—dishonouring his mother's name—tells his own admiral where his duty lies! Who could conceive of it?" he bellowed gleefully.

Houghton held up his hand for silence. "And so it will be hard for me to take my leave of *Tenacious,* a ship we have all grown to love and respect, but the needs of the Service must rise above all."

"Hear him! Hear him!" The wardroom resounded to the thump of hands on the table, the rattle of glasses.

"But who can say, gentlemen? We may meet again—at sea." Knowing growls indicated that it was not lost on the officers at the table that Houghton was going on to the command of a powerful 74, the mainstay of the line-of-battle, and it would be remarkable if he so much as noticed the humble *Tenacious* if they did sight one another.

"Now, before I sit down, there is one concern that is of particular satisfaction to me. And that is in the matter of promotions." The table fell instantly silent. "As you must be aware, my own removal into a seventy-four might have been expected, but following a successful action it is the custom of the Service to bring forward deserving officers."

Kydd's pulse quickened: was his star now ascending to take him onward and upward?

"It has been difficult to choose which among you, but as of this morning I received word from Sir Horatio that he has graciously acceded to my recommendation." He paused, surveying his officers gravely. "I therefore selected an officer who to me appears particularly forward, one whose ardent spirit in the face of the enemy has been so often remarked. I know you will all join with me in congratulating . . . Lieutenant Bryant!"

There was a moment's pause as the news sank in, then the wardroom broke into good-natured shouts of envy and felicitation.

"He has been made commander into *Dompteur* sloop-of-war and late prize, to join Earl St Vincent before Cadíz."

Kydd was startled by the intensity of his reaction to this news: envy was turning unworthily to jealousy. As a commander, Bryant was now lifted out and above them all to a different and higher plane of existence as captain of his own ship. Kydd forced a smile as he looked across at Bryant, who was red-faced with pleasure, loudly admitting his good fortune. Independence, prize-money, the prospect of leading a ship's company to honour and glory in his own name . . . Bryant had it all now.

Then the feeling passed. No doubt Kydd's turn would come—he couldn't be the junior for ever, and there was still a chance that there would be further promotions after the Nile. Kydd's natural generosity of spirit returned and he leaned across to shake Bryant's hand. "Give you joy of y'r step, sir," he said, with a broad smile. "We shall wet y' swab afore ye leave!" On his plain lieutenant's uniform Bryant would henceforth ship a golden epaulette to larboard for all the world to see and know by it that he was now the captain of a ship.

Captain Houghton left his command in the morning of the following day. As was the custom the officers rowed him ashore in his barge, still leaving unanswered the all-important question of who would succeed.

"Ah, yes," said Adams, reflectively, in the wardroom afterwards. "This is all very well, but it's who they'll find for premier that I'd be more concerned with. Stranger coming in, doesn't know our ways, a new first luff can be a deuced awkward party."

Kydd agreed—the first lieutenant was responsible for so many vital domestic arrangements, from apportioning the watch-and-station bill of the hands to ensuring before the captain that the appearance of the ship was taut and seaman-like. There was plenty of scope for tyranny or slackness, both equally dismaying within the confines of a man-o'-war.

"Sir?" It was the duty master's mate at the door. "What do we do wi' this'n?" It was a plain message, scaled, and addressed to the first lieutenant, HMS *Tenacious*. "Been waitin' these several days fer the new first l'tenant, and we don't rightly know what t' do with it."

"Well, now, and here's a puzzler," said Adams, turning it over and trying to glimpse its contents. Very obviously it was not of the usual flow of administrative trivia for it was of different quality paper and the seal was a private one.

"Return it," Bampton said flatly. "There *is* no first lieutenant."

"Open it," Pybus and Kydd said together. Renzi frowned: reading a gentleman's mail was a sad lapse in propriety.

Adams grinned. "Since there's no indication on the outside of who sent this, I propose to open it and discover where to return it."

He fumbled at the seal, broke it and began reading the short letter. "Good God!" he gasped. "It's the new Owner. He's asking the first l'tenant to prepare the ship for his arrival—this afternoon!"

In the space of two hours there was little of substance that could be done to the ship's appearance and when, at precisely four bells, a boat was reported putting off from the shore the officers gathered, expecting the worst.

The boatswain's calls twittered bravely as a lone figure in the full dress uniform of a post-captain, Royal Navy, mounted the side. The piping ceased as a tall, precise-looking officer doffed his hat to the quarterdeck and again to Bampton at the head of the waiting line of officers.

"Er, Bampton, second lieutenant," he said, removing his hat. "I regret to say, there is no first lieutenant at the moment."

"Thank you, Mr Bampton," said the officer, after a pause.

"Sir, might I now introduce Mr Adams—"

"Later, Mr Bampton." Stepping to the centre of the quarterdeck the officer withdrew a parchment, which he unfolded. Clearing his throat he began to read. "By the Commissioners for executing the Office of Lord High Admiral . . . Captain Christopher Main Faulkner . . . hereby appointed to the command of His Majesty's Ship *Tenacious* . . ." The man had a high, penetrating voice, which to Kydd came oddly from such a tall figure. ". . . whereof you shall answer at your peril . . ." Faulkner concluded, folded his commission and returned it inside his coat—and HMS *Tenacious* had a new captain.

"There will be a meeting of all officers in the great cabin in one hour. Thank you, gentlemen."

It allowed just enough time to hoist aboard the new captain's furniture and other baggage before the officers assembled as instructed.

"Please be seated," Faulkner began. Rather older than the captains Kydd had known, the man's manner was careful and fastidious. "I am happy to make your several acquaintances," he said evenly. "In the matter of the first lieutenant we have a difficulty. Only this morning was I told that Mr Protheroe, designated for the post, has unfortunately been struck down with a fever, a most vexing circumstance. Clearly this vessel requires a first lieutenant but in the time available I have been unsuccessful in finding an officer of sufficient seniority. Therefore I am going to ask Mr Bampton to accept the post."

Bampton started with surprise, then gave a barely suppressed smile of triumph.

"Mr Adams will advance to second lieutenant, but concerning the remaining two gentlemen I have my reservations—their slight length of service in this vessel does not warrant my confidence that they are ready for service at a more senior level."

Kydd coloured. After the Nile and service on the North American station he knew he was more experienced than most at his age.

Faulkner steepled his fingers. "Sir Horatio has been kind enough to find me an officer prepared for immediate employment, and he will be joining *Tenacious* tomorrow." He paused, his brow furrowing in annoyance. "However, there is a difficulty. That officer is a passed midshipman only, newly promoted to acting lieutenant. Thus I am obliged to appoint him as fifth lieutenant and therefore signal lieutenant, and trust that Mr Renzi as third and Mr Kydd as fourth lieutenant will find they are able to discharge their responsibilities in a correct and timely manner, as befits their new station."

He looked soberly round the room. "It is particularly regrettable that there are so few officers of seniority available in this part of the Mediterranean, but haste is necessary in this instance. I refer, in fact, to the sailing orders that I have just received.

"Gentlemen, *Tenacious* being in all respects ready for sea, she will be proceeding to a secret rendezvous to assist in an enterprise of great importance, the nature of which I may not divulge to you until we are ten leagues to seaward."

# Chapter 8

"Minorca! Of course . . ."

"It has t' be," agreed Kydd, offering the remaining whitebait to Renzi. It did not take much deliberation to understand why an invasion of the easternmost of the three main islands of the Balearics was thought so necessary. Britain had re-entered the Mediterranean, but her victorious fleet was alone in a hostile sea; it was urgent that a forward base be established to maintain it. In Port Mahon there was a compendious harbour and a fine dockyard—and Minorca was an island, therefore defensible once taken. And, unlike Gibraltar, with reliable winds.

Kydd glanced up the table. It was odd to see Bampton at the head, president of the mess. He looked to the other end where their new junior mess member sat quietly. "Mr Dugdale, did y' ever visit Minorca at all?"

"Why, yes, Mr Kydd," the man said warily, reluctant to imperil his position with any ill-considered move. He was older than almost all of the other officers, far from the green newly promoted midshipman they had expected. He had found a place as a midshipman in the last war, then been left without a ship at its end, and had eked out a penurious existence ashore until the outbreak of the present war. Only now had he the good fortune to secure an acting lieutenancy.

"Well, spit it out, man!" Kydd said, helping himself to the last of the haunch of rabbit.

"It was only a brief visit, sir. As you'll know, it had been British for twenty years before. The people were used to our ways and, dare I say it, contented with their lot, for the Spanish rule was not always welcome to your average Minorcan. There are two main towns—Ciudadela to the west and Port Mahon to the east. The Spanish kept mainly behind the city walls of Ciudadela while we were happy with Mahon. A first-class harbour, it is, splendid careening and repair, fine quarters ashore in English style and guarded by great forts. Should this be our base in the future, why, I cannot think of a finer."

Bampton stirred. "*If* it becomes so. You're rather forgetting that it's been in the hands of the Spanish these sixteen years and they're not about to present their fortresses to us upon our request. We shall have to fight for them—and this means nothing less than an assault, an amphibious landing. Has anyone here had the joy of going into battle with the army? No?"

Kydd kept quiet, the ill-fated descent on Guadeloupe in the Caribbean he had experienced as a young petty officer would probably not count.

"Then consider yourselves fortunate. An opinionated and ignorant tribe, I fancy we'll need every mort of patience we can muster on the day."

"How's th' island defended?" Kydd asked Dugdale.

His brow wrinkled. "There are big forts on each side of the entrance to Mahon. The biggest as I remember is Fort St Philip, which would stand next to any in Europe, and many minor forts and batteries around and about."

Bampton gave a thin smile. "It's as well, then, that I can tell you this is not our task. We shall not be going ashore," he announced flatly.

"Thank God for that," murmured Adams. "But how do you know this?"

"The captain has seen fit to entrust me with certain confidences," Bampton said smoothly, "and I'm able to tell you that the main task of our squadron under Commodore Duckworth is to defend the landing against any ships of force that the enemy sees fit to send to oppose the assault. We shall see out the operation at sea."

Dugdale opened his mouth to speak, but said nothing.

"What is it, Mr Dugdale?" Bampton said caustically.

"Er, after the late complete destruction of the French at the Nile, surely they have nothing left to throw at us?"

"You are forgetting Cartagena," Bampton said heavily, "the Spanish battle fleet."

"And Mallorca," added Renzi. "It would be strange if the Spanish do not maintain a standing force there for mutual protection—and less than eight leagues to the west from Minorca, half a day's sail. This could do us a real mischief at the time of our landing even if we have the advantage of surprise. Cartagena is ten times the distance and the issue could be decided before they receive any intelligence and are able to respond."

"We cannot discount that our intentions against Minorca are known. The Spanish may well be at sea and lying in ambuscade for us," Bampton said irritably. "In any case, Captain Faulkner has set me a task."

Renzi raised an eyebrow. "Presumably involving us."

"As a matter of fact it does. I'm to put before you all that one liaison officer from each ship has been requested by the commodore to attend his councils with the army command." He paused. "Any officer interested is asked to put himself forward. Should there be none, the commodore will be under the necessity of detailing one himself. As too vital in the management of the ship I am to be excluded, as is Mr Dugdale on account of his junior status. Therefore I am open to suggestions from the remainder."

Adams glowered. "It'll be jawing all day, notes and reports all night. Not if I ever have the choice."

Renzi stared into space.

"Then I'll do it," Kydd said. "At th' least I'll get t' know what's afoot." But foremost in his mind was the possibility of notice and the first chance of seizing any prospect of active service that came his way. Yes—this was a positive, Nelson-style move.

The secret rendezvous was the line of 40° 25' north latitude, where it seemed at first glance a mighty fleet was gathered. But closer observation revealed that there were only two ships-of-the-line other than *Tenacious,* and half a dozen assorted light frigates and cutters; the rest were transports and supply craft. With fifteen enemy ships-of-the-line in Cartagena, or possibly at sea close by, Kydd wondered whether this was showing great confidence—or disastrous folly.

In the great cabin of the 74, HMS *Leviathan,* Commodore Duckworth, a large, well-built man with an open, seamanlike face, started proceedings. "I have the honour to welcome aboard Lieutenant General Sir Charles Stuart, field officer commanding the expedition."

By contrast, Stuart was an aristocratic, sharp-featured officer with an impenetrable air of authority. "The reduction of Minorca will not be an easy task," he said briskly, "but the commodore has assured me of the steadfast support of the navy, and I'm satisfied that the operation may proceed without delay."

"You'll understand—" began Duckworth, getting to his feet, but was interrupted by Stuart's continuing.

"This officer is my second in command," he said, nodding at a short, fierce officer who half rose, revealing the tartans and kilt of a Highland regiment. "Colonel the Lord Lynedoch, laird of Balgowan, known in the regiment as Colonel Graham."

Duckworth sat heavily. The navy were not to be the leading players on *this* stage.

"I shall begin with an overview of the enemy force awaiting us. Our information derives from a hodge-podge of sources and is therefore not necessarily reliable, but opposing us are about five thousand troops, some, it seems, heavy dragoons, others garrisoned in the major fortresses guarding Port Mahon, our prime objective.

"There are as well a considerable number of small forts and gun-towers on the coastline, which we would do well to avoid. My intentions in summary are these. Draw near, if you please," Stuart said sharply, tapping an opened map with a slender polished stick.

"Although Port Mahon is our objective, the landing will be here in the central north, at the Bay of Fornells—there is a good harbour, quite sufficient to bear our transports and larger ships. Having established ourselves ashore, we drive south to the centre of the island and to the town of Mercadal, here. At this point I will split my forces. One division will press west to invest the administrative capital of Ciudadela on the west coast. This is merely to occupy the Spanish while the more important division strikes east to take Port Mahon from landward. Is this clear?"

"Aye, sir, but I foresee that—"

"We shall have opportunity to discuss your objections later, Colonel. Now to the order of battle. The navy: its primary task is to prevent the Spanish fleet interfering with the landing. But equally vital is the need to keep the expeditionary force well supplied and in a timely manner. Finally, I look to the navy to deny the enemy resupply. Therefore as I have mentioned in another place previously, there will be no role for the navy ashore. The twenty-eighth Regiment of Highlanders, Colonel Paget, will be the main field force and will be accompanied . . ."

The flow of military verbiage washed over Kydd as he pondered Stuart's strategy. It sounded straightforward enough, but even with his limited experience he could think of many reasons why it could all go wrong.

"Now, Colonel Graham, you have objections, sir?"

"I do, sir. In any venture to put troops ashore we are critically reliant on our understanding of the enemy's positions, that they are not in sufficient numbers to prevent our disembarkation by any means. What intelligence do you have, sir, that encourages you to believe Fornells is open to us?"

Stuart paused. "I do not have direct information, true. There is a species of revolutionary Minorcan zealot opposed to Spanish rule assisting us but their intelligence leaves much to be desired." His lips thinned. "It were better we rely on our own estimates, Colonel. If it transpires that the enemy presses us too hard in Fornells we must abandon the attempt—and strike elsewhere. Addaya to the east has been mentioned."

"With respect, sir."

"Colonel?"

"Just three miles inland there is a road marked, here, passing between the two. If the enemy uses this to transfer forces rapidly between, we will not see them—we will have no warning until they fall upon our exposed landing."

"Colonel Graham! In war, risks must be taken. The landing must take place somewhere—have you any other suggestion? No? Then, sir, we land as planned in Fornells, accepting casualties if need be. Now, on to the details. In the matter of—"

"Sir!" Kydd felt the same exhilaration, the same unstoppable conviction that had carried him on to make the fateful decision to hand over his signal codes to the American navy. Now he was stepping forward in a council-of-war to propose a seaman's solution to an army difficulty.

Stuart stopped, raising his eyes questioningly.

"Sir, L'tenant Kydd o' *Tenacious*—we can't see th' soldiers from where we are, coming in fr'm the sea as we will."

Stuart continued to look at him stonily, the rest of the cabin turning curiously to look at the usurper. "Yes?"

"Sir, Minorca is a low island, not many hills as you'd say, but in th' sea service when we navigate past we always take a sight of Monte Toro, a single mount y' can see leagues out to sea without ever ye sees the island.

"Should anyone climb t' the top with a spyglass, then nothing can be hid from him—all th' motions of the soldiers will be made clear, it bein' less'n four miles distant, and by this you shall know for a surety in which place to throw in your own forces."

Graham thumped the table. "Preposterous! How is your spyglass man then going to advise General Stuart? Run helter-skelter back down the mountain?" There were sniggers from the other army officers. "Even with a fast horse—"

"Colonel Graham, I am—er, was, signal l'tenant in HMS *Tenacious*. Gen'ral Stuart, I'm sure, will be very satisfied should he take intelligence on th' quarterdeck of *Leviathan* that informs him hour b' hour of where the Spanish are. We have a fine enough set o' signals in the navy we can use for th' purpose."

The murmuring died away as Stuart contemplated Kydd. "Possibly. For this it will mean crossing unknown territory occupied by the enemy . . ."

"Aye, sir, but did I not hear about y'r Minorcan patriots? They c'n see us through t' the mountain right enough."

"Commodore?"

"Er, I can see nothing wrong in principle at this stage, sir, but—"

"Mr Kydd, you are prepared that you may be taken up as a spy, as most assuredly you are?"

"Sir."

"One moment, if you please, sir." A young army subaltern stood up and banged his head on a deck-beam, which made him sit again abruptly. "This is an army operation, sir, and on land. I cannot see how the navy can be expected to recognise military movements. Therefore I do volunteer for the task."

Kydd bristled. He swung on the young officer. "I think I c'n be trusted to recognise a parcel o' Spanish redcoats. But can *you*, sir, tell if the wind is foul f'r a landing if we have to shift from Fornells? I have m' doubts of it . . ."

"Quite so," said Stuart. "But do I understand you to mean that you can undertake to observe the enemy from their rear, signal over their heads to my headquarters at sea to advise on just where their forces are massing to oppose us?"

"Yes, sir—and give ye warning should reinforcements be afoot."

"Hmmm. Reliably?"

"Sir, a line o' frigates ahead of a fleet c'n watch sixty miles o' sea—an' there's three hundred signals in the book they can use t' advise the admiral." Kydd did not mention there was no signal hoist in the book he could remember for "Fornells" or "marching towards" or any other military terms for that matter.

"Very well, we will take this forward, Mr Kydd. Be so kind as to consult with the adjutant on how best to proceed." Stuart hesitated then declared to the meeting, "For the purposes of this operation we press on as before. If—if this signalling fails in its intention we have lost nothing and will resume the assault without the information. However, if your scheme succeeds we will be greatly in your debt, Mr Kydd."

Kydd bowed politely, but inwardly he was exulting. He had seized the moment. This was what it was to be a Nelson! He resumed his place, but before he had settled, Duckworth leaned across and said testily, "A word with you afterwards at your convenience, Mr Kydd."

"Say y'r piece, Nicholas, but please t' make it speedy. The landing is set f'r only two days hence." Kydd rummaged in his chest, looking for anything that he could put over his uniform. He had a dim recollection from somewhere that he could not be shot as a spy if he was in uniform.

"Tom, my friend . . ."

"Do ye lend me y'r watch, I'd be grateful."

Renzi untagged the expensive hunter from his waistcoat. "It's not too early to reconsider the plan," he said softly. "You see, it is not the fear of failure that troubles me, it is your unthinking trust that so many things will go *right* for you."

Kydd stopped and looked directly at Renzi. "If Nelson let fear o' what *can* go wrong come t' the front, why, he'd never have sailed against the enemy at the Nile. Nothing was ever won b' holding back, Nicholas."

Renzi bit his lip. "Then how will you set up for signals without you provide a mast and halliards?"

"I'll find a way. Pass the lashing, if y' please."

Renzi tried another tack. "If you are taken, you can expect no mercy. There are tales told of the Spanish treatment of prisoners that make ugly—"

"Enough! I have t' be ready by six bells. If you can't help, be s' kind as to stand clear." Kydd tested the lashing round a small seaman's chest. Inside was a full set of naval signal flags and tack lines that would allow the sending of any message in the book. And all the while *Tenacious* cruised ever closer to Minorca's east coast for a secret night rendezvous with the revolutionary group.

"What is your plan, brother?"

"Not so rarefied, m' friend. After we get ashore it's just four an' a bit miles to Monte Toro through scrub 'n' a few farms. We've got good charts o' the island from when we were here in 'eighty-two. I've copied a track from them. There's a path up to th' top where the ladies used to go for the view an' up there is just a nunnery. I'll not disturb 'em if I set up on their roof, I believe."

"And you *can* see the Spanish from there?"

"A prime position! Fornells t' the north, five miles, turn about to the nor'east to Addaya, four miles. An' with a height of eye up there close t' a thousand feet there's nothing that moves I can't see."

Renzi murmured words of general unease as he helped bring the chest on deck.

"Sir, ready in all respects," Kydd said to Faulkner.

"Very well. You have no qualms at this stage, Mr Kydd? It is not too late . . ."

"Ready, sir," Kydd said stoutly.

"Then we will proceed. Lookouts to your stations! Mr Pearce?"

"Aye aye, sir," said the boatswain, and the darkness was suddenly split by the ghostly blue of the light of a flare reflected on sails. It sputtered and fizzed, sending dark shadows dancing about the deck, illuminating the faces of the men. In a few minutes the flare died to red sparks and blackness clamped in once more.

"Absolute silence!" Long minutes passed. Nothing could be heard but the easy creak of the ship in the placid seas and the distant cry of a seabird. Kydd clutched a rope tightly. *Tenacious* was his true home, where he had been formed as a king's officer, faced death and destruction, crossed whole oceans: now he was leaving her warm security for the unknown perils that lay out in the darkness.

A faint cry came out of the night and was immediately followed by a hail from the foretop. "*Deck hooooo*, an' it's three points t' larb'd."

"Mr Pearce!"

"Sir." He took his speaking trumpet and roared into the night, *"God save King George!"*

An answering cry came and minutes later a small fishing-boat appeared. The boatswain gave a signal for it to come alongside and Kydd prepared to board. Bowden was standing close. "Bear a hand with m' chest, Mr Bowden," he asked, trying to keep the tension from his voice.

Upturned faces in the boat watched as Bowden passed a hitch round it and went down the side to the boat to receive it from the seamen lowering away.

Kydd turned for a farewell sight of his ship and a handshake from the captain. Renzi waited until last—his grip was tight. No words were spoken.

"Good luck t' ye, sir," came a low cry from the anonymous darkness forward, and a lump formed in Kydd's throat. He lifted an arm in response and went into the boat.

A jabber of nervous Spanish greeted him and a woman's voice cautioned, "Pons he say as 'ow we must not waste th' time."

Taken aback, Kydd muttered something and took the chest from Bowden. "Away y' go, m'lad," he said, "an' thank ye."

"Can't do that, sir," Bowden said quietly. "I'd be disobeying captain's orders!"

"Wha—"

"He asked me to accompany you, sir." Kydd realised that this was probably not the way it had happened, but already the anonymous figure in the bows had poled off and the comforting bulk of *Tenacious* was receding into the blackness.

"Y'r a rascal, Bowden, but I thank ye all the same."

"Pons ask you, do not spik—he listen for danger!" In the sternsheets the woman was close enough for him to be aware of her female scent.

A darker mass loomed and the boat stopped in the water. The fitful half-moon laid a fragile luminosity over the water, revealing a third figure, whom Kydd presumed to be Pons. He was listening with rigid concentration. At length he signalled to the rower, who skimmed the boat about and glided in to the shore.

There was just enough light to make out a rickety landing-stage. The boat bumped against it and the rower went forward to secure the painter. Pons stood and made his way clumsily up behind him while Kydd prepared to land on enemy soil.

There was a flurry of movement in the dimness forward—and in a sudden chill of horror Kydd saw the flash of moonlight on an arc of bright steel and heard a gurgling cry, then a dull splash echoing in the tiny bay.

"Wh-why did—"

"Is th' only safe way," the girl said flatly. "Even if he want, he can tell no tale now."

Shaken, Kydd motioned to Bowden to help sway up the chest.

They took a barely visible path over the low scrub-covered hillock and Kydd could smell the scent of wild thyme and myrtle on the air. It led down to a wider bay with a small village of fishermen's dwellings by a beach.

Pons held up his hand for them to stop. There was no sound on the cool breeze beyond the distant bray of a donkey and laughter from one of the white stone houses. The walk resumed. A hundred yards short of the village Pons growled something to the woman.

"We wait," she said. "Here!" she added urgently, moving into the scrub. They crouched down, Kydd's senses at full alert. Pons entered a brightly lit dwelling, and emerged a few minutes later with an imperious wave. The woman rose warily and gestured towards the village. "Es Grau."

A smoke-blackened interior revealed it to be some form of taphouse, but the conversations ceased as they entered. Kydd followed Pons to a small room at the back, which reminded him of the snug in an English hostelry.

"Sit."

Kydd slipped into a chair next to Bowden.

"Are we safe?" Kydd whispered to the woman. "Those people know we're here."

"Here you will not find th' Spanish."

"They are Minorcan?"

"*Minorquin!*" the girl said impatiently. She wore a distinctive red cowl, which she let down to reveal black hair swept back severely into a queue, not dissimilar to the familiar tarry pigtail of the seaman. "The Minorquin do not love those 'oo seek to master them." Then a brief, wistful look stole over her as she introduced herself. "Isabella Orfila Cintes—when I a little girl, you English sailor call me Bella."

"L'tenant Kydd, an' Midshipman Bowden." Kydd was reluctant to release his boat-cloak to display his uniform coat beneath, but he was stifling in the heat of the room.

"That is Pons—Don Pons y Preto Carreras." She threw the words at the sullen man opposite. "Our leader," she added.

Pons snapped something at her.

"He ask, what do y' want of him, that the gran' navy of Englan' send you to Minorca?"

Kydd felt disquiet. Why had they not been told details by Stuart's staff? Were they trustworthy? And were they in possession of the secret of the invasion—its time, its place?

"I volunteered t' come," he mumbled. Without their help his entire mission was impossible. Surely he would not have been put in contact with the Minorquins unless he was expected to make use of them. It was being left up to him to decide how much to reveal. "Do ye know what is being planned for Minorca?"

"Planned?" Isabella looked puzzled.

Kydd saw Bowden's anxiety and knew he was thinking the same thing, but there was no help for it. "We mean t' take this island from the Spanish," he said quietly, "an' very soon."

"You—you will come wi' soldiers an' ships . . ."

"Aye. An' we need your help."

She stared at him then leaped up, knocking the table askew. "God be praise!"

"*¿Que? ¿Que?*" Pons seized her arm to force her round. She replied in low, urgent tones, then Pons stood to proclaim dramatically what sounded like patriotic slogans.

Kydd gestured frantically for him to sit. "There's much t' do before they come. We are here t' signal to our general where the Spanish are an' where they march to."

Isabella's expression sobered. "That is ver' dangerous," she said darkly. "What is your plan?"

"There is a big hill, a mountain called Monte Toro." Isabella said nothing, her concentration growing intense. "We mean t' climb up and see . . ."—something stopped him going further—". . . all of Minorca, and there we'll set up a little mast an' signal to th' ships at sea." She made no comment, so he tried to explain further. "Y' can see these flags fr'm a long distance an' send any message y' like." He pulled the chest over and threw back the lid, then held up some of the flags. "You see?"

"That is your plan?" she said icily. Pons affected disinterest at the sight of the bunting.

"It is."

"You are all fools! Do you know what is up there on Monte Toro?"

"I've heard there's a nunnery, a convent," Kydd said warily.

"It is. An' you know else? The army agree wi' you—a fine

place for flags an' signals. They have their own post for flags. Guarded by th' heavy dragoons. So where is your plan now?"

Kydd tried to keep dismay from his face. "We will find a place out of sight, o' course. Somewhere up there, on a roof—"

"Where is your money? In th' box?"

"Money?"

She took a deep breath. "How you going to pay th' soldier to look away while you wave y'r flags?" Kydd kept an obstinate silence, his face burning. "You must! If your ship can see th' flags so can the Spanish Army." Her shoulders drooped. "How . . ."

Kydd had no answer. Then she looked up into his eyes. "Ver' well, I will help you. But first—"

She went to the door and opened it. "*Juan!*" she called loudly. There was movement inside and a nervous pot-boy arrived, carrying a jug and mugs on a tray.

"When you English here before, you teach us abou' gin. We learn well an' make our own. To hell wi' all the Spanish!"

The gin owed more perhaps to myrtle than juniper but it had its own attractive character. "Damn right!" Kydd responded.

The darkness outside seemed all the more intense as they stumbled along a beachside track and crossed a small stream. The chest was an irritating encumbrance and Kydd felt the effects of the gin fall away. He took off his boat-cloak and uniform coat and tied them to the chest, going in shirt and breeches alone.

What had become of his plan? If he could not signal the invasion would certainly still go ahead—and men's lives would pay for his failure.

It was only a little more than four miles to Monte Toro but no map could take into account the endless dry-stone walls of small plots of land, the deep ravines in the limestone bedrock, the sudden thick woods.

At one point Pons stopped with a hiss of caution: ahead was a moonlit clearing and beyond a dark tower. "We go one b' one," Isabella whispered. Pons crouched low and scurried to the other side to disappear into the shadows. He reappeared further towards the looming tower and beckoned. Hearts thumping at the unknown danger Kydd and Bowden complied, Kydd awkwardly humping the chest. Then Isabella flitted across swiftly and they resumed the march.

They reached a road. "How far, Bella?" Kydd gasped. The chest was taking its toll of his strength.

"Don't stop here! Anyone is moving at night, he must be *bandido*." She went to help him with the chest, but he brushed her away and crabbed across the road to the anonymous shadows of the other side.

"It is not s' far now, Mr Keed," she said. "We get to Sa Roca before the daybreak. There we fin' a new plan." Pons stalked on ahead at a merciless pace, the terrain growing ever steeper and rockier, the track leading through fragrant pine woods that pulled and snagged constantly.

It was more than an hour before they arrived, the immense dark bulk of Monte Toro dominating ahead—a lone, rounded peak that he had last seen from the deck of *Tenacious* but whose brooding presence made Kydd's heart quail. "Sir, quite the ticket for signalling," Bowden said brightly. Kydd did not reply.

Their hiding-place was well chosen: a small shadow in the side of a craggy hill turned out to be a dank but secure limestone cave. From the smell of its contents, it was probably used for farm storage. Kydd let the chest drop thankfully as Isabella found a small lantern. "We will return in th' morning. On your life, do not show ou'side!"

Sleep was a long time coming. Kydd had not counted on the presence of an army post on the summit. Rigging a makeshift signal mast was going to be impossible under their eyes and he despaired. Perhaps daylight would suggest a way.

• • •

The grey of dawn stole into the cave turning sinister dark shapes to ordinary dusty kegs and sacks. It also brought Isabella and a wrinkled old man, with their breakfast of bread and onion soup. "This Señor Motta, an' this his *finca,* his farm. He want t' help."

His beady black eyes watched them steadily as they ate, while Isabella waited impatiently and Pons stared out moodily.

"Now! What our plan?" she said, as the last of the meal went down. It was time to confront their situation—and, above all, the vital question of whether he could trust her with the secret of the landing-place. She was practical and intelligent, and if anything was to be rescued of the mission it would have to be through her.

Before he could speak she answered his unspoken question: "On Monte Toro is my brother José. He cook for the dragoons." It was what Kydd needed; she would not have trusted him with that knowledge unless she believed in him and, therefore, in turn, he could trust her.

"There is a way *you* can visit him," she added cagily, "but not wi' your big box."

"What's it like up there?" Kydd countered. "That's t' say, how many soldiers? Where do they—"

"There are twenty-two soldier, an' five sailor t' work the flags," she said crisply. "They are in a fort an' barracks, not so big. The *monasterio* gate are closed, th' nuns not interested in them."

Now he just needed a reason to be up there and a hiding-place. He was on his way back with a chance. But without signalling flags? On the quarterdeck of *Leviathan* they would be expecting standard naval signals—without flags and a mast to hoist them, what use was it to get up there?

"How do ye pass the soldiers?"

"Is easy—I wash th' clothes for the soldier and 'is family," she said. "I must take them up—what soldier want to stop his washing?"

"Then can ye tell me how *we* will get past 'em?" Kydd asked.

"Easy as well. You are cousin of José, you deliver onion an' garlic to him on a donkey. This young man not go."

"But—"

"You cannot spik Spanish 'cos you are idiot of the village. Can you be idiot? Señor Motta will 'ave clothes for you."

"Mr Kydd, sir," Bowden said, in a low voice, "our flags an' ropes?"

"They look inside th' box an' we are betrayed." She folded her arms. "No."

Kydd knew there was everything to win—if only his wits could come up with a solution. But without flags to signal . . . At the back of his mind something stirred. Flags—and something she had said. The idea struggled for form and consciousness. Fornells, Addaya—and the waiting fleet. Then it leaped into focus.

"Bowden!" he snapped. "I have an idea. I'd be obliged should you help me t' reason it through."

"Aye aye, sir," said Bowden, mystified. They moved deeper into the cave for more privacy.

"Do ye agree that . . ." The idea took shape: a plan was possible. He explored further, testing each part against Bowden's loyal opposition.

He returned to Isabella. "We have an idea. Here's what we're going t' do—"

"I won't hear you!"

"You—"

"If I don't know your plan, how can I tell th' Spanish if they catch me?" There was nothing Kydd could say to that.

She looked at him squarely. "Jus' tell me—when you wan' to be on Monte Toro?"

"Before ten, tomorrow."

"We will be there."

There was one last matter. "My midshipman needs t' return to the gen'ral. Can—"

"Pons will take 'im tonight."

In the cool of the morning Kydd and Isabella set out over the steep tracks towards the rearing bulk of Monte Toro. Dressed in the homespun of Minorca, a waistband of faded red with abarca sandals and a low-crowned dull brown hat, Kydd led a donkey laden with onions in panniers, strings of garlic bulbs round its neck and two laundry baskets.

They did not speak as they reached the base of the massive mount and began to trudge up the steep spiral road. A thousand feet to go—the surrounding country began to spread out as they rose and the glimmer of sea appeared on the horizon. Further still and the limits of the horizon extended until even without a telescope the unmistakable winding shape of the Bay of Fornells became apparent. The panorama of low, rolling country out into the far distance was spectacular.

The gritty noise of a cart sounded behind. Kydd snatched a look and saw it was an army conveyance. He let Isabella chat on incomprehensibly. She stopped to give a cheery wave to the soldiers, who responded with catcalls.

They wound round the last few yards of the road, and suddenly were on the airy summit, a flat area with a squat, square reddish fort and a line of barracks one side, a white stone building the other, well shuttered. A hut and signal mast was atop the fort.

Playing his part to the full, Kydd stood and gaped vacantly until Isabella tugged angrily at him to move forward.

Two sentries ambled across. "*Oye! Isabella, para! Tenemos que registrarte a ti y la colada!*"

As Isabella told her story Kydd shrank fearfully from the men, scrabbling to hide behind the donkey as the men fumbled among the onions in a perfunctory search, laughing at his clumsy consternation. *"El Coronel dice que los ingleses están cerca y no quiere jugarsela."*

They turned to the washing baskets; Kydd started to whimper in distress at their behaviour. *"Dejadlo en paz, cabrones!"* Isabella shouted, pulling them away. They complied meekly while she comforted Kydd with soothing words and firmly led him on.

At the sound of raised voices several people came into the courtyard. The cook, fat, jovial and impatient to see what they had brought, emerged from the barracks. He fingered the onions doubtfully and inspected the strings of garlic. They were apparently judged satisfactory; the donkey was unloaded and led away, and the cook promised to find a little something for the visitors after the long haul up.

Inside the cook's quarters there was nervous chatter, but Kydd's first concern was the room. To his vast relief there was a large jalousie window facing north. He looked out cautiously. It was one of many in the outer wall, whose face fell vertically from a dizzying height to the rocky flank of the mount. In the next room there was a smaller window. It would do.

He raised his eyes to the distance. Fornells was in plain sight, and shifting to the right he saw the complex of islands and bays that was Addaya. Perfect! He would not be seen while he did the observations and the signalling—it was all very possible.

Isabella brought the cook forward. "Mr Keed, this José." He shook hands, aware of a shrewd look.

"What do we do now, Mr Keed?" The door was thick and had bolts but if they were discovered in their nefarious activity there could be no exit through the window—they would be trapped.

"My spyglass." It was covered in sacking at the bottom of a washing basket. He went to the window and settled down with a chair. To seaward there was a bright haze; this would conceal the approach of the fleet until it was about five miles offshore. He hauled out Renzi's watch: in only an hour or so there would be sudden alarm and dismay as the rumours of an English fleet took on an awful reality.

He must work fast. Methodically he quartered the country along each side of the narrow Bay of Fornells. On one side of the entrance there was a medium-sized fort and on the other a town. An army encampment was easy to see, the regularity of the tents, the glitter of equipment and even a caterpillar of men drilling. He located and traced the road away from the base: this would be the avenue for reinforcement or retreat.

Then he switched his glass to Addaya where he saw little military activity; there seemed to be nothing but small fortifications and only one concentration of soldiery. He searched for and found the connecting road. Finally, he carefully scanned the countryside round and about for any evidence of defences in depth. As far as a sharp seaman's eye could tell there was none of significance.

As he had feared, most troops appeared to be at Fornells, and would cause grievous damage to the landing. There were some at Addaya but not enough to indicate that they considered a landing there to be in prospect. Tensely, he settled down to wait.

Less than half an hour later a trumpet sounded urgently outside. José started and hissed at Isabella. "They call th' soldier to arms," she told Kydd.

Kydd lifted his glass seaward, but the bright haze lay uninterrupted in all directions. He searched in other directions, then realised it was probably Fornells signalling the approach of a hostile fleet, which he could not yet see in the haze.

Kydd waited, his glass trained out to sea, until his heart

skipped a beat as the gossamer shapes of first one then several ships appeared close-hauled and standing steadily towards Fornells. The two 74s led the fleet; further out he saw the frigates and in the far distance the transports. There would be English soldiers aboard who, before the day was out, might owe their lives to Kydd's actions in the next few minutes.

"Isabella, bring y'r washing." He had just rigged an endless loop of washing-line passing out of one window and in the next.

"I'll have th' red shirt, y'r lady's shawl an' the pantaloons, if y' please." A deft twist to form two bights, and a clove hitch secured the shirt first by one corner and then spaced to the other. The shawl and pantaloons followed, then Kydd hauled on his "halliard." The washing disappeared out of the window to hang innocently suspended along the wall outside.

He grabbed his glass and stared at *Leviathan*'s mizzen peak until his eyes watered. Had Bowden reached the flagship in time? Did they believe his improbable story? Minutes dragged.

There it was! The answering pennant hoisted close up. Feverishly, Kydd hauled once more on his horizontal halliard to rotate the clothing inside, around and out again, the "signal" repeated. The answering pennant whipped down—he had been seen. Near delirious with excitement he focused on what was next: "troops are concentrated at Fornells." "M' dear, I'll trouble you for th' black bodice an' that fetching yellow skirt."

The flagship's quarterdeck was tense and silent. Ahead was the enemy coast, the narrow entrance of Fornells Bay dominated by a fortress with a huge Spanish flag flying defiantly. A single massive peak was visible inland, with a monastery or some such squarely on the summit.

Duckworth stood with General Stuart, their expressions grim. A gun from the fortress thudded defiance, the sound and gunsmoke telling of a great thirty-six-pounder or more.

The signal lieutenant of *Leviathan* clattered down from the poop and saluted. "Sir! We have signals established from shore."

"Thank God," said Stuart. "What do they say? Quickly, man!"

"Er, at the moment, only that they have correctly authenticated."

"Then tell me when you receive anything useful."

The lieutenant returned to his post but was back just as quickly. "Sir, signal received: 'enemy troops concentrated at Fornells.'"

"Can we trust this?" demanded Stuart. "It would mean postponing the assault, and that I'm not prepared to do—"

"Another signal, sir: 'negative,' and 'troops concentrated at Addaya.'"

"No formations at Addaya? That will do. How far to Addaya from here, Commodore?"

"But four miles. Say, an hour's sail."

"We land at Addaya as provided for."

It was hard for Kydd, watching a battle unfold yet having such a restricted role of activity.

"They take no notice!" wailed Isabella. It was true: far from moving away from Fornells the two bigger ships moved closer, followed by others.

Kydd's heart sank. Then, in the flat image of his telescope, he saw activity at the rear of the fleet. Ships were hauling their wind to the other tack, moving back out to sea.

Inland he saw a line of dust arising. He focused on it: it was a column of soldiers marching fast on the road to Fornells. "Bella, quick—th' apron and that small curtain!" It would read, "reinforcements marching on Fornells."

He took up his glass—and his heart leaped: they had not misread his signals. The ships at the rear were the transports, the soldiers, and they were heading to Addaya while the warships in the van made a feint against Fornells to draw forces there.

It was all unfolding to those who had eyes to see it: some ships advanced on the fortress, others disappeared into the haze to re-appear suddenly off the rock-strewn entrance to Addaya. Boats hit the water and through his glass Kydd saw them pass between two low islands and head for the shore. One or two scattered guns opened fire but two frigates were in position and, over the heads of the boats, thundered in their broadsides. There was no further firing.

Kydd pounded his fist with glee and swung his telescope back to Fornells. There was chaos in the town—no doubt news had reached them of the landings in Addaya. It gave him a piquant thrill to think that while the signal station above them was frantically passing the dread news, his own signals beneath were having their contrary effect.

What was more significant were the soldiers now pouring out of the fort and flooding down the road. Where were they going? Were they reinforcements for Addaya? Whatever, this called for a "negative" and "heading for Fornells" and Kydd briskly plied his red shirt, the bodice again and a woman's shift.

When this had been completed he turned his attention back to Addaya. The experienced Highlanders had stormed ashore and he could catch the glint of their bayonets as they spread out in the brush. They were not meeting much resistance and Kydd saw why: the rough road away was streaming with soldiers in disorder—they were falling back, not prepared to be cut off in a heroic last stand. That would be a definite "negative," "troops at Addaya," then.

Now the road from Fornells was streaming with men moving away—no question that these were reinforcements for Addaya: this was a "negative," then "troops at Fornells," and suddenly Kydd realised his job was done.

. . .

"Sir—they're abandoning Fornells."

"Or reinforcing Addaya." Stuart was not to be stampeded. The landings at Addaya appeared to be well in hand—Duckworth had a repeating frigate relaying news from there—but there was every reason to expect the Spanish to throw everything into a savage counter-attack.

The signal lieutenant reported once more: "Sir, they're on the retreat from Addaya." Stuart harrumphed and stalked up and down, but there was no mistaking his look of triumph.

Commodore Duckworth, however, was not so easily satisfied. He left the general, moved to the lee side of the quarterdeck and called the signal lieutenant to him. "This is damned irregular, sir! I have not seen you refer once to your signal book and all the time you're advisin' the general of the conduct of the war. Where is this shore station you say is passin' the signals?"

"Er, I think Mr Midshipman Bowden can answer to your satisfaction, sir."

Bowden touched his hat respectfully and explained: "Mr Kydd found it impractical to rig a mast and halliards ashore, sir, but conceived of a private code. If you'd take the telescope and spy out the top of Mount Toro—yes, sir, more to the top of the outside wall at the end—there you'll see his last hoist."

"I see a Spanish signal mast, none else."

"If you'd look a little lower, you'll find hanging out the three-flag hoist, 'negative,' 'at Addaya.'"

"I see nothing of the sort! Only . . ."

"Yes, sir. A red Minorquin shawl, a black bodice and a blue pair of men's pantaloons."

"Explain, damn you, sir!"

"Mr Kydd reasoned that everything the general had to know could be sent by two significations, the first, location, being one of

Fornells, Addaya or Mercadal, the other to be the military event, being one of marching towards, or massing at, the location. It requires then only a 'negative' prefix to reverse the meaning and the code is complete."

"And the flags?"

"We could not use our flags. It would have alerted the Spanish. And, as you can see, sir, the distance is too great to make out detail. Therefore he used colours: in this way he could make use of anything, as long as the colour could be distinguished. Red for 'negative,' white for 'marching towards,' blue for 'Addaya.'"

"Yes, yes, I see. Most ingenious. Hmm—I look forward to making further acquaintance of Lieutenant Kydd."

From his eyrie Kydd watched marines make their way ashore in Fornells; they would take possession of the forts and the English would be established irrevocably ashore. It was certain to be victory—and he had played a central part in it. With a welling of contentment he raised the spyglass again to watch the consolidation at Addaya.

"We must go," Isabella said, distracted.

Kydd could not tear himself from his grand view, and the thought of another night in a dank cave was not appealing. He remembered that the next planned move was a march on Mercadal close by. If the English forces had reached so far already then it was more than probable they would reach the town and Monte Toro the next day.

He would sit it out where he was. "Isabella—if y' understands—I'd like t' see how it ends. Can y' ask José if I could stay here tonight?"

She left in tears of emotion and Kydd resumed his vigil at his spyglass. More men landed at Fornells; with a tug of pride, Kydd saw seamen rig lines ashore to land artillery pieces. Once there, they passed drag-lines and began man-hauling the guns along the roads inland. The end could not possibly be in doubt.

*"Brindemos por la victoria!"* José's affable toast came as he handed Kydd a glass of Xoriguer.

"Thank ye—whatever y' said! Must say, sir, this is a rare drop. Y' good self, Mr José!"

"Who the devil—?" stuttered Colonel Paget, in command of the approaching troops. Kydd was wearing his begrimed uniform recovered from the cave, without cocked hat and sword.

"L'tenant Kydd, HMS *Tenacious,* y'r duty, sir. I make apology f'r my appearance."

"As you should, sir," the colonel replied, eyeing Kydd askance. "And may I know why you are not on your ship?"

"Sir?"

"The Spanish fleet at sea and not you? Hey? Hey?"

"Sir, I've spent several days behind th' Spanish lines an' have not had news. I'd be obliged if you'd confide th' progress of the landing."

"I see. Well, sir, be assured we're rolling up their rearguard in fine style and have this hour taken Mercadal. The Spanish are retiring on Ciudadela—General Stuart is in pursuit but has required me to take a fast column to lay against Port Mahon. I am at this moment at the business of forming it up."

"The Spanish fleet, sir?"

"Yes, yes," Paget said testily. "It seems they were sighted falling on us from the west and the commodore took all his ships to sea to meet 'em. There's none still here, Mr Kydd."

Kydd ground his teeth and cursed his luck. That morning while he had been cautiously making contact with the advancing soldiers *Tenacious* was now possibly in a climactic battle that would decide the fate of Minorca. If this was the Cartagena fleet they were in serious trouble.

"Sir, what ships were sighted?" Kydd asked urgently.

"Dammit—five, six big ones, I don't remember," the colonel said, clearly tiring of the exchange.

For Kydd it was mortifying news—and left him stranded with no way to rejoin his ship. But he could not stand idly by while others went on to face the enemy. "Sir, I do offer m' services to ye. Mahon has a dockyard an' big harbour and it would be very strange if there weren't any ships there. I could help ye secure 'em as prizes."

Paget raised his eyebrows. "And, no doubt, put yourself in the way of some prize-money." Kydd bristled but Paget went on genially, "But you're in the right of it, sir—I'll need someone who knows the ropes to make sure the dons don't set the dockyard afire or any other foolishness. Right, sir. Your offer is handsomely accepted. Do ask the quartermaster for something a little more fitting for an officer, if you catch my meaning. We move off at dawn."

In a startling mix of buff army breeches, a navy lieutenant's coat and an infantry cocked hat, Kydd went out to meet the seamen just arriving after man-hauling the guns overland. The pieces would soon be finding employment in laying siege to the walled town of Ciudadela.

"Good Lord above! Of what species of warrior are you, sir?" said the young naval lieutenant in charge of them.

"Why, in th' uniform t' be expected of the officer-in-charge o' the naval detachment in the assault on Port Mahon," Kydd said loftily.

"Naval detachment?" the man said, puzzled.

"Yes. I mean t' press half a hundred of y'r men, if y' please." A quick glance told him that at fifty men each on the dozen or so guns there were more than five hundred in all, probably contributed evenly by each ship in the squadron including his own: they could spare a tenth of their number.

"Press my men!" the lieutenant stared in amazement and began to laugh. At Kydd's glare his mirth tailed away.

"We must secure th' dockyard, board all ships in harbour and attend t' any prisoners," Kydd said, in a hard voice. "I don't think fifty men overmuch f'r the task, d' you?"

He looked past the officer at the weary men coiling down the drag-lines, pulling off encamping kit and flexing tired muscles. He strode over to them, leaving the lieutenant to hurry along behind. "I say, this is out of order, sir! You may not—"

"If I have t' ask th' colonel he'll make it a hundred," Kydd snapped, without looking back. He had spotted Dobbie from *Tenacious*.

The stocky seaman's face creased with pleasure as Kydd went up to him. "Sir! Never thought ter see yez again, goin' ashore with them dagoes."

"Dobbie—I want fifty good men f'r particular service in Mahon. Seamen I must have, knows the difference between a buntline and a bobstay an' can be relied on in a fight."

"Aye aye, sir."

"Have 'em mustered here for me in an hour."

There was one further matter he had to attend to. There was every prospect of his meeting the enemy on the morrow and the quartermaster had offered him the loan of a heavy sabre or a token small-sword, but neither appealed. He went to an arms chest on the limber of one gun and helped himself to a cutlass; this would be of use only in close quarters fighting, but a defensive action was all that he expected for the seamen. It was not the fine sword he had now grown used to, but the heft and balance of the plain black weapon was familiar and pleasing, and he slipped the scabbard into its frog, settling it comfortably on his belt.

Later that night, after he had seen to his men, Kydd dined

with the officers in their mess-tent. It was both strange and comforting. The singular appearance of the red check tartan of a regiment of Highlanders, with their arcane mess rituals and free-flowing whisky, was another world to the ordered uniformity of a naval wardroom. But the loyal toast was sturdily proposed and the same warmth of brotherhood reached out to Kydd. "Give ye joy of y'r victory, sir," Kydd acknowledged to the army captain sitting to his side.

The officer raised an eyebrow. "You think so?"

"Why, yes! I know nothing of y'r military affairs but t' land and take a town seems t' me to be a fine thing for such numbers."

The captain examined his whisky, holding it to the light so the glass twinkled prettily. "It was fine done the landing, I'll grant—but the general must have had inside intelligence to change the place of landing at such notice. Quite took the dons on the hop."

Kydd glowed, but now was not the time to claim recognition.

"But then I don't envy Quesada—an impossible task, I'd say."

"Quesada?"

"Their commander. One can feel pity for the man. His soldiery has rotted from too much garrison duty and they're near useless. And reinforcements? All he got before you fellows cleared the seas of 'em was a couple of battalions of Swiss."

"The Swiss?" Kydd was hazily aware of the tangled complexity of allegiances in Europe but had not heard they were at war with Switzerland.

"Yes, German-Swiss mercenaries. Austrians took 'em prisoner, then sold them to the Spanish for two thaler a head. Not my idea of a bargain. When we landed at Addaya they were opposing us. Then your frigate let fly a broadside or two and in twenty minutes they broke and ran."

"Still runnin'?" Kydd chuckled.

"In fact, no. We took a hundred deserters and told 'em that if they could bring in their friends we'd see them right in the matter of employment. Gen'l Stuart is thinking of forming up a foreign corps of some sort, and now we have the lot—a thousand and more."

Kydd agreed. With rabble like that Quesada could do nothing to stop the English. Then he remembered, with sudden apprehension: "Did ye see the Spanish fleet at all? If we're beat at sea . . ."

"The fleet? I'm not sure about that. I did catch a sight of the Spanish, but they weren't your big fellows, only one line of guns." Frigates, realised Kydd, with jubilation.

"And last I saw of 'em was the gallant commodore haring off over the horizon, tally-ho, after them with all flags flying."

Kydd grinned. "So *we* c'n sleep tight tonight but y'r Gen'ral Quesada has a mort t' reflect on."

"He has. Without command of the sea of any kind he can't get supplies or reinforcements, nothing. And he'll never get the Minorcans to fight for him."

"So ye'd say we've won?" Kydd said cautiously.

"By no means. Quesada is off with the bulk of his troops to Ciudadela—their major town with city walls and fortifications. A siege will be a tedious thing with no certainty at the end of it. And tomorrow we march on Mahon, which is even more heavily fortified. While we hold the country, Quesada will hold the towns—and we can't wait for ever."

It was another kind of war but in the warmth of the evening's cordiality it seemed far removed. Yet here he was, enjoying the regiment's hospitality not only in the middle of enemy country but presumably on a battlefield with enemy soldiers perhaps creeping through the night.

"What's out there? I mean, what's to stop th' Spanish coming suddenly while we're enjoyin' our supper?" Kydd did not mean it to come out so nervously but he preferred the direct ship-to-ship fighting at sea where the foe was visible rather than the uncertainties of land.

"Well, armies don't fight at night as a rule," the officer said, with only the glimmer of a smile. "But if the Spanish see fit to counter-attack in the dark—presuming they have precise knowledge of our position—then first they must find a way to get past our vedettes and outer pickets before our sentinels can take alarm, but even then you may sleep soundly, I believe."

The brass baying of trumpets woke Kydd. Before he had struggled into his clothes the stillness was rent by hoarse cries of sergeants and shouts of command from impatient officers as the camp came to life. First light appeared as the soldiers bolted down their breakfast and prepared for the march, buckling on equipment and loosening limbs.

The damp smoke of breakfast fires still hung about in the greyness of the pre-dawn as Kydd drew up his men to address them. "I'm L'tenant Kydd, and this is th' Port Mahon naval detachment. You're not going t' pull the guns any more—but you are going t' march. This is what th' lobsterbacks call a 'flying column,' which is to say we're going to move *fast*. We're heading f'r Port Mahon, an' there we'll find a harbour and dockyard fit f'r the whole o' Nelson's fleet. But only if we take it from them—there could be quite a deal o' fighting before we're done, but I've got no doubts about that with English hearts of oak by m' side."

His hand dropped unconsciously to his cutlass hilt as he continued, "We're not here t' do the assault. That'll be the lobsterbacks' job, an' they're good at it. What we'll be doing is t' wait until they've got a breach and marched into the town. Then we'll follow and go to the harbour an' set about any shipping we find—not forgettin' the dockyard, that the Spanish don't start fire-raisin' there."

He regarded the men dispassionately. Lithe, intelligent, these were the skilled seamen who were achieving more at sea than any before them and he felt a deep pride. "So we'll be on our way—this is Kane's highway to Mahon an' it was laid by us eighty years ago. Now let's use it!"

But they had to stand aside as the professionals formed up. Scouts clattered off ahead into the early morning and others fanned out to each side of the line-of-march. Yet more galloped urgently backwards and forwards for some arcane military reason. Finally, officers on splendid horses took their place at the head of their men and with a squeal and drone of bagpipes skirling and the rattle and thump of drums the column set off.

Kydd had refused a horse, feeling unable to ride while his men marched, but after the first hour he regretted the decision. It was good to swing along to the stirring music, seeing the soldiers moving ahead economically and fast but he was unused to the discipline of the march and felt increasingly sore.

After five miles they reached the small market town of Alayor. The inhabitants watched them pass, some with grave expressions, others fearful. On the far side they stopped for fifteen minutes' rest. The soldiers joked and relaxed, some not even bothering to sit, but the sailors squatted or sat in the dust.

A cheerful sun was abroad when they got under way once more; there were no disturbances or threats of attack and after another five miles in a countryside of sinister quiet they were pressing close to Port Mahon. A halt was called while the town was still hidden in the low hills ahead, orange orchards and neat garden plots betraying its proximity.

But there was no sign of the enemy. Could it be that they were lying concealed, waiting for the whole column to enter before springing their ambush? The soldiers did not appear unduly concerned, and Kydd reasoned that as the detachment was only about three hundred strong, it was more a reconnaissance in force than an assault and could withdraw at any time. His worries subsided.

Then his mind supplied a new concern: was the main body for the real assault approaching from another direction? The anxieties returned—not that he had any doubts about his courage, but as an officer of rank what would be expected of him should the army "beat to quarters"? He forced his eyes closed.

"Sir."

Kydd opened his eyes and saw a youthful subaltern saluting him in the odd army fashion with the palm outwards.

"Colonel Paget desires you should wait on him."

At the head of the column Paget was at the centre of an animated group of officers, each apparently with a personal view on recent events. Kydd took off his hat and waited for attention.

"Ah, Mr Kydd. Developments." He looked distracted and barely glanced at Kydd. "Scouts have returned, they report that the Spanish in Mahon want to parley."

"Sir?" It could mean anything from abject surrender to an ultimatum—or a Spanish trick, Kydd told himself, to control his sudden rush of excitement.

"I'm inclined to take it at face value. I shall go forward under flag o' truce and see what they want. I should be obliged if you would accompany me in case they try any knavish tricks concerning sea matters." He glanced at Kydd. "Kindly remain silent during the proceedings unless you perceive anything untoward at which you will inform me, never addressing the enemy. Do you understand?"

"Aye aye, sir."

Paget heaved himself up on his horse, which was patiently held by a soldier. "And get this man a horse, for God's sake," he threw at an officer, as he looked down on Kydd's rumpled, dusty appearance.

The little group of officers walked their horses down the road, preceded by a mounted trooper holding a pennon with a vast white flag attached. Ahead, in the distance, a blob of white appeared, resolving by degrees into a group, which to Kydd looked distinctly non-military.

"Halt!" A trumpeter dismounted and marched smartly to the exact point of equidistance and sounded off an elaborate call. There was movement among the figures opposite but no inclination to treat that Kydd could discern.

They waited in the sun: Kydd could hear Paget swearing under his breath, his horse impatiently picking at the ground with his hoof. At length there was a general advance of the whole mass towards them.

"What the devil!" Paget exploded. "Stand your ground!" he roared back over his shoulder to his officers.

It was apparent that any military component of the Spanish group was conspicuous only by its absence. The florid garments and general demeanour of the leading members seemed more municipal than statesmanlike as they nervously approached. "Tell 'em that's far enough," Paget told an aide.

"*Ni un paso más!*" The group stopped, but a man stepped forward uneasily with an old-fashioned frilly tricorne in his hands. Words were spoken and the man regarded Paget with a look that was half truculent, half pleading.

"Sir, this is Antonio Andreu, *alcalde* of the councillors of Mahon. He wishes you a good day."

"Dammit! Tell him who I am, and say I'm expecting three more battalions to arrive by the other road presently."

"He desires to know if there is produce of the land that perhaps he can offer, that you have come such a long way—red wine, olives, some oranges."

"Also tell him that our siege train arrives by sea tonight, and before dawn Mahon will be held within a ring of iron standing ready to pound his town to dust and rubble."

"Mr Andreu mentions that Minorca is famed for its shoes and leather harnesses, which we English will have remembered from the past—I believe he is talking about our last occupation, sir."

"What does the man want, for God's sake? Ask him!"

"Sir," said the lieutenant, very carefully, "on behalf of the citizens of Port Mahon he wishes to surrender."

"He what?" Paget choked.

Andreu's face was pale. He spoke briefly, then handed up a polished box. "He offers up the keys to Mahon, sir, but deeply regrets that he is not certain of the ceremonial form of a capitulation and apologises profoundly for any unintended slight."

Taking a deep breath, Paget turned to his adjutant. "I can't take a surrender from a parcel o' tradesmen."

"Sir, it might be considered churlish to refuse."

"They haven't even got a flag we can haul down. There are forms an' conventions, dammit."

"An expression of submission on their part, sir? Purely for form's sake . . ."

"Tell 'em—tell 'em this minute they're to give three hearty hurrahs for King George."

"They say, sir—er, they say . . ."

"And what do they say, sir?"

"And then may they go home?"

At the head of his seamen Kydd moved through the town. They padded down to the waterfront, past gaping women leaning from windows and curious knots of townsfolk at street corners. Most were silent but some dared cheers at the sight of the English sailors.

The dockyard was deserted: there was a brig under construction but little other shipping. That left only the boom, set across the harbour further along. Helpful townsfolk pointed it out, then found them the capstans to operate it.

There was little else that Kydd could think to do. It was a magnificent harbour with its unusual deep cleft of water between the heights where the main town appeared to be. It was long and spacious, its entrance flanked by forts. Out to sea were the men-o'-war of the Royal Navy.

Once more the two frigates put about and beat upwind outside the harbour. The Spanish flag flew high over the forts that made the harbour impregnable to external threat. The army was going to have a hard time when it came to the siege.

"Boat putting off—flag o' truce, sir."

The captain of HMS *Aurora* held up his hand to acknowledge. It was a rare sight, as the blockade around Minorca was as tight as could possibly be. Still, the diversion from duty would be welcome. "Heave to, if you please."

Under sail out in the open sea the boat made heavy weather of it but came on stubbornly in sheets of spray. As it neared he could see only a few figures in it. It was one of the straight-stemmed Minorcan *llauds* that he had seen fishing here. The boat rounded to, the soaring lateen sail brailed up expertly as it came lightly to leeward.

"*Aurora,* ahoy! Permission t' come aboard!" hailed the deep-tanned figure at the tiller in a quarterdeck bellow, to the great surprise of the frigate's company agreeably passing time in watching the exchange.

"One to come aboard, Bosun."

The boat nuzzled gently against the ship's side and the figure sprang neatly for the side-ropes and pulled himself aboard, correctly doffing his hat first to the quarterdeck and then to the captain.

He was a striking character. Strong in the frame and attractively open in the face, he was nevertheless in a wildly inappropriate mix of English army and navy uniform—a Spanish ruse? "L'tenant Kydd, sir. Late o' the Port Mahon naval detachment t' Colonel Paget." His English was faultless if individual.

"What may we do for you, Lieutenant?" the captain of *Aurora* said carefully.

"Sir, Colonel Paget desires y' should not fire on th' Spaniards on any account, but that ye proceed into harbour without delay."

"I see. I should sail my frigate under the guns of the fortress yonder, and forget the presence of the boom across to the Lazareto?"

"Oh, pay no mind t' the boom, sir. We've just triced it in this hour."

"Are you not forgetting something, Lieutenant?"

"Sir?"

"That fortress flies the Spanish flag, which I have observed unchanged these three days."

"Ah—I should explain. Colonel Paget came upon the town, which surrendered a little precipitate before they could fin' a military man. Y'r flag flies above Fort San Felipe where the only soldiers are t' be found. The fort is in ruins, havin' been demolished by the Spaniards t' discommode us but the soldiers say they won't surrender until they've found the king's lieutenant and get a proper ceremony.

"Meanwhile, sir, we have the possession and occupation o' the whole port. If ye'd kindly sail upon Mahon directly the colonel will be obliged—he is anxious to make inventory of the ships and stores that have fallen into our hands."

# Chapter 9

The ordered calm and routine aboard HMS *Tenacious* was a welcome reassurance of normality and Kydd paced the decks with satisfaction. His ship was now moored inside the deep emerald harbour of Port Mahon with the rest of the fleet; watering parties were ashore in Cala Figuera.

Kydd contemplated the prospect of an agreeable summons from the commodore in the near future. It had been an extraordinary achievement—the entire island was now in English hands, from the time of landing to capitulation no more than a week, on their side without any loss. And he had played what must surely be seen as a central part in the success.

"Sir, if y' please . . ." One of the smaller midshipmen tugged at his sleeve.

He turned, frowning at the impropriety, then softening at the boy's anxiety to please. "Aye?"

"Mate o' the watch sends his duty an' the commodore would be obliged should you spare him an hour."

"Thank ye," said Kydd, a little surprised at the informality. He had been expecting something of a rather more public character, but supposed that this was preparatory only. After all, while this was a commodore he did not have the standing and powers of a full admiral. Any form of honours would have to come from the commander-in-chief, Admiral Nelson, still in Naples. His heart beat faster.

After reporting to Captain Faulkner in full dress uniform, as befitting a visit to the flag-officer, he was stroked across to *Leviathan* in the gig, thinking warmly that life could not be bettered at that moment. The day before, he had come back aboard and spent an uproarious evening in the wardroom telling of his adventure, being heartily toasted in the warmth of deep camaraderie. Now, dare he think it, he had been noticed and therefore was on the golden ladder of preferment and success. His instinct had been right—Nelson was showing the way. Seize the moment when it came!

He was politely received by a flag-lieutenant and conducted to the commodore in his great cabin. "Ah, Kydd. Sit ye down, I won't be long," Duckworth said, waving Kydd to a chair. The commodore was writing, a frown on his open face as he concentrated on the task. He finished with a scrawl and put his pen down with a sigh. "L'tenant Kydd," he said heavily, "I do believe that you should bear much of the credit for the success of this expedition. From what I hear, your initiative and courage did much to secure the safety of the force. Do tell me now what happened."

Kydd began, careful to be exact in his recollections for this would be a matter of record for all time. But as he proceeded he became uneasily aware that he did not have the commodore's full attention. He fiddled with his pen, squared his papers, inspected the back of his hand. Somewhat put out, Kydd completed with a wry account of his boarding of the frigate and told him of the conclusion of hostilities, but the commodore failed to smile.

Duckworth stood. "May I take the hand of a brave man and a fine officer?" he said directly, fixing Kydd in the eye. "I see a bright future for you, sir." Kydd glowed. "Good day to you, Mr Kydd," the commodore said, and took up his papers once more.

Kydd hovered uncertainly. "What is it, Mr Kydd?" the commodore said testily.

"Sir, dare I say it, but should I be mentioned in y'r dispatches, I'd be infinitely obliged if you'd spell m' name with a *y*—Kydd, sir, not like the pirate Kidd." There had been instances of promotion awarded for valour to the wrong officer entirely, which regrettably it was impossible to undo at the Admiralty.

Duckworth leaned back, eyeing Kydd stonily. "The dispatches for this engagement will be written by another. I haul down my flag tomorrow, Mr Kydd."

At a loss, Kydd excused himself and withdrew.

"I would have thought somethin' a bit more rousin'," Kydd said morosely, not sure at all of what had been transacted in the great cabin.

Adams was sympathetic, and put down his book on the wardroom table. They were alone and Kydd had returned disconsolate from what should have been a memorable interview.

"Luck o' the draw, old trout. You'll understand that Duckworth is out of sorts. His mission complete, he has to strike his flag and revert back to plain old captain now."

"But his dispatches—"

"Dispatches? He's not the expedition commander, Tom, Stuart is. And I've strong reason to know from a friend at Headquarters that he's a man to seize all the credit that can be scraped together. His dispatches will say nothing of the navy—all we did was sally out to meet half a dozen Spanish frigates, which instantly put about and had the legs of us. No creditable battle, no mention for anyone."

"I should've smoked it," Kydd said. Stuart was certainly the kind of man to dim another's candle in order that his become the brighter. "So the general won't want th' world to know that he'd got special intelligence as would give him th' confidence to stretch out an' take Minorca?"

"I fear that must be the case," Adams murmured.

"I was present at th' takin' of Port Mahon!" Kydd continued stubbornly.

"Dear chap, any battle won swiftly, efficiently and with the minimum of bloodshed must be a bad battle by any definition. For your triumph and glory you need a good butcher's bill, one that has you blood-soaked but standing defiant at the end, tho' many at your side do fall. And we had the bad luck to lose not a single man . . ."

"You're bein' cynical, I believe."

Adams shrugged.

"Besides, m' name must be mentioned once in high places in the navy, must it not?"

Adams gave a small smile. "I should think not. The successful practice of creeping abroad at night is not an accomplishment that necessarily marks out a future admiral."

As he strolled along in the sun with Renzi on the road to Mahon, Kydd brooded; no doubt there would be other opportunities for dash and initiative but unless a similar conspiracy of circumstances came up how was he to be noticed? Duty was not enough: he must show himself of different timbre from the others.

They had landed below George Town, Es Castell as it was now known. From there it had been a precipitous pathway to the top—the harbour of Port Mahon was a great ravine in a high plateau, opening to a capacious sea cove three miles long. The town of Mahon was perched along the top, the skyline an exotic mix of medieval casements, churches, windmills and several inclined roadways to the water's edge.

A pleasant two miles of open country lay ahead. Wearing plain clothes in deference to the sensibilities of the inhabitants, they passed through Es Castell, a relic of past English occupation, still with its parade-ground four-square in the centre, and found the road west to Mahon.

"So grateful to the spirit," Renzi mused. At sea there was a constant busyness; even in the most placid of days the flurry of waves, the imperceptible susurrus of breeze around the edge of the sails and the many random sounds of a live ship were a constant backdrop to life aboard. It was only on land, where a different quietude reigned, that its absence was noticed.

Kydd's naturally happy temperament bubbled to the surface. "S' many windmills—you'd think it Norfolk or Kent."

"Yet the soil is poor and difficult of cultivation, I think," said Renzi, as they passed tiny garden-like plots and endless dry-stone walls. A little further on the wafting scent of orange groves filled the air. "But there could be compensations . . ."

In front of each white stone farm there was a distinctive gate of charming proportions, an inverted V, probably made from the ubiquitous wild olive wood. The road wound round the end of a deep cleft in the cliffs, a sea cove a quarter of a mile deep with buildings on the flat ground at its head. Kydd recognised it as the chief watering-place, Cala Figuera—English Cove. The English ships, *Tenacious* among them, were clustered there.

Mahon could be seen ahead, past a racket court in use by two rowdy midshipmen, the houses by degrees turning urban and sophisticated. The two nodded pleasantly to local people in their pretty gardens; Kydd wondered how he would feel if conquering officers passed his front door. Nevertheless there was more than one friendly wave.

Several paths and avenues led from the one they were on and it became clear that they needed directions. "Knock on th' door?" Kydd suggested.

After some minutes they heard, "*¿Que quiere?*" A short man wearing round spectacles emerged suspiciously.

"Ah, we are English officers, er, *inglese,*" Kydd tried.

Renzi smiled. "Your Italian does you credit, my friend, but what is more needed now—"

"Goodness gracious me!" Both turned in astonishment at the perfect English. "So soon! But—dare I be as bold—your honourable presence is made more welcome by your absence, these sixteen year."

Kydd blinked. "Er, may we ask if this is th' right road f'r Mahon?"

"Ah! So many years have I not heard this word! Only the English call it *Marn*—the Spanish is *Ma-hon,* but we Minorquin call it *Ma-ó,* you see."

"Then—"

"You are certainly on the highway to *ciudad Maó*—forgive me, it has been many years . . . Sadly, though, you will now find Maó in the comfortable state we call *siesta.*"

He drew himself up. "But, gentlemen, it would be my particular honour to offer you the refreshments of the road."

"You are too kind, sir," Renzi said elegantly, with a bow.

They were soon seated in an enchanting arbour in a small garden at the front of a Mediterranean white house, all set about with myrtle, jasmine and vines and with a splendid view down into the harbour. The man withdrew and they heard shrill female protests overborne with stern male tones before he reappeared.

"My apologies. I am Don Carlos Piña, a merchant of oil of olive."

The officers bowed and introduced themselves. A lady wreathed in smiles appeared with a tray, murmuring a politeness in what Kydd assumed was Mahon-ese. On the tray he recognised Xoriguer and there were sweetmeats that had him reaching out.

"Ah! Those are the *amargos*. If they are too bitter, please to try the *coquinyales* here." Piña spoke to the woman, who coloured with pleasure. "My wife remember what you English like."

The crunchy anisette indeed complemented the gin and lemon cordial but Kydd had to say what was on his mind: "D' ye please tell me, sir, why you are not offended at our bein' here?"

Piña smiled broadly. "Our prosperity is tied to the English—when you left in 'eighty-two our trade suffer so cruel where before we trade with the whole world. Now by chance it will return."

"I'm sure it will," Renzi contributed.

Piña flourished the Xoriguer. "I toast *His Majesty King George*—King George th' Three! I hope he enjoy good health?" he added anxiously.

"He is still our gracious sovereign," Renzi replied.

"Please! Gentlemen, you may toast to the return of Lady Fortune to Minorca!"

Renzi asked earnestly, "Sir, this is such an ancient island. The Moors, Romans, Phoenicians—surely they have left their mark on the land, perhaps curious structures, singular artefacts?"

"There is no end of them," Piña said brightly, "but there are also the *navete* of the Talaiot—before even the Roman, they build boats of stone! No man know what they are. We never go near." He crossed himself fervently, bobbing his head.

"Excellent!" said Renzi.

"And if you are interested in Minorca, good sir, I recommend to your attention the town of Migjorn Gran, in which you will find many learned in the ancient ways of our island."

Kydd put down his glass. "And Maó is not far ahead?"

"I'm delaying you!" Piña said, in consternation. "Before you leave, the *abrazo!*" To Kydd's embarrassment he was seized in an embrace. "So! Now you are for us the *hermanito*, our ver' good friend!"

• • •

Mahon bustled with excitement. It seemed a declaration of open trade was to be gazetted immediately by the English, and merchants scurried to prepare for prosperous times. The dignified but sleepy town was waking up and the purposeful hurry of the population was in marked contrast to Kydd and Renzi's leisured pace.

Noble churches stood among a maze of busy streets; an ancient archway glowered at the top of one, and there were shops of every sort between lofty residence with balconies. Kydd was charmed by the little town, which had in parts an almost English reserve. On impulse, he stopped as they were passing a handicrafts shop. "Nicholas, I'd like t' take something o' Minorca back to m' mother as a remembrance. A piece o' lace?"

They entered the quiet interior of the shop. It took a few seconds for Kydd's eyes to adjust to the gloom after the glare of the sun but then he saw the girl behind the counter. "Er, can I see y' lace—for m' mother . . ." He tailed off, seeing her grave attention.

But she gave a delighted squeal. "You are Engliss? *Que suerte haberte conocido!* I always want to meet an Engliss gentleman, my mother she say—"

"If we are to make the cloisters by angelus we must step out," said Renzi, sharply.

"Cloisters?" said Kydd, distracted.

"We have much yet to admire, brother."

*Tenacious* was first to be warped across the harbour to the dockyard for survey: she had suffered at the Nile with her lighter framing, and a worrying increase in bilge pumping was possibly the result of a shot taken between wind and water.

It did not take long to find the cause: two balls landing not far apart below the waterline had damaged a run of several strakes.

They would have to be replaced. With the ship canted to one side by capstans to expose her lower hull she was barely inhabitable and, with the prospect of possibly months at the dockyard, her officers quickly realised that lodgings ashore would be much more agreeable. The best location was evident: Carrer San Roc in the centre of Mahon, where fine town-houses in the English style were to be readily engaged.

A small but comfortable establishment with quaint furniture from the reign of one of the previous Georges met the bill, and Kydd and Renzi moved in without delay. It was a capital headquarters for further exploration of the island.

Renzi laid down his *Reflections on the Culture and Antiquity of Iberia*. "It is said that the western Ciudadela is of quite another character," he mused, nursing his brandy. "Suffered cruelly from the Turks but still retains splendid edifices—but the people are of the Castilian Spanish and have no love for an Englishman."

Kydd picked up a dog-eared newspaper and settled into his high-backed chair. "An' I heard fr'm one o' the midshipmen that t' take away a boat and sail around the island would be prime—there's snug coves an' beaches all up the coast."

"Where, then, is your warlike ardour, your lofty aspirations to laurels?"

"With our ship in dock? Little chance t' find such . . . but there are compensations," Kydd said, with a private smile and raised his paper again.

"Oh?" Renzi said.

"Nicholas, I saw *Love's Labour's Lost* is t' be staged tonight. Do ye fancy t' attend at all?"

"Well, if we—"

"Unfortunately the captain wants t' sight m' journals, I must complete 'em. But do go y'self, I beg!"

"Actually, this volume is an engrossing account of your

Hispanic in all his glory. I rather fancy I shall spend a quiet evening here."

"Nicholas, m' friend, you will do y'r eyes a grievous injury with all this readin'. In th' big church they're presentin' a concert o' music especially t' welcome the English. Why not go an' enjoy this? There's all y'r favourite composers, er, Pergylasy and—"

"I see I must," Renzi said flatly, and Kydd coloured. Later, leaving for the concert, he nearly collided with someone walking in haste. He had last seen her at the lace counter.

Kydd had to admit the forced idleness was not altogether an imposition. He was seated at a table in a small *taberna* with Renzi, enjoying a good bottle of red wine and the fine view from their position at the top of the cliff-like edge of the town into the glittering emerald length of the harbour. "Y'r good health, Nicholas," he said complacently, raising his glass.

"A most underrated and priceless gift," Renzi murmured, lifting his glass and staring into it.

"Er, wha—?"

"Robust health, in course, brother. Worth more than diamonds and rubies, this can never be bought with coin—it is always a gift from nature to man, which never asks aught in return."

"Just so, Nicholas. But do you mark that barque comin' around th' point? She's English." This was a welcome sight in the Mediterranean that, before Nelson's victory, had been cleared of English flagged vessels. "A merchantman," Kydd said lazily, and pulled out his little spyglass. "Cautious master, fat 'n' comfortable—wonder what she's carryin'."

The vessel went into the wind, brailing up and coming to a standstill. Lines were carried ashore by boat and in one movement the ship was rotated seaward again and brought alongside the landing-place near the customs house, just below where they sat.

Curious, Kydd focused on a colourful group on her after deck. From attentions given they must be passengers, and important ones at that: the brow was quickly in place for their disembarkation before the sailors had even begun snugging down to a good harbour furl.

Something about one of them, however, caught his attention: unconscious cues in the way she walked, the movement of her hands, which he knew so well . . .

"Nicholas—I'd swear . . . It must be!" He jumped to his feet. "I'm goin' down. It's Cecilia!"

A narrow inclined pathway zigzagged to the water and Kydd hurtled down it, then finally emerged on to the busy wharf.

"Cecilia, ahoy!" he shouted, waving furiously, but an open-topped carriage drove away just as he came close.

He stared after it foolishly but a woman's voice behind him squealed, "Thomas! Is that you?" He turned to see his sister flying towards him. "My darling brother!" she said happily, embracing him. When she released him, her eyes were glistening.

"Cec—what are y' doing *here?*"

"We're to establish in Minorca, Thomas. Lord Stanhope is to treat with the Austrians to—But why are *you* here?"

Kydd pointed across the harbour to where the ugly bulk of *Tenacious*'s hull lay on its side. "This is now th' home of the Royal Navy in the Mediterranean, Cec, and *Tenacious* is bein' repaired."

A disgruntled wharfinger touched his hat with one finger. "Where'm they ter take yer baggage, then, miss?"

"Thomas—I have to go. Where can I see you again?"

"An' it's a shillun an hour ter wait for yez." The arms were folded truculently.

"Here, sis." Kydd pulled out one of his new-printed calling cards. "Tonight it's t' be a rout f'r all hands—an' you're invited."

• • •

The evening promised to be a roaring success—other than Renzi, no officer had met Kydd's sister and all were bowled over. He had to admit it, Cecilia was flowering into a real beauty, her strong character now veiled beneath a sophistication learned from attending many social events in her position as companion to Lady Stanhope. But what really got the occasion off to a splendid start was the discovery that Cecilia had been in London when the news of the great battle of the Nile had broken. "Oh, you cannot possibly conceive the noise, the joy! All of London in the streets, dancing, shouting, fireworks—you couldn't think with all the din!

"There were rumours for weeks before, it's true, but you must know we were all in a horrid funk about the French! All we heard was that Admiral Nelson had missed the French fleet and it was taking that dreadful General Buonaparte to land an army on us somewhere—you cannot imagine what a panic!

"Then Captain Capel arrived at the Admiralty with dispatches and the town went mad. Every house in masses of illuminations, bells ringing, cannon going off, Lady Spencer capering in Admiralty House, the volunteers drilling in Horseguards firing off their muskets—I can't tell you how exciting it was."

Under the soft touch of the candlelight her flushed cheeks and sparkling eyes hushed the room and had many an officer looking thoughtful.

"Lord Stanhope would not be denied and we left England immediately for Gibraltar, for he had instructions to establish in the Mediterranean as soon as it was practical. It wasn't long before we heard that Minorca was taken—and so here we are!"

"And right welcome y' are, Cec—ain't that so, Nicholas?"

His friend sat back, but his eyes were fixed on Cecilia's as he murmured an elegant politeness. She smiled sweetly and continued gaily, "Thomas, really, it was quite incredible—in every village we passed they had an ox roast and such quantities of people supping ale and dancing on the green. In the towns they had special illuminations like a big 'HN' or an anchor in lights and several times we were stopped until we'd sung 'Rule Britannia' twice!"

It was strangely moving to hear of the effect of their victory in his far-distant home country. "So, Jack Tar is well esteemed now, sis," Kydd said lightly.

Cecilia looked at him proudly. "You're our heroes now," she said. "Our heroes of the Nile! You're famous—all of you! They're rising and singing in your honour in all the theatres. There's poetry, ballads, broadsheets, prints—there's talk that Admiral Nelson will be made a duke and that every man will get a medal. There's been nothing like it this age, I swear."

Kydd hurried into their drawing room. "Nicholas! We've been noticed, m' friend. This card is fr'm the Lord Stanhope, expressin' his earnest desire t' hear of the famous victory at th' first hand—that's us, I believe—at afternoon tea at the Residency on Friday."

"So, if this is a species of invitation, dear chap, then it follows that it should contain details of our expected attire, the—"

"An' here's a note from Cecilia. She says Lady Stanhope will be much gratified should we attend in full dress uniform . . ."

It was odd, on the appointed day, to leave their front door and simply by crossing the road and walking to the end of the street to be able to present themselves at the door of Lord Stanhope's discreet mansion, such was the consequence of the English propensity to stay together.

"Lieutenants Kydd and Renzi," Kydd told the footman. It seemed that the noble lord could afford English domestic staff—but then he remembered that Stanhope was in the diplomatic line and probably needed to ensure discretion in his affairs.

They entered a wide hallway where another servant took their cocked hats. Kydd was awed by the gold filigree on the furniture, the huge vases, the rich hangings—all spoke of an ease with wealth that seemed so natural to the high-born. He glanced at Renzi, who came of these orders, but saw that his friend had a withdrawn, preoccupied look.

They moved on down the passage. "My dear sea-heroes both!" Cecilia was in an ivory dress, in the new high-waisted fashion—which gave startling prominence to her bosom, Kydd saw with alarm.

They entered a drawing room and Kydd met, for the first time since very different circumstances in the Caribbean, the Lord Stanhope and his wife. He made a leg as elegantly as he could, aware of Renzi beside him.

"Dear Mr Kydd, how enchanting to meet you again." The last time Lady Stanhope had seen him was in the Caribbean—as a young seaman in charge of a ship's boat in a desperate bid to get vital intelligence to the British government. *Seaflower* cutter, in which the Stanhopes had been travelling, was beached ashore after a storm. Lord Stanhope, although injured, could not wait for rescue and Kydd had volunteered to take to sea in the tiny vessel.

"Your servant," Kydd said, with growing confidence, matching his bow to the occasion.

"And Mr Renzi. Pray do take some tea. Cecilia?"

The formalities complete, they sat down. Kydd manoeuvred his delicate porcelain cup manfully, privately reflecting on the tyranny of politeness that was obliging him to drink from a receptacle of such ridiculous size.

"Now, you must know we are beside ourselves with anticipation to hear of Nelson and his glorious triumph. Do please tell us—did you meet Sir Horatio himself?"

Suddenly shy, Kydd looked to Renzi, but his friend gave no

sign of wishing to lead the conversation. He remained reserved and watchful.

"Aye, I did—twice! He spoke t' us of our duty and . . ." It was easy to go from there to the storm, the long-drawn-out chase, the final sighting and the great battle itself. At that point he saw Cecilia's intense interest and felt awkward, but again Renzi seemed oddly introspective and offered no help. He therefore sketched the main events of the contest and concluded his account with the awesome sight that had met their eyes on the dawn, and their rapturous welcome at Naples.

"Well, I do declare! This will all be talked about for ages to come, there can be no doubt about it. Pray, where is Sir Horatio at the moment? Is he not with the fleet here?"

"No, y'r ladyship. He's still in Naples—y' understand, the King o' Naples has been uncommon kind t' us in the matter of fettlin' the ships an' entertaining us after our battle, and . . ." he tailed off as he noticed Stanhope's eyes narrowing suspiciously ". . . he'll probably be with us directly."

He sipped his tea although it was now tepid. His admiral's disposition was no business of his and he could not understand Stanhope's disquiet. Now would be a good time for Renzi to contribute a sage comment on the strategic implications of their victory but, annoyingly, he sat still as a statue, staring into space with unfocused eyes.

"Er, I think it has somethin' to do with the admiral wanting t' rouse 'em up to face the French. An' with the Austrians our, er, friends t' help—not forgettin' that the Queen o' Naples is sister t' the emperor," he added weakly.

"The late emperor," Stanhope corrected automatically, but his frown had deepened and Kydd felt out of his depth.

"Sir, if ye'd be s' kind, can we know how th' news has been received aroun' the world?"

"Certainly." Stanhope's face cleared. "Yet, first, I could not forgive myself were I not at this point to express my deepest satisfaction in your change of fortune. Your conduct in the Caribbean will never be forgotten by me and it must be to the country's great benefit that your resolution and professional skill has been so justly recognised."

Cecilia clasped her hands in smothered glee and Kydd flushed.

"I do also remember your particular friend." He directed a meaningful look at Renzi, whose attention seemed to snap back to the present.

"Indeed, sir." Renzi's distracted look was replaced by urbanity. "I have the liveliest remembrance myself of past days, not all of which have been tranquil." Relieved, Kydd let Renzi continue. "It would seem, however, that we have been attended by a very welcome measure of success that should be a caution to all."

Stanhope smiled grimly. "There are nations who have sought to find common cause with the French. Now they are obliged to gaze upon their great Buonaparte stranded helpless."

"A prime spectacle!" chuckled Kydd. "Do ye think he'll last long?"

"He may flounder about, win a battle or two against the indolent Turks who inhabit that part of the world, but the great sand deserts that ring him about will end his ambitions before long, you can be sure."

Kydd turned to Renzi but his look of distraction had returned. It was not in character and Kydd felt unease, which deepened when Renzi did not appear to have noticed that the talking had stopped.

Cecilia leaned across. "Nicholas, is anything wrong? You're as quiet as a mouse."

Renzi looked at her unhappily. "Er, today I received a letter." He swallowed. "From my mother . . ."

# Chapter 10

Renzi stared into the fire as it crackled and spat, sending sparks spiralling up the inn's chimney. Winter in England was a sad trial after the Mediterranean; he snuggled deeper into his coat and sipped his toddy. His mother's letter, pleading that for her sake he return, had come as a shock. His father was in such a towering rage at his continued absence that he was now making her life unbearable.

In Halifax Renzi had received a letter from his brother Richard, advising him that his brother Henry was trying to have Renzi declared dead so that he could assume the place of eldest son. This had been easily dealt with: Renzi had immediately sent a letter to his father calmly setting out the reasons why he had chosen his term of exile and informing him of his elevation to the quarterdeck as a king's officer.

His father's contemptuous reply had dismissed any justification of conduct based on moral grounds and had demanded he return instantly to answer for his absence. Renzi had decided to face him when *Tenacious* returned to England but his mother's letter had forced the issue.

With the Mediterranean quiet and his ship in the dockyard for some time, there had been no difficulty in securing leave and he had taken passage in a dispatch cutter to Falmouth, then a coach to Exeter and the bleak overland trip to Wiltshire. He was staying overnight in the local inn and had sent ahead for a carriage, knowing that this would serve as warning of his arrival. Tomorrow he would return to Eskdale Hall, the seat of the Laughton family and the Earl of Farndon since King Henry's day.

It had been nearly seven years, and Renzi had changed. Gone was the careless, unthinking man who had dissipated so much of his youth and means on his Grand Tour. And he was no longer the naïve young fellow who had been so shocked by what he had encountered on his return that he had taken the moral course of self-exile for a term of five years. His time on the lower deck of a man-o'-war had shaped him, hardened him. Now he looked at life with a detached, far-seeing regard. There would have to be a reckoning, however, for as eldest son his situation was circumscribed by custom and law. He felt the chill of foreboding.

The long night ended with a cold dawn, and after a frugal breakfast Renzi waited on the benches outside, trying to let the sights and smells of the country enter his soul once more, but the bleakness and mud were depressing.

Eventually the carriage came into view, its gleaming black sides spattered with winter grime. The coachman and footman wore careful, blank faces but the noble family crest on the door seemed accusing. Renzi settled into the cushions—despite everything he could feel himself assuming only too easily the mantle of the high-born, with its habits of hauteur and expectations of deference.

They reached the local village of Noakes Poyle where many of the estate labourers lived. As they clattered through the cramped high street, he caught sight of old shops, the busy market; besmocked agricultural workers respectfully touched their forelocks. All conspired to peel away the years and thrust him back to what he had been.

Out into the country again they turned into a road with an elegant gold-filigreed iron gate. Old Lawrie emerged from the gatehouse, grinning like a boy. "Oi see thee well, Master Nicholas, sir?" he asked. It was the first cheeriness Renzi had experienced since he arrived.

The carriage pulled grittily up the drive, which, flanked by trees, led to the splendour of Eskdale Hall. He could see figures assembling on the front lawn: the servants turning out to mark his homecoming. He forced a composure.

The carriage began its final wide curve towards the house and Renzi found himself searching for familiar faces, friendly looks, then saw his parents standing together at the top of the steps. The carriage swept past the servants and came to a halt. The footman got down and swung out the step. Renzi descended. Amid a deathly hush he went up to greet his mother and father.

His mother was set and pale, her hands clasped in front of her; the ninth Earl of Farndon's granite expression showed no emotion.

"Father," Renzi said formally, extending his hand. It was coldly ignored. Renzi felt the old anger and frustration build but clamped a fierce hold on himself. He bowed politely, then turned to his mother, who stood rigid, staring at him as if he were a ghost. Then he noticed the glitter of tears and went to her, holding her, feeling her fierce embrace, and hearing just one tearing sob before she pulled away and resumed her position next to his father.

For a long moment there was silence, then his father turned on his heel and went inside. His mother reached out and took his hands. "Go to him, Nicholas," she said, her face a mask.

Renzi followed his father into the dark wood-panelled main

study. "Close the door, boy," the earl snapped, and took his seat behind the desk more usually employed for dealing with tenants behind in their rent. Renzi was very aware of how little provocation might set tempers ablaze.

His father barked, "An explanation, if you please, sir."

Renzi took a deep breath. "I find I have nothing to add that I have not set out in my letter, Father."

"Don't feed me that flim-flam about moral duty again," his father roared, his face red, eyes glinting dangerously. "I want to hear why you've seen fit to disappear for years, absenting yourself from your rightful place of duty to—"

"Sir, I've as lively a sense of duty as any—"

"Sir, you're a damned poltroon if you think there's an answer in running away—"

Renzi felt his self-control slip. He had taken to logic and rationality as a means of establishing ascendancy over his own passions and it had served him well—but now he could feel building within him the selfsame passionate anger at his father's obstinacy that had prompted him to leave. "Father, I made my decision by my own lights. Whether right or wrong it was done and cannot now be undone." He forced himself to appear calm. "It were in both our interests to recognise this and address the future instead."

They locked eyes. Then, unexpectedly, his father grunted and said, "Very well. We'll talk more on your future here later."

Renzi got to his feet, but the earl did not. "Go and make your peace with your mother, Nicholas," he said bleakly.

She was waiting in the Blue Room. "Shall we meet the rest of the family, Nicholas?" she said brightly. "They are so looking forward to seeing you." They were assembled in the drawing room, and Renzi was gratified to see Richard, whom he had last seen in very different circumstances in Jamaica where Richard owned a sugar plantation—they exchanged a brotherly grin. Fourteen-year-old Edward had no doubt about a welcome and little Beatrice shyly dropped him a curtsy. A warning glance from his mother prepared him for his next younger brother. "Henry, are you keeping well?"

"Tolerably, tolerably," was all the answer Renzi knew he was going to get from that sullen young man, and he turned back to the others.

"Nicholas, old fellow, we've missed you," Richard said breezily. "Why don't we take a turn round the estate before we dine and see what's changed? You don't mind, Mama?"

As soon as they were out of earshot Richard dropped the jolliness and looked at Renzi keenly. "I hope you don't believe I broke confidences when I told Mother you were safe and well, and had taken to seafaring? She did so grieve after you, Nicholas."

"No, Richard, it was kind in you. I should have considered her more."

"Father was in such a fury when you left—he swore he would whip the hide from you when you returned. Then when you did not, he went into himself, if you understand me. Mama dared not tell him of—of where you were. The shame would have been too much."

Renzi said nothing: his time before the mast had been hard and the experience was burned in his memory, but it was also the first time he had felt truly a man. He had won his place in this world by his own courage, skill and fortitude—and the depth of friendships forged in the teeth of gales and at the cannon's mouth. It was wildly at odds with life ashore and he had lived life to the full. He would never forget it.

As they talked they passed so many things of his childhood remembrance: the high-walled garden, the winding path to the woodland park, the pond where once he had ducked Henry for impudence. So much of his life was rooted here.

• • •

Renzi supposed that he would dress for dinner: his luggage did not cover more than travel clothing. To his wry amusement the odd things he had left here did not fit his now strong, spare figure—his father would have to take him as he was.

The meal began stiffly: no one could ignore the glowering presence of his father at the head of the table, Renzi once more at his right hand. Fortunately, Richard sat opposite and took a wicked delight in teasing out amiable platitudes to the point of absurdity, much to their mother's bafflement and their father's fury, but it eased Renzi's feelings.

Henry sat further down, pale features set, eyes fixed balefully on his elder brother. "So, you conceived it a duty to go on a boat as a common sailor? Then praise be that you have regained your senses and are restored to us."

Renzi half smiled. "It's said that sea air is a sovereign remedy—is this why the King takes the waters at Weymouth? I have found it the most salubrious of all in the world."

Henry smiled thinly. "No doubt of it. Nicholas, do tip us some sea cant—I find excessively droll Jack Tar's way with words. So plain-speaking, as we might say."

"Boys!" Their mother reproved them in much the old way. "Remember where you are. I will not have bickering at the table."

Uncharacteristically, his father had made no contribution, although Renzi had felt his eyes on him. When the cloth was drawn and the brandy made its appearance, he spoke. "You others, get out! I want to speak to Nicholas." Meekly, they followed their mother from the room, leaving the earl and Renzi alone in the candlelight.

Renzi's father drew a candle to him and lit a cigar, puffing until it drew to his satisfaction. Renzi watched, not moving. His brandy remained untouched. "Help yourself, my son," his father rumbled, and pushed the humidor across the table.

"Thank you, sir, but I've lost the habit of late," Renzi said carefully. A cigar-smoking able seaman was such a bizarre concept that, despite the circumstances, he felt a smile tug at his lips.

"Suit yourself, then." He inspected the end of the cigar closely, then opened with the first salvo. "I mean to hear your intentions, sir. You've come to your senses at last and have returned—but I've heard no talk that you plan to take up your place here. You're the eldest and one day Eskdale Hall goes to you—but you've shown no interest in the estate management, tenant rolls, income. How do you expect to run the damned place without you know how?"

The blue cigar smoke spiralled up into the blackness while his father fixed him with a glare of unsettling intensity. "Sir, as a sea officer," Renzi began, "it is not acceptable that I leave the ship without so much as a by-your-leave. There are forms, customs of—"

"Humbug! You're no jack-me-hearty sailor—you're heir to an earldom of England, which you seem to have forgotten. I want you here—now! When is it to be?"

"I—I need time," Renzi said defensively, "to settle my affairs . . ."

"You'll give me a date when you'll present yourself now, sir, not when you see fit."

"Father, I said I needed time. Impatience will add nothing to—"

"Then, dammit, get on with it!"

Their talk did not stop until past midnight.

Renzi knew that he was only delaying the inevitable. Of course he had been aware from childhood that, in the fullness of time, under the rules of primogeniture, he was destined to be an earl and the master of Eskdale Hall. It was natural, it was expected, and he had never devoted much thought to it.

His father had accepted his Grand Tour without a word—the sowing of wild oats was almost expected of him. Then, the swaying body in the barn and the burning shame of witnessing his father's summary dismissal of the broken family's claims had changed him.

His high-minded exile at sea, however, had had unforeseen results. Apart from the insights into human nature that the fo'c'sle of a man-o'-war had provided, he had found that much of his book-learning had come to life: it had so much more meaning in the context of the sea and exotic shores. How easily could he turn his back on it?

On the staircase, candle in hand, he knew there had to be a resolution. He blew out the candle, turned and tiptoed down again until he came to a small window. The catch was still the same, the window stiffly protesting, but then his childhood escape route was open to him. It was the work of moments to swing out into the night and down the matted ivy to the flower-bed.

A cold winter's moon rode high and serene, bathing the slumbering countryside in brightness. He strode forward, following the near invisible but well-remembered little path to the woodland, letting the air clear his head. He entered the woods; a curious owl gave a low hoot and he heard scurrying in the bracken, nocturnal animals surprised at finding him suddenly among them.

There was no avoiding the fact that his father wanted him installed at Eskdale Hall with no further waste of time—probably because he wished to devolve management of the estate on Renzi so that he could spend more of the Season in London, where he kept up the pretence of attendance at the House of Lords.

Nevertheless, whatever the reason, he must consider his retirement from the sea. But his heart rebelled: he had found himself on the ocean, much as his friend Kydd had done, albeit in a different way. He relished the paradoxical freedoms it gave: there could be no care for the morrow when his actions were preordained—he could not alter the course of the ship or wish it elsewhere, so his horizon must shrink to the compass of that snug little world. All else was in vain. Relieved of worldly fretting, his mind could expand and soar in a way that was impossible with the distractions of land. And now, with the intelligent and worldly company of a whole wardroom of officers, he could find an agreeable conversation at any time of the day or night.

And there was Thomas Kydd, a friend like no other, who had seen him through grave and wild situations in a voyage round the world. Now they must part. Kydd was growing confident and ambitious in his profession, and would no doubt go on to achieve wondrous things, while he . . . His father was in robust good health and might haunt him for many more years to come. Renzi would be confined to the endless social round of the country where a major excitement was the arraigning of a horse-thief.

It was galling—but there was no middle way. And it was becoming more than plain that perhaps his father was right: Renzi had used exile as a means to escape his situation. The realisation stopped him cold. Was he indeed running away? Did he not know his own mind?

Suddenly a shadow loomed dark against the moonlight and a blow thumped off his ribs as a heavy man brought him to the ground. Renzi twisted away and pulled himself upright. Seeing the silhouette of a raised cudgel, he drove inside it, cannoning into the man's stomach. The man staggered back, but when Renzi stepped into a patch of moonlight he stopped. "Is ut you, sir? Master Nicholas?"

Renzi took a breath to steady himself. "It is, Mr Varney. This will teach me not to creep about at night like a poacher. You did right, and I apologise if you were winded."

• • •

He came down early for breakfast; the years of watch-keeping at sea had made late rising distasteful to him, and he was surprised to see his father.

"Sleep well?"

Renzi thought he detected a sly undertone and answered neutrally, "As may be expected, Father."

"Attending the assizes today. Do you want to come? What's-his-name—jumped-up magistrate—won't do as he's told, need to learn him some manners. Do you good to take in a piece of the real world."

Renzi could not trust himself to say anything civil and remained silent.

"Come to any conclusions yet? I want to be able to say something in the House about the Rents Bill at the February sessions, if you take my meaning."

"Sir. I've been plain with you—this is not something I can arrange immediately. It takes—"

"And I've been plain with you, sir! My patience is wearing thin. Your boat will float without you on it, damn it all. All it takes is a date I can work to, for God's sake."

Renzi stood up, boiling. "I find I must take some exercise," he said thickly, then left the room, trembling. He stalked over the straw and mud of the stables forecourt, shouting for the groom.

Prince, the fine black gelding, was still in his stall and, miraculously, remembered him. The horse nuzzled his hand with a now grey-fringed muzzle. Renzi's eyes smarted as he swung into the saddle, clopped noisily out of the yard, then broke into a gallop on the long stretch of grass to the front gate. He pulled up, panting, and wheeled about to take the long way round the boundary of the estate.

A coppice worker going to the woods looked up in astonishment. Mrs Rattray, fat and buxom, stood at her cottage door and waved shyly. Further along chickens scattered with loud squawks ahead of him; nearby lived the simple woodcutter Jarge who had been told time and again to keep them cooped . . . Renzi felt a lump forming in his throat. His canter dropped to a walk and his eyes took in the land—his land, his tenants, his people, if he wanted them.

Powerfully, startling him with its intensity, came the sudden knowledge that at that moment he did not: he was not yet ready to leave the sea life in all its terror and beauty for this, however comfortable and secure. He could not!

He whipped Prince to a gallop and screamed defiance into the wind. Then he became aware of the thud of hoofs out of rhythm behind him. He snatched a backward glance and saw his father low on his horse's neck, striping his mount mercilessly. Renzi swerved aside and headed for a gnarled oak tree standing stark and alone in the middle of the field.

They dismounted without a word, the earl tight-lipped and dangerous. "Boy, I will not tolerate your peevish ways. You'll put your sailor days behind you and take hold of your responsibilities now, damn you, or I'll know the reason why."

Renzi took a deep, shuddering breath. He felt a light-headed exhilaration, a species of liberation. No longer was he going to be in thrall to the red-faced tyrant before him. He was different from the man he had once been and had seen far more of life than most. "Sir, you must allow that—"

"Be damned to your arrogant posturing!"

Renzi was pale and determined. He said nothing. This seemed to goad his father, who roared, "Unless you see fit to return and find it in yourself to act as my son and heir, I know someone who will!"

So it had come to that. Renzi was tempted to dare him to do his worst, but knew that, once said, his father would never take back his words. "I have told you that I cannot abandon my post—"

"Damn your blood, sir! I will not take this—" but Renzi had turned on his heel and led his horse away.

"Where are you going to? Come back this instant, or I—I'll—" His words were lost in a splutter as Renzi walked away. "I'll disinherit! Never fear, sir, I'll do it!" The choking rage was fearsome but it settled the matter as far as Renzi was concerned. Now the only way back was to grovel and beg, and that he would never do. He walked on.

The voice bellowed after him: "Three months! Three months—and if you're not returned I will go to law and have the title reverted. I can do it, do ye hear? And I *will* do it, God rot your bones!"

# Chapter 11

"If there's any more o' that lobster salad, I'd be obliged," Kydd said lazily, from the long seat in the sternsheets of the officer's gig, where he lay sprawled under an unseasonably warm sun.

"No, you shall not!" Cecilia said crossly. "There'll be none left for the others." However, more preserved sardine fillets, it seemed, were on offer. The two midshipmen were ashore on the rocks of the little cove, trying without success to conjure a fire to grill their fish and Adams was out of sight inland.

The sun beamed and the plash of the waves was soothing. "Do you not feel a pity f'r Gen'ral Buonaparte, sis," Kydd teased, "that he's cast away in Egypt with no hope o' rescue, him 'n' his great army all alone in the desert?"

"I do not! Such a wicked man! I hope the sun quite dries him up like a wizened prune."

Kydd's grin at his sister's pout broadened as he considered how things had changed for the better. "Ye've heard we're in Leghorn now, Cec—that's in the north of Italy—"

"Thomas, I'm not ignorant."

"An', best of all, Our Nel has stirred up Naples enough that they've marched north an' taken Rome."

"'Our Nel'?"

"What we call Admiral Nelson."

"The common sailors, Thomas, not the officers!"

"They love him, Cec. When we were chasin' the French and everything looked so bad, he called across his captains then started asking 'em if they were feeding the men enough onions! And makes sure they get full measure o' grog with wine he buys himself. They'd sail through hell for him—truly."

"And you?" Cecilia pouted. "Will I see you run after a man with one eye, one arm, the most junior admiral in the list?"

"You will, Cec," Kydd said. "Nelson is th' greatest leader I know, and if he says that this is the way t' do it, why, that's the way t' do it."

"There are some who are not so easily persuaded . . ." Cecilia said archly.

"Who? They're jealous, is all!"

"Lord Stanhope, for one."

Kydd paused. Stanhope's discreet position as a diplomat was mysterious, and involved much travel, but it was known his allegiance was to London alone. His presence in Minorca would not be coincidental. "What is *he* saying, then?"

"Well, he doesn't even tell things to Lady Stanhope," Cecilia said, "but when he heard that Sir Horatio had caused King Ferdinand to move on the French he was very uneasy—and even the news that Rome was restored didn't bring him to humour."

"Is that all? Well, now Nelson is a peer o' the realm—Baron Nelson o' the Nile! An' there's talk that the King o' Naples is going to make him a duke. Doesn't that tell you what the world thinks of him?" He sat up and tested the holding of the little kedge anchor. "Cec, we've got the mongseers on the run. Everywhere they're losin' battles—and it could be," he said, with a sudden wrinkling of his brow, "that this war is going t' be over soon."

Sir William Hamilton entered the room quietly. Nelson, scrawling at a great rate in his peculiar crabwise fashion, was at his desk by the window with its magnificent view of the Bay of Naples. He was grey with exhaustion and his slight body seemed shrivelled, but his expression nevertheless retained a fierce vitality. "Is it true?"

"I fear so. I have a letter from General Mack. In essence he cannot be sure of holding them, even at Capua. It's the very worst news—I'm sorry." It had been so extraordinarily swift: Rome had been taken but the regrouping French had rapidly struck back, vengefully striking south into the heart of the Kingdom of the Two Sicilies. And now it seemed that the Austrian commander of King Ferdinand's forces, Mack, with an army far larger than that of the French, had contrived to lose every encounter with them so far.

Nelson stared out of the window, then said heavily, "Our situation in Leghorn becomes insupportable. The grand duke must shift for himself."

"Our reputation would be irretrievably ruined, should—"

"I didn't mean that," Nelson said testily. "I shall send a frigate, should his household be put to hazard."

"As it appears it will . . ."

Nelson threw down his quill, got to his feet, and paced the floor as if it were a quarterdeck. "Charles Emmanuel of Sardinia escapes to Cagliari, now the Grand Duke of Tuscany flees before his own people—what kind of rulers are they? And from London I've received only reproaches—never any soldiers. How can I steady these cowardly wretches without English soldiers?" He stopped pacing. "I will leave Malta to Ball. That is all I can retain of this shambles."

Hamilton murmured sympathy but Nelson interrupted, "General Buonaparte! To give the devil his due, he's now crossed an impassable desert and kept his army together, which is more than any man would credit. Now he's marching north into the Holy Land and could be anywhere. God damn his French soul!"

A young army captain covered with dust entered hurriedly and handed over a dispatch satchel. "Sir! From Capua." He saluted. "Sir, you might give thought to your safety—Naples is in a rare state of disorder. The people are terrified they are being abandoned to the French, that the King will depart privily and—"

"Thank you, sir. Now go," growled Nelson, unbuckling the satchel and scanning the single sheet. He looked up slowly. "Good God . . ."

"What is it?"

"Mack has been defeated! His army is now only a rabble—more than two thousand have deserted, he's lost communication with his rear. There's nothing between us here and General Championnet's veterans." Nelson went to his desk and slumped into the chair. He stared into space for a moment, then picked up the papers he was working on and tore them up, one by one.

When he had finished he looked up with an odd smile. "There is now nothing to detain us in Naples. You may wish to make your dispositions for leaving, Sir William."

Hamilton opened his mouth but closed it again, then said, "Yes. I shall be within call," and left as quietly as he had arrived.

Nelson's head drooped in despair. The door opened again. "Why, what's this? England's Glory in a stew, is 'e?" Lady Hamilton crossed to Nelson, whose face lit up. "The conqueror of th' Nile cast down? For shame!"

"Your ladyship has only to bestow a smile and I shall be made new again."

"There's somethin' wrong, isn't there?" she said, her hand on his shoulder.

Nelson stood up, as though to throw off her touch. "We are to evacuate Naples, I believe," he said harshly. "That is to say, the King and Queen and their household—they must not be allowed to fall into the hands of the French."

She went pale. "You mean—well, we must, o' course. But if—"

Outside, from the cold corridors of the *palazzo* came shouts and the sound of people running. She looked fearfully at Nelson—and the Queen burst into the room. *"Siamo persi!"*

Emma crossed to the frantic woman and held her, stroking, comforting. "She's hearin' the tumbrels comin' for her too," she said. The Queen's sister, Marie Antoinette, had been guillotined by the revolutionaries in Paris. *"Non i preoccupare, signora, cara, Nelson ci sta con noi,"* she added in spirited Italian. Looking over her shoulder at Nelson, she said, "If we're t' do it proper, it's best we 'ave a good plan. What are we to do, Adm'ral?"

There were ships enough. *Vanguard* lay at anchor in the bay with other warships, and there were smaller vessels, which Nelson ordered to be prepared for the evacuation of English residents—but no indication of the Royal Family's departure could be even hinted at.

As if on a visit of state, Sir William Hamilton and Admiral Nelson made the short journey from the embassy to the vast Palazzo Reale, palace to the kings of the Two Sicilies for centuries and a fortress in its own right.

"Your Majesty," Nelson murmured, bowing low to King Ferdinand. A repugnant figure, with the raw-boned build of a farm labourer, the King had small, sly eyes each side of a grotesquely long nose, and gave a doltish impression—yet the safety of this monarch was Nelson's prime duty.

"Do acquaint His Majesty of our intentions, if you please, my dear." Emma Hamilton was fast becoming indispensable with her warm, practical handling of the royal couple, whom she had long known, not to mention her easy familiarity with the language. It seemed there would be no difficulties from them, as long as the

Queen's hysteria could be kept in check. Nelson crossed to a window and pulled aside the curtain to peer out: the waterfront was seething with angry crowds converging on the palace.

"We're not going to be able to get to the boats through that," he said soberly, "even with a regiment of soldiers."

"Don't be fooled, sir. They love the King an' would never 'ave a revolution," Emma came back.

"That is quite true," Hamilton said. "The *lazzaroni,* the common people, adore their king. It's the lawyers and petty bureaucrats who see their opportunity at this time. We must ensure that their loyalty is not tested by, er, their sovereign's precipitate flight. Sir Horatio is quite right in his concern—I rather fear we may find ourselves trapped here." In the rich surrounds of the immense gold-vaulted room they were as helpless as any felon in the local prison.

"There is one course that we may consider." Hamilton's cool words were in English; his warning glance at Emma kept her mute. "It would be a coup beyond compare should the famous Horatio Nelson be taken by the French. At all costs this must not happen. I suggest that as we are English, the mob will let us pass . . ."

"No," Nelson said crisply. "There will be another way to get them out—at night perhaps. We prepare for evacuation now. Troubridge will arrive soon and we shall conceive a plan together."

"Then might I recommend that the treasury be not left to the French? It is reputed to be of several millions in specie alone." There were also rich paintings, hangings, gilded carvings beyond counting—but these would have to remain. Only the state reserves could be taken.

Darkness fell. More crowds gathered below, chanting and restless. There would be no flight from the palace even at night. Troubridge arrived at last: grave and polite, he listened while

Nelson gave his orders, then slipped away to prepare communications with the ships.

The chanting grew in volume and Hamilton peeped out. "Dare I ask that Their Majesties show themselves to the crowd?"

The King and Queen of the Kingdom of the Two Sicilies appeared on the balcony of the palace to tumultuous applause, bowing and waving, held for an hour by the baying crowds before they could move inside, pale and shaking.

"We move the treasury to the embassy," Nelson snapped. "I want every cask and barrel that the kitchens can find, and we'll stow it all in those." The embassy in the Palazzo Sessa was conveniently on high ground at the back of the palace, and before long, gold ducats, silver from a dozen countries and even gold sovereigns were being nailed into hogsheads and ankers, Emma loyally scrawling in chalk on each one "Stores for Nelson."

The howls of the mob grew louder. Hamilton eased back the curtain again. The streets were alive with packs of men, some carrying torches, others weapons. "They're staying around the palace," he murmured. "We dare not leave.

"There goes Ferreri," he said, and stiffened. A figure in a dark cloak thrust across the waterfront road and began to board a boat not a hundred yards away. The boatman gestured angrily, shouting at the crowd. Ferreri was a valuable man to Hamilton, a royalist Frenchman with a line to secrets within the Jacobin underworld.

With horrifying swiftness the mob closed round him. His French accent had triggered suspicions and he was dragged from the boat on to the quayside where he disappeared under a flailing pack. They punched, kicked and tore at the black figure until it moved no more, then a rope was tied round one leg and the corpse was dragged over the cobblestones towards the palace, leaving a slime of blood to glitter in the torchlight. A maniac chanting started from the upturned faces below the balcony.

"My God," said Hamilton. "They want to show the King what they've done for him!"

Queen Maria Carolina dropped into a swoon; the King made odd gobbling noises. Nelson turned to Hamilton. "We have to leave now, sir. Do you know—"

The Queen came to herself, muttering strangely.

"Be quiet! Everyone!" Emma listened intently, then threw a triumphant look at Nelson. "She says there's some kind o' door—a gate. It connects her rooms to th' old caves an' passages under Naples."

"That could well be so," said Hamilton. "We know of the *sottosuolo,* where the Romans left underground catacombs and tunnels after excavating for *tufo* building stone. Huge voids, some, and artefacts have been found that date—"

Emma gave a twisted smile. "She says she hasn't told us before as she's always worried a thief might get to know of it an' rob her in her sleep."

"Do any of these connect with the sea?" Nelson demanded.

"Apparently most of them do, yes," Hamilton said.

"The sea!" Nelson's cry was heartfelt: to an Englishman the sea was a friend, a highway to freedom. "At which point?" he added hastily.

"The Molosiglio."

"That's all I need. I'll get word to Troubridge directly. Please to inform Their Majesties to prepare for their departure."

Soon after midnight Nelson stood grimly at the top of a dark stairway, listening to the hollow sound of approaching footsteps. A naval officer came into view, blinking uncertainly in the bright light. "Cap'n Hope, *Alcmene* frigate, sir, with a party of men," he said, touching his hat.

"Well met, sir! Shall we proceed?"

"Aye aye, sir."

"Light the torches—I shall go first." Nelson descended the dank stairs and paused at the bottom to inspect the seamen. They were in their familiar sea rig and all had drawn cutlasses, which gleamed in the flickering torchlight.

"Keep station on me," he snapped, drew his sword and plunged forward. It was ghostly quiet in the ancient tunnels and stank of damp antiquity. The flickering light fell on rough-hewn tunnel walls and the black of anonymous voids.

The men hurried to keep up, the only sound their footsteps and heavy breathing. Nelson was in front, his sword at point. From behind came occasional female squawks of protest but the pace never slackened.

A petty officer pointed to an open iron gate. "Th' entrance, if y' please, sir." Beyond, the stars glittered in the night sky. "All's well," he hailed into the blackness and an anxious lieutenant appeared.

"Sir, your barge is at the mole."

"I shall not board until Their Majesties are safely embarked."

"Aye aye, sir," the lieutenant said reluctantly.

When the Royal Family arrived, there were cloaks to conceal them and men to carry their belongings. Seamen stood guard on the short distance to the mole, facing outwards with naked blades. With heartbreaking sobs, the Queen, clutching her baby, was bundled aboard the admiral's barge, the King rigid with fear beside her.

"We're going t' be jus' fine, sir," Emma said stoutly, smoothing the distraught Queen's hair, "an' lookin' forward to a bit o' sea air now, aren't we?"

*Vanguard* was soon in a state of chaos: the Royal Family included young princes and princesses, ministers, ambassadors—any, it seemed, who feared the imminent catastrophe—all of whom had to be found accommodation.

As soon as Nelson came aboard he had only one question of his flag-lieutenant: "What is General Buonaparte doing?"

"Sir, I'm truly grieved to say he has triumphed over the Turks yet again. At Jaffa, and with three thousand prisoners butchered in cold blood. He is now unopposed, sir." Jaffa was in the Holy Land, far from the European war, but ominously north of Egypt and therefore in a direct path to Constantinople and the trade routes east to India. Napoleon Buonaparte had succeeded in breaking out of his desert prison and was now on the march north in a bid to outdo Alexander's conquests.

"And, sir, Captain Sidney Smith begs to inform you that he is attempting a defence of Acre just to the north with two sail-of-the-line."

# CHAPTER 12

KYDD STEPPED OFF THE BOAT in Acre, ruefully contemplating the fortunes of war. While he had succeeded in Minorca, he had failed to gain the notice he had sought, but his part in the recapture of the island had ensured that when a lieutenant for service ashore in Acre had been called for, his name had been the first that was mentioned. He had heard that the commander, Sir Sidney Smith, was a daring, unconventional officer who, no doubt, would welcome initiative and ambition.

*Tigre,* with *Tenacious* and a hodge-podge of small fry, was all that had been available to Smith and he was going to try to hold on to this old town, which lay directly in the path of the French advance north. With a handful of troops and seamen to call on, against an army of thirteen thousand with siege artillery and the legendary Buonaparte at its head, he could not last for long, but if he could delay the French advance even for a short time, perhaps the Turks would take heart and make a defence of Constantinople.

While the crew transferred his gear from *Tenacious*'s pinnace, Kydd looked around. It was a squarish walled town of immeasurable antiquity on a low, west-facing promontory. The golden-yellow stone walls were grey and gnarled with age, crumbling towers and empty gun embrasures testifying to its dilapidated condition. A tiny, silted harbour to the south-east had been created by a mole, but breaking water over rocky shoals offshore showed it was useless to larger ships. The dry, arid odour of sun-baked rocks was overlaid with the pungent goat-like smell of camels, together with the heady aroma of spices and dried fish.

A small gateway opened and a marine sergeant came forward. "Sah!" he said, saluting smartly. "L'tenant Hewitt, sah, welcomes you ashore an' would you come wi' me?" Kydd followed him through narrow streets swarming with people in every form of dress. They emerged into a small square, on one side of which was a building with a marine sentry on guard beneath a flag hanging limply.

Inside, a naval lieutenant, writing at a desk, looked up at Kydd's entry. "Ah, you're expected, old fellow. I'm Hewitt, third o' the *Tigre.*" He extended a hand and listened courteously as Kydd introduced himself.

"I expect you'll be interested to know that this is, *pro tem,* the headquarters of our commander ashore, and therefore our place o' duty also."

Kydd's interest quickened. "Duty?"

"Ah. That is our aggrieved leader being mysterious. He means us to be in turn a duty officer ashore in his place. We take watch 'n' watch, sleeping here where we can be found."

"Aggrieved?"

"Why, yes—I'm amazed you've not heard the tale! He was at Toulon with Hood in 'ninety-three, personally setting the torch to near a dozen French sail-o'-the-line. Next he gets himself captured in a river action and is taken to Paris. There he's accused by our fine friend Buonaparte of being an incendiary and is thrown into a condemned cell while they prepare a public trial. But he made a daring escape before they could do the deed and now he's facing this same Buonaparte again and vows he will make him smart for it."

"He's really going t' see out a siege against the whole French army?" said Kydd. It was bold and courageous, but was Smith imagining he could stand against an army of conquest with siege guns?

Hewitt went on drily, "Do not judge Sir Sidney by standards you'd use on others. He's unique, completely fearless and most inventive in the arts of war. You'll find him . . . different. Many dislike him for his ways. As my captain, I've found him amiable enough. And he's devilishly well connected—his brother's our top diplomat in Constantinople, and he takes his orders direct from the Foreign Office as plenipotentiary, which has probably put Our Nel's nose somewhat out of joint."

"What are our orders, then?" Kydd said.

"We'll both discover shortly—he's coming ashore to plan his defences." Hewitt looked at Kydd shrewdly. "As I said, make no hasty judgements. He's damned clever and brave to a fault."

Smith arrived promptly at noon. Fastidiously dressed, he had made no concessions to their surroundings. His uniform coat even bore the bejewelled star of some order. Kydd noted the delicacy of his grip as he shook his hand, the sensitivity of his face.

"Conference now, if you please, gentlemen." He led the way to an upper room with plain furniture scattered about and pulled a table to the centre. There he spread out a large hand-drawn map, showing the land features that were necessarily missing from the familiar sea chart. "This, gentlemen, is the town of St John d'Acre. As you can see, walled around, open ground without. Two sides to the sea, two facing inland—here at their corner is a large square tower. It has good observation possibilities. The locals call it the 'Cursed Tower.'" He added lightly, "It seems it was paid for with Judas Iscariot's thirty pieces of silver."

Kydd was not interested in a Biblical allusion. "Sir, ye're thinking on making a stand against Gen'ral Buonaparte here?"

Smith's smile vanished. "I most certainly am, Mr Kydd. Can you be one of those wretched crew who cringe at the sound of his name? I mean to show the world that he can be bested—and, remember, we have the sea at our backs."

Kydd felt Hewitt's eyes on him. "Sir, with no soldiers it'll be a hard job."

"You're forgetting Djezzar, the ruler of this region. He is providing three thousand of the best troops—Anatolian, Albanian, Kurds, Africans—and will reside within these walls while the French do their worst, trusting us to effect its defence."

Something of Kydd's scepticism must have shown, for Smith went on, "Our object is simply to hold the town until relieved. And I can tell you now that at this very moment a Turkish army eight times the size of Buonaparte's is preparing to advance towards us. Not even the victor of Italy may prevail over that."

There was the sound of movement and voices below. "Ah, he has arrived." Smith went to the window and stared out until an older officer, with a deeply lined face, wearing a uniform that Kydd did not recognise, entered. Smith turned and, with a warm smile, greeted him in a stream of mellifluous French, gesturing first to Hewitt, who responded with a bow and murmured French, and then to Kydd, who could only bow and mutter in English.

"For those without the necessary accomplishment I will translate," Smith said. "This gentleman is Lieutenant General the Count Phélippeaux, an honourable Frenchman of the *ancien régime*. He is in the first rank of those learned in the arts of fortification and will tell us how best we may prepare for our siege."

Kydd's expression altered, but Smith, mistaking the change,

went on, "Set aside your concerns. This was the officer who, in the most handsome manner, assisted in my escape from the prison cell in Paris. He has every reason to detest the revolutionaries, you may believe, Mr Kydd."

The conference moved forward quickly. Whatever else, Smith was clear-headed and energetic. Within the hour they had settled on immediate priorities: with an unknown time before Buonaparte appeared, their defences had to be completed as soon as possible.

The most effective would be in the deploying of their two ships of force, which amounted to the equivalent of a regiment of artillery. Each ship would be anchored in position so that it could fire down the length of one side or the other of the walls, their line of fire intersecting at the end. The open ground in front of the walls across which the enemy must pass for an assault could therefore be kept under fire. The only problem with this was that shallow water with rocky shoals extended in places for several miles, making it a dangerous and exposed anchorage for ships of size. They would be firing at extreme range.

The count engaged in long, earnest discussions with Smith, which Smith summarised tersely. It seemed that, without effective artillery of their own, they would be at a grave disadvantage: they had to keep Buonaparte's siege guns at a distance or they would effect a rapid breach.

"I shall land guns from *Tigre* and *Tenacious* with volunteer seamen gunners to serve them. The men relish a jaunt ashore and I shall oblige them." More discussion yielded their number and position.

Things were looking up for Kydd: with seamen to command and a worthy task ahead, there was every prospect of distinguished service.

Smith stood and stretched theatrically. "At this point it would appear appropriate to involve Djezzar Pasha." He began to pace about the room, his hands behind his back. "I would have you understand the importance I attach to our alliance. He alone has the men close at hand whom we need, and without him we are lost. Now, before we make audience, allow me to say something of this worthy gentleman. He is pasha of this region, holding nominal allegiance to Sultan Selim in Constantinople but has always been an independent spirit."

He glanced significantly at the other two officers in turn. "'Djezzar' means Slasher or Butcher and it is an apt name. When he was young he sold himself into slavery to the Mamelukes and by sinister means made himself indispensable as an assassin until he turned his blade on his master. He is cruel and has the morals of a polecat, but is the ruler and will be accorded all possible marks of respect. Is that clear?"

"Understood, sir," said Hewitt. Kydd nodded.

"Then we shall proceed to the harem."

"Sir?" both officers said, in astonishment.

"All official business with Djezzar Pasha is conducted in his seraglio. Shall we go now?"

With an increasing sense of unreality, Kydd followed Smith through noisy ancient streets to a complex of buildings to the north and a tent surrounded by chattering Arabs in a courtyard with palm trees and a fountain. A tall man in a turban approached and bowed in the eastern manner.

"To see His Excellency," Smith said, with practised hauteur. This was the man, Kydd had been told, who had recently won over the Sublime Porte in Constantinople to secure a treaty—he would be no stranger to eastern ways.

They entered the tent: rich hangings, soft carpets, riotous colour, unknown tongues—it was all an exotic wonder to Kydd.

To one side a man sat cross-legged and others stood round

him obsequiously. The man, whom Smith indicated was Djezzar, rose: well-built and mature, he wore the full burnous of the desert Arab and carried himself with dignity, a diamond-hilted dagger at his waist.

Smith bowed deeply and Kydd hastened to do likewise. Smith spoke in French to Djezzar, and the four then retired to the interior where they all sat cross-legged. Kydd refused a bubble-pipe but Hewitt accepted out of curiosity. Kydd looked furtively about for ladies of the harem but, disappointingly, saw none.

Smith conversed urbanely and at length with Djezzar, whose harsh, booming voice had a hard edge of authority. Kydd leaned over to Hewitt. "What's the drift?" he whispered.

"Asking for men to build up the fortifications," Hewitt replied, in a low voice, "and about the Turkish cavalry promised to us." There was a snarl and impassioned words from Djezzar. "He says he told them to go out and attack the enemy and not to return until they had done something worthy of his notice."

The audience had apparently been a success: on the way back to their headquarters Smith made light commentary on the sights, approving the purposeful hurry of gangs now setting about clearing detritus and rubble from the walls, labouring at the stonework, shoring up weak bastions.

In their campaign room Smith looked in satisfaction at the map as he made corrections and notes. "So far, so good," he said briskly. "El Djezzar is proving most co-operative, and I'm sanguine that if we do our part we shall have a good chance of delaying the French long enough for the Turks to bring them to battle.

"There is much to do—I shall be returning aboard *Tigre.* I want those guns landed before sunset and placed in position without delay. Your orders are here." He produced a slim sheaf of papers. "In essence they require you to act for me ashore.

Djezzar Pasha has been notified that you may do so in my name. Therefore you will acquaint yourselves thoroughly with my orders so that nothing is overlooked."

He considered for a moment, then said, "We have no reliable knowledge of the French advance. It might be prudent to begin a regular reconnaissance south until their presence is detected. One of you will take a boat away at dusk for this purpose."

"So, we have our orders, an' our task is tolerably clear. I only hope we can get away in time."

"You are not confident of a favourable outcome?" Hewitt responded coolly.

"Are you?"

"I know my duty, I believe," Hewitt said stiffly.

"F'r me . . ." Kydd began, and thought better of it. "Then let's be started. Where's Suleiman, the translator we've been promised?" He turned out to be the tall man at the seraglio.

"Er, Mr Suleiman, I want t' see the *serang*—whatever you'd call th' chief of the workers on the wall. There's not a moment t' lose."

The first gun from *Tigre* was landed at the mole soon after midday: a heavy twenty-four-pounder, laid along the thwarts of a launch, and its two tons of cold iron swayed ashore by improvised sheer-legs. A gun-carriage followed, then boats with powder and shot, some with stores and rum casks.

Soon after, the grinning faces of Dobbie, his close friend Laffin and others arrived in *Tenacious*'s cutter, volunteers all, ready to man the guns that would soon face the great Napoleon Buonaparte. Their twenty-four-pounder, which had come earlier in the launch, was man-hauled through the streets and into place.

"Dobbie, you're gun captain here. There'll be a Frenchy along presently as will tell ye where, er, you'll best direct y'r fire." There would be no looming enemy ship to fire into: presumably it would be columns of men or random waves of attackers. He ignored the puzzled looks of the men at the word "Frenchy."

The *Tenacious* gun was mounted at the end of the wall where it met the sea to the south and commanded the open ground in front of the town, now being broken up to form a discouragement to attackers. Kydd let his gaze move across the littered landscape: wild fig trees and hovels had been levelled out to line-of-sight of the nearest high ground some quarter of a mile away. Beyond that was the anonymous dry, scrubby country that stretched inland to distant purple hills. It would be from this direction that the army of Napoleon Buonaparte would come.

Kydd watched Dobbie dispose his men in imitation of shipboard, handspike and crow to hand. He had ensured that there was a semblance of a magazine along the inside of the wall and gave orders for the safe handling of powder and shot. But he was becoming uneasy in this unfamiliar world and hoped their withdrawal would not be long delayed; it had been in a similar siege on land at Calvi that Nelson had lost the sight of one eye to the splintering stone of a ricocheting shot.

Hewitt had concluded his gun dispositions at the other end of the wall—they could now converge fire and, judging from the chattering fascination of gaping onlookers, they were giving heart by their presence.

They met later back at their musty headquarters for a snatched meal. "We get marines t'morrow," Kydd said, through the last of his lamb stew, "t' use as we please."

"Orders are strict enough in the matter of sentries. I'd far rather trust a leatherneck on sentry-go than a Turk, if you take my point."

"I do. An' I notice that we're on watch an' watch—days on an' split the nights?"

"Alternately?"

"Agreed." Kydd lifted his cup in acknowledgement; the wine was dry and resinous but pleasant enough. Hewitt looked disapprovingly at the china cup but drank.

"And the dusk patrol?"

"That's f'r me," Kydd said quickly—the chance for some sea-time was not to be missed. It was also an opportunity to show Smith what he could do.

"Then I'll take the first watch."

"Aye."

Hewitt seemed moody, distracted. Kydd sensed that he was having misgivings. "Rum sort of place," Kydd tried. "Ye can see how old it is."

"Old? You might say that," said Hewitt bleakly. "This is Canaan—that is to say, the Phoenician lands from centuries before Rome. And that's the road to Nazareth over the hills—St Paul was here, and this was the very place, St John of Acre, where Richard the Lionheart and the crusaders marched against Jerusalem. It's been fought over by all the tribes of man for thousands of years, and now we are come to add our blood . . ."

Kydd would not be depressed: this was a passing strange and unusual task for a sea officer but it was also the best and only chance in sight for notice and advancement.

"Laffin, get a boat's crew t'gether for me. Cox'n an' six, the launch under sail and I'll have the thirty-two-pounder carronade shipped in the bows." There was no harm in being well prepared: a boat action could be the most brutal form of combat at sea. "Ready in half an hour, if y' please."

He examined the charts with Hewitt: communications with the south were a road following a fertile strip along the sea at the edge of the desert—if the enemy were to come they must choose between the coast road and a long swing inland from the interior to reach the gates of Acre.

"I'll press south t' this Mount Carmel," Kydd mused. "Ten miles or so. They'll come along the coast road's my guess."

"Mount Carmel—Elijah discomfits the prophets of Baal, two Kings something . . ."

Kydd could not bring it to mind: this was half a world away from the boredom of the Sunday service in Guildford town where the dry words of a preacher speaking of the Holy Land bore no resemblance at all to this arid country.

". . . the Samaritans, even. Christ passed by here on his way to Jerusalem . . ."

"Um, that's right—an' I'm takin' a carronade in case they have gunboats out. Do ye keep a watch f'r gunfire, as will be y'r signal they're abroad." He left Hewitt to his Biblical musings and collected his sword belt from the corner. He favoured a shoulder carriage to spread the weight, leaving the belt loose for a brace of pistols. His fighting sword had a satisfying heft and in the warmth of the late-afternoon sun he strode down to the mole.

Laffin, the hard petty officer Kydd remembered from his "duel" in Canada, touched his hat at his approach; also in the boat was the lofty Poulden, forward at the stubby carronade, and several other Tenaciouses along the thwarts. A stout enough crew, he thought with satisfaction.

"Pistols an' cutlasses?"

"In th' arms chest, sir," Laffin said immediately.

He boarded the big launch and settled in the sternsheets, leaving Laffin the tiller. "We'll shove off now, if y' please," Kydd told him.

The soft westerly meant they did not even have to ship oars as the gaff-headed main was hoisted. "I'll have th' running bowsprit out with jib an' stays'l, I believe." The carronade would not bear forward while this was rigged but it would add considerably to their speed and could be struck in a hurry if need be.

The boat left the mole, slipped past the roiling white of the

Manara rocks, then headed out to sea to preserve an offing before shaping course south. It was most pleasant, Kydd had to admit; the sun sinking out to sea in shimmering splendour, warmth still in the air, and in the other direction, the low, nondescript coast taking on the wistful indigo of evening. Along the endless virgin sands was the startling white of breakers, the purple of far mountains now a deep ultramarine.

Olive gardens and small clusters of the flat-topped dwellings were dotted along the shore. Several times figures stopped, watching them curiously. The cheerful splash of their passage and the occasional grunted conversation of the men lulled Kydd into a reverie—he pulled himself together. What *did* a great army look like, apart from thousands of bayonets? He had no idea, but knew that if he saw one his duty was to get the news to Smith with the utmost urgency.

The bay curved round. At one place he saw classical ruins enough to make Renzi stare—but he was not present: he was in distant England, resolving his personal life. A string of camels plodded along the skyline. Kydd idly counted nearly a hundred on the dusty road with their riders in flowing desert cloaks looking as if they had stepped out of a picture book of his childhood. He followed their advance, their riders rhythmically jerking forward as though in a boat in a rough sea—*jerking?* Surely a desert Bedouin had a more comfortable style of riding.

He looked about quickly. "Laffin—put about an' go beyond that spit o' land." They had passed a tiny headland, no more than a small twist of sand. The boat went about smartly and returned the way they had come. As soon as they were out of sight of the riders Kydd said urgently, "Set me ashore, an' stand off 'n' on until they're past, then collect me."

The boat scrunched into the fine sand beyond the point and Kydd leaped off, scurrying to get into the fringing grasses of the sand dune. He crouched, waiting. There were no sounds of sighting or pursuit but he kept very still. At length came the soft chinkle of a camel harness and the murmur of voices on the evening air. A delicate, unknown but haunting fragrance warred with the dry pungency of the desert and the nearer salty sand of the dunes—he flattened among the reedy grasses, rigid with concentration.

He felt the thumping of camel feet through the ground as they drew nearer. The voices were louder—and it was not Arabic that was being spoken but French.

It seemed to take for ever for the camel train to pass. He heard muted laughter, sharp words and an occasional snatch of song above the rustle of shuffling feet and the leathery slap of harness. Finally the last one passed. Cautiously Kydd raised his head: they were receding along the road without looking back. He delayed for a while longer, then slid down to the beach and waited for the boat.

"Load with canister!" he growled at Poulden, as they shoved off. There was no doubt in his mind of what he should do—the sound of the cannon would be as good as a personal report to Smith of their presence.

The launch leaned purposefully to the wind; they passed the camel train once more, the riders took no notice of the little sailing boat offshore. Kydd chose his move carefully: if the boat took the ground they could expect no mercy from the enemy riders.

At a stipple in the line of dunes ahead he doused the sails and took in the bowsprit, using oars to rotate them shoreward. "Out kedge," he snapped. The little anchor plummeted and bit and the line tautened over the transom. He paid it out to allow the boat to nose close in, the deadly carronade trained steadily on the shore. Still the camel riders did not take alarm: in the uncertain light and against the setting sun it must have seemed a fishing-boat.

The line of camels came on, some heads turned curiously. "As they bear, Poulden," Kydd growled, "an' make it count." There was a great army following behind and he had no compunction about the blood he was about to spill, but his heart beat faster as the train of camels passed the cold black muzzle.

The carronade crashed back in its slide, the gun-flash nearly blinding in the fading light. The effect on the column was instant—sleeting balls tore into them, and with squeals and screams it dissolved into panic. One riderless camel fled back down the road as others shed their mounts and scrambled in terror over the dunes. Hoarse cries of command mingled with shrieks. Poulden reloaded, and Laffin deftly lined up the boat for another crashing discharge.

In total disarray, the camel train was no more, still dark forms and wildly scrabbling men and animals all that were left. Kydd recalled from the map that inland there was nothing but salt-marsh: the French would find themselves trapped.

"Secure the gun," he ordered. They had made contact with the enemy and alerted the defenders—there was no glory in useless bloodshed.

Smith arrived late for the morning conference, and wasted no time. "So Buonaparte's advance guard now has a bloody nose—well done, Mr Kydd." He grinned without humour. "We can expect therefore that they'll abandon the coast road and swing inland to come at us from the north. There's no time to lose. We're nearly complete with the fosse—that's our surrounding ditch—and all the gunboats I can find are anchored here in support."

He bit his lip. "Regrettably it would appear that the Muhammadans have got wind of Buonaparte's behaviour at the siege of Jaffa—he induced the garrison there to surrender, then took them all down to the beach and slaughtered the lot. Had the cold-blooded gall to use bayonets to save powder. Now half our own Mussulmen are streaming out of town and heading for the hills." Unexpectedly, he smiled. "But this means that those who remain will be staunch. We're well rid of the rest—useless mouths to feed.

"So! We expect Buonaparte on our doorstep directly. I have given orders concerning the illumination of the wall in the event of a surprise attack and other matters, do you both ensure they are carried out—" He was interrupted by a messenger. Unfolding the dispatch he chuckled grimly. "From *Tenacious*. Good news indeed, for once. In fact, magnificent news." Dancing a jig and flourishing the paper aloft, he grinned boyishly at the dumbfounded officers.

"This will take the shine off the morning for Mr Buonaparte. *Tenacious* fell in with a French convoy off Mount Carmel and took nine—nine o' the beggars, mark you!" Kydd and Hewitt politely murmured their surprise, but Smith continued, "And the best thing about it is, those were Buonaparte's entire siege train! He has no ammunition, no heavy guns—we're reprieved, gentlemen. Unless he gets another such, we have a chance."

Kydd felt an unworthy envy: he could visualise the convoy, within sight of safe harbour and then a ship-of-the-line, no less, appears from round the point. Boarding parties are sent away in every boat, seizing vessel after vessel, all under the helpless eye of the French army ashore.

"Count Phélippeaux will be exceedingly satisfied with this morning's work—we shall mount the guns ourselves and pound 'em with their own metal," Smith concluded.

Later in the morning there was a blurring of the horizon to the north-east, a broad ochrous veil of dust rising from the countless thousands of a great army. Kydd climbed the narrow steps inside the Cursed Tower to see for himself. His pocket spyglass added details of the serried glitter of bayonets, columns of dusty blue coats, cavalry, vast numbers of wagons, light guns, more columns.

In its creeping, menacing, unstoppable progress it was a sinister sight. It would take some time yet to reach them but when it did it would clamp a vice-like grip on Acre before an overwhelming assault.

Kydd went cold as he considered the larger scene and realised the stakes could hardly be bigger. Buonaparte was a ruthless, gifted general: there was no reason why he could not complete his march north by taking Constantinople from the weakened Turks. Then he would stand astride the route to India and the world. Only one thing was in his way: Acre.

If he bypassed it on his thrust north he would then have a port in his wake through which his enemies could pour troops to fall on his rear at any time. Even in his ignorance of military affairs Kydd could see that this would be intolerable. While Acre still stood Buonaparte's triumphant advance was halted. He had no alternative but to throw everything he had into its destruction.

Kydd descended the tower stairs slowly. This was no longer a simple duty in a far-off land: it was now the crux of the whole war against the French and he had been called to the fore at this critical hour. Acre *must* be held.

A sea mist over a calm sea was lifting as Kydd made his way back to the headquarters, but the road out of Acre was full of people, some on donkeys or camels, others in wooden wagons, all hurrying away from the doomed town.

Smith was still at the headquarters, crisply ordering the disposition of the captured guns. Kydd took up the order book to make sure he was aware of any changes. In addition to sentries there were outlying pickets who would be the first to catch sight of the siege army. They would retire quickly and sound the alert. A small force of gunboats would patrol to seaward from now on, not only to give warning of hostile naval forces but also to deny the attackers any seaborne supply.

Hewitt returned from his inspection of the northern flank with *Tigre*'s gun, propping his sword in the corner and wiping his brow, ready to hear Smith's latest news.

"Ah! Now, gentlemen, let me apprise you of some intelligence that has come my way. It appears that while *Tenacious* dealt ably with the convoy, four vessels escaped. These, it turns out, are sailing barges laden with stores for the army. I don't have to tell you, if the enemy is denied these he will find it hard to forage hereabouts . . ."

Kydd could see where it was all leading. "Sir, where are they?"

"In the port below Mount Carmel, which is Haifa. There's no doubt it will require a bold cutting-out expedition if we wish to take them from the enemy."

"Three boats enough, sir?" Kydd said casually. A smart operation would at the very least mean a mention in dispatches.

"I would think so," Smith said, with satisfaction.

The little flotilla set off in longboats and cutters in the last of the daylight, Kydd's boat in the lead, the other two under a senior midshipman on either flank. In all there were sufficient seamen to fight any reasonable waterfront opposition and work the captured vessels out to sea.

He had studied the charts: Haifa was a small haven, a lengthy quay enclosing an inner harbour. If the barges were alongside this quay on either side it would be a straightforward matter but if they were further in it would complicate things.

The Bay of Haifa was calm; a quarter-moon gave adequate

visibility and there did not seem to be any other shipping about, apart from the lateen sails of the ubiquitous trading feluccas. Nevertheless things could happen quickly—he felt once more for the comforting presence of his fine fighting sword. There was every prospect that this night it would taste its first blood.

The land was dark and anonymous; occasional lights flickered but nothing to show the presence of a great army. They had diverted inland, Kydd reasoned, and were probably close to taking up their positions around Acre. His resolution firmed—their action would bring results out of all proportion to their numbers and justify risks.

They approached the end of the bay, the bold bluff of Mount Carmel easy to make out; the small port of Haifa was at its base. Kydd strained to see into the harbour—there were some lights, but not enough to reveal the situation, and the quarter-moon was now veiled in high cloud. "Keep together!" he hailed to the others.

The barges were probably inside the long quay, but where? The further in they were the longer they would be under fire as they sailed out with their prizes. But on the other hand there did not appear to be formal defences—in fact, there were neither gunboats at the entrance nor soldiers guarding the quay. Could they be so lucky?

Closer, there were no sudden shouts or signs of alarm. Tense and ready to order an instant retreat, Kydd took his tiny fleet round the end of the quay and into the inner harbour. The barges came into view—at the far end, rafted together, probably to unload in the morning into the tall warehouses that lined the wharf.

It was quiet—too quiet? The cheery splash of their passage could be heard echoing back from the tall stone of the quay. The waterfront buildings were in complete darkness, the nearest lights in the small town on the slopes above. He could not see anything of concern but the silence was unnerving.

Kydd felt uneasy with the long passage they were having to make up the harbour. If they had encountered opposition, even just well-placed muskets on the quay and the inner shoreline, they would not have been able to penetrate more than yards towards their prizes, so close to were they on each side.

Barely two hundred yards away Kydd looked about for the easiest way to board. One or two curious Arabs glanced their way, and on one of the barges a curious head popped up. "Red cutter t' larb'd, longboat th' other side," Kydd called quietly to the other boat crews. They would fall on the barges from each side, working inboard.

The order was barely uttered when Kydd's world tore apart. A single hoarse shout came from somewhere, then the crash of muskets, screams and violent movements in the boat slammed into his perception. The stroke oar took a ball in the head and jerked before slithering down, his oar flying up and tangling with the next. A shriek came from forward: a man rose, then fell over the side.

Kydd's mind snapped to an icy cold, ferocious concentration. The firing was coming from *behind* and it was coming down from the upper storeys of the warehouse and the quay. The soldiers had done well to lie concealed while the boats, with their lower line of sight, had gone right past them, the trap well sprung. There could be no return the way they had come. Kydd realised bitterly that the source of Smith's intelligence had also betrayed them to the other side.

There was only one course. "The barges!" he bellowed. There was just a chance that the enemy would be reluctant to fire on their own vessels. It was only twenty or so yards, a dozen frenzied strokes . . . A young seaman clutching his cutlass was struck in the throat by a musket-ball with a *splutch* that sounded curiously loud above the general uproar. He fell forward, kicking, into the bottom of the boat with a strangled bubbling, gouting blood. Kydd could feel the constant slam and thud of bullets into the boat's side as he fought the tiller to counteract the wild slewing as more oarsmen were hit.

The boat thudded woodenly into the side of the outside barge—its freeboard was lower even than that of the longboat. "Take cover on board!" he yelled, clambering over the side to the deserted deck. Others crowded after him. On deck he drew his sword for the first time in deadly earnest and ran forward.

Any hopes that the French would slacken fire on their own ships were proved false—the lethal *whup* and strike of bullets continued about him with no diminishing. There was no cover on the upper decks of the ungainly barge and with its hold full there was no shelter there either.

With a wrench of the heart Kydd saw that the other boats had loyally made the longer distance round to the other end of the rafted barges in accordance with his last orders and the sailors were clambering up, white faces and bright steel in the moonlight.

"Go f'r the warehouse!" He had to buy time. They rushed forward and over a rickety gangplank to the wharf. Panting hard, Kydd dashed to the doors of the nearest building. He drew his pistol, shot off the padlock and swung the door wide. Inside a musket fired and he saw two or three soldiers frantically reloading. Maddened seamen got to them and slaughtered them in an instant.

The rest of his men threw themselves inside and the door was slammed shut. The darkness was lit only by a single lantern. Kydd shouted at a petty officer to search out any remaining enemy hiding in there and tried to force his mind to a cool rationality. He had probably about thirty men left, far too few to stand up to a regular army force, and only a handful of muskets. Most seamen were equipped for standard boarding with pistols and tomahawks and, of course, a cutlass; their main task was to get sail quickly on the prize.

Peeping through cracks in the door he could see the aimless drift of their abandoned boats and, worse, out of range he could detect enemy soldiers assembling for a rush on them. There was no more time.

His men, seamen he had known through long night watches, out on the yardarm in a gale, at a cannon in the titanic battle of the Nile, were looking to him to make a decision, take firm action and save them.

A lump grew in his throat as cold desolation flooded in. Trapped in an old warehouse with soldiers closing in, they could only burst out and meet the enemy in a last desperate stand—or was it time to call a halt to the killing and dying?

Slowly he turned to face his men. "I do believe—it's not m' duty t' throw away y'r lives," he said thickly. "Hang out somethin' white, if y' please." There was a rustle and some murmuring, but no argument. A seaman shinned up to a high, barred window, worked through it a white waistcoat, then shook it awkwardly.

A single voice called loudly several times. Kydd could not understand the words but their import was plain. "Open th' door," he said, then stepped outside.

The voice called again from out of the darkness, this time in a more commanding tone.

"L'tenant Kydd, Royal Navy," he replied, and waited. The soldiers advanced warily, their muskets trained on him. They stood in a semicircle while a French officer in high boots and cockaded hat stalked forward.

*"J'exige votre reddition,"* he snapped.

Kydd had no idea what he had said. "Sir, I ask terms f'r my capitulation," he said wearily.

"You surrender, ees it?" the officer said, smirking.

"What are y'r terms, sir?" Kydd repeated stiffly.

"Terms? You surrender, you safe your lifes. You not, then . . ." He shrugged.

"Very well. We, er, surrender." It was done.

*"C'est excellent, Lieutenant."* He held out his hands. Kydd was at a loss to understand. Then he realised. He unbuckled his fine sword, still unblooded, and gave it to the officer. Bitterness threatened to choke him as he watched the man put the cherished sword under his arm, then turn to give the orders that must send them into captivity.

# Chapter 13

Kydd was imprisoned in a former office above some sort of trading floor. Two sentries stood guard outside. As far as he knew, his men were below, crowded into the odorous basement room he had seen briefly as he mounted the stairs.

There was an echoing quiet in the barely furnished room, which contained a table, two chairs to one side and some untidy rubbish in the corner. A palliasse had been thrown on to the floor with a grey blanket. Moonlight entered through the window, which was barred, ironically, to prevent entry rather than exit. The view outside was limited to the slab side of another building. Kydd had no idea where he was.

He crossed to the palliasse; it was going to be a long night. Using an old seaman's trick, he thumped it several times in the centre with his fist and saw dots scrabbling in the indentation. He kicked it aside and sat moodily in a chair. He felt shame at surrendering, giving up in the face of mere musket fire when at sea he had stood firm against decks of heavy cannon. It was hard to accept in a service where hauling down one's flag was a rare and final humiliation.

His mind raced over the events, probing mercilessly for evidence of stupidity, neglect, cowardice—had he done his duty as a king's officer to the full? Would he be able to stand before a court-martial and swear he had done all that was possible?

Hot, accusing images of men screaming at their death-wounds flooded in. Did the survivors blame him? What did they think of him as an officer? What did he think of himself?

But he was torturing himself to no purpose. He fought down the whirling thoughts but his feverish mind found a new tack: these soldiers were the same troops who had recently taken out three thousand surrendered men and massacred them on the spot. Would they do the same with them? It made little sense to guard and feed them in the middle of a full-scale siege. And probably Smith would not have heard of their fate . . .

The night passed slowly for Kydd, full of phantoms and dread of the unknown. With the first grey light came another question: what lay in store for the day—for the endless time that lay ahead? Smith had endured years in a Paris prison before his dramatic escape. Escape! But as soon as the thought had flowered, it died. Kydd had no mysterious friends to help him, no funds and, above all, he could not abandon his men to the French army. He vowed to share their fate, whatever it might be.

A breakfast of flavoured rice and gruel arrived, but it was not until the morning sun had come to full strength that he received a visitor, the officer who had accepted his sword in surrender. "Ah, *bonjour, mon brave,*" he said, gesturing to the guards to wait outside. He took a chair and sat. "I am Lieutenant d'Infantrie Cadoux. An' you are Lieutenant Keed, *n'est-ce pas?*" He smiled. "Of ze ship-o'-ze-line *Tenacious?*"

Kydd remained silent. The French could only have known this if his men had been interrogated.

"*Alors,* eet is of no consequence. Do you know, Monsieur, zat you are famous? No? Then let me tell you, ze great General Napoleon Buonaparte 'imself knows of you. 'E wish to offer 'is condolences on your misfortune, but regrets 'e cannot receive you at zis moment. 'E is engaged on an important matter."

Kydd said nothing. No doubt Buonaparte had heard of him—his capture would have been quickly reported by the triumphant officer in charge, but whether the general had any real interest in him he very much doubted.

"Ze general wonders if you can be of service to 'im. 'E would be much oblige eef you are able to assist 'im with 'is unnerstanding of ze geography of Akker. For zis 'e wants you to know zat 'e will be grateful. Very grateful—eef you unnerstan' me?"

"No," he said defiantly.

Cadoux drew his chair closer. "M'sieur—you do not comprehend! One does not refuse ze general's politeness. Did I not express mysel' sufficiently?" He tried again. Then, frustrated at Kydd's lack of response, he stood and left.

The day drew on. Clearly the defences of Acre were of vital interest to the French and there was little they would not do to secure the intelligence. Kydd's capture must have seemed a godsend. His stomach was in a knot and he could not bring himself to eat; he wondered what his men had been given, but seamen were inured to poor food when victualling declined and would probably eat whatever was put before them.

He paced round the shabby room trying not to think about what must follow his stubbornness. The sun gentled into evening and Cadoux returned. He entered slowly, his right hand concealing something behind him. Kydd went cold: if this was the end he would not go meekly.

"Lieutenant Keed, you are a very fortunate man."

Kydd tensed. Then Cadoux whipped out his beloved fighting sword from behind his back. "You are to be exchange. General Buonaparte graciously agree, you may return to your ship." He bowed elegantly and proffered the scabbard as though Kydd had absentmindedly left it behind.

Hesitating in disbelief, Kydd reached out for his sword.

Another figure entered the room, Smith's secretary. "True enough, sir," the man said drily. "As soon as he heard, Sir Sidney sent me to Gen'ral Buonaparte, flag o' truce. You—and your men—are to be exchanged for two Frenchmen we hold. If you'd come with me down to the quay . . ."

"Fortunate? I'd say you were damn lucky, Kydd!" Smith, in his cabin in *Tigre,* did not seem to share Kydd's relief at his deliverance. "You know that you've cost me my only two French captives of worth?" With a sigh he stared through the stern windows. "Buonaparte taking up his positions, bombarding me with demands to turn over the town to him immediately—I can do without these distractions." He turned to Kydd. "Now, pray tell me, sir, what the devil happened?"

Kydd swallowed. "Sir, there was no sign o' the enemy—he must've lay down atop the quay."

"No doubt. In the event you couldn't be sure, perhaps you should have first thought of sending a man to peer over the top?" Kydd held his tongue. "And your retreat. Whatever possessed you to go to ground in a warehouse? Why did you not put about immediately and return?" he added in disdain.

"I lost five men, just in making f'r the barges," Kydd said. "The firing coming fr'm behind, I would've lost far more going against 'em until I got t' open water." He felt Smith's scorn at his words and added forcefully, "Someone tipped 'em off. An' that can only be y'r precious source of intelligence."

"That's as may be, Lieutenant, but I'll trouble you to keep your temper in my presence," Smith said acidly.

"Sir."

"In war, casualties are inevitable. I'll have your written report before sundown, if you please. I imagine you'll want to get back to your ship now?"

"No—sir. If you will oblige me, I should want t' go back ashore an' finish the job."

"Very well," Smith said, with a slight smile. "Let it be on your own head, sir."

Hewitt looked up from some Arab dish he was eating off a chipped plate. "Well, I can't say that I find your good self unwelcome." He went to the window. "See there?" He indicated to the north-east. Just out of range a city of grey tents in three main blocks, regular as a chessboard, was springing up row by row and covering the terrain facing them. "I've been watching 'em. And I believe we are looking at General Buonaparte's headquarters in the centre, with the engineers to the left and artillery to the right."

Kydd took his telescope and slowly traversed the ridges. "I can see 'em," he said, in a hard voice. "Any word on th' relief army?"

"Smith heard that the Turks are taking time to mass a huge force, one that'll outnumber Buonaparte's by far. We just have to resist until it arrives."

Kydd lowered the glass. "Do ye know what we c'n expect next?"

"According to the Count, they'll establish their advance lines within range of us first. Then they'll push forward and start their parallels—that is, trenches matching the line of our walls—and it's from these that they'll begin digging saps, deep tunnels, direct towards us. The idea is to bring up guns near enough to pound a breach in the walls."

His expression hardened. "If a practicable breach is made, it's customary for the defenders to seek terms. If they insist on fighting, it's equally customary for the attackers to put the entire population to the sword without mercy."

"What does he say are our chances?"

Hewitt shrugged.

"I'm going t' see my gun," Kydd said, and left him to finish his meal.

The experience of being captured, possessed by the enemy, had shaken Kydd's confidence. And although Smith had not directly criticised his conduct, how could he be sure he had done everything possible in that situation? In a black mood he made his way through the malodorous alley to the corner of the wall where the *Tenacious* gun was sited. It was fully in place, complete with wooden runners cunningly inclined upwards to slow the recoil and help bring the gun back to the firing position.

Dobbie stood to greet him and touched his forehead. "Good ter see you again, sir. An' Black Bess 'ere's all ready 'n' correct fer your inspection." He slapped the long muzzle of the big gun affectionately. Some seaman artist had embellished the sides of the carriage with an heraldic ribbon bearing the name.

Kydd looked at Dobbie closely. He had not been on the cutting-out expedition but would know about it. However, his face showed only honest satisfaction at his return. "It's going t' be a hard fight before it's over," Kydd said, then felt uncomfortable that he had perhaps sounded pompous and affected.

"Aye, sir, but we'm ready f'r when the beggar shows 'imself at last." Dobbie's gun crew had prepared faultlessly, handspikes and rammers neatly against the inner parapet, powder cartridges stowed in a case out of sight below.

"When it starts I want every man t' wear a cutlass even when working th' gun," Kydd said. "I'll see about pistols." He looked out over the broken ground. "They'll be moving t' their advance lines afore long—then you'll have work t' do."

There was no point in waiting about so he walked back slowly to the headquarters. "Don't much fancy kicking my heels here,"

Hewitt said. "Shall we go to the Cursed Tower and see what there is to see?"

The antique square tower stood at the corner of the wall: they climbed the old stairs to the top room and Hewitt trained his telescope towards the French encampment. "Busy enough," he grunted, and brought it further round. "Ah, what do we have here? Well, well—I do declare!" He passed the glass to Kydd. "Do you mark the mound to the nor'-east? That is Richard Coeur de Lion's mound. Now, tell me what you can see."

There was general activity around the mound but at the highest point a solitary group was looking directly towards the tower. In the centre, in plain dress contrasting with those on each side, stood a single figure. Even at that distance Kydd could sense a presence, a maleficent will. "General Buonaparte," he said, in a low voice, and handed back the glass. In the same view he had seen a dozen or so big field-pieces being hauled forward across the uneven ground. On all sides there were ominous signs of encirclement, entrapment. In its slow but certain progress, it held a deadly fascination.

That night Kydd paced along the walls. This ancient, foreign land was not the right place for a sea officer—he was completely out of his element. But he had accepted this duty, and it was here that he would prove himself. Or . . .

Dobbie and his gun crew lay about their post. Some were sleeping, others spun yarns, much as they would in a night watch aboard *Tenacious*. Kydd nodded to Dobbie and passed by. At four points along the walls watch-fires blazed, throwing ruddy light over the open ground. He looked out into the black of the night, aware of the line of marine sentries placed within sight of each other along the walls.

The Turkish and Arab troops chattered noisily together within the wall. The seamen were there only as gunners and it was these soldiers who would repulse any assault. They seemed outlandish, with their turbans and scimitars, and were an unknown quantity in close combat, but Kydd would lead them and the marines into battle. The seamen would act as a reserve if fighting came down to close quarters.

His thoughts were rudely interrupted as a musket went off near the centre of the wall, then another. Out in the darkness, at the extremity of the light thrown by the watch-fire, he could see the suspicion of a moving shadow, then several more. He ordered the oil fire lit, which flared up with a satisfying *whoomf*.

Caught in the sudden light, scurrying figures darted about. Muskets blazed up and down the parapets, the first shots of the siege, but with little effect. "Cease fire!" roared Kydd. It had probably been a reconnaissance party, spying out the terrain. His men had achieved what they wanted: there would be no more French creeping about at night. He gripped his sword. They knew what to expect in the morning.

At dawn Buonaparte's cannonade began. During the night his guns had been drawn up in a breach battery directly opposite the Cursed Tower and they opened up in a continuous roll as the light strengthened. Through his feet Kydd felt the vicious thump of solid hits. Some stray balls tore through the air above him, while others struck noisily but ineffectively off the slope of bastions and casemates.

He could distinguish the deep smash of twelve-pounders above the more strident eight-pounders and the bark of lesser pieces, before their own artillery replied. Their siege mortars were now turned on the besiegers, antiquated bronze guns of Djezzar's own and, most satisfying of all, the twenty-fours landed from *Tenacious* and *Tigre*.

Dobbie needed no special instructions. He laid the gun calmly himself, then sent ball after ball into the French positions, making them pay for the privilege of coming within the range needed for their own guns. Kydd could see the earth parapets before the enemy guns flung aside, leaving broken muzzles pointing skywards.

But the ancient Cursed Tower, built at a time before modern iron guns, suffered. The French had correctly estimated it the weakest part of the wall and concentrated savage fire upon it. Under the remorseless battering the masonry started to crumble, then fall. For five hours it endured bombardment before the last French gun was destroyed.

The facing wall of the tower was now a gaping ruin. Kydd left the gun and hurried to the scene. The tumbled stonework had left the lower part of the tower a dusty cave, a wide pathway to the interior of Acre—a breach in their defences.

Among the babble of excited Turks Kydd caught sight of Phélippeaux, clambering over the fallen rubble. If the customs of war were to hold, they should now treat for a capitulation and withdrawal or later suffer the carnage of a sacking. But if they did, what would be the fate of this brave and resourceful royalist Frenchman?

As the dust settled, all sounds died away in the enemy direction, then came the thunder of massed drums: the *chamade*, a demand to parley. A white flag appeared above the enemy earthworks and waved to and fro. Then a single figure appeared, standing erect with the white flag on a banner staff. Kydd noticed that Smith had arrived next to him.

The figure began a rigid march towards them, stumbling occasionally on the broken ground. At a point within shouting range the man stopped and demanded something in French. Smith stepped forward and replied with a bow and mild words. The man came on: he was an officer of proud bearing with scarlet sash and feathered cockade. His eyes flickered rapidly from side to side as he marched.

Gawking onlookers made way for him as he stalked through the breach. He halted, then began a staccato tirade but was interrupted with a gesture from Smith, who turned contemptuously to Hewitt, speaking in English: "The rogue came without a blindfold—he thinks to come as a spy!" He turned back to the officer and barked a command; Turkish soldiers seized him and dragged him away.

"Well, that's settled," Smith said. "I'd be obliged, Mr Kydd, if you'd give a reply to Mr Buonaparte on my behalf with your twenty-four?"

"Aye aye, sir!"

The die was cast. Buonaparte would never forgive the insult.

The breach was stopped up hastily with baulks of timber and rubble. At noon there was a sinister movement across the whole width of Kydd's vision. Unseen trumpets blared at each end of the line, colours were raised and drums began their volleying summons to the flag.

Kydd looked along the wall to the soldiers at the ready. Obviously frightened, they were calling to each other and looking about them as if to escape. Kydd brandished his sword and strode down the walls. This steadied them to a degree but then the skyline erupted into a mass of advancing troops, Buonaparte's finest, who had defeated a hundred thousand Mamelukes in an hour at the Pyramids, been victorious at the siege of El Arish and butchered in cold blood the survivors of the Jaffa siege. Firing wildly, many Turks and Arabs broke and fled. Kydd shouted himself hoarse and some hesitated, but most tumbled off the parapets and ran. Kydd returned hastily to the gun, shaken.

Dobbie and the others acknowledged him calmly and a surge of feeling for them came over him. "Grape, then canister," he croaked, with renewed determination. There would be time to get away only two shots before the French were upon them. Smoke was obscuring his view but he could make out the advance guard running in front. They carried scaling ladders and equipment, and close behind were their armed supporters.

The sheer numbers appalled Kydd, dense masses of troops that faded into the distance, all tramping forwards in an unstoppable wave, even over the bodies of those who fell. In his gut he felt the terror of the helpless. The main wave was going against the Cursed Tower, and their close-packed ranks quickened as they drew nearer, their swords and bayonets rising and falling with a terrible glint.

The final battle for Acre would be won or lost at the tower. He hurried to the breach and saw that it would never stand a determined assault. Kydd stood there with bared sword, waiting for the onslaught. He sensed others forming up behind him, filling the breach with their bodies, and suddenly felt exhilaration, a curious exaltation that he was alive and a man on such a day.

The first wave of the assault reached middle ground, then came to the final distance. Then above the tumult of battle came an avalanche of thuds. Seconds later the entire front of the attacking army crumpled. Whole columns were slapped to the ground or flung skyward, and military formation dissolved into panic-stricken scrabbling. Offshore, *Tenacious* and *Tigre* delivered their ferocious broadsides again, their shot rampaging the length of each wall and converging in front of the Cursed Tower in a welter of blood and corpses. Nothing could stand against what amounted to whole regiments of heavy artillery, and Buonaparte's assault crumbled.

Most turned to flee, to find the rear of the army still pressing them forward. Others stormed on heroically but when they came close to the walls they discovered Phélippeaux's fosse, a ditch twelve feet deep that made a mockery of ladders intended only for the height of the wall. Rallying, the Turks ran back to the parapets and threw grenades and heavy stones into the ditch, which quickly turned into a killing ground.

Trumpets sounded distantly—the retreat, Kydd realised. He looked down into the fosse. Those surviving, abandoned by their own army, held up their hands. It took main force to prevent the Turks killing the prisoners, who were led away by marines.

It was a galling blow for Buonaparte. Cheated of an easy victory by the same navy that had destroyed his hopes for an Oriental empire, he could no longer expect to take Acre in a frontal attack. Sliding his sword into its scabbard with a satisfying snick, Kydd watched the last of the assault wave scramble to the rear. He was still breathing deeply, aglow with the intoxication of battle on a scale he had never seen before—and he had been ready! He turned and made his way to the gun, but although the columns were repulsed in such disorder, cooler regions of his mind told him that Buonaparte would not be thwarted in his march to glory.

At sunset Kydd left the headquarters where he had been in conference. He had been grateful for the activity: the day's events had disturbed him. In a man-o'-war there were casualties and he had seen his share at the Nile, but he had been unprepared for the scale of slaughter in a land battle. Hewitt was on the first watch and he must try to catch some sleep—but could he close his eyes on the images of blood and death?

His evening walk took him to the *Tenacious* gun. One of the seamen, whom Kydd remembered only as a reliable member of the afterguard, was sitting on the gun-carriage with his grog can, singing to the others in a low and compelling tenor:

*The topsails shiver in the wind,*
*The ship she's bound to sea;*
*But yet my heart, my soul, my mind,*
*Are, Mary, moored with thee . . .*

Kydd stood transfixed: in this harsh and unfeeling land, away from the clean simplicities of a sea life, these sailors had brought their world with them and were drawing strength from their age-old customs.

He turned to go, but his seaman's instincts had pricked an alert and he faced back, sniffing the wind. Since morning, it seemed, it had backed a full three points. He had no barometer or other instruments but he felt uneasy.

The dawn came and, as he had suspected, the winds were more in the north, a cooler touch to them after the dry warmth of the desert *khamsin*. The giant bowl of the deep blue sky, brassy with sunlight and usually innocent of cloud apart from playful tufts, was becoming overcast.

Kydd climbed the Cursed Tower with Hewitt. Nothing in the French camp gave a clue to Buonaparte's plans, but Hewitt seemed unusually reserved.

"Wind's gone to the nor'ard," Kydd said.

"If you'd been in the eastern Mediterranean as long as I have, you would have your concerns. It could soon be a nor'-westerly," Hewitt told him.

Kydd nodded gravely. Any wind of force from the north-west would place *Tenacious* and *Tigre* on a lee shore. Anchored as they were, as close to the scattered rocky shoals as was possible, they would have to weigh and proceed to sea to make an offing until it was safe to return. And while the ships were away they could no longer maintain their broadsides—Buonaparte would have his chance.

"I hold to my small hope that Buonaparte is as much a seaman as my sainted aunt Betsy, and will not in anticipation plan a descent, and will be caught off-guard. Is that too much to pray for?" Hewitt said.

The wind strengthened: it blustered and the first raindrops fell. Soon curtains of rain squalls were marching in from seaward, laying the dust and forming myriad rivulets in the drab, yellowish-brown dust but turning the dull iron of cannon to a lustrous gleam. Those who could pulled on rain slicks; others endured. The squalls passed but behind them the wind set in from the north-west, hard and cold.

"Stand to! All hands, *get on th' wall!*" Kydd roared, driving wet and bedraggled Turks to their stations. An assault would come, it was certain; it was only a question of when.

They stood to for an hour—then two. Hewitt had been right. As dusk approached it was certain that Buonaparte was not going to mount an assault that day. Now everything depended on the weather: if the wind shifted back during the night the ships could return, but if it stayed in the same quarter the defenders of Acre would face an assault.

With the dawn came the wind, relentlessly in the north-west. Before the day was out, they would be fighting for their lives, and Smith was still somewhere out at sea in *Tigre* and could play no part. It was entirely up to themselves.

The enemy came without fanfare, a sudden purposeful tide of attackers. The defenders' guns blasted defiance, but without whole broadsides from the ships there was no deterring their deadly advance. Kydd lost no time in placing himself at the breach, now choked with hastily placed timber and rubble.

On the tower above him the muskets banged away but against such numbers they had little effect. Then a deep rumble sounded. The front ranks faltered. Kydd's heart leaped: if the ships had returned they stood a chance. But a crash gave the lie—it was a thunderstorm.

As the French bore down with scaling ladders to throw up against the walls from the fosse, blustering and chilling rain squalls came. The open ground grew slippery with sticky yellow mud. Firearms were useless in such conditions yet still they came on—hurrying lines, the dull glitter of wet steel, a sea of anonymous faces and a continuous shouting roar.

The first wave reached the fosse. Ladders were thrown down awkwardly, but Phélippeaux had designed well: the width of the ditch did not match the height necessary to reach the parapets and the ladders ended in a tangle of bodies and bloody corpses.

The first breathless Frenchmen arrived at the breach, hard, brutal faces in sketchy blue uniforms, bright weapons, the cutting edge of Buonaparte's will. Pistols banged out and they scrambled over the rubble to close at last with the defenders.

Kydd braced himself, his sword warily at point. A soldier reared up with a short carbine and threw it to his shoulder, aiming at Kydd's face. It missed fire but he hurled it at Kydd, yanked a long bayonet from its scabbard and came at him. Used to the confines of shipboard fighting, Kydd whirled away and his blade flashed out and took the man squarely in the side. He fell and was immediately trampled by another whose bayoneted musket jabbed at Kydd's face. He dropped to one knee and as the man lurched forward he lunged for his bowels. The sword ran true and the man dropped with a howl, but his fall jerked the weapon from Kydd's hands. On his knees he scrabbled for it desperately—but towering above him was a giant of a soldier. Before the man could plunge his bayonet down, bloody steel shot out of the front of his chest. With a squeal the man half turned as if to see who had killed him, then toppled, trapping Kydd under his wet carcass. Struggling to move Kydd felt the body shift. It was heaved aside to reveal the grinning face of Suleiman, his curved Ottoman dagger still dripping red.

Kydd shook his head to clear it. The fighting had moved down the rubble and into the ditch. He picked up his sword and looked about. Rain now hammered down in earnest on his bare head and his eyes stung with a salty mix of sweat and blood.

The well-sited guns from the ships were still tearing great holes in the waves of attackers. A musket ball slammed past his cheek with a vicious slap of air, but he could see that the rain and mud were severely impeding the assault.

In the fosse, grenades and infernal devices thrown at the hapless survivors exploded loudly in bursts of flame and smoke. Kydd saw a skull split and crushed by a heavy stone flung from the upper storey of the Cursed Tower. The attack was faltering. Then, as quickly as it started, it faded, leaving Kydd trembling with fatigue atop the rubble of the breach.

He stepped inside the tower out of the rain and wiped his sticky sword on a body. He looked at the now bloodied and muddy weapon, then slid it neatly into its scabbard: it had proved its worth.

There would be a reckoning when the weather abated; there would be no rest. At the *Tenacious* gun the men sat exhausted on the ground, heads in their hands. Dobbie looked up wearily with a smile of recognition. "Got 'em beat again, sir," he croaked.

Kydd could not trust himself to say the words that lay on his heart and ended with a gruff "No chance o' Buonaparte getting what he wants while there's a Tenacious in th' offing." It seemed to serve, for several of the gun crew looked up with pleased grins. "Don't know where I'll find it, but there's a double tot f'r you all when I do."

At the headquarters he found Hewitt slumped in his chair, staring at the wall with the map of operations spread out before him. "That damned relief army had better show itself before long or we're a cooked goose."

"Aye," said Kydd, and searched for words of cheer. "We came close t'day—but doesn't it tell us that Buonaparte is getting impatient, running scared, that he throws his army at us without he has a plan—an' in this blow?"

Hewitt looked up, an odd expression on his face. "Pray see things from his point of view. Before now he has taken the strongest fortresses in Europe, defended by the most modern troops. What does he see here in Acre? An ancient, decaying town ruled by a bloody tyrant and defended by a ragged mix of sailors and Orientals. No wonder he thinks to sweep us aside quickly and get on with his conquests."

"He's tried—"

"He has not yet! But I'll wager he's already sent for a second siege train to pound us to ruin even with our wonderful ships, supposing he is not at this moment up to some other deviltry! Remember, he made his name at Toulon at the head of the artillery—he is no stranger to such works."

They worked together on the defences, Hewitt's halting translations of Phélippeaux's schemes of fortification serving for them both. They divided between them the main tasks: Hewitt consulted Djezzar on matters concerning labour for the works and Kydd saw to the lines of supply from the victualling stores and magazines to the guns—but always many other details demanded their attention.

The winds blew themselves out and veered more easterly as the rain cleared. With the first blue sky all eyes turned to the French encampment for signs of a new assault. But the sodden ground remained impractical and, to the cheers of the defenders, the two ships sailed back cautiously to take up their positions once more.

Smith came ashore immediately and energetically visited all parts of the old walled town, demanding particulars of each. He finished at his headquarters. "Well done, gentlemen," he said, with satisfaction. "Yet I would rather you had kept a better eye on Djezzar Pasha—he is a man of decided opinions concerning his enemies, and I have just learned that in my absence he seized thirty of the prisoners, had them sewn into sacks and thrown into the sea, including our French officer spy. I shall have to be firmer with him in the future.

"And now I have news. Good news, believe me. You will be happy to learn that the Turkish relief army in Galilee has left Damascus and is even now on its way south. A mighty army indeed: seventy-five banners of Mahgrebi infantry and Albanian cavalry, two hundred Janissaries, Dalat and field cannon, Mamelukes and Kurds beyond counting—near eight times Buonaparte's numbers. They march fast and will reach the Jordan in a day or so. Then he must fight, or retreat and abandon the siege. I believe he will fight, and in that case he will be obliged to divide his forces. It will be an interesting time for Mr Buonaparte."

Kydd's heart lifted. Perhaps in a few days he could return to his rightful place in *Tenacious*—the warm fellowship and ordered sanity of the wardroom.

There was other news: Bedouin fighters were joining from the country—more exotic fighters to prowl the walls with their flowing robes and wickedly curved knives. And it seemed agents in India had discovered that Buonaparte had told the Sultan of Mysore, the scheming Tippoo Sahib, to prepare for a victorious host that would descend on his country from Persia in the footsteps of Alexander.

"However, we have a more immediate worry. Count Phélippeaux has confided that he believes the French have begun a sap, a mine. Protected from our ships' gunfire they are tunnelling towards us from their forward trenches and when they are under the wall they will explode a great charge to bring it down."

Kydd and Hewitt exchanged a glance. In one stroke another dimension of war had started. While they walked and talked above, French engineers were driving their unseen mine ever closer. In a single instant they could be blown to pieces.

"Sir, does he know where it is? How far it's gone?" Kydd wanted to know.

"No doubt about it—he has seen an advance parallel grow earthworks and men go down into it. The closest trench to the Cursed Tower."

"Is there anything we can do?" Hewitt looked drawn and tired.

"The usual in these cases is for us to counter-mine, to drive our own pit towards theirs and stop them."

Kydd shuddered: he could not conceive of a worse scene than in this black underground the breaking through into an enemy mine and the savagery of hacking and stabbing in such a confined space that must follow.

There was no attack that day, or the next: it was becoming clear that Buonaparte was not going to risk another frontal assault in the face of the ships' broadsides and was either biding his time while his sappers did their work or was away, deploying his forces to face the Turkish hordes.

It gave Smith, Hewitt and Kydd precious time to repair and regroup. One thing they could be sure of, which Kydd kept close to his heart: they would never starve—the little feluccas bringing food ensured that. It was something their enemies could only dream of without command of the sea.

On the following day Smith brought grave news. "Gentlemen, I have to tell you now, the Turkish reinforcements are beaten—outnumbered many times. That devil Buonaparte won a victory over them at Mount Tabor in Canaan. They're fleeing north as fast as they are able and we can expect nothing from them now."

"May we then know your intentions, Sir Sidney?" Hewitt asked, in a low voice.

Without any relieving force in prospect their main reason for holding out was gone. Slowly but surely the mining was reaching their walls, and a victorious General Buonaparte was returning with his booty and no threat in his rear to distract him. When the news got out who knew how it would be received? An evacuation was the only real course left.

"We stay," Smith said calmly. "To yield up Acre is to hand Buonaparte a highway to Constantinople and the world. While we are still here he dare not proceed further with us in his rear. Therefore our duty is plain." It was the cold logic of war. "We bend every sinew to defend ourselves, every man to bear a hand in doing whatever Count Phélippeaux desires in the article of fortifications. We send away any who cannot hold a weapon. Let there be nothing left undone that can help us resist the tyrant."

Hewitt got to his feet and reached for his sword. "Then we had best be about our business. Mr Phélippeaux has the idea to place a ravelin outside the walls. I have no idea what species of animal this is, but I look forward to finding out. Good-day, gentlemen."

Kydd looked nonplussed. "Outside the walls?"

"Certainly. We raise an earthworks on each flank of the wall—this in the shape of an arrowhead pointing towards the Cursed Tower. Each will contain a twenty-four-pounder and they will have an unrivalled field of fire when they play upon the approaches to the breach." Building these ravelins in the open would be a bloody affair, Kydd mused.

"And I desire you, sir, to attend to our port. I'm sure there's much that can be done to dismay the French. Take what you need and tell me about it afterwards—and thank you, Mr Kydd."

A brass eighteen-pounder was found and, in consultation with the gunner of *Tenacious,* mounted on a platform high up in the lighthouse. This gave a deal of grave joy to the seamen, who were employed to rig complicated sheer-legs, parbuckles and all manner of tackles to raise the long gun to its final eminence. When finished, the height provided a most satisfying range into the French camp.

Kydd turned his attention to the mole: here was a potential hostile landing place. Remembering his first success in the dunes, he moored a barge there with spring cables to bow and stern. A thirty-six-pounder carronade was mounted in it, the ugly muzzle capable of blasting hundreds of musket balls at any who were brave enough to attempt a landing.

There were fishing-boats, gunboats, every kind of small fry—why not use them? Capable of clearing the shoal water inshore they could render the entire southern approaches impassable by soldiers. Each craft could be equipped with the smaller guns of the ships anchored offshore, then spaced close around the walls, ready for immediate service at any point.

When dusk brought a halt to the work Kydd returned to the headquarters. Smith had the map laid out and courteously enquired what steps he had taken. Kydd told him, puzzled that Hewitt was not present as was their usual practice when setting the night watch. Smith's expression did not change. "I'm grieved to say that Lieutenant Hewitt was gravely wounded in the discharge of his duty and has been returned to his ship. I have asked for another officer." Kydd's heart went out to the dry, sensitive Hewitt, who had suspected from the first that his own blood would join that of others in the history of this ancient, holy land.

"Therefore I will assume the first watch," Smith said, in a controlled tone.

"Aye, sir. May I ask if the ravelins—"

"They are secure and their guns will be in place tomorrow."

. . .

Kydd tossed in his cot. The endless striving, the blood-letting, and the knowledge that under the ground a mine was advancing that would end at any moment in a deadly explosion—all this, and the exhaustion of days and weeks facing the worst that the most famous general of the age could throw against them—was bearing down on his spirit.

At daybreak he went to the parapets to scan the distant French encampment with his signal telescope. There were no signs of untoward activity: perhaps today would be quiet.

At breakfast the new lieutenant was announced. Kydd lifted his eyes—to see Renzi standing there. "Have I lost m' reason in the sun—or is it you, m' dear friend?" he cried, lurched to his feet and gripped Renzi's hand. He broke into a smile—the first for a long time.

Renzi greeted his friend warmly, and Kydd brightened. "Why, Nicholas, but I had hoped you were safe in England," he said. "How is it I find you in this place o' misery?"

"And leave all the sport to your own good self?" Renzi said lightly. "Besides, I am only returned these two days, and seeing this is set fair to be the most famous siege of the age, I could yet find myself noticed . . ."

They paced slowly along the scarred walls of Acre, Renzi blank-faced as he learned of the perilous state of the siege and the imminent return of the victorious Buonaparte.

"Did your visit to y'r family go well?" Kydd asked, after a space. Renzi had said nothing to him before he left, other than that a family concern required his attention.

They walked further before Renzi replied quietly, "It was a matter involving a decision of great importance to my future and, I confess, it is not yet resolved."

Kydd knew his friend to be one who cared deeply about moral

issues and worried at them until he had drawn all the threads into a satisfactory conclusion. Perhaps this was one such instance. "Should you wish t' debate a little, Nicholas . . . ?"

"That is kind in you, dear fellow, but the nature of my dilemma does not readily yield to the powers of rational philosophy."

"Then I shall no longer speak on it," Kydd said firmly. Renzi would come out with a fully reasoned decision when he was ready, and at the moment they had other more pressing concerns.

"Did I mention," Renzi said, in quite another voice, "that our good chaplain Peake comes ashore shortly? Knowing his extreme distaste for the effusion of blood I tried to dissuade him from this charnel pit but he is a stubborn old horse." He considered for a moment and added, "Do bear him with patience—he's been aboard an anchored ship for an age while he knows that there are men here dying without comfort, and he devoutly wishes to do his duty in some way."

The morning conference opened with the news that Buonaparte was drawing close, and the dismaying intelligence that because he no longer had to look to a threat from inland he could bring up and deploy every resource to the one object—the reduction of Acre.

"This, then, is the climax," Smith declared. "Buonaparte has all his forces present and if he cannot triumph over us with these he never will. I recognise this as our supreme moment. My intention is to deny him his victory and, to that end, I am stripping our ships of every man that can be spared and bringing 'em ashore to fight. Gentlemen, we shall not be beat!"

It was crazy—a few hundred seamen, a handful of ship's guns and the Turks and Arabs, who could at best be only a few thousand against the might of Buonaparte's army.

"We must hold," Smith went on. "I have word from Constantinople that a Turkish fleet is on its way to us, and troops are summoned from Rhodes. We have but to hold and we're assured the final victory."

He felt for a satchel under the desk and swung it up. "Taken from a French supply vessel yesterday. See what our devilish friend is up to now."

Inside were leaflets. Renzi picked one up: "'To all Christians! I am come to deliver you at last from the unholy practices of the Muhammadans . . .'"

Smith grimaced. "And the other?"

"'. . . am the Defender of the True Faith; the infidels shall be swept away . . .'"

"You see? Very well. I will not stand in the way of such devout protestations. I will have these delivered to Christian and Muhammadan alike. However, the Muslim will read that this general is a champion of the Christians, while the Christian will read it was the same Buonaparte who bore away the Pope to captivity."

Chaplain Peake came ashore by one of the boats streaming in with the reinforcements, an unmistakable figure. Kydd went to meet him and was struck by the peculiar mixture of reverence and disgust playing on his features. "Mr Peake, I'll have you know we expect hourly t' have the French about our ears, an' this will not be a sight for eyes as cultured as y'r own, sir. I beg—"

"And have me sit on the ship in forced idleness, hearing the dread sounds of war at a remove, knowing there are wolves in human clothing rending each other—"

"Have a care, sir!" Kydd said tightly. "Such words aren't welcomed here. If you wish t' remain, you'll keep y'r judgements to yourself." Peake kept his silence, but his expression was eloquent. Kydd sighed. "Be aware I have nobody t' look after ye, Mr Peake. They all have a job t' do. Keep away fr'm the walls, sir—you'll find th' wounded in the town. And, er, the Djezzar will not welcome instruction on the conduct of his harem. Good luck, Mr Peake."

Rawson and Bowden found their way to the headquarters and saluted smartly. "Our orders, sir?" Rawson said, his eyes straying to exotic sights: the Bedouin with their swaying camels and veiled ladies, fierce Turks with scimitars and turbans, the ruin of bombardments.

"Do you stay here until you understand th' situation, if y' please." Kydd made room at the table where the situation map lay open. "Then I shall want ye to take position inside the walls here, and here, at opposite ends, with a parcel o' pikemen and cutlasses. There's a breach at the Cursed Tower here, where we've been takin' the assaults. If the French get through an' into the town, you close with 'em from your side. Clear?"

Bowden looked absurdly young—his hat was still too big, but now there was a firming of his shoulders, a confidence in his bearing. "One more thing. Leave aside y'r dirks an' ship a cutlass. This is men's work. And—and remember what you've been taught . . . and, er, good luck."

Kydd left for the guns with a sinking heart. The French encampment had swollen, and rumour had it that the unorthodox Druse sect was siding with the French against Djezzar Pasha to settle old scores. Now hundreds more were against them. Hurrying along the wall, Kydd placed his men alternately with the Turks and Arabs; if some broke and ran there was a chance the seamen could hold for a time, but there were among their ranks some whom Kydd had seen fighting like demons—their harsh cries had stiffened the others.

He could not suppress his forebodings. It was possible that he might not survive to see the night. And what of these men, who had to take his orders as an officer and obey? Whether wise or ill-conceived, they had no choice. Would his orders be lucid and reasoned or would he, in the chaos of the moment, waste their lives?

Along the wall he saw Renzi shouting to the gun crew in the redoubt. "Nicholas, I—I just wanted t' say . . . the best o' luck to ye," he said gruffly, holding out his hand. "I have a brace o' the best claret waiting f'r when we get back, an' we shall enjoy 'em together."

Renzi looked up with the familiar half-smile. "In the event, it will—" He was interrupted by a shattering roar from the bowels of the earth. A gust of super-heated air threw them to the ground and showered everything with debris. As it settled Kydd picked himself up, dazed and choking on the swirling dust. The mine had exploded! One half of the Cursed Tower lay in rubble and there was an opening in the wall wide enough for fifty men abreast to march into the town.

"T' the breach!" bellowed Kydd. It was crucial to meet the inevitable assault with as many as could be mustered until more effective resistance was ready. He dropped from the wall to the top of the rubble and faced outwards, his sword ready. Several seamen with boarding pikes and cutlasses joined him, then Turks and Arabs with their daggers and scimitars. Others arrived, until there were a hundred or more.

The horizon rapidly filled with soldiers advancing towards them, more massing behind. A dismayed murmur spread through the defenders. Kydd raised his sword. "Give 'em a cheer, m'lads!" he shouted, above the increasing noise. The seamen raised their voices and, encouraged, the Turks gave their harsh war-cries. The attackers came on in a headlong charge, the numbers beyond counting.

The other ships' guns mounted in the ravelins opened up. Grape-shot ripped into the attackers. From to seaward came the heavy rumble of broadsides in enfilade, which tore into the advancing mass at appalling cost. Even before the first had reached the rubble-strewn fosse the retreat had sounded and the grim marching had turned into a disorderly scramble out of range of the merciless naval guns. They left the ground before the walls a wasteland of pain and dying with new dead joining rotting corpses, wild dogs howling and tearing at the bodies, a sickening odour of death catching in the throats of the defenders.

Kydd felt a hot hatred for Napoleon Buonaparte and his towering ambition to conquer at whatever cost, a tide of anger that took him above his exhaustion and anxieties and left him only with a burning determination to thwart the man. "Stand fast!" he bellowed. "They'll be back!" His voice broke with emotion but he did not care. They would stand until they were victorious or were overcome.

But the midday sun beat down without a sign of the enemy. Kydd stood down half of the men and sent them for rations and an hour's rest. Smith came to observe the breach, coolly taking notes. "I'll send you all the help I can, Mr Kydd," he said, scanning the wasteland beyond the walls. "They have to defeat us, of course—Buonaparte's very reputation and the future of the world rides on this."

In less than an hour the drums beat again and trumpets pealed the *pas de charge* up and down the lines, but with one difference: this time it was the grenadiers in full array leading the assault, Buonaparte's finest troops at the advance edge. They came on steadily, marching with standards held high. In their distinctive red-plumed hats and long muskets aslope they were a different calibre of soldier.

The first shots from the ravelins found them. Men fell, but they closed ranks and marched on. The anchored ships opened up with a massed thunder, tearing into the columns like a scythe. Still they advanced. All along the parapets every man that could hold a musket blazed away. The noise was horrific and smoke hung over the battle as a pall—but the grenadiers still came on.

At the breach Kydd braced himself. Then someone jostled him from behind and he caught a glimpse of Renzi moving up to his side, pale-faced but with a steely resolution. "I do believe, dear fellow, we're in this together," he said, with the ghost of a smile, flourishing his blade.

The first rank of the grenadiers carried pikes and as their moustachioed faces became distinct Kydd gripped his sword and prepared for what must come. In the last few yards they levelled their weapons and broke into a trot, coming at them with a fierce snarl. Kydd tensed. In theory the same principles must apply as with boarding a ship in the face of a pike—get inside it and the man was yours.

With a vicious lunge at Kydd's eyes a dark-featured grenadier hurled himself at him. Kydd swayed just enough to avoid the pike, yanking the man forward by it to his waiting blade, but another dropped his pike and drew his sword. Kydd snatched out one of his brace of pistols and pulled the trigger in the man's face, whirling to meet another who was coming in low. He smashed his pistol down on the man's head but at the same time felt the searing burn of a bayonet under his arm. Wildly he spun about for his next opponent but saw only an unstoppable flood of soldiers pressing forward through the fierce musketry and explosions of grenades thrown from the walls.

Renzi was backed against one side, hacking and slashing at two soldiers. Kydd threw himself at one, his sword taking him in the back. His victim let out an animal squeal and a fountain of blood. Renzi's blade flashed out at the other and transfixed him, but he had seen something behind Kydd and with a shout he pulled out his sword and made ready. Kydd realised what had happened and wheeled about but the man had disappeared back into the mêlée.

"Retire!" Renzi shouted, above the guns and death screams. Retreat—to the second line of defences Phélippeaux had prepared—was the only course: the press of invaders was so great that they were jostling each other in their eagerness to break through.

"Fall back!" Kydd roared in agreement, edging round the jagged end of the wall and gesturing with his sword. Seeing the remnants of the breach crew disengage or be swept aside he turned and ran to the inner line—an improvised parapet of rubble on each side and loop-holed houses on the far side. He vaulted over and crouched, panting.

A shout of triumph went up from the grenadiers as they found themselves flooding into the town. It was taken up outside the walls and excitedly echoed back from the advancing columns.

"Stand y'r ground!" roared Kydd, seeing the pitiful line of defenders wavering. "Get 'em while they don't know where they are!" The second line of defence, a square a hundred yards distant inside the breach, was crude but effective, temporarily containing the invaders. The French milled about, unsure of where to head next, penned in and without a clear enemy.

Some tried to climb over the rough barrier but had to lower their weapons to do so and were easily dispatched. More pressed in through the breach to add to the confusion and were met with musket fire. Above it all, Kydd could hear the crash and thump of heavy guns outside—the battle was by no means over.

Suddenly his eye was caught by a flutter of colour from the top of the Cursed Tower—a French flag had replaced the English: the citadel that dominated the town had fallen to the enemy. Now it only needed them to expand their toehold in the town and they would be unstoppable. Acre would be Buonaparte's before sunset.

Then a harsh, alien braying sounded from the breach. Kydd stared, trying to make out what was happening through the smoke and dust. Inwards, from each side of the breach hurtled a whirling frenzy of men in gold turbans and flowing trousers. All flashing blades and demonic screams, they fell in a murderous fury on the French grenadiers pouring in. The two sides met in the middle of the breach and as the grenadiers gave way they joined together—one line facing outwards, another inward.

These were Bosnian Chiftlicks, sent by Sultan Selim from his personal bodyguard; Smith had kept them for just this occasion. With a surge of hope Kydd saw how they had severed those penned inside from the support of their comrades outside. They had a chance! He rose with a shout: "Finish the bastards!" He kicked at a nearby seaman. "Move y'rselves, we have a chance if we move *now!*" Several looked at him as if he were a madman. "Get off y'r arses an' fight!" he yelled hoarsely, and leaped over the parapet into the dismayed Frenchmen, who now saw that they were, in effect, surrounded, their cohesion as a military unit demolished.

Seamen rose up and joined Kydd in the vicious fighting that spilled out, but now there was a change in the spirit of the invaders. Turning to retreat, they found their way barred. Ululations of triumph became howls of terror, for the Turks now had the enemy at their mercy and flooded into the area from all sides, slaughtering and mutilating without mercy.

Kydd's battle rage fell away at the sight and he stood back with bloodied blade as the last of the interlopers was hacked to death and the area cleared up to the breach. The line of Chiftlicks, facing out, capered and menaced with their strangely curved weapons at the demoralised columns, which fell back into the fire from the ship's guns.

Kydd pulled at the sleeve of one, gesturing up at the Cursed Tower and making suggestive motions with his sword. The man's eyes were glazed, uncomprehending, as though he was drugged. Then he grinned fiercely, shouted for others and rushed for the gaping ruin.

The wavering column began to disintegrate. Buonaparte's brave grenadiers had broken and they fled out of range of the merciless broadsides in a *sauve qui peut*—every man for himself.

Trembling with emotion, Kydd watched them flee but suddenly a dark, round object soared through the air to thump at his feet—and another. Grenades? His heart froze. But they were the heads of Frenchmen who had had the misfortune to be stranded in the Cursed Tower and found by the Chiftlicks.

His gorge rose, as much at the sight as at the sickening repetition of killing. He left the line and stalked back through the breach. There were now only corpses and those picking over the bodies. But where was Renzi? At last he saw him standing bowed at one corner of the killing field. Relief chased dread as he crossed over to him. "Nicholas! You . . ." There was a tear in his friend's eye.

In a low voice Renzi pointed to a body and croaked, "Mr Peake—he must have got lost." He cleared his throat and continued, "Of all I know, he was a man of conviction, of courage and did not fear to stand for the cause of humanity over the world's striving for vanities . . . a gentle man, and the world is now the poorer for his loss." Kydd walked away, leaving his friend to his grief.

"Sir—sir!" Bowden raced down the steps of the parapet. "Mr Smith's duty, and if you should cast your eyes to the nor-west you shall see such a sight as will fill your heart!"

Kydd mounted the steps to the top of the wall and looked out to sea. On the horizon, perhaps a dozen miles off, was a cloud of sail, sprawling over most of the west. "The Turkish fleet, sir." They were saved—Buonaparte was thwarted. Deliverance meant cessation of this madness. All Kydd could think about was his little cabin aboard *Tenacious* and the precious benison of sleep.

He snatched Bowden's telescope and saw about nine warships, the rest transports, presumably with soldiers. "That's them, sure enough," he grunted. Something made him raise the glass again: the image had suffered from the glare of the sun on water, but it was plain now that the whole fleet lay becalmed, helpless. There would be no quick end.

The first guns started, and others, until the whole enemy line seemed to be alive with the flash and shock of artillery. No longer were they battering at the fortifications: now they aimed at random: cannon balls, explosive shells, incendiary carcasses—all fell on the town of Acre, setting alight houses, mosques, camel stables, tenements. Screaming women ran about the streets. Buildings crumbled and burned.

Kydd got hold of Dobbie. "Get all th' men behind the wall an' on their hunkers." Ironically, the walls were now the safest place to be and, following his example, many rushed to flatten themselves against the inside of the wall.

"Sir, why?"

"I don't know, Dobbie. M' guess is that Buonaparte knows that if he c'n break into Acre afore the fleet arrives he's won. Some sort o' ruse to rush us in the confusion—trickery of some kind, for sure."

"Aye, sir. Then we'll stand to th' gun, by y'r leave, sir."

"Thank ye, Dobbie."

The guns pounded all afternoon. It was not until dusk drew in that the cannon-fire slackened and finally stopped for want of aim. Kydd peered through the breach at the darkening countryside now being speckled by the light of campfires; there would be no more suicidal assaults, but what deviltry would they meet tomorrow? The Turkish fleet still lay distant offshore, unable to come to their help if there was another mine or if the renewed bombardment set fire to the town.

He resumed his pacing at the breach, his mind a turmoil after the day. Dobbie came up with Laffin. "Stand down th' gun, sir?"

"Yes. I'd get y'r sleep while you can. Who knows what we'll be facing tomorrow?"

"Sir." Dobbie turned to go, but some trick of the light, the last of the sunset, touched the top of the Cursed Tower and Kydd noticed the French flag still hanging limply atop it. On impulse he told him, "Afore ye turn in, douse that Frog rag and bring it t' me."

Dobbie touched his forehead and loped off, emerging on the top of the ruined tower. There appeared to be some sort of difficulty, which Kydd guessed was that the flag halliards had been shot away. Dobbie lifted a hand to point up to the flag and began shinning up the bare mast, an easy feat for a seaman. At the truck he tugged on the flag until it came free, and stuffed it inside his shirt. Then he slid down the mast awkwardly and disappeared inside the tower. He emerged from its base and stumbled towards Kydd, the flag outstretched, a look of grim concentration on his face.

Kydd stepped forward in concern, but before he could reach him, Dobbie fell face forward to the ground and lay still, the victim of a sharp-shooter in the outer shadows. With a hoarse cry Laffin pushed past Kydd and dropped to his knees next to the unmoving Dobbie. "No!" he screamed blindly, holding up a bloody hand and staring at it. "He's dead! An' it's you, y' glory-seeking bastard," he choked at Kydd.

• • •

Kydd keeled over into his cot, shattered in mind and body. The death of Dobbie and Laffin's accusation brought an unstoppable wave of grief and emotion. He tried to fight it, but the weeks had taken their toll. A sob escaped him.

It had been a cruel taunt: Kydd knew only too well from his time before the mast that a glory-seeker as an officer was worse than an incompetent, inevitably resulting in men's lives sacrificed on the altar of ambition. He could understand Laffin's reaction, but how could he say that his order to Dobbie to take down the flag and bring it was only so that he could present it to Smith as a tribute for what he was achieving?

But was this more of a general indictment? Were his actions in leading from the front during the siege seen by the lower deck as an ambitious bid for notice, to their cost? Was he, in truth, a despised glory-seeker?

Kydd tossed fretfully in the close air of the little room above the headquarters. His motivations in stepping forward into danger at the head of his men were, he had believed, those of duty and understanding of their desperate situation, but could there be within him a hidden impulse to glory and ambition?

And what kind of leader was he? His capture, along with that of the men who had trusted him, still smarted in him for it had been only by the greatest good luck that Smith had had French captives on hand whom Buonaparte had needed. What was being said at the mess tables when they took their grog? What judgement was being passed on him? Perhaps he would be perceived as an unlucky weight around whom men seemed to get themselves killed and, indeed, many had since the siege of Acre had started.

Kydd knew that this was at the core of himself as an officer. If the seamen regarded him as square and true they would follow him through anything; if he was seen as a glory-seeker, he might one day find himself alone on an enemy deck.

He could not sleep—the torturing thoughts rioting through his mind made it impossible—and when the marine private arrived at midnight to call him for his watch he almost welcomed it.

Renzi was below at the operations table, staring at the map with its lines and erasures enumerating the many assaults and savage encounters they had endured. So tired, the friends spoke little more than a few words and, after the customary hand-over, Renzi left for his room above.

Kydd had the watch until dawn. If it was quiet it was usual to stay at the headquarters where any could find him, but his heart was so full of dark thoughts that he told the sentries gruffly he would be at the wall.

Hearing the burr and chirp of night insects he paced along the parapet past the occasional sentries next to watch-fires. Out there, in the vast unknown velvet darkness, their mortal enemy lay and plotted their destruction. In the other direction was the inky sea and anchored offshore *Tenacious* and *Tigre,* the warmth of golden light from the wardroom windows and clustered lanthorns on their fo'c'sles so redolent of the sea life, but at the same time so remote from Kydd's place of trial.

He continued pacing, the cool breeze bringing with it the ever-present stench of death, overhead the calm splendour of stars in the moonless heavens. What would they face tomorrow? If the guns kept up their bombardment there would be ruin and panic. The only course would be evacuation and a suicidal rearguard action. His mind shied from the implications.

He heard someone approach in the stillness. It was Laffin. The seamen had no night watches: the man had no reason to be about at that hour. "C'n I talk, if y' please, Mr Kydd?" His expression was indistinct in the gloom.

"What d' ye want?"

"It's Bill Dobbie—sir."

"If ye want to say you're grieving f'r him, then I'll have you know—so am I."

"He were m' mate, sir."

Kydd waited warily.

"We was two-blocks since 'e came aboard in Halifax. 'E was 'appy 'n' did well in *Tenacious,* 'e did—wanted t' make gunner's mate but didn't 'ave 'is letters, an' so I learned him."

This was by no means unknown but spoke of a deep friendship born of common hardship, which Kydd recognised, with a stab of feeling.

"Has a wife in Brixham an' a little girl—"

"Laffin, why are you telling me this?" Kydd said sharply.

The man hesitated, then straightened. "Sir, I wants ye t' know that I was hasty wi' me words when I called ye a—"

"Aye, well, thank you f'r telling me."

"—an I think as how y' should read this'n. Comes across it while I was makin' up his gear t' give to his wife." He held out a paper, then disappeared into the darkness.

Kydd went to a watch-fire and realised, with a sinking feeling, that it was a letter. Back in the privacy of Headquarters he took the lanthorn across to the table and smoothed out the paper. The writing was strong but childish. Kydd remembered that in Canada not much more than a year ago, Dobbie had been obliged to make his mark on the ship's books, the tell-tale sign of illiteracy.

"My sweet Mary" it began. A letter home to his wife. "Anuther day in this god-blastd hole whi the bedoo like it I dont know for the lif of me."

It was hard to continue—he felt it a violation to read the precious words that would be all that the woman would know of her man's thoughts and feelings before . . . Kydd wondered why Laffin had wanted him to read this.

*I hav saved for you my dearist mor than eihtgteen gineas to this date. I doant know when wi will return it is a hard time wi are having but my dear it wuld make yuo smil to see the rare drubbing we ar giving the frogs and we not lobsterbaks but jack tar!*

Kydd felt his eyes sting but he kept reading.

*Wi will win, sweethart there is no dout of that. Yuo see we hav the best men and the best oficers and yuo may beleive that like sir sidny and mr kidd who I hav seen miself with his fine sowrd at the breech in the wall. He giv hart to us all to see him alweys there he is a leson in currage if we see him in charg of us wi will allways tak after him wher he tell us to go . . .*

The rest dissolved in a blur of tears. Any torturing doubts were now behind him for ever.

"Sir? One hour t' dawn."

Renzi was fully awake but politely thanked the marine, who touched a taper to a little oil-lamp. He lay for a few more moments, then, with a sigh of resolution, threw off the single sheet. He had barely slept and wondered at Kydd's stamina after the much longer perils and hardships he had endured.

Something had spoken to him during the night, a tendril of presentiment reaching out that the day would see a culmination of all their striving. For himself, Renzi had no doubts. When it chose to strike, death could come in so many ways—disease, shipwreck, a round shot. It really was of no consequence. What was of importance was the manner of leaving life. With courage, and no regrets.

In the mirror his face looked back at him, grave but calm. He raised an eyebrow quizzically and silently acknowledged that there was one matter, trivial in the circumstances, but a loose end that his logical self insisted should be resolved to satisfaction, if only to impose a philosophic neatness on his life to this date. It was the decision in the matter of his father's demand that he take up his place as eldest son and heir-apparent to the earldom.

The stakes were plain: if he acceded he would be in the fullness of time the Earl of Farndon and master of Eskdale Hall. If he did not, his father would have no compunction in taking the legal steps necessary to disinherit and disavow him in the succession.

Therefore, in this hour he would make his decision, before he and Kydd went together to meet the dawn and all it would bring. He knew too well the arguments—his life at sea had opened his eyes to the human condition and made all the more precious the insights he had gathered on his adventures. This would cease: the vapid posturings of society were a poor substitute.

Then there was the undeniable fact that he had matured in the face of calls upon his courage, fortitude and skills—he had become a man in the true sense of the word. And had about him the society of others who had been equally formed. Where would he find these on a country estate?

No, he was deluding himself. If he was honest, the true reason was that in essence he wanted excitement before security, stimulation before tranquillity, change before monotony. The sea life.

His instincts were telling him that he should refuse his

father. But was this the proper course? He must examine the consequence.

Could he foresee his life as a disavowed son of the aristocracy? He was content to continue with his persona as Renzi. He had means, a small enough competence, but his needs were little as a sea officer. He valued his books far beyond a fashionable lifestyle—it would be sufficient.

This, therefore, should be his decision.

Why, then, was he not convinced of it? At heart he knew that there was one looming consideration that forced the issue, one that his father had used against him without realising its power to move him. His duty. It was his obligation and responsibility to prepare himself to inherit the earldom, and no consideration of personal preference or taste could be allowed to take precedence.

Therefore this was his proper answer, his determination.

"*No!*" The passion in his outburst surprised him. Hypothetical the argument might be, yet it was not a natural conclusion. It had been forced upon him and, with rising excitement, he saw another path of reason that led to a different decision.

The true meaning of his duty was not solely to his father—or even to his family. It was to the wider community: to those who would depend on him—tenants, families, the estate men of business. It was to the caring husbandry of the land, the enlightened management of the estate—it was to descendants unborn. Would he make a worthy earl to them all? Or would he be a crabbed, uninterested and ultimately miserable aristocrat of the species he had seen so often before? No, indeed—he would leave the title to Henry and may he have the joy of it.

A shuddering sigh overtook him. A burden had been lifted that had weighed on him since he realised his five-year exile had turned first into a blessing, then a fear that it must all end and he would be compelled to return to the claustrophobia of a sedentary life. He was free at last! He buckled on his sword in a glow of deep satisfaction.

Renzi found Kydd alone at the top of the Cursed Tower, staring into the void of the night even now delicately touched with the first signs of light. "Brother," he said softly, but he could not find the words befitting this time of supreme trial that lay so close for them both. Instead he held out his hand, which Kydd took solemnly. Neither spoke as the dawn broke.

After the ladies had withdrawn the gentlemen settled comfortably to their brandy and port, replete after as fine a dinner as ever had graced the table at No. 10. The guests looked appreciatively at the Prime Minister as he raised his glass.

"A splendid repast as always," Addington said affably, noting Pitt's evident contentment, "and, if I might remark it, improved upon only by the intelligence you have disclosed to us tonight."

"Indeed," Pitt said, with satisfaction. "And the damnedest thing it was too! At dawn Smith and his doughty mariners stand to, expecting to fight for their lives, but what do they see? Nothing but an empty landscape. Our glorious Buonaparte—crept away in the night. Gone!"

"Does this mean that Buonaparte is finished at last?"

"Umm. We shall see. We do have intelligence that's unimpeachable for once—I can tell you in confidence that we took the singularly aptly named *La Fortune* at sea, and aboard by extraordinary good luck we found the general's dispatches to Paris." He smiled boyishly. "And in them he tries so hard to find a victory in his ruination that I nearly feel pity for the man. Now he has to explain to France how his grand design for glory and empire has failed. How the fine army that he led to victory and conquest across all Europe is now lost to plague and starvation in the deserts of Syria. And also why he has cynically abandoned his men to their fate—it seems he seeks to flee secretly to Paris."

Pitt's smile widened. "But when he arrives, the hardest task he will face is to explain the fact that the army he vastly outnumbered yet who defeated him—for the very first time on land—was not in the character of the military at all, but common sailors!"

# Author's Note

It is one of those happy coincidences that *Tenacious* was first published in 2005, the year of the Bicentenary celebrations of Nelson's great victory of Trafalgar—and a time when we had the opportunity to value anew the achievements of such a great sea leader. This book is dedicated to Sir Horatio Nelson.

When I began the Kydd series, as I plotted out the general content of each book, I knew my central character Thomas Kydd would meet Nelson at some time. No writer in this genre can tell of the stirring events in the great age of fighting sail without being aware of Nelson at the centre. But it was not Trafalgar that I selected for this first meeting; it was at the Battle of the Nile—in my mind Nelson's finest hour.

In the course of my research for this book my admiration for Nelson—which was already considerable—has increased immeasurably. He was undoubtedly a true genius as a leader of men, but he also had a great humanity, and such respect for the lower deck that he insisted on adding common seamen to his coat of arms.

In terms of background historical material for *Tenacious* I was spoiled for choice. It was a time of titanic global stakes. If the Nile or Acre had been lost we would have seen Napoleon dominating a world which would have been very different today. And it was a time of deeds so incredible that they may seem like fantasy but are not—Nelson personally saving the king and queen of Naples at cutlass point, Minorca taken without the loss of a single man—and above all, the astonishing but little-known fact that Napoleon was first defeated on land not by a great army but a rag-tag bunch of sailors.

As usual, I do not have the space to acknowledge all the institutions and people I have consulted in the course of writing *Tenacious* but there are a number to whom I owe a special debt. The National Maritime Museum holds priceless material on the thrilling Nile chase, much of which is now going online. In Minorca, Roy Wheatley and his charming wife Mary took Kathy and myself under their wing when we were there on location research. The Admiralty Hydrographic Office at Taunton could not have been more helpful in sourcing charts of the time, including one of the actual maps used in the siege.

And, my deep thanks are due to my wife and literary partner, Kathy. As well as maintaining a strict and professional eye on my developing manuscript, she has contrived to become my "reality manager," keeping the intrusions of everyday life at bay to enable me to fully immerse myself in the eighteenth-century world I write about. It is a source of great gratification to me to know that so many of you share my passion for these fascinating times and I look forward to sailing with you for many books to come . . .